ROSES

IN THE

DUST

Jon—
Thanks for devoting your time to support a worthy cause and a great sport!
Steve McCarthy

ROSES IN THE DUST

SHERRI MCCARTHY

TATE PUBLISHING
AND ENTERPRISES, LLC

Published by Tate Publishing & Enterprises, LLC
127 E. Trade Center Terrace | Mustang, Oklahoma 73064 USA
1.888.361.9473 | www.tatepublishing.com

Tate Publishing is committed to excellence in the publishing industry. The company reflects the philosophy established by the founders, based on Psalm 68:11,
"The Lord gave the word and great was the company of those who published it."

Book design copyright © 2013 by Tate Publishing, LLC. All rights reserved.
Cover design by Joel Uber
Interior design by Joana Quilantang

Published in the United States of America

ISBN: 978-1-62854-436-7
1. Fiction / Historical
2. Fiction / General
13.09.18

DEDICATION

For my grandfather, who taught me through the example of his own life the value of love and service to all.

CHAPTER ONE

THE OLD GENERAL

Eddie shivered and pulled his coat closer about him. The wind whistled by, dislodging some of the freshly fallen snow from the boughs. He leaned against the towering tree, wrapping his arms around the wide trunk as far as his thirteen-year-old reach allowed. "Well, General," he began, "how's my little sister? Is she safe? Is she with the angels, like Papa says? Will we see her again like Mama swears, or is that just a story? C'mon, old man. You can tell me the truth."

For as long as he could remember, this had been his "thinking tree." Eddie found a strange sort of peace here, in this glen near a stream, with the tall, stately incongruent oak tree rising amidst the maples. In his mind, the tree had always been "Old General," wise and weary from many battles and full of a hidden wisdom he sought to tap, like he tapped the sap from the maples for sweet, sticky syrup he helped his mother jar. He wasn't sure where the tree's name had originated; maybe from one of the adventure stories he read so avidly, or a poem Miss Welch, his teacher, had asked him to memorize. Perhaps he had taken it from a tale that his father, a colorful and animated storyteller, had told him long ago. Regardless of where the inspiration had come from, the name suited the tree, and the tree was his most intimate companion. Eddie told his secrets to the gnarled bark. He poured his heart out to the leaves and branches, finding peace beneath the boughs. Right now, he desperately needed peace. Baby Flo, his beautiful little sister who was barely eight months old, on whom he had lavished so much love and attention, was buried in the cold ground, not far from the tree.

"I told Mama not to take her out in the storm," he lamented. "I told her I could warm the milk and keep her safe until she returned from delivering the Bowen's baby. It was too far in a blizzard for little Flo. It was too far." He self-consciously wiped one of the bitter tears that were falling down his cheek. He didn't want to cry; it wasn't manly.

As the oldest child of a family homesteading in Alberta, Canada, Eddie had been responsible for his brothers and sisters for as long as he could remember. "You're my little man," his father always told him before setting out on long journeys to earn money, building the Canadian frontier with his skill as a carpenter or working on railroads throughout the western US and Canada. "Take care of the ranch for me. Take care of your mama." And Eddie had always done his best to obey.

"I need to go deliver a baby in Lethbridge. I'll be back in two days. Can you take care of the little ones until then?" or "Mr. Smith, on the ranch to the north, is very ill and I need to tend to him. I'll be back tomorrow. Can you keep things in hand?" his lovely mother, the only trained nurse in the province of Alberta, would often say. From the time he was only four or five years old, he always had taken care of things, so it was not surprising that now he blamed himself for his little sister's death. She had died of pneumonia, caught after the long night ride in the snow with Mama to deliver yet another baby. His father was still away and would not even learn of this tragedy until he returned next month.

"We should be grateful that all the rest of you are healthy and alive," Mama had said, in her stoic German accent, through her tears. "Why, your father's family in Ireland lost four little ones, two before he was even born. My little brother in Switzerland died when I was six. We've lost only one child of eight, Eddie. We should thank the good Lord for that." Somehow, Eddie was having a hard time taking her advice to heart and thanking the good Lord for this pointless, tragic loss and he hoped his "thinking tree" would lend some comfort. "If only she'd stayed home by the fire with me," he wailed, hitting the tree with his fist. "If only Mama hadn't taken her out in the snow. She's a nurse; she should know better!" Then, chastising himself for daring to criticize his beloved Mama, he bit his lip as the tears continued to fall.

It wasn't that death was a stranger. Since his family had come here, when he was too young to even remember, he had experienced the rugged life of the western Canadian frontier. Trying to tame a cold and savage land was hard work and left little time for sentimental reflection. Winters were fierce, only occasionally lightened by the warm coastal Chinook winds that blew in from British Columbia. Food was scarce. Neighbors died; classmates died, victims of pleurisy or pneumonia or smallpox or flu. Animals he loved and cared for were slaughtered routinely for food. Life was difficult for all of the families struggling to create homes for themselves. His family had gotten by more from his father's extended trips to work as a carpenter and his mother's medical skill than from any sustenance they could force out of the land. They were much better off than many of their neighbors, he knew. They always had food to eat and warm clothes to wear. They had a large, well-heated house his father had built; he even had his own room, a luxury most of his classmates at school sharing quarters with their many siblings in small, two-room homesteaders' cabins, could barely imagine. The other children in his family had plenty of space, too. His two brothers shared a fine bunk bed in their own quarters on the third floor, heated by a warm fireplace. His four sisters had two rooms between them, with mattresses and cozy comforters. They all had warm clothing—several changes, even. Some of the children in the area only had one suit of clothes. On the rare occasions those clothes were washed at the stream, they had to stay inside and shiver in a thin blanket during the long hours or even days the clothing took to dry or, worse, wear it wet and shiver more.

Compared to the small cabins most of the other homestead-ers survived in, his family lived in a palace. They dressed well and ate well. He knew he should be very grateful; there was no reason for him to complain. But that hadn't mattered at all for baby Flo. She would never enjoy it. He thought of the many nights he had held her and rocked her, singing her to sleep while Mama worked or rested. He wondered why he was alive and she was cold in the ground.

"I guess I'd better make my life a good life, old man," he told the tree now. "I guess I'd better make it really count and do enough good things for both of us." He gazed at the snow-capped moun-tains rising in the background and the quiet trees. He heard the creek burbling beneath the coat of ice. Then, Eddie wiped the last of his tears away and trudged through the snow toward the barn to finish his chores before Mama called him in for dinner.

CHAPTER TWO

ALMOST A PRIEST

Even in a time of mourning and sadness, Eddie noticed how much happiness his father's return brought. His little sisters all pranced and laughed, wearing their prettiest dresses that Mother made them. Papa told them how beautiful they were, and what fine ladies they would be someday. The lines on his mother's face softened, and she smiled much more often. There was a lilt in her step and a shine in her eyes that he only observed when his father was home; although sometimes after receiving a letter from him after he had been away for a very long time, the same soft smile appeared. This was not lost on Eddie. "If I ever marry," he told himself, "I will never be gone from my family. But," he added in his thoughts, "I will probably never marry. Too much work!"

Spring was slowly descending on Alberta. The snow had melted. Sprigs of bright flowers shining blue, purple, and yellow were gracing the fields. The sun appeared more frequently. Heavy boots and mittens were laid aside. Between the happy changes in the weather and the joy of his father's return, Eddie was almost able to forget the sadness in his heart. Almost. He still missed baby Flo tremendously, and because of the immense responsibility he had always shouldered for his siblings' care, he still felt partially responsible for her death. He should have truly been the "man of the house" his father told him he was and forbade Mama to take Flo out in the blizzard, even though he knew he could never disobey Mama or tell her what to do. It was a dilemma.

Eddie felt he should have done something. But what could he have done?

As if he sensed this weight on Eddie's shoulders, his father called him aside one early morning as his young sons were feeding the horses. "The Lord giveth and the Lord taketh away," he said gently. "We mortal men just do our best to understand." Eddie knew he was speaking of Flo, and he nodded. "We should have a service for her, sweet soul," his father added, almost whimsically. "A family memorial in the Catholic tradition, followed by a good Irish wake. I'll preside. Did you know I was almost a priest?"

Eddie shook his head. He hadn't known. He'd often crept into the small cathedral in Pincer Creek, near the one-room school he attended, to look at the beautiful stained glass images of saints and the haunting statue of the Virgin Mary. He'd learned the Stations of the Cross from his classmate Josie. But he'd never known his father was Catholic, or had been, at least. "Why weren't you a priest?" he asked, with the candid, innocent curiosity of a child just beginning to enter adolescence.

"It's a long story," his father sighed. "A very long story best kept for a long winter's night." Seeing the disappointment on his son's face, he added "But I'm not here in the winter very much of late, am I? So maybe I'll make this a spring tale. We'll have some storytelling tonight after your mother's fine dinner, eh? Would you like that?" Eddie's nod and smile confirmed how much this gift would mean.

School that day seemed to drag out even more than usual. Eddie helped the younger students with their lessons, and read a story to the class while Miss Welch graded writing exams. But his mind was on the story he would hear tonight after dinner. His father was a fine storyteller. He had a magical way with words, using them like a paintbrush to give color and drama to every scene he described and every person he spoke of. Eddie loved his father's stories.

Miss Welch looked fondly at her favorite student. She would miss Eddie after he left her classroom this year. She'd already told his mother that he had learned all she could teach him, and she knew that was true. She'd never had a finer student—well behaved, disciplined, and intelligent. He was also an excellent teacher. She knew that much of the progress her younger pupils made was more a credit to Eddie's fine tutoring than anything she did. His sisters were very bright, too. She was sure, with the knowledge born of teaching for over a decade in a one-room schoolhouse in a small frontier community where she knew all the families and their children that his sister Inez, two years younger than he was, would probably replace her when she retired. Inez admired her brother so much, mimicking his actions with the young students. She, too, was a natural teacher.

Eddie deserved a good education. He could teach at the university in Calgary, or one in the USA, as his uncle did. He had a fine mind. But she also knew instinctively that he would not have that opportunity. His family needed him too much. He hadn't even begun attending school until he was eight years old, almost nine, despite her pleas and protests. "I just can't spare him yet," Johanna McCauslin had explained, having already enrolled two of her younger daughters, Inez and Allie, and one younger son, Joe, before their sixth birthdays while Eddie remained at home. "He takes care of the little ones when I'm gone. He takes care of the ranch. Maybe next year, when Gene is a little older and more responsible, he can come to school. Eddie's bright. He'll catch up quickly."

He certainly had. He would leave her charge this summer, having completed eight grades in less than four years and scoring higher on her final exams than any other student ever had. She knew he would leave her to work twelve-hour days, taking care of his young siblings again so his brother Gene could now attend school, and maintaining the family's small ranch and large house during the times his father was away—which was almost always.

She looked at the handsome young man who would soon be leaving her care without receiving the educational opportunities he was due, that he could make so much of. She shook her head sadly. That was the way of the frontier.

Eddie was a handsome youth, already taller than she was, with thick, wavy dark hair and intelligent green eyes. He was strong and athletic, well proportioned with wide shoulders, a narrow waist, and long legs. He had high cheekbones and a broad, open smile. He shared some of his father's rogue Irish features, including his musical voice and way with words, but he also had the quiet Swiss-German discipline and unassuming intelligence of his mother. His mother, Miss Welch knew, had delivered most of the children she'd been teaching for the last few years. She'd also been responsible for saving many of their lives and the lives of their parents. The little nurse, in addition to having eight children of her own and maintaining a homestead while her husband worked far away from home as a carpenter, or on the railroads, single-handedly provided medical care for over half the province of Alberta. She was often riding on long missions of mercy, surviving it seemed on little sleep herself and miraculously remaining healthy no matter what blights she nursed. The people called her "our ministering angel," which she was. She helped whoever was sick, regardless of their status. If they couldn't pay, she never asked; just said she would appreciate a jar of preserves or a prayer for one of her children. Good nurses were in short supply in the cold, western Canadian frontier and Johanna's presence there was a godsend for all. That was another reason Miss Welch hadn't complained about Eddie's late arrival to her classroom doors. And that was another reason that, although she would always regret Eddie's missed educational opportunities, she would be happy with Johanna's promise to send Inez to normal school after her graduation so she could teach, and Allie, who also showed promise, to nursing school. Thus, two of the women who held southern Alberta together, she and Johanna, were guaranteed to be replaced. The third McCauslin daughter, Lizzie, hauntingly frail and beautiful with a sunny personality, would marry well, perhaps to a wealthy American or an Englishman, and thus be able to help her family. Maybelline, only eighteen months now, was too young to have yet been assigned a role in the minds of parents, teacher, and community. The three bright young McCauslin boys would be left to care for their family as long as was necessary and then seek their own fortunes. It was a bit sad, perhaps, but inevitable. Elizabeth Welch understood. That was the way of the Alberta frontier, and the parents who had come to homestead had made that choice for their children long before the children were ever born.

Because the children knew no other life, perhaps for them it was not so sad. But for Miss Elizabeth Welch, born and raised in Toronto and aware of the many opportunities life held, it was regrettable. She had come here nearly fourteen years ago, at the age of eighteen. Two years out of Toronto Teacher's College, she had come to recover from a broken heart. Intelligent and stubborn, her life path had seemed simple and straightforward. She had fallen madly in love with someone hopelessly out of her social class. Burt was the son of a British nobleman relocated to Canada, two years her senior and strikingly handsome. The surprise was that he had ever given her a second glance, not that he had left her to seek—not his fortune, because that was unnecessary—but whatever adventures he craved. He left her suddenly though, without an explanation, after she had given herself to him, body, and soul. She was despondent, deciding if she could not marry the man she loved, she simply would not marry. One of the few options available to educated, intelligent women who chose not to marry was to accept a position teaching in one of the many one-room schoolhouses on the Canadian frontier. In fact, remaining unmarried was a requirement of employment. One could not marry while under contract. One could not marry and retain a position. She liked that requirement.

Miss Welch never regretted her decision. She had come here depressed and heartbroken, too distraught to notice the sparse conditions and harsh surroundings, so different from what she had known in her comfortable Toronto home. She had buried herself in her work, and found she loved it. Elizabeth knew she had made a difference in the lives of many of her students. Many who would otherwise not have learned to read, write, or do numbers now could because of her patient efforts. Her old-maid status was now acceptable; her family could explain that it was because of her career if they were so inclined. And she would never need to worry about another broken heart.

Just past thirty, she was still very attractive. Tall, slim, and stately, she had a regal profile and wavy hair that fell in wisps past her shoulders. Her walk was light and graceful, and her sparkling eyes were robin's-egg blue. She had a full, pouty mouth and bright cheeks. Elizabeth had been a beautiful girl and was now a beautiful woman. Only her students appreciated her beauty, though, in her remote cottage next to her remote schoolhouse in this remote town in Southern Alberta, Canada in 1904.

Eddie, in his polite, observant way, appreciated her beauty and often wondered, sometimes aloud, why she had never married. "Because then I could not have been your teacher," she always answered sweetly, and he was content with that answer. He did his best to help in class, and cut firewood for her in winter, unasked. Sometimes, he brought fresh butter and cream from the cows he milked each morning. Eddie seemed a bit bemused today, as if his mind wasn't focused on the story he was reading aloud to the class. She'd heard his father was back in town and decided that was probably why. Children reacted to things like that. Changes in home environment were translated to changes in their emotions, thoughts, and ability to concentrate. She had seen this many times in her students. It must be difficult to only have a father's presence a few weeks or months each year, she reflected. Yet Eddie was so intelligent, so mature. The lack did not appear, at least by all apparent indications, to have done him any harm.

As Miss Welch reflected about Eddie, he was busy reflecting about his father's comment this morning. Almost a priest. His father had almost been a priest. What fascinating story awaited him after dinner tonight? It made the day slip by even more slowly than usual at school.

After school, he walked the three miles home at a fast pace. The weather was warmer; wildflowers graced the pastures on his way and the sun was bright. His afternoon chores seemed to last an eternity. He checked on Old Bessie, the family milk cow, and her latest calf. He exercised Redwing and Sparky, making sure the horses had plenty of water and fresh grain. Then he checked to make sure the younger children had slopped the pigs, fed the chickens, and gathered eggs as he'd taught them. The spring garden was planted. It appeared Allie and Gene had already weeded it while harvesting tomatoes and early vegetables. Eddie hoped the girls had visited the woods to gather berries this afternoon. He could almost taste the wonderful berry pie his mother usually made when his father returned. Finally satisfied that his responsibilities were met, he walked down toward the creek to bring in water, stopping by his "thinking tree" on the way.

"Hey, General," he greeted the tree before settling in against the trunk for a short rest. "How're things?" He leaned against the comforting bark and watched the billowy, white clouds drift leisurely past in the sky. "Did you know Papa almost became a priest? Can you imagine?" There appeared to be a dragon in one cloud; a knight on horseback in another. Eddie laughed, pushing a few strands of thick, dark hair back from his eyes. His father's storytelling even influenced what he saw in the sky! But tonight's story would be far more interesting than Papa's tales of St. George and the Dragon or his perfect, theatrical recitations of *Charge of the Light Brigade*. Tonight he was going to learn about his father's life when he was young, about how he had nearly become a priest.

Eddie rested a few minutes longer then walked down to the water to fill the waiting buckets and carry them to the house.

On entering, he smelled delicious scents of Mother's cooking. She was preparing a wonderful dinner, as she always did when his father was home. During the days his father was away, especially when she was off tending to the sick, the children often subsided on the meager dinners Eddie put together. Bread with his mother's fruit preserves and fresh milk, or boiled potato stew made with vegetables from the garden was the usual fare. But when his father arrived, that changed. There would be fresh rolls and jam with a chicken prepared as only his mother could, infused with mushrooms and spices. There would be steamed cabbage with fresh butter and a delicious fruit pie with whipped cream for dessert. There might even be blackberry brandy afterward as they gathered around the fire to listen to his father's stories. He wondered idly if the family would always eat as well if his father stayed with them every day of the year, then shook his head, bemused. Of course not! They could never afford it. His father's long trips away from home to work earned the money they needed for feasts when he returned. Life was always a trade-off, it seemed. You just had to decide what you wanted and what you were willing to give up for it, as his parents had.

"There you are!" his mother greeted Eddie as he entered. "Just in time with the water. How's my favorite oldest son?" She kissed him on the forehead as he put the pails down in the kitchen. "Dinner will be ready soon. Can you go make sure the little ones are finishing their lessons?" He smiled and nodded, heading upstairs. He knew they would be. The McCauslin children who had begun school, Allie, Inez, and Joe, all loved their teacher and their books. Eddie never had to prod them to finish their work; they were usually well ahead of their classmates, anyway. He suspected that Gene, Lizzie, and Maybelline, once they started, might not be quite so studious. But he also suspected he wouldn't be the one to worry about that. Allie and Inez would be in charge of the lessons at home by then, and Joe would be in charge of the chores. He would be finished with school and off to seek his fortune. Or at least find what he wanted to do with his life, besides take care of Mama and the children. Maybe his father's story tonight would give him some ideas.

Eddie enjoyed the food his mother cooked as he always did, eating lightly and stopping before he was quite full. A full stomach always made him sleepy. Tonight, he wanted to be wide-awake for his father's tale. He listened happily to the pleasant banter among the younger children. He was eagerly waiting for the time the meal would end, however. He knew that, after the girls cleared the table, his father would gather everyone around the fire to tell the story promised earlier of how he had almost become a priest. Eddie had been eagerly awaiting that moment the entire day.

Once the family was settled around a warm fire, Eddie relaxed and let his father's words fill his imagination. Liam McCauslin was a fine storyteller; each phrase painted a new picture for the eyes of his listeners, and each rise or fall or pause of his voice enhanced the narration. Tonight, he began by recounting his own childhood in County Cork, Ireland. Parts of this tale were familiar, but even so the lilting words kept Eddie's attention and provided new, vivid details.

✳   ✳   ✳

The family listened as Liam recounted his childhood, letting his vivid words paint pictures in their minds as they sat around the roaring fire. Liam, like Eddie himself, had been the oldest son in a large family. But, unlike Eddie, he had a sister eight years older who had inherited much of the responsibility of caring for the younger children. Irene was his father's special love, his favorite sister. "She always spoiled me so, saving me from many a whipping by taking the blame for things I hadn't done—or had!" Although he didn't dwell on it, his narration made it clear that life had been hard. His parents had both worked long hours to maintain a tailor's shop "for the gentlemen of the region." Although they'd had more than many families, the potato famines and economic hardships of Ireland in the mid-nineteenth century took their toll. Two sons had died before he was born. One younger sister and one younger brother died before he turned six. Food was scarce, weather was cold, and times were difficult. But he and Irene had lived and thrived, as did his younger sister and his little brother Peter.

As befitted their station in life, the children received an education at a good Catholic school in Cork. The girls attended grammar school before apprenticing with their parents to learn the trade of tailoring. Peter would be expected to someday manage the shop. Liam, as the eldest living son in a reasonably well-off Irish family, was given to the Church to become a priest. After completing grammar school at the age of thirteen, he began attending the seminary. Liam actually embraced his fate enthusiastically. He had always been a sensitive, religious youth, shy around the ladies and eager to serve mankind. He could easily see himself happy as a priest and was a model seminary student for his first three years. The monastic life seemed to agree with him despite his spirit of adventure for he saw bringing souls to God as the greatest adventure of all. Living the earthier and more unpleasant aspects of life vicariously, through the confessional, suited him fine. He loved his religion, and knew all of the rituals and ceremonies in detail. Liam seemed destined to be a fine priest in southern Ireland. Then, his sister Irene changed his fate unaware, by eloping to the United States of America shortly before his seventeenth birthday.

"She's disgraced the family!" his father declared. "Leaving her homeland and her family and her church without a second thought to sail for America with a renegade. What was he doing here anyway? Just come to steal our fair daughter and take her back to his harem of wives across the sea, no doubt. And the fool

ROSES IN THE DUST

girl let him do it. She left with him!" The event was certainly the talk of the town of Cork in 1884. Everyone heard the tale of the tailor's daughter and the renegade, godless heathen. "She's no daughter of mine anymore!" declared Patrick McCauslin. "Mary and I never gave birth to such a rebellious, worthless child. I've disowned her completely. If she came begging to my door, I'd not let her in. She's no child of mine."

Liam knew his father was a proud man, and prone to overreact and dramatize. But he sensed that the underlying sentiment was true—his father had disowned Irene, who Liam loved dearly and to whom he felt he probably owed his life, and certainly his happiness. His favorite sister was gone and, if his father's threats held, would be gone forever from his life and the life of his family. He couldn't imagine it. This sad condition went against everything Christian in his being.

It became Liam McCauslin's sole quest to convince his father to forgive Irene. He visited his family frequently, beseeching them as both a son and a soon-to-be priest, to forgive. He recounted the story of the prodigal son in many variations. He devoted every waking moment to trying to soften his father's heart. His father was a stubborn man, though, and refused to recant his disownment. "She's none of mine," he repeated sullenly whenever Liam pled for her. It became a moral crisis in young Liam's life. Finally, he decided that the only way to make peace with himself and God was to reunite Irene with the family.

He became convinced that if his father were to see her again on his doorstep, he would not be able to remain cold and hardhearted. He would embrace his repentant daughter and welcome her back. So Liam, not yet seventeen, knew what he must do. He must go to America, that vast, strange, faraway land, and find his sister. He must find her and convince her to return to Ireland, to return to her family, and to return to the Catholic Church. His father would not refuse if he went to all the trouble of finding her and convincing her of the error of her ways. He was sure of it.

That left just one major problem. How would he manage to leave the seminary, get to America, and find Irene? He'd always been resourceful, but finding the means to accomplish what he now felt was his true purpose in life was beyond him.

First, he visited Stuart MacKenzie, the wealthiest man in town, a banker. He entreated him for a loan to cover passage to America and back, colorfully recounting his sister's disappearance from the family and explaining how he felt it was his God-given duty to find her and return her to the town, the family, and the flock. Mr. Mackenzie listened respectfully. "Ah, ye be a fine brother, young McCauslin. A fine son. And ye'll be a fine priest. But tell me, how would you ever repay this loan? Do you have any inkling how expensive round trip passage to America is on one of the ships? Young men studying to take the cloth don't have the means, my lad. How could you ever repay it?" This wasn't a question Liam could easily answer. He offered to work it off, swore he would find a way. MacKenzie shook his head. "I don't know what work you could ever do for me for that kind of money and besides, I'll not be interfering in your father's business or taking you away from your calling in the church, either. I'm sorry, lad. I know this is important to you, but I can't help you out with this one. Maybe you should talk to the good father and see what his advice is."

Liam had been avoiding that. He could well predict what Father O'Donelson would say, given that Irene had already been the topic of many a sermon and lecture about the sins of disobeying one's parents and the rebelliousness that led to misery and degradation. There'd even been a few sermons about the evil of listening to heathen ideas. He didn't foresee much help from the old priest—at least, not until he had already accomplished his quest and brought a penitent Irene back into family and fold. That would possibly be worthy of forgiveness for his unannounced disappearance and gain him readmittance to the seminary. Possibly. Even that was uncertain. Liam knew that he was potentially threatening his own calling in the priesthood. If he forfeited that, it would truly break his parents' hearts.

No, Father O'Donelson was the last person he wanted to learn of his plans. If he asked permission, he knew it would certainly not be granted. If he asked and then disobeyed, he knew he would never be allowed to reenter the seminary. It was better to just go with the impulsiveness of well-meaning youth, succeed in his effort, and then return. That was his best chance. But now, if Stuart MacKenzie began wagging his tongue about his request, that hope would be gone, too. He realized he hadn't thought things through as well as he should have. It had simply seemed impossible that his request for a loan would be refused. He had imagined he would be on a ship bound for America that night. Not that he had even checked to see if there were ships bound for America leaving anytime soon. It occurred to him that, since the harm in letting MacKenzie know of his plans was already done, he could perhaps at least find out some necessary information from the man.

"Perhaps I should talk to the good Father," he said. "Perhaps I shall. But, Stuart, you know how poor our parish is, and I would never want him to feel he needed to—you know—assist me with the matter. How much is passage? Do you know that?" Now he was thinking ahead.

"Ships don't leave that often, and generally only from Dublin or Belfast," the banker replied thoughtfully. "It's been months since one docked in Cork bound for America. Hasn't been that much of a call since everyone left with the last potato famine before you were born." He shook his head sadly. "That was a tragedy. Lots of families separated. Lots of little ones and old ones lost to starvation. Why, your own family lost several babes, as I recall. Sad times. Sad times." He looked wistful. "I wonder if any of those lost ones will ever come home? Wonder how they've fared in the New World? Is it better for them? Or worse?" He shrugged. "A few sent word back, the ones that succeeded sometimes even sent money to their old ones. Many just disappeared. The ships from Belfast and Dublin going now, though—those are mostly just for rich folks on a journey. They usually set sail in London and stop on our shores to pick up a few passengers or hire crewmen, since the Irish will work for less than the English. Passage on one of those liners will cost you hundreds upon hundreds of pounds, Liam. More than you'll make in your lifetime, sure. More than your father has, probably. Sorry, lad. It doesn't seem likely you'll be headed for the United States of America anytime soon. I hear they are united again, more or less, now that that war to free the black men has ended," MacKenzie continued, glad to have an audience. "Do you know how many Irish lads lost their lives fighting for that cause? On both sides, mind you."

Liam shook his head. "It's a tragedy to enslave a fellow human being because of the place of his birth or the color of his skin," he said passionately. "They fought a good war and I am glad they succeeded! But, Stuart, don't mention my request to my family or Father O'Donelson, please. If I pursue this, I'd rather tell them in my own way and in my own time. And, from what you've told me, it isn't likely I'll pursue it now, is it?"

Liam hoped his entreaty would persuade McKenzie to keep silence; perhaps it did. He probably was not the one who actually told Father O'Donelson or Patrick McCauslin. He certainly told at least one of the townsfolk, though, who told another who told another, until everyone was babbling about it, and about what a fine, well-meaning young man he was and what a good trait this desire to return a fallen one to the fold was in a future priest. Again Liam's family was the talk of the town. He knew neither Father O'Donelson nor his own father would treat his planned impudence nearly as kindly as the prattling townspeople. When his father called on him at the seminary three days later, he steeled himself for a resounding lecture.

"As if it isn't enough to have one smug, rebellious child who disowns her kin and runs off with a heathen to a faraway shore!"

began Patrick McCauslin. Liam noticed how, in his father's mind, it was now Irene who had disowned the family rather than the other way around, but he said nothing. "No, that isn't enough pain for a poor man to bear," he continued, becoming increasingly dramatic. "Now, my fine, first-born son wants to forsake his calling, forsake the honor he was meant to bring his family, and go chasing off to find her. I won't have it! I won't have you even thinking such thoughts! It is beyond disrespectful. It is no way for a man in your position to act. In fact, I've already discussed this shameful behavior with the good Father"— he motioned toward Father O'Donelson who now rather sheepishly entered the small quarters—"and told him I'd spare him the embarrassment of having to deal with this abysmal plan of yours by withdrawing you from the order myself!"

"At least temporarily," interrupted the mild-mannered priest. "Just temporarily, until you have had the time to think things through and make sure this is the life you want for yourself. Your father has entered a petition to have you return home to assist the family in times of hardship. The work your sister did, it seems, needs to be replaced for the family business to survive. Once that has been solved, you can of course return here and complete your studies and your preparations. If you choose to, of course," he added, as if it would be impossible for Liam to choose otherwise.

Liam felt a little dizzy; he hadn't expected such a repercussion for his actions, and he certainly hadn't expected it so quickly. Dazed, he said nothing and slowly gathered the few possessions he had been allowed—a change of clothes, a Bible, a few books on the lives of saints—and followed his father back to the family house.

When he arrived, he wondered how much of his father's request had been altruistic to spare the priest a scandal—which Father O'Donelson could certainly have avoided just by a good sermon on brotherly love with Liam as the hero, reinforcing what most of the townsfolk were already saying—and how much had been due to a desire to have him home to take over some of the work Irene had left behind. Irene had always been a hard worker. In addition to working every day around the house and caring for the children, she was also a talented seamstress and devoted several hours each day to sewing. The family's tailoring shop had done well lately in large measure because of her tireless efforts. Now that she was gone, it was apparent work was far behind. Mother and the little ones couldn't keep up with the orders, and so the orders were falling off and being given to the competition—the O'Reillys' small business up the street. Irene's departure had certainly not been good for the family financially. Liam wondered now, realizing how hard she had worked here in this shop, how much of her departure was out of love for the young man she followed back to "the promised land" and how much of it was just an attempt to have a life of her own. If she'd stayed here in Cork, she would likely have remained at home, helping with the sewing, her entire life. She'd had no social life and was past twenty-five years old when she left, very old for a Cork lass to marry.

Patrick McCauslin seemed to have every intention of keeping it that way, too—perhaps, Liam now realized, for selfish, economic motives. He began to see his sister's actions in a new light and found himself wishing her well on her voyage to a new life where she would, he hoped, be as happy as she deserved. He was still determined to find her and reunite her with the family, though—even more so because he did not want to spend his days nipping and tucking and measuring for suits and trousers. He had helped a little in the trade as a child, but Irene had usually secretly done most of his work for him. She knew he detested sewing, and it was another of her gifts as she spoiled him. Focusing on his studies and preparing to be a priest had actually been a very good escape from the drudgery of a trade in which he found no pleasure. If finding a way to go to America and look for his sister got him out of hemming and sewing several hours a day, he couldn't wait to depart! Besides, he reflected, in a way things were working out well. His father had saved him from burning bridges with Father O'Donelson who, otherwise, would probably have called him in for a chat the next day, told him he understood his feelings and admired them, but then forbade him to go. Since he was now no longer in the seminary in the priest's charge, he would not be disobeying if he sailed to the United States. He could still, perhaps, go back to the order upon his return to Ireland and become a priest. He wouldn't be forfeiting his career. "The good Lord works in mysterious ways," he told himself, renewing his resolve to find a way to America, now even more certain that it was what he was meant to do.

He remembered that Stuart MacKenzie had said the ships sometimes stopped in Belfast or Dublin to hire crewmen. Well, if that was true, then he just needed to get to Belfast or Dublin and get himself hired as a crewman on one of the ships. That solved the problem of passage completely in his mind. It never occurred to him that he wouldn't be hired. He only had to get to one of those cities. After two weeks of pricking his fingers on pins and needles and taking measurements, he decided to trust his fate to God. Liam set off walking in what he thought was the general direction of Dublin with a canteen of water and a loaf of bread—hardly enough for a two-hundred-mile walk. But luck was with him, and not more than an hour out of the city, he met a tinker band traveling from Claire toward the city. The group had stopped to fix a broken wheel spoke. Always a good carpenter handy with tools, he endeared himself to all by helping with the repairs. When the old grandmother heard his story, of how he had left the seminary to walk to Dublin and hire on to a ship with only a loaf of bread, she insisted he travel with the troupe.

He had heard of the tinkers; the townspeople were suspicious, accusing them of stealing horses and children wherever they went and of being in league with the devil, fortune-telling along with crazy dancing and music. He'd never met a tinker before. But this group of twelve men, women and children with three horses and two carts between them, loaded with tin cups and pans they were planning to sell in Dublin, hardly struck him as sinister. They seemed interesting and kind. When the old grandmother read his fortune with her tarot cards, telling him he would succeed in finding his sister but his voyage would not turn out as he expected, he thanked her, offering her the rest of his bread. She chuckled and took it. "You'll need potatoes more than bread, anyway," she said, "though bread'll help you, too." The tinkers shared what little they had with him throughout the two-week journey. He learned their songs and stories and even some of their dances. Liam had always liked to dance; he still happily broke into Irish jigs on occasion when he was at home on the ranch, and had since taught Eddie and the rest of the children the energetic steps of jigs and reels—and some of the tinker steps, as well.

When the group finally reached the outskirts of the city and joined the large tinker camp gathering there, one of the older sons gave Liam a ride on horseback to the docks several miles away. "Here ye be," he said, pressing a few coins into Liam's hands and giving him a bag with some fruits and cakes. "Fare thee well."

The docks were a busy place. There were several small fishing vessels, many looking for helpers, but no streamliners or schooners headed for America. Liam tried to hide his disappointment when the men on the boats told him the big ships didn't come often and since there had been one docked here barely a week before, it could be months before another arrived. Now becoming more practical, he decided that if he planned to hire on to a ship to America when it finally did arrive, he had better get some experience. He had never been onboard a boat in his life. He didn't mention that, though, as he tried to convince one of the skippers of a large fishing vessel that he would be a good dockhand. "Ye can handle a net, can ye?" asked the gruff old man, pleased with Liam's youthful enthusiasm and energy. "And swab the decks and help with the cookin' besides? Well, I guess I can give ye a try. We'll be off tomorrow for two weeks at sea. Be puttin' in at Belfast, then either back here or on to Canary Wharf, depending. You be here sharp at sunrise!"

Liam didn't mention that he had nowhere else to go and found what appeared to be a fairly safe corner just off the docks to sleep. No one bothered him but the prostitutes, and they mainly offered good-natured advice and tried to mother him, seeing his youth and inexperience. One, with an intuitive generosity he would always be grateful for, even gave him some tablets to fend off seasickness that she'd liberated from one of her clients earlier that evening. "Just in case," she explained. "You say you've never sailed before, so they just might come in handy for you. Me, I don't plan on doing any sailing." She laughed and covered him with her shawl. "Sleep tight, little one," she said. "I'll wake ye in the morning if the sun doesn't do it first."

The sun woke him long before her promised return. He pocketed the pills and, seeing no safe place to leave the shawl, folded it under his arm, promising himself he would find her when the boat returned to Dublin. Weeks later, shivering as a stowaway in the moat of a ship bound for Boston, he would again bless her kindness as he wrapped himself in the shawl for warmth.

Now, he was just eager for his adventure on the high seas to begin. A few hours later, pale and retching with what seemed to be a fatal case of seasickness, his eagerness completely disappeared. The skipper quickly ascertained the boy had never been aboard a boat before in his life and alternated cursing his judgment for bringing him on board with cursing Liam. He was hard pressed to find anything Liam could assist with. "I'll feed you while we're at sea, teach you what I can in between your vomiting, and put you off at the first port we stop at," he said. "No pay. No siree." The tablets that the kind prostitute had given him helped a little, although he used them sparingly. He did learn a little about sailing and a little about fishing during his brief maiden voyage, but he learned more about cleaning latrines. When the vessel put in at Belfast not quite two weeks later, he was almost relieved to be put off the boat. Now he had another problem, though. He needed to figure out how to feed himself while waiting for the mythic ship that would sail him to America to arrive.

He found himself drawing strength from the kind old tinker's tarot reading. "You will succeed," she had said. He needed that assurance to keep from losing faith as he took stock of his situation. He'd never been in Belfast. In fact until recently, he'd never been out of County Cork. The city was dirty and bustling and more than a little frightening for a country lad of sixteen. Remembering the kindness of the prostitutes in Dublin, he decided the ladies of the evening may be his best source of good advice, and he set out to find the areas they frequented. The docks seemed strangely empty of women, though, and well patrolled by cops in English garb.

Finally, Liam got his courage up enough to approach one of the burly sailors on the dock. "Excuse me, sir," he said, "but do you know where I might find—might find a lady of the evening?" The burly sailor's expression changed rapidly from disbelief to amusement, and he began to chuckle.

"Well, I'll be blessed!" he exclaimed. "A young lad like you with the face and manner of a seminary pup lookin' for a whore!" He chuckled some more. "Guess I wish I'd known about them fine lasses at your age," he continued. "Guess I wish. I fear you won't find any near here, though. Been a moral cleanup campaign lately. Them English coppers be protecting us from our vices by rounding up our ladies and puttin' 'em in the clinker. If you head downtown, though," he continued, motioning over his shoulder to the left, "you'll find a place called Maddie's Boarding House where many of the fine ladies have taken up residence of late." He winked. "You go there and knock three times lightly on the door, then tell whoever answers that Simon sent ye." He guffawed then leered. "But you leave Maddie alone, lad, mind ya. That one's mine!" Then, as an afterthought, he laughed again and pressed a couple of silver coins in Liam's hands. "Reckon you might need these, too," he said. "The prices as well as the ladies get a bit uppity when they're off the docks."

Liam stammered a thank you. He added the coins to those he still had in his pocket from his tinker benefactor and the few shillings the skipper of the boat on which he had spent such a miserable two weeks of his life had finally relented and given him before putting him off at shore. He wandered up the road in the general direction the sailor had pointed, determined to find a sympathetic friend at the "boarding house" who would help him finally find his way to America to locate his beloved sister.

When he arrived at Maddie's, he knocked three times lightly, as he had been instructed. When the door was opened by a plump, blonde woman in her early thirties with laughing blue eyes and a bright smile, he said "Hello. Are you Maddie? Simon sent me." She broke out in a hearty laugh.

"He did, did he? That rogue is corrupting the young now, is he? And what, pray tell, did he send you for?" Now Liam was on his own.

"A warm shower and a place to sleep," he said, proffering the coins he had in his pocket. "You see, I was just put off a boat because I couldn't fish and had no sea legs, and I'm trying to get to America to find my sister who eloped and got disowned by the family. I left the seminary to find her and—"

"Enough, enough," said Maddie. "Come in. No one could make up a story so ridiculous so you must be telling the truth. And whatever inspired Simon to send you our way, we'll take care of you for a spell. He is a warm-hearted fellow for all his gruff ways, he is. Come in. Come in. We'll find a way for you to make yourself useful and give you a place to sleep until you figure out what you're about." She motioned him in. "Flossie! Gina!" she called. "Come here, girls. I have someone for you to meet. Help me figure out what to do with this young would-be priest!"

✸   ✸   ✸

"So there you have it," his father concluded. "I went from being a seminary student to cleaning spittoons in a whorehouse, all in a matter of days. How's that for a bedtime story?" Then his eyes clouded a bit. "I suppose it's a blessing my poor parents never knew. How mortified Papa would have been. I wonder, Mama," he mused, looking toward Eddie's mother, "how the old man is doing now? Do you suppose it's time to send another letter?"

His mother met her husband's eyes with a loving, soulful look that spoke volumes of unspoken shared pain and regret. "Perhaps so," she said quietly. "Perhaps he'll answer this time. We can write one tomorrow, if you like."

His father nodded. "That would be good," he said. "Surely he won't hold his grudge past twenty years' time. If he is still alive, that is," he added sadly. "But I suppose we could check with the county recorder in Cork about that, couldn't we? As we always have before?" Again, his mother nodded.

"What happened next, Papa?" said Gene, still awake by the fire. "Tell us how you got to America. What happened next?"

"Tomorrow," said Liam. "We'll have more storytelling tomorrow. Right now, the little ones are dozing, and it's time for us all to be off to bed."

Eddie slept well and awoke looking forward to the rest of his father's story that evening. His mother had fixed pancakes and fresh jam for breakfast. Papa was eating breakfast when Eddie reached the bottom of the stairs. "Good morning, son," he greeted him. "How would you like to ride Redwing to school today rather than walking? That will give you more time to enjoy this fine meal. Besides, I worked her out a bit yesterday, and I think you have her broken enough to ride now."

"Do you really think so?" Eddie asked, feeling his pulse quicken a bit. He loved the beautiful roan filly his father had traded from "the Chief" in exchange for a fine table and chairs he had carved a few months ago, but the horse was very spirited. She didn't let people near her—except for Eddie and the Chief—and her moods were unpredictable. Eddie loved working with Redwing; he had a natural ability with horses and was an excellent rider. But, other than around the ranch, he hadn't dared venture far with her. "I'm not worried about riding her, mind you. But I don't think she'll take kindly to being tied up outside the school while I do my lessons. She'll likely try to break her tether—or the post. And she might succeed!"

"Well, we have to break her in as a mount eventually, and might as well do it now. Besides"—he winked—"you can tell that pretty teacher that your dad's in town and needs you back early. Then, Redwing will only have an hour or so to face off against the tethering post, eh? After you leave school, you can go see the Chief. Invite him to join us for dinner. Tell him I'm in town."

Eddie liked the idea. He enjoyed a leisurely breakfast before saddling the pretty mare, then hummed to her as she loped toward his schoolhouse. "Oh, the moon shines tonight on pretty Redwing," he sang. "The maid is crying; the night bird's sighing. That's your song, Redwing!" As he sang and rode, he thought about Chief, Redwing's previous owner. "She's a fine pony," the Chief had told his father. "She needs a special touch. That boy of yours would do. But tell him he must visit me so I can show him how to talk to her…"

"Chief's a little eccentric," Eddie's father had told him. "But humor him. Go by once in a while. He doesn't live too far." Eddie had actually enjoyed the visits he made to the Chief's cabin ten miles outside of town. The Chief was a Blackfoot Indian, one of the few who had learned English and interacted regularly with the settlers in Pincer Creek. He taught Eddie lots about handling the horse. He also taught him how to track animals in the mountains by recognizing their signs, footprints and scents, and how to imitate birdcalls and recognize all the various edible berries and barks in the wilderness. Eddie actually preferred this education to the one he received with Miss Welch. He wished he could spend more time with Chief.

He arrived at school, dismounted, and tried to calm the horse, who did not like the idea of being tied to a post and left alone. Miss Welch heard the commotion and came to the classroom door. "Ah, it's you, Eddie," she greeted him brightly. "Is that a new horse you're riding?"

"Not quite," he said. "I've been trying to break her in for several months, but she doesn't always cooperate. Papa wanted me to ride her to school today. I'm not sure it was such a good idea…" He looked helplessly at the horse that was pawing the ground, whinnying at the post and pulling the rope in a tug of war between her neck and the building. "Maybe I should take her back?"

"If your father is in town, he probably wants you home anyway."

"Yes," Eddie agreed. "He did say that. But if you need me to help with the little ones' lessons first…"

"No, we'll be fine without you. Inez can read to the class today. She needs the practice. You take that wild beast home and help your papa. I'm sure there's lots to do."

Eddie nodded. "Thank you. I do appreciate that!" He untied the restless horse and jumped on her, soon galloping into the mountains toward the Chief's strange abode, half deerskin teepee and half logger's cabin. Chief's home held a weird mixture of his father's hand-carved furniture and animal skins, pipes, and beads. Chief was curious about the white settlers and a bit of an outcast from his own tribe as a result. He was a loner, almost a hermit. He lived by himself miles from anyone, with lots of beautiful horses. Chief had a way with all animals. There were rumors he sometimes kept bears and wildcats for pets. Eddie had never seen that, but it wouldn't surprise him. Chief was also a wonderful storyteller—almost as good as Papa. But his stories were different. They were about talking animals and insects; people from underground cities and faraway stars; nymphs and nature spirits.

They were epochs of mythic proportion. Eddie loved listening, and sometimes he thought he understood the underlying lessons and meanings Chief tried to impart. Maybe Chief and Papa would "swap stories" tonight.

At present, the Chief was quietly whispering in the ear of one of the lovely young foals his beloved Spider had recently given birth to. Eddie approached quietly—or as quietly as was possible on the excitable Redwing who was always happy to come here—so as not to scare the horses. When Chief acknowledged him with a nod, he spoke softly. "Papa's in town, Chief. He wants me to invite you to supper tonight, a little before sunset." Chief nodded again, accepting the invitation, and turned his attention back to the colt as Eddie rode away. "Moose there," Chief called after him, motioning to a wooded area past a large clearing to his left. "Near the lake. Go see 'em. Meet their eyes."

Eddie turned Redwing toward the lake. She eagerly trotted into the woods. Not too far in, she slowed and Eddie looked through the trees toward the water. There were, as the Chief had predicted, a group of five large, stately moose drinking from the lake. The largest raised his head as Eddie reined in Redwing. Their eyes met. It was an eerie sensation. Eddie felt the moose startle, then become apprehensive. Next, he had the eerie feeling he saw Chief's face briefly reflected in the animal's large, dark eyes. The animal held Eddie's gaze a moment longer with a calm, timeless stare that seemed to echo of the mountains and lakes it had recently traveled through before returning its attention to the water. Eddie turned his horse away and rode back toward the ranch, puzzling over the strange sixth sense the Chief possessed that seemed to always, unfailingly, tell him when animals were near and where they were located. He'd never known Chief to be wrong.

"How do you do it?" Eddie would ask. Chief would laugh.

"See here," he would say, pointing to his forehead. "Listen here," he would say, pointing to his heart. "You can do, too. I teach." Eddie was still trying to learn.

That night, Chief arrived well before dinner with fresh venison. "Cook," he said, giving his offering to Mama. She smiled and took it, returning with two jars of Chief's favorite berry preserves and honey from the beehives Eddie's father kept. Chief happily put the jars in his elaborately beaded and feathered leather saddlebag before trotting his horse toward the barn, where hay and oats were waiting.

After his horse was comfortably settled in for the night, he returned to the house and sat down by the brightly burning fire. "Early spring," he said. "Good summer crops." Papa nodded. Just then, Gene and the girls appeared.

"Their lessons are done," announced Gene. "Can we hear the rest of your story now, Papa? About the boat to America?" Chief looked interested and began asking questions about the boat. How big was it? What kind of wood was it made of? Papa shrugged.

"I don't know, Chief. As you will soon learn, I was never much of a sailor! But let's eat first. When our stomachs are full, I'll finish my story."

Dinner was good as always, followed by Mama's delicious pie with fresh whipped cream and ground chicory coffee. After the meal, the family gathered to hear the rest of the story about Papa's journey from Ireland. "Let's see. Where did I leave off?"

"You were in the whorehouse!" Gene said.

"Gene!" Mama exclaimed. "Where do you get these notions at the grand old age of seven?"

Papa laughed. "Now, Mama, the boy just pays attention. He's a good listener, that one. You'll recall that is where I finished last night. Maddie and her girls, thanks to Sailor Simon, had saved me from the streets of Belfast. I was cleaning spittoons, listening to gossip and trying to find my way on to a ship." Papa resumed his story. Soon Eddie was seeing the streets of Belfast's busy ship docks as if he was there from the skillful way his father wove together words.

*   *   *

Liam was comfortable at Maddie's. He ran errands, kept the place clean, and generally made himself useful in whatever ways he could. The ladies liked this fresh-faced, innocent young man determined to get to America and find his sister. They spoiled him just as she had. He learned their stories, too. Flossie had been orphaned very young, so Maddie had taken her in. Gina supported a younger sister and child through her earnings. Maddie, in her gruff, practical way, was one of the kindest, most generous women he'd ever met. Liam began to seriously rethink all he had ever been taught about sin. Life wasn't nearly as simple as the rights and wrongs he'd studied. Maddie and her girls lived more Christian lives in their actions than many of the women who attended church regularly in Cork. Liam was quickly developing an appreciation for grey areas of theology. His naturally compassionate, philosophical nature was broadened.

Whenever a ship bound for America docked, Liam applied for work, but his youth and inexperience rendered optimistic persistence futile. He was overlooked in favor of the many capable sailors who sought positions. Just as he was beginning to lose hope, Flossie came to his rescue. One of her clients was loading supplies into the hull of a ship scheduled to depart for Boston in three days. She told him Liam's story, and he took pity. Liam could hide in one of the large burlap sacks of provisions he was loading. He could load Liam into a safe place in the hull among the potatoes without arising suspicion. Liam could stow away on the ship. It was a risky, romantic idea that Flossie was sure would work. "You'll be able to eat if you stay with the provisions; there will be water, too. Maybe you can even slip in among the passengers without attracting attention. Shall I arrange it?"

The plan seemed to be his best chance of getting to America, so he readily agreed. Maddie gave a "bon voyage" party for him. He was sad to leave these kind ladies, but on his way to America at last.

All went well with the plan initially. He hid in a burlap bag of potatoes, with holes that allowed in light and air, and was carried safely onto the ship without suspicion. "Wait'll she sails before you stir at all," warned his mysterious benefactor, slipping a canteen of water into the bag as he lowered it. "Twelve hours, maybe more. Good luck." Soon, all went dark. Liam forced himself to sleep, difficult because of the excitement he was feeling. After he slept, he remained wrapped in a shawl inside the bag, barely moving despite muscle cramps for what seemed like days. It was probably no more than a few hours.

Once the ship was underway, he knew it for sure. The high seas still had the same effect on him as they had on the fishing boat. Retching and vomiting forced him to leave his hiding place among the potatoes. It also made his presence very apparent to the first sailor who entered for provisions. The ship had been gone less than three days when he was discovered.

"We got us a stowaway, Cap'n," the burly man who dragged him out said, holding the thin, pale boy up to the man in charge of the ship and crew. "Shall I throw 'im overboard to swim back to Eire?" He laughed menacingly.

"Normally, I'd consider it," said the captain. "Stowaways expecting free passage irk me. But one of the cook's assistants has taken ill. If he's clever enough to get on board, he's probably clever enough to work for his passage. He's a young one. At cook's assistant wages, he'll earn his ticket price before he's forty or so. Take 'im to Cookie." Thus, Liam became an indentured servant on the good ship *Philadelphia*. He was given a small, uncomfortable bunk in a tiny berth shared by the cook's two other assistants, both at least twenty years older than he was. One seemed to be suffering from pneumonia. He had a raspy, constant cough, wild eyes, and a high fever.

"Take his seasick pills," said his bunkmate. "He won't be needing 'em now." Liam did, but he felt guilty for doing so and spent many hours trying to comfort the sick sailor, bringing him cool, damp towels for his forehead at night, talking to him, and praying.

"Just mind you wash well before you peel my potatoes, bleeding heart," warned the cook. Liam always did. When the dying man learned Liam had been in the seminary, he begged him to hear his final confession and perform last rites. With new perspectives on life from Maddie's, Liam didn't think twice about agreeing, even though he'd never taken his final vows. He administered the rites very naturally, then performed a simple memorial service before the sailor was cast into the sea.

Liam's life on the ship was miserable. The cook declared him a good helper, which satisfied the captain, but he never received wages. Just a bunk, food, and medicine for his seasickness. "Those wages are goin' to your passage," said the captain.

When the ship finally docked in Boston, the captain locked him up on board and had other sailors stand guard. Liam spent the next three years of his life on board the ship, miserably peeling potatoes. He spent many long hours considering his plight, trying to plan some way to escape from his indentured servitude. One morning outside of Boston Harbor, as the ship was bound back to Europe for the third time, he made a desperate attempt. Liam jumped as the ship sailed, swimming as hard as he could to escape from the undertow current of the engines. "Man overboard!" he heard someone shout. He kept swimming away from the ship toward the shore, hoping no one would respond to that call.

Fortune favored the foolish as usual. No one did. He was free. He dragged himself to land exhausted, kissing the sand after what seemed an eternity. He had made it to America. Now, all he had to do was find Irene. After what he had been through, that should be an easy task. Wet and shivering, he walked along the narrow stretch of rocky beach toward the city. He arrived two hours later on the outskirts, seeing a group of brownstone homes that, by Irish standards, looked like estates. He watched amazed from a distance as a woman entered an alley and threw what appeared to be bread into a large metal container. People here threw food into the garbage! This really was the land of plenty! He could hardly believe his good fortune.

A few minutes later, pangs of hunger rumbling through his stomach after his long, exerting swim, he approached the trash-can. It was deep, and he had to rummage to find the crusts of bread. As he did so, the lid he'd balanced on his shoulder fell, crashing to the ground.

"Bums rummaging through garbage cans!" A gruff voice with a trace of an Irish brogue resonated from a nearby gate, now open. "I'll not have it in this neighborhood! You come with me peacefully, you drunkard, or I'll pull my nightstick on ya. I'm off duty now, but you'll be goin' with me to the station when I report tonight, that's sure."

"I mean no harm, sir," Liam said, replacing the lid on the large metal container and approaching the man. "I'm a stranger here, and hungry. I'll do any work you have need of to pay for these crumbs of bread. I—"

"I'll say you're a stranger!" the man replied, a little less gruffly now. "Are ye from Donegal? I recognize that accent. Came here from Tipperary myself, near twenty years ago. Best thing I ever did. You look like a drowned rat, boy."

"I'm from Cork. My name's Liam McCauslin. I—"

"What's the racket, Paddy?" a female voice called, also with an Irish accent. "Quit talkin' to yourself and get in here, or you'll miss dinner, you will. You been drinkin' that whiskey again and seein' leprechauns?"

"Shush, woman, I've been doin' no such thing," he called back. "I've just found me a young pup to save from a life of crime.

Come with me," the man said to Liam. "The missus'll feed us both and make a fuss over you because you're a young Irishman. You can tell your story inside."

"Am I really under arrest?" Liam asked innocently as he followed the man through the gate. "I didn't mean any harm, honestly. Is it against the law to take food others don't want? I couldn't believe my eyes when I saw bread being thrown away! If I'd known it was wrong to take it, I—"

"Come with me, get cleaned up, and enjoy a warm meal. I'm a police sergeant in this town. Whether or not I arrest you depends on your story, lad." He still sounded gruff, but his tone had softened as a smile formed. Sighing involuntarily, Liam crossed himself as he walked inside. "A good Catholic, too!" the sergeant observed. "That'll help your case, I'm sure!" He turned to the plump woman busily setting the table. "Add another plate, Mrs. Mac. I found this young tadpole from our homeland digging through garbage for food. Why don't you help me figure out what to do with him?"

She bustled back with an extra plate and silverware, continuing to set a table with what looked like a feast. There was roast beef, baked potatoes, steamed carrots, fresh bread and large glasses of milk. He couldn't recall ever eating so well at home. As if reading his mind, the sergeant laughed. "Boggles the stomach, doesn't it?" he said. "Welcome to the land of plenty."

Liam told his story to the McConnells over dinner. Hearing Liam had jumped ship, a shadow crossed the sergeant's face. "That just may be an illegal activity. There are no laws against going through trash, though it rarely happens. But escaping indentured servitude is an infraction. I can't be harboring a fugitive, lad."

Molly McConnell interrupted. She'd taken an immediate liking to Liam, as her husband had predicted. "Now, Mr. Mac, just be reasonable. This event happened less than three hours ago. It isn't a crime unless the captain filed a complaint. Since he's bound for England, that isn't likely to happen for a very long time. Whatever happened, a young man can't bring incriminating evidence against himself so it's just hearsay. It happened in international waters outside of your jurisdiction, so your conscious needn't be bothering you. This boy is just looking for his sister to take home. He's going to be a priest, for the love of God. So don't you be entertaining thoughts about arresting him, or you'll have no more fine dinners from me!"

"Hush, missus. I'm thinking of no such thing. I can't be doing anything improprietous, seeing as how I'm a pillar of this community. I'm just thinking you'll want to take this young man in, and it won't be possible if there's any questionable circumstance, that's all. There may not be any now, but there's bound to be eventually if he's stowed away, been discovered, and jumped ship."

"There's a solution for that," she came back with quickly. "I'll tell the neighbors he's a cousin of my friend Mamie from south Boston come to help me paint that porch that's in need of a good whitewashing. That'll be the end of any questions. He can paint that porch and do all the things around here you've been promising me for the last six years. I'll pay him with my own household money I've saved if necessary to get him a ticket to find his sister!"

"Been pocketing me money I'm giving you in good faith for the house, have you, woman?" he said, but there was warmth and humor in his voice. "I knew it! And a liar besides. Me ma told me never to marry the likes of you!"

Liam's fate with the McConnells was settled by this exchange. He stayed with them, painting, making home repairs, and refinishing furniture, for over three months. He helped with landscaping and gardening, too. The McConnells soon had a beautiful garden of roses in their front yard with lovely hand-carved benches Liam designed. He had found, serendipitously, two great loves and talents—carpentry and gardening—as a result of Mrs. McConnell's charitable kindness. Whenever he would mildly suggest that he needed to be on his way to find his sister, Mrs. McConnell would always rave about what a wonderful job he was doing and how her fine home was at last becoming the showplace of the neighborhood, as it always should have been. Mr. McConnell would think of one more upgrade or repair that needed tending to. Finally, over dinner one evening, Liam said he really needed to be on his way. "I was sixteen when I left to find Irene," he said. "Now, I'm nearly twenty-one. I still haven't found her. I really must go."

"America's a big land, lad," said Mr. McConnell in a fatherly voice. "It isn't a little island like Ireland. Hundreds of Irelands could be laid out here back to back! You may have been able to walk to Dublin, even though you didn't have to, by God's grace. You certainly won't be able to walk up to every door in this great, vast land looking for your sister. You have no idea where she went, do you?"

Just then Mrs. McConnell said "I heard those people that call themselves Mormons walked all the way from New York to Utah, thousands of miles, some of 'em. Took over ten years and a lot of 'em died. But you'd be surprised how far you can walk."

That caught Liam's attention. "Mormons," he repeated.

"I think so, yes," replied Molly. "Strange bunch, I hear. Pagan religion. Seemed to bring misfortune to folks wherever they went, it's said. But to walk all that way 'cause they claimed their God told 'em to—well, you got to give them credit. Sounds like Moses in the Bible, almost…"

"Where's Utah?" asked Liam. "Is that where they all are? Do they call it the promised land?"

Mr. McConnell shrugged. "Haven't heard of them anywhere else for a very long time," he said. "Utah's darned near to California, though. Far stretch from here! You can probably get a good part of the way by train, but you'll need a stagecoach for part of the journey."

"That's where she is," Liam said simply. "I know it. A place called the Great Salt Lake is where the fellow was taking her.

That's where I'll find her. Please help me figure out how to get there."

In exchange for his labor, Molly McConnell generously bought him a train ticket as far west as her funds allowed and Sergeant McConnell solemnly gave him several more dollars for his journey. "We'll be saying our Hail Mary's for you, me lad," he said. "Not too many young men would undertake such an adventure. The Lord's been with you so far, and I trust he'll help you finish your journey and bring your sister home. You look us up if you come back this way." Then, he sobered for a minute and shook his head. "Better you don't, maybe. That Captain Bly of yours is likely to have sailed back by then. He may report you. Even if he doesn't, not many ships sail for Ireland and word spreads. Go back by way of New York," he advised. "Not here. We'll miss you, though, and you'll have our prayers go with you on your way."

Liam boarded a westbound train. He had been miraculously fortunate on his journey, he reflected. The miserable years on the ship allowed him to mature enough to make the journey to its end. He realized, had he been more mature at the time he set off on foot for Dublin so many years ago, he never would have attempted it. But he had been convinced then he was doing the right thing, and he still was convinced. Besides, after all he had gone through, he was now even more committed. The Tinker woman had predicted long ago he would succeed, and he had never since doubted that he would. She had certainly been right about things not turning out as he planned. He chuckled. She'd even been right about needing the potatoes more than bread! So there was no reason to doubt that she would also be right about finding Irene. Heartened, his faith renewed, he watched the land pass through the window of the train for days on end. Sergeant McConnell was right. This land was much bigger than Ireland. Liam couldn't imagine anyone walking this far.

✳   ✳   ✳

Chief interrupted, seeking more information about the train. How fast did it go? Did it belch out smoke like a giant dragon? The Chief always seemed fascinated by transportation. After Eddie's father answered questions about the train to his satisfaction, the Chief asked for some blackberry brandy. As he sipped the brandy, Chief began a tale of his own, a strange tale his grandfather had told him about a time when trails would tie up this land like ribbons. "Tiny boxes belching smoke follow each other down the trails. That'll be the end of the Fourth World," he said knowingly, as if everyone should understand exactly what he was talking about. "That train, though. That wasn't it. Must not be ending yet."

"Have some more brandy, Chief," offered Eddie's father. "You sleep here by the fire tonight. It's a cold night out there." The Chief grunted happily, and Eddie understood that signaled the end of storytelling for the evening.

"Aren't you ever going to tell us if you found your sister?" complained Inez. "I don't want to go to bed until I know!"

"Of course he found her, silly goose," said Gene. "The gypsy said he would, remember?"

Inez looked at her brother as if he'd lost his mind. "You think that means anything?" she said with a superior air. "Gypsies! Like they would know!"

"Gene's right," said his father. "She knew. But never fear, little one. I'll tell you the rest of the story tomorrow. If you all do your chores quickly so I get an early start on my story, I might even tell you how your mother came to America, and how we met."

This offer was especially appealing to the girls. "C'mon," said Allie. "Let's hurry to bed so we can get up early and finish before school!" The children scurried off to bed, except for Eddie. He stayed by the fire until late in the evening, sipping brandy and talking with his father and the Chief. The men talked about crops and weather. The Chief told another of his stories, this one about people coming from underground after a flood.

"They sang a song to the sun every morning, and ran toward the rainbows to chase away the rain," he said. "That was how the Third World ended. Rain. Floods. People quit singing and running like they should. The Second World ended in fire. This one will end when the ribbons that hold the smoke-belching boxes strangle the land. You'll do important things after the world ends, Eddie," he heard Chief say just before he fell asleep. "First, you gotta learn to find the animals. You gotta let me teach you how to see with your soul. You gotta let me teach you how to listen with your heart."

CHAPTER THREE

IN SEARCH OF HIPPOCRATES

As they had planned, the children were up before sunrise, getting their assigned tasks done in record time before heading to school. Chief asked Eddie to spend the day with him, tracking animals in the woods. His father liked the idea. "Our family could use a good hunter. Chief might not always be around to bring us that venison your mother likes so much. Miss Welch won't mind if you miss another day. Joe," he called, "you tell your teacher I needed Eddie to stay here and work with me today, okay?"

Eddie didn't mind. He found the hikes and rides with Chief infinitely more fascinating than helping the children at school learn their numbers and letters. Chief knew the name of every tree, berry, and plant in the area—in his own language as well as in English. Eddie readily absorbed this information. He also loved to listen to the stories the old Indian told about how each plant and tree and berry had originated, and what its purpose was for human beings. Eddie was vaguely aware that the information he was learning might be valuable someday. Chief, in his strange way, was teaching him which plants were edible, which were medicinal and which were poisonous. He was teaching him how to tell, by undergrowth, where to find the nearest stream or where to dig for a well. He taught Eddie how tints and colors of flowers predicted seasonal changes or forthcoming droughts, and how this, in turn, signaled the travel patterns of deer and wild turkey; of moose and wildcats; of elk and bear. He was teaching him too, in more subtle ways, how to earn the trust of animals, starting with Redwing, his skittish, spirited horse.

Eddie's day with the Chief passed quickly and happily. They tracked a pack of wolves deep into the woods, gathered mushrooms and berries to take back to Mother, and found more moose. Eddie heard stories about the rock people, and learned how to start a fire with stones and sunlight, his pocketknife, and dry wood. "Didn't have matches when I was your age. You might not always have them, either." Chief also told him how to protect himself in a blizzard, how to keep warm in snow, and where to locate the nuts squirrels stored for winter. Eddie listened, filing it all away for future use. They returned to the house in early evening. Chief seemed to take it for granted that he would stay another night and hear the rest of Liam's story. Eddie knew his parents wouldn't mind. They always welcomed the Chief in their home. He would probably stay with them all weekend. Eddie hoped they could spend more time together in the woods.

After another delicious dinner, the family settled around the fire for stories. This was a rare treat. Generally, Papa would devote at least one night of his visits home to telling stories to the children, but other nights were spent visiting friends, or talking softly with Mama. This story was more interesting than usual, too. Stories from the Bible or imaginative stories Papa made up or remembered from his childhood were fascinating. Learning about his father's own life, though, held even more magic for Eddie, who now was thinking about what his own future life might hold.

"Tell us about how Mama came to America!" said Inez brightly as everyone gathered.

"No, no," said Gene. "First we have to hear about how Papa found his sister. Don't you want to hear that part?"

"I need to finish one story before beginning another," Papa said, resolving the argument before it began. "But since these two are related, I can tell you both at once. When my train arrived in

Colorado, I had a problem. It was coming on winter, and I had no idea how to finish my journey. I decided, despite what the Mormons had supposedly done, I was not walking through the towering mountains stretching across the horizon to the Great Salt Lake!"

* * *

Liam first sought out the local whorehouse, based on the good fortune he had enjoyed at such locations in the past. Perhaps it was because he was older now, no longer a fresh-faced, innocent sixteen-year-old boy from the countryside. Or perhaps the ladies here were more hardened than the ladies he'd known in Ireland. Whatever the reason, the ladies weren't interested in him except as a paying customer, and he had no interest in that—at least none he would admit.

He began asking around town for work. There wasn't much available, but he learned of a couple of mining towns to the south where silver had been discovered and, though the mother lodes were nearly mined out, there was a need for mine workers and good carpenters. Getting there without money was a problem. Since he was well-educated and polite, Liam may have been able to work in the post office or a similar position, but the fact that he had never been legally accepted into the country and had no papers to verify his citizenship or even his true name made that impossible. He found himself caught between a rock and a hard place as the snow began to descend. Still determined, believing in the Tinker's words and the rightness of his quest, he didn't give up, eventually finding work as a dishwasher in the restaurant of the town's railroad hotel. The pay was poor, but he got two meals a day as a benefit, sharing a room with the cook that cost most of his meager wages.

That was how Liam spent the winter. He saved what money he could, planning to head for Silverton, the once-booming mining community, in the spring to try his luck prospecting. He hoped to earn enough to get him comfortably to Salt Lake. He had no idea how to work in the mines, but he had plenty of confidence. He'd made it this far. He was sure he would make it further. While he washed dishes, surprised by how much more severe the winters were in Colorado than they had been back home in Cork, Johanna Schneider was sailing to America.

Johanna's route to the New World was somewhat different than Liam's. Her father made his living as a watchmaker in Zurich, Switzerland. She was one of four children. Her elder brother would take over as a watchmaker. Her younger sister had already married a local businessman. Her younger brother was a bit of a dreamer; the family assumed he would help in the shop, making and repairing watches, but he wanted to study—perhaps to teach at the university someday. He attended courses in geology, while Johanna attended nursing college, seeking a career in medicine. She had always been intelligent; also spirited. Her family and neighbors did not go quite so far as to call her rebellious, but that was sometimes in their minds.

As a child, she had insisted she would be a doctor. Her father had loved and humored his favorite daughter to the extent that he could. When it became clear this was not just a childish whim, he even sent her to nursing school, but pointed out a woman should not work as a doctor and that, given her station in life, it was expected that she would marry a well-off husband so that a career in nursing would not be necessary—or even acceptable.

Johanna had other plans for her life. Just as she finished nursing school, her brother became acquainted with two young men from America. They were missionaries for a religious group that believed in visions and revelations proselytizing in Switzerland to find others to join their church. They were especially interested in finding people with skills that were needed in their new community on America's western frontier. As it happened, teaching—especially university-level geology teaching—and nursing were among these skills. With the promise of work in the careers they sought and their passage to America guaranteed by the church these young men belonged to in exchange for their services, little persuasion was needed. Johanna and her brother were soon bound for "Zion." Because it allowed both to do what they had always wished, the religion appealed to them. His philosophical nature and her strong belief in a higher power made accepting the religious doctrine easy—even welcome. It was as palatable as the Calvinistic Lutheran sect in which they had been raised. Johanna, feeling fresh, youthful, and ready for adventure, eagerly boarded the ship, sailed to America with her brother, and accompanied the young men they had met far across the vast continent by train and stagecoach to assume their roles—roles they had always dreamed of.

Heinrich—now Henry—began the department of geology at a newly formed college in Salt Lake City. Johanna became the head of the main city hospital's nursing department very quickly, for her skills easily surpassed those of most of the country doctors there. They appreciated her seemingly supernatural ability to heal and her broad medical knowledge. Soon, most of the doctors refused to perform surgeries without her advice. She followed her inner motivations. She followed Hippocrates. This intelligent, spirited young Swiss woman found the life she wished to live when she and her brother settled happily in Salt Lake City.

The Mormon practice of multiple marriages did not appeal to her, however. There were far more women than men in Salt Lake City, and in the interest of community stability, reproduction and child rearing in a land that needed tamed, most of the Mormon men had several wives. She understood the logic of it, but wasn't interested. Johanna had several marriage offers, but she kindly explained she was married to her career. She was the bride of Hippocrates, and the time she put in at the hospital precluded a family. Because it was so obvious she was needed at the hospital, and because her explanations were always so kind and unassuming, the community accepted her wishes. She had traveled far for it, but she had found the life she wanted. She used her skills to save lives. Johanna was appreciated for her abilities, and it didn't matter that she was a woman, not a man—something that in her homeland at the time would have mattered very much. She and her brother learned a new language, a new culture, and a new religion together. They had each other's company and never regretted their decision. He married two women and had several children; she spoiled her nieces and nephews and was very happy in Salt Lake City. Not marrying seemed a small price to pay. Until she met Liam in a rather dramatic way, the idea had never appealed to her anyway.

While Johanna was managing the nursing staff and healing the sick, Liam was making his way through Colorado in search of his sister. In early spring, he joined a small group of men bound for Silverton. He obtained a job in one of the mines there and did some wildcat prospecting on his own when he had time. Silverton was a rollicking mining town. Now twenty-two, far away from home and full of energy and youth, he rollicked with it. His love of dancing and music kept him at the local bar and dance hall when he wasn't in the mines, making it very difficult for him to save the money he made. Spring and summer passed. When snow began to fall, he was no closer to finding Irene than he had been several months before. Then, during one of his whiskied evenings out, he made friends with a young stage-coach driver named Edward who had fallen in love with one of the local belles at the dance hall. The driver was supposed to bring the coach safely as far as southern Arizona on the Butterfield trail, where another driver would relieve him. He and Liam came up with a plan. Edward would stay on in Silverton with his ladylove and take Liam's position in the mine. Liam would drive the coach the rest of the way, then resign. Edward had never been to Arizona before, so no one would know what he looked like. This would bring Liam to a passable trail to Utah in the winter.

Providence continued. By November, Liam was bound for Arizona with legal ID as a US citizen. Besides, he was able to collect the wages due Edward when he resigned in Yuma, where he bought a horse and provisions to head north toward Salt Lake. His route was even simplified because several of the Mormon settlers had begun moving down into Arizona, founding settlements along the way to raise crops, spread the Word of the Lord and escape the harsh winters and crop blights they faced in Utah. They'd established good relationships with local Indians along the way. All he needed to do was follow their migration trails in reverse, telling them he was headed for Zion to join his sister, and he had directions, food, company and, given the harshness of the land, a very easy trip to Salt Lake City. Five years after leaving Ireland, he had nearly accomplished his goal. Now, all he had to do was find Irene and convince her to return to Cork. He'd need to figure out how they were getting back, too, of course. But he wasn't worried. He'd made it halfway around the world on wits, charm, and good fortune. He was sure he could get back to Ireland the same way.

As Liam recounted his trip north through Arizona, Chief became especially interested. He seemed to know quite a bit about the landscape, inexplicably. He asked specific questions about rivers and canal systems. He wanted to know about the dwellings of the various tribes in detail. Were they high in cliffs, or on the land? What food did they eat? What stories did they tell? Liam only had limited details for Chief's many questions. He had enjoyed the hospitality of a few clans on his way north, despite a language barrier, but he had only limited information from his short visits. Chief listened intently to every word. "Sky people," he announced as Liam was describing his progress through the beautiful, haunting, rock formations in what Eddie later knew as Bryce and Zion National Parks. "Been there since the Second World ended. Sky people." Eddie made a note to question Chief more about this later, but for the moment he was lost in his father's adventure. Liam was making his way on horse-back slowly north toward the Great Salt Lake. The year was 1890. He described the desert as like no landscape he had ever seen before, with a brilliant carpet of stars overhead at night punctu-ated by the subtle beauty of cactus, lizards, rock and sand. He talked of the mountains and towering pines he passed through, describing peaks, valleys, and high plains. He told of rocks and sand that appeared to be painted with every color of the rain-bow, and marbleized pieces of ancient wood, brightly colored and scattered in the sand. He described deep canyons carved by rivers, which seemed to drop forever to depths below the earth. The pic-tures his father described haunted Eddie. He wanted to see that place someday. For now, he listened as his father recounted how his excitement grew as he neared Salt Lake.

Liam passed through many settlements along the way. The Mormon people all seemed friendly and welcoming, especially willing to give him food, directions and company after they heard the purpose of his journey. They welcomed him into their homes, sharing their stories of coming to the west and settling the land.

Gradually, he made his way to the land called "Zion" by the people he had met. When the city came into view, he was impressed by what he saw. Laid out in a grid pattern, several homes and buildings towered in view. For a group of people who had been here less than thirty years, these Mormons had accom-plished a great deal. Farmlands surrounded the valley; a large church, or temple, was the centerpiece of the town and a hospi-tal, school, central offices and homes surrounded it in an orderly fashion. He entered the city with a sense of elation. Now, he just had to find his sister.

He would be so glad to see Irene again, to hear of her adven-tures and to tell her of his own. Not sure where to begin his search, since Salt Lake appeared to be at least twice the size of Cork, he stopped in what appeared to be a general store. "You in need, brother?" the proprietor greeted him. "What do you need from the warehouse today, and what can you offer in exchange?" It turned out he had entered a sort-of charity warehouse. People who had extra gave freely to the church warehouse; those in need took what they required, offering services or other goods in exchange. It was an interesting system. He wondered how long it would last before people began giving less than they could and taking more than they needed. For now, though, it seemed to be functioning.

"I'm looking for my sister," he said. "I guess what I am really in need of is directions to find her. She left Ireland's shores over five years ago to come to this city, and I'm hoping I might locate her. Her name is Irene McCauslin—or was," he added. "She may have married before she arrived here."

"Don't recognize the name," said the man. "But that's not surprising; there are many saints in this town. Check with the Stake President. He's likely to be able to help you locate her. His name's Brother Smith. I'm Brother Johnson. Here, I'll draw you a map to his place."

Armed with directions, Liam left in search of Brother Smith. He conscientiously ran his fingers through his thick, dark hair. It had been months since he'd had a haircut or shave; the clean-cut proprietor made him keenly aware of that. And he wore the clothes of a miner, not of a refined townsman. It wouldn't do to greet Irene looking like this. He turned back and asked Brother Johnson for directions to a barber. He also asked about what he might do in exchange for a fresh suit of clothes. "What can you do?" Brother Johnson asked affably. "We always need help at the fire department. You look like a hardy, practical sort. Want to do a shift there for the next couple of weeks? I'll give you a fresh set of clothes as well as a fire uniform and some boots if you're up for that. Even let you bathe at my place if the missus agrees so you don't get those new clothes dirty. Your sister and her family will likely give you a place to stay once you find her, until you get on your feet. They'll explain to you where to find the station and

how to report for duty, too. It'll take me a couple of days to process your promissory anyway. I'd say two weeks is a fair exchange
for your clothing. If you don't stay on, just leave the uniform at
the station after your two weeks. If you like the work at the fire
station, you can stay on there. If not, there are plenty more opportunities for a bright, strong young man like yourself in Zion."

Liam immediately liked the man as they located a nice suit—
probably the nicest he'd ever had—along with socks, shoes and
underclothes, as well as heavy boots and a bright red firefighter's
uniform. He accompanied Brother Johnson home for dinner
when the shop closed, bathed, and enjoyed a hearty supper and
pleasant company among the three wives and six children that
lived in and maintained a pleasant, three-story wood house. There
was a large garden on the grounds, a workroom, and a small barn
for the horses. The Johnson's obviously had all they needed. They
seemed healthy, happy, well educated, and well fed. If his sister
had fared as well, he reflected, she had made a very good decision.
Not many families in Cork lived so well. She certainly wouldn't
have a home as nice as this if she had stayed. Their own parents'
little house, one of the better ones in town, could not compare.

It occurred to him for the first time that it might not be so
easy, after all, to convince Irene of the error of her ways and return
her to Ireland. She might not want to return. B'gore, HE might
not even want to return! Liam had been so focused on his quest
that he had never entertained that thought before. But he did
now. Based on all he had seen here, did HE really want to go back
to Ireland? Or had his experiences, and all the vast possibilities in
this new land, made that an impossible dream? Perhaps he could
never go home, either. For, even if he did, it would never be the
same. He would not ever be able to be content in his small village parish again after all he had seen, all he had experienced. "I'll
think about it tomorrow," he told himself, pushing the doubts
from his mind. "For now, I'll just enjoy this fine full stomach

and this wonderful warm fire and the pleasant company of the Johnsons. I'll find Irene tomorrow. We'll see what happens then."

He had the rare gift of being able to shut troubling or confusing thoughts out of his mind completely when he wished. He did so, and had one of the best nights of sleep he'd enjoyed for months, on a soft mattress near a warm fire, covered with a beautiful, thick hand-made quilt one of the Johnson women had just proudly finished. The next morning, rested, he visited the barber and then, looking like a new man, went in search of the Stake President named Brother Smith who could lead him to Irene.

He wasn't disappointed. Brother Smith was a friendly, fiftyish man with nervous, harried mannerisms. Liam introduced himself and explained that he had come from Ireland to find his sister. He didn't mention his plan to bring her back to Ireland. He had gathered from his brief interactions with the people here that it would be better not to bring up that topic. He also included the information that he would be supporting himself during his stay by working at the fire department. Brother Smith seemed satisfied with that. His problem, which seemed to be making him more nervous than usual, was that he didn't immediately know who Irene was or where to find her. "Not good," he muttered. "I should know all the saints in my stake. Lots of Irenes I can think of. But from Ireland? I just don't know. You wouldn't happen to remember the name of the young man she came with, would you?" Liam shook his head. He couldn't recall the man's name.

"She arrived in 1884," he offered. "Would that help?"

"It might," said Brother Smith. "Or it might not. Just depends on how the records clerk has organized the records. You wouldn't know if she has an active temple recommend, would you?" Seeing Liam's puzzled look, Brother Smith shook his head. "No, you wouldn't know that, being as you haven't yet accepted the Lord's gospel. Never mind. I'll find her. But it may take a bit. Have you a place to stay?" Liam shook his head. "It appears I must hurry, then," said Brother Smith, chuckling at his own joke. "I have a few things to tend to at my furniture shop, and then I'll see what I can do for you. Would you like to come with me to the shop first? I'm guessing you've nowhere else to go right now."

Liam nodded. When he arrived, he was delighted to see the beautiful, hand-carved tables, chairs and cabinets there. "Do you make these?" he asked, obviously impressed. "I tried a bit of carpentry, and found I really enjoyed it. I've made a few benches and restored a few tables and chairs."

"No, I'm the merchant," explained Brother Smith. "I display and make them available to those who want to purchase. Not," he hastily added, "that they wouldn't be given freely to any saint who needed furnishings in exchange for service, but—well, our economy is an interesting blend of commerce, free enterprise and communal property right now." He shook his head. "Hard to explain to an outsider. But we are leaning more toward free commerce and a man's right to earn a living than when we first arrived. These are for sale to those with means to afford nicer furnishings. My brother-in-law and nephews make most of them. A few of my sons work on these, too. If you've a talent for this type of work and you'd like to give it a try, I'll introduce you after your time at the fire department is up. Now, just look around and make yourself comfortable while I take care of this paperwork and arrange a delivery. Shouldn't take me long."

Liam looked at the fine woods and lovely inlaid designs of the tables and the intricate carvings on chairs and cabinets. He would enjoy learning how to produce work like this. There was a special feeling that carving and working with wood had always given him, from the time he was a child whittling small musical instruments and toys. He promised himself to meet the brother-in-law to ask if he wanted to take on an apprentice after he found Irene.

Brother Smith took longer to finish the paperwork and arrange the deliveries than he had intended. Flustered, near evening, he hurried off with Liam in tow to check with his records clerk and access files at the church. The chapel was another example of fine woodcarving and carpentry, Liam noticed. The pews and benches were elegantly designed. Every piece seemed to fit together perfectly. "Did your brother-in-law build the church?" he asked.

"Everyone helps to build a church in Zion," replied Brother Smith. "We all had a part. But, yes, I believe Steven did oversee most of the carpentry, as I recall, and train the men who put on the final touches." He turned his attention to rummaging through drawers of papers. "These are the baptism records of all of the Saints who have joined us in Zion" he explained. "Unless she was baptized before she arrived, which isn't very likely, I should find some record of your sister here. She came around 1885, you say?" Liam nodded and waited patiently while Brother Smith continued rummaging. "Here's a possibility," he finally said. "Irene McCauslin arrived in October of 1885. Baptized on October 14; married to Heber Jensen on October 17. Lives on South Temple, not far from here. If you like, I'll walk there with you. Be good for me to see the Jensens. I should know all the saints in my charge," he chastised himself again. "I really should."

Liam appreciated the offer. "I can return for my horse later, I suppose," he said. "Thank you." The two men left the furniture shop and walked what seemed to be about two miles through downtown. They arrived at a large but not particularly well-maintained house with several children in the yard arguing.

"Now, now," said Brother Smith to a little boy about to hit his sibling. "The good Lord says we are our brother's keeper. That's no way to be acting." The freckle-faced child looked up.

"He took my favorite marble and he won't give it back! I'd say he deserves a lickin' for that!" By now, the other child had disappeared into the house.

"The women should be tending to these children," complained Brother Smith, shaking his head. "I wonder where they are?"

They approached the door and knocked. The child who had reportedly taken the marble from his brother opened the door. "Hi, young man," said Brother Smith. "Where are your parents?"

The young child looked surprised. "Mama and Sister Lucy are working at the cannery," he replied. "Sister Irene is sleeping; she hasn't been well. Papa died last month." Now, Brother Smith looked surprised.

"I should know these things," he said apologetically, to no one in particular. "I had no idea. I'm Brother Smith, your Stake President. What's your name?"

"I'm Heber, Junior," replied the child, who appeared to be about six years old. Just then, a pretty young girl, not more than two, appeared.

"You're supposed to be taking your nap, Mary Lee," Heber said. "Well, c'mon," he added to the men. "If Mary Lee's awake, I'm supposed to get Irene anyways." He grabbed the child's hand, and they disappeared up the stairs. Liam knew as soon as he saw the little girl's face they had come to the right place. There was no doubt that she was his sister's child. The bright blue eyes and wild red hair, and the scattering of freckles across her face, looked just like he remembered his sister looking when they were children.

Several more minutes elapsed before Irene appeared on the stairs. She was pale and drawn, obviously not in good health. She also appeared to be about seven months pregnant as she lumbered heavily down the stairs. "I'm sorry for the state of this house," she apologized. "Brother Smith, I know I should be taking better care of things, but with Heber gone and the baby on the way, trying to watch all the children while the other women are away so much at the cannery to earn enough to get us by, I just can't seem to…" Then, her eyes fell on Liam and she cut off her apology mid-sentence. A look of pure radiance and peaceful joy spread across her countenance. "Praise the Lord!" she said, catching her breath. "He does provide! He does answer prayers! Liam, is that really you? How did you find me? How're Papa and Mama and Peter and the girls? Oh, Liam!" She ran to embrace him, tears running down her face.

"This is a miracle," observed Brother Smith, slowly making an exit. "Young man, I'll have one of my boys bring your horse and belongings by this evening. I'll send some supper with him, too, ma'am," he added kindly to Irene. "You're in no condition to be preparing the feast you'd no doubt like to give this brother who has come to take care of you." With that, he left Irene and Liam to get reacquainted with each other after their long separation. It was clear a lot had happened in both of their lives since they last had been together.

Liam found it hard to believe he had finally found his sister. They spent the evening happily in each other's company. He recounted his adventures for her in detail. When he'd finished, she told him of her life. "Heber was a good man," she said wistfully. "He was. It took a little adjusting on my part to get used to the way of things here, but Lucinda and Magda have been kind to me, especially since…" She began to cry. It was still difficult for her to talk of her husband's recent death. "Well, never mind. You have no idea how much I have missed you, and Mama and Papa, and Ireland. I thought I was doing the right thing to come here. I was so tired of stitching those suits! But, looking back, it was a good life. I could see my accomplishments, you know? Here, with these brawling children…" She wrung her hands. "You were always such an easy child, Liam," she said fondly. "Little did I know that not all children would be like you!" Hearing screams in the yard, she began to rise and fell back, short of breath.

"You wait, sister," said Liam. "I'll take care of things." He headed for the yard, introduced himself to the children in an intentionally gruff manner, and soon had each of the five engaged in some type of task, gathering up toys or picking vegetables from the garden. When he returned, he queried his sister about her health. He learned that when she had given birth to her daughter, Mary Lee, two years before, it had been a very difficult pregnancy. She had nearly died herself, losing lots of blood, and had never really regained her strength. The doctor had told her sternly not to have any more children. But her husband, whom she loved, had wanted to "follow the word of the Lord, be fruitful and multiply," as she explained. She had faith that all would be well. She had become pregnant with another child due to be born in less than two months. When her husband had been killed in a fire at the cannery, she had been devastated. The strength she thought she had to get through a difficult pregnancy had been sapped. The other women left her at home during the day to watch the children—they had six under seven years of age amongst them—while they tried to honorably make a living for the family. The effort was taking its toll.

"Just last night," she said, still crying, "I was sure I could not go on. I prayed so hard for the strength. And here you are! You are my strength!"

Liam felt many conflicting emotions. He, too, was happy to be here for his sister who now needed him so much. He was sorry for her difficulties, but another part of him was aware that the current situation would make his own task much easier. He knew, now, that he could persuade her to return with him to Ireland. Not immediately, of course. He would stay with her through the pregnancy and wait until she regained enough strength to travel. It would be more expensive and more difficult with her two children. But Papa, seeing his widowed daughter and grandchildren, would never be able to hold a grudge. He would welcome Irene back. He would help her as she worked in the tailor shop. They could raise her children at home in Ireland, where they all belonged. Liam could return to the seminary and, older and wiser, assume the priesthood. His quest would be successful. It was sad that her experiences were as they were—but perhaps necessary, too. He regretted leaving this new land, but realized he must. This was what he had come to do. Find Irene and leave. He had been blessed on his voyage. He would realize his goal. Now, he knew, was not the time to broach the subject of returning to Ireland. There would be time to do that soon enough. For now, he just wanted to help his sister. He wanted to comfort her and let her rest. He told her of his two-week obligation at the fire department, wishing inexplicably he had been there a month earlier to perhaps save her husband.

"After that," he said, "I'll stay on. I can do carpentry, too. I'll help support this household so one of the other women can stay home to tend the children—and you. You need rest." He stroked her hair. "Dear Irene," he said. "You do need rest."

Brother Smith's eldest son returned shortly, with Liam's horse and belongings as well as a bag full of meat, potatoes, rolls, and cakes—enough for Liam, Irene, and all the children to eat, and still have leftovers for a small army. Liam rummaged through the kitchen enough to set a good table. He gathered the children to eat first, then set about getting them cleaned up and ready for bed while his sister rested peacefully on the sofa, content that he was here.

Once the children were sleeping, he roused Irene. They ate together. The other women returned home and joined them before the meal was finished. Liam met Lucinda and Magda, two women slightly younger than Irene. Both looked sad and tired. His winning charm cheered them, though, as did the prospect of someone else to help maintain the household and earn a living. The two agreed that Magda would stay home to care for Irene and the children, beginning tomorrow. They would make up a room for Liam; the two young girls could share Magda's bed for now. Life already looked better. The Lord had provided.

"And so," finished Liam, looking at his drowsy children and the snoring Chief, "now you know the story of how I found my sister. That's enough for the evening."

Inez yawned. "But I want to hear more about Mama," she said. "Do we have to go to sleep now?"

"Most of you look like you are already asleep," he chided. "I won't be leaving until Monday. We still have two more days for storytelling. I'll tell you more of these tales of my life tomorrow,

children." Slowly, everyone left the fire and curled up in their
beds for the evening, leaving Chief snoring quietly on the hard-
wood floor while Papa and Mama stayed by the fire, talking softly
to each other and holding hands.

❋   ❋   ❋

Eddie awoke early on Saturday, just after dawn, and dressed
hurriedly. He wanted to finish his chores so he would have plenty
of time to spend with Papa and Chief. He fixed some oatmeal
for himself quietly so he wouldn't wake Mama or the rest of the
household. He liked warmed oats boiled in water and mixed with
cinnamon and syrup from the maples covered with rich, fresh
cream. It was his favorite breakfast. After he ate, he quietly left
the house, walking outside into the beautiful spring morning. The
air was crisp, but not cold. A slight breeze was blowing. Sunrise
was magnificent, with shades of gold and pink reflecting in the
scattered clouds across the bright blue Canadian sky.

This was a beautiful place, he reflected, looking at the rugged
mountain peaks punctuating the horizon. From this little clearing, he could see the magnificent peaks of Jasper to the north and
Banff to the west. The Grand Tetons were barely visible to the
south. Snow still remained on the peaks, but the fields around
him had been thawed for several days. Bright wildflowers formed
a carpet of lavender, blue and gold across the pasture. He could
hear the burbling of the creek in the woods, and the songs of
the many birds that were returning home for summer. The places
his father had described—Ireland and Boston and Colorado
and Arizona and Utah—all sounded interesting, but he was sure
those places didn't have the majesty and beauty of Alberta in
springtime. "I will find out someday, though," he told himself.
Eddie wanted to travel. Unlike his brothers and sisters, he had
actually been born in the USA before his parents came to homestead in Alberta. He realized now that he considered it home, in
a way. He planned on going back when he grew up. Just from his

father's tales, he knew there was much there to see. Not that there wasn't lots to see in Canada, too. He had time, he assured himself. He would see many places, just as his father had, before he found a place that he called home. He continued musing as he milked the cows, gathered eggs and tended the garden. Then he fetched water from the spring and made sure there was plenty of cut firewood piled near the house. He knew the girls were planning to collect berries in the woods later and help Mama make jam. He hoped during that time to be tracking deer with Chief and his father. The weather promised to be beautiful today; it would be a fine day for hunting.

When he returned to the house, everyone was up, eating pancakes. Finding himself hungry again, Eddie joined them at breakfast. "I promised the Bowen's a crib in exchange for some canned preserves," his father announced. "Who wants to learn some carpentry today?"

"I do!" said Joe. He loved working with wood just as his father did.

"I'm teaching Gene to read," announced Inez. "Miss Welch told me I could and gave me a book for him." She already loved playing school. She was a natural teacher.

"That's good," said Mama. "Can you keep an eye on Maybelline while Allie and Lizzie help me find berries for jam?"

"Sure," Inez agreed brightly. "I'll teach her, too!"

CHAPTER FOUR

THE PROMISED LAND

Soon, breakfast dishes were cleaned and cleared. Everyone set about their chosen tasks for the day. Only Eddie and Chief remained. "You come with me," said Chief. "We hunt. I teach you to find the animals. Teach you how to listen, how to talk." That suited Eddie fine. It is what he had hoped to do. Eddie spent a fascinating day in the woods with the Chief. He'd actually been able to lead them to a fine elk by following Chief's strange instructions.

"Easy," he'd said. "Pay attention to what you really know. Feel animals. Feel their spirits. See what they see. Then you find 'em." After their successful expedition, as they were headed back home, Chief stopped their horses for a moment on the trail. "Now what you feel?" he asked. Eddie shivered.

"I don't know. A little anxious, maybe?" Chief nodded.

"Grizzly up there," he said, pointing left toward the mountains. "Mama bear's fierce and hungry, protecting her baby. We go fast, before she comes down."

Eddie was fascinated. "How'd you learn all this, Chief?" he asked. The old Indian shrugged.

"Human beings just know. Just gotta listen inside." He paused for a moment. "Some of my people think you new ones, with your strange ways and your strange God, not human beings. They're wrong. You can listen; just need to be reminded." Eddie enjoyed his time with Chief, "being reminded." He spent much of his free time in his company, learning how to "listen," how to name and use the plants and trees, and how to track animals. These skills proved very valuable to him later in his life. Today, though, he was just anxious to return home with the fine elk meat, settle down, and hear the rest of his father's story. He knew that Papa would be leaving again soon to work on the lodge being built down near Waterton, and he wanted to hear as much as he could of this epoch tale about how his family had arrived here in Canada before then. He wasn't disappointed. Liam finished his story as everyone who listened stayed awake long into the wee hours of the morning.

"While I was settling in to this strange land of Zion and learning the ways and the religion of these people," he began, "your mama was right there close, but I hadn't met her yet."

"If you'd just gone to church and accepted the Lord's truth," Mama said, "you would have met me far quicker and with much less fuss! I'll never forget the bloody mess when I pulled that scorched boot off your leg. Watching a big, strong hero faint at the sight of his own blood!" she teased. "Now that was quite a sight! Do you know when I first agreed to see you alone it was because I thought you were embarrassed about that, and wanted to swear me to secrecy?" She laughed. "Brother Orm told me I shouldn't be socializing with someone who wasn't a convert, you know," she added. "I told him I was sure it would just be an innocent thank you for saving your life."

❋　　❋　　❋

Liam had completed his two weeks with the fire department successfully, and stayed on. In less than a month, he'd been promoted to fire chief. His youth, strength, and optimism, not to mention his experience in the mines, made him a natural leader among the men. He also worked evenings with Brother Smith's son-in-law. He found carpentry, especially the creative work on fine, inlaid tables and elaborately carved chairs, relaxing and would have continued even if he wasn't getting paid well for it. His natural talent made the items he carved popular. They sold for high prices, and the Smiths were fair in their distribution of profit. He learned the Saints had only begun using U.S. currency recently, since Utah had become a territory. In the past, their economy had been a barter system and a communal exchange. Some were a little uncomfortable with the new system. "Let's greed in, and that's the devil's calling card," they said. "Better when we just all care for each other and everyone has what they need."

"The Lord helps those who help themselves," said the others. "This system just rewards hard labor in the Lord's vineyards, as should be." Liam noted those were the folks who seemed to have the money to buy his fine furniture.

He didn't think much about the philosophical aspects, or even about the interesting experiment in living that was going on in his midst. Later, he would listen to his wife's brother, a professor, debate the fine points and nuances long into the evening. For now, he was satisfied working at the fire department, and creating fine wooden furniture when he wasn't on duty. His income helped Irene and her deceased husband's other wives and children survive more comfortably, and he knew his sister was happy he was there.

"It's so good to have you with me," she told him repeatedly. "I was beginning to lose my faith for a bit, but no longer." He'd hold her hand as they sat near the fire on the evenings he was home. She liked hearing about Ireland and the family and she wanted to return to Cork. "Will you take me back after the baby comes?" she asked one evening. "There's nothing for me here now that Heber is gone. Little Iris deserves to grow up on Irish sod, she does."

Liam promised he would take them back, observing how every obstacle to his original plan to return Irene to Ireland had gradually fallen away. Now she herself was asking him to bring her home! He also realized that his sister did not know of his father's reaction to her departure, and decided now was not the time to tell her. She looked so pale. He was very worried about her health. "Nothing to do but pray," the doctor said on one of his frequent visits. "She shouldn't have been put through this, but there's no going back. If anyone could help her," he added, "it would be Nurse Schneider at the hospital. You try to get her to deliver that baby."

Liam had been meaning to go by the hospital to meet Nurse Schneider and make this request, but between both jobs and spending time with Irene, he hadn't gotten around to it yet when the fire at the stables broke out. He and his crew were battling the flames as he watched fire jump to a house nearby. He heard a scream and, without thinking, ran through the blaze up the stairs. He emerged later, choking from smoke while carrying a woman and a baby. One of his boots was melted to his skin. He had obvious burns on his arm and shoulder as well. Weak with pain, he didn't argue when one of his men left the scene to take him to the hospital on his horse.

"So," he told his audience, "I certainly met your lovely mother at a weak moment! She thinks I fainted at the sight of my blood when she cut my boot off, but I never even saw it. I passed out from the pain long before.

I remained in the hospital for days under her care. Besides, she was taken with me immediately. She never left my side until I was well!"

"You were the town hero." She laughed. "It would never do to have anything happen to you in my hospital! Besides, that pain medicine inspired some very nice dreams about me, as I recall, that you still don't remember telling me about!"

"It was love at first sight," agreed Papa. "It's just that she caught sight of me first; I was in no condition to be seeing for a few days there. But thanks to your mother's skill, I recovered very quickly. I was fit as a fiddle in no time."

His sister, however, did not fare so well. Once Liam was conscious and only slightly delirious, he told Johanna about Irene's condition. She looked at him gently as he asked her to please take care of his sister and the baby. "She'll want to come see me," he said. "I know she will. But she's due any day and weak. She shouldn't leave the house. Please tell her I'm okay and go check on her condition." Johanna nodded sadly. She didn't tell him then, but it was too late to help his sister. When word of his accident and the fire had gotten to her—inaccurately, no doubt, as gossip generally is—she had become hysterical. "It's not fair to lose them both!" she screamed as she went into labor. Magda stayed, trying to calm her. She sent Heber, Jr. to find the doctor. But the baby had come quickly and painfully, breeched and choked by its own umbilical cord. Magda didn't know what to do; she was not a midwife. Both Irene and the baby were dead by the time the doctor arrived.

Liam only learned of this when he was well enough to leave the hospital, and the tragedy took a heavy toll. It had seemed his quest to find Irene had been blessed until now. Despite the extra and unexpected time on the ship and the slow progress coming west, everything had fallen into place. His initial plan conceived five years before to return his sister to Ireland and to the family had guided his life. Now, his sister was gone. It would be impossible to ever return Irene to Irish soil. It would be impossible to offer his father a chance to recant his cold abandonment of his daughter. Liam's grief was profound. Here he was, far away from home and lost to the life he and his family had planned for him in the priesthood. He felt alone among strangers. He questioned his beliefs. Fortunately Johanna, the kind nurse who had saved his life, was there to comfort him. Otherwise, it is hard to say what may have become of him.

Johanna, for her part, had been taken with the young Irish fireman from the moment he entered her life. He was a fallen hero in uniform. This was a romantic introduction, as townspeople were already recounting his worthy rescue of Sister Young and her son by the time she first saw him. She would, of course, have devoted the same careful attention to any patient in her charge, she told herself. This one, though, with his hero credentials, dark hair and shining eyes, really compelled her attention and devotion. When she learned he was not a Saint and did not believe in multiple marriages, this made him even more appealing to her, although she knew she should not feel so selfish. Regardless, she had never been more fascinated by any man she had met. She found many excuses to stay at his bedside while he was recovering. Once he had recovered, in part because she knew of what had happened to his sister and how hard he would take this, she still felt compelled to stay by his side. They had a whirlwind courtship. Within three months of the time they met, they had married. Neither had ever regretted it since.

Liam, in his philosophic way, now felt his quest to find his sister had really been a quest to help him find his life. He thanked Irene and felt she was the one person who had more influence on his life than anyone else—even in death. He hadn't become a priest, but he had become a very happy husband and father. If not for her, that never would have happened. Liam and Johanna remained in Salt Lake for the first two years of their marriage. Liam continued working as both a fireman and a carpenter. Johanna continued at the hospital. Eddie was born during that time, on a bright September morning. Johanna, always hardy and healthy, was back at work within two days, bringing her baby with her. After watching his poor sister's difficult pregnancy, this was exhilarating for Liam.

The couple remained happy in Zion, but when they heard that there was land available in Canada for any families willing to settle it, the opportunity was appealing. Both were adventurous. They had already left their homes in Europe and adjusted to very different lives in Zion where they could work hard and maintain a pleasant home. But, if they were willing to head north, they could claim several hundred acres—enough for all of their potential offspring to comfortably live on. The opportunity sounded far too good to pass. When Johanna also learned there was a need for anyone with expertise in medicine, the decision was made. She wanted to share her knowledge and healing ability. There were now enough good nurses and doctors in Salt Lake City to care for the sick. She was ready to do her best to keep others, more in need of her skill, alive. Since Alberta was just being settled, Liam's carpentry skills would also be in high demand. The decision was easily made. Before Eddie's second birthday, they packed what goods they thought were necessary—mainly tools and medical supplies—in a wagon and headed for Canada.

The sad part of this adventure for Liam was leaving his sister's daughter. She was happy with her brothers and sisters living with Heber's other wives. It would not have been wise to take her; he knew that. But she was the last concrete tie he had to Irene, his beloved sister. It was difficult to leave her behind. Before they left Salt Lake, he sent a long letter to his father, explaining all that had happened to Irene and to him, and telling him of his granddaughter. He waited for a reply, but a reply never came. Johanna said it was probably due to the unreliability of the mail. It was difficult to send letters from Zion to places within the U.S.—never mind Ireland.

Liam hoped that was the reason he never had a reply, but he knew Johanna and her brother received regular letters from Switzerland, so he wasn't convinced. Finally, on the advice of a friend, he sent a query to the Cork town recorder, inquiring whether his parents still resided there. Although the reply took months, he received one. Yes, Patrick and Mary McCauslin were still alive and living in Cork. He sent another letter to his parents, which also went unanswered. He assumed that he now shared Irene's fate in the family; he, too, had been disowned. This saddened him tremendously, but there was little he could do but grieve the loss of his family along with the loss of his sister. Liam did so as he moved his young family to the Canadian frontier of southern Alberta as the nineteenth century drew toward a close.

Life on the Canadian frontier proved harder than expected. For the first few years, building their home and trying to eke enough food out of the land to survive took all of his energy. Johanna's medical skills allowed them to acquire a few cattle and other animals through barter; he was grateful for her skills. He often stayed home building and planting during the first few years while she traveled to assist doctors with operations as far away as Calgary and Edmonton, to deliver children and to attend to the sick. When Eddie, Allie, Inez, and Joe were young, their father was often their primary caretaker while Johanna traveled.

Once the ranch house was finished, the fields were established and livestock were acquired, there were enough other settlers to provide her with plenty of work closer to home. Then, Liam had been able to use his skills at carpentry to work away from home, building resorts and railroad hotels. Life on the Canadian frontier had not been easy, but it had been rewarding. They had been able to create a pleasant home for themselves and their children and to contribute to society. They were happy here in this cold northern land, and they were still very much in love. Their children were responsible, secure, and well cared for.

"The Lord always provides," Papa said as he finished his tale. "Even when times seem difficult, it is for a reason; for a greater purpose. We are all here now together. Life is good."

But we aren't all together, Eddie found himself thinking as he crawled in bed that night after the storytelling. Life isn't good for all of us. What about Baby Flo? He still missed his little sister, and he didn't have the easy faith in God that seemed to characterize the rest of his family. He trusted action, reason, and planning more than providence. In contrast, however, he also trusted Chief's odd insights and the intuition he was developing as a result of their time together. As he fell asleep that night, he saw himself reflected in the eyes of an elk.

CHAPTER FIVE

THE HUNTER

Eddie's father's visit seemed too short, as always. At least now he was working on a new resort hotel only forty miles from the ranch, so he would be able to return more frequently. The southern Alberta frontier was growing rapidly, becoming a popular frontier destination to visit for hunting and sightseeing. The spectacular mountains and landscapes were attracting the attention of several big game hunters and tourists. A wealthy investor began building a hunting lodge nearby. Liam invited Eddie to spend the summer working with him as an assistant and an apprentice, for he would be graduating from school soon and needed to learn a trade.

"Joe's old enough to help Mama with the children," Liam said. "We will be working nearby, so we will be back often." Eddie was pleased his father invited him, but he had other plans. He shared his father's love of gardening, but not his love of carpentry. Besides, he had invested too much time in raising the little ones to give up that role quite yet. Joe was the one who really loved carpentry. He had always taken pleasure in whittling wooden toys and in building things with his hands.

"Take Joe instead, Papa," Eddie said. "It's nearly summer, so he won't miss classes. Mama needs me here. Besides, I plan to talk Chief into starting a business with me. We'll take all these big game sportsmen that stay in that lodge you are building hunting in the mountains!"

Liam looked at his son with interest. "Is that Chief's idea?" he asked.

"No, it's mine," Eddie replied. "But I'm sure I can convince him."

"Perhaps you can," his father assented. "It's a very good idea, you know. I'm sure there will be guides from the east that descend on this place like pirates when the lodge opens, but Chief knows these mountains like no one else. If you and he are ready, and I'm able to assure Mr. Rigall, who is financing the lodge, that I can guarantee him the best trail guides in the province, the two of you will have quite a business on your hands! You talk to Chief about your fine idea. I'll talk to Joe."

Joe was delighted, as Eddie knew he would be. He was a natural carpenter, and the opportunity for refining this skill with Father's guidance brought a bright smile to his face. Chief was somewhat less thrilled by Eddie's plan. Eddie wasn't discouraged, though. He still had another month of schooling to complete, and several more months until the lodge was finished. It would be nearly a year before the first hunters began to arrive. That would give him time to convince the old Indian of the worthiness of his plan, he hoped. If not, he would learn all he could from Chief about the area, and guide hunting parties on his own. He began spending as much time as possible with Chief, always finding excuses for trailing animals or exploring further and further into the mountains. Everything he saw and learned, he filed away mentally. Nothing was forgotten.

His mother and father both seemed to like his plan. It would keep him home to help at the ranch most of the time. It would be a good way to earn extra money; perhaps lots of extra money, if the stories his father had heard about the wealthy hunters who would be frequenting the lodge when it was finished proved to be true.

Miss Welch also listened to his plan with interest. She learned of it in the final essay she asked him to write just before his graduation from school. "It's time to be thinking about your life ahead, Eddie," she told him when she gave the assignment. "But this doesn't need to be completely practical. You can dream a little, too. I want you to write a paper for me telling how you plan to use what you have learned."

As usual, she was moved and even surprised by the work of her favorite student. His essay speculated about how he could make the world a better place. He noted he didn't plan to marry, but also indicated that, if he did, he would always remain to care for his wife and children. He talked about how important knowledge was, indicating that literacy opened many doors in the mind as well as the world. Eddie wrote that he would always work to make sure that every child he came into contact with had the same educational opportunities he had enjoyed. Not surprisingly, he mentioned he would always take care of his brothers and sisters and help his parents. But he also revealed his desire to travel, and he revealed his plan to earn money to do so by leading hunting parties in the nearby mountains. He provided detail about the lodge his father and Joe would build this summer, including the type of clientele it was likely to attract. This caught her attention, and she asked him about it in more detail.

"It's a good idea, Eddie," she told him. "You know I'd prefer to see you go on to the university, or even the normal school, but it sounds like you've thought ahead."

"I have," he assured her. "Besides, after having you as a teacher, I've learned everything I need to know. I can read. I can think. I'm good with numbers and trigonometry. There's really nothing else I have a desire to study, Miss Welch. I've always known you wanted me to go on, but I honestly don't want to. It isn't just the family, either. If I were really passionate about learning more— like Mom was about medicine, for example—I'd go. But I'm not. Anything else I need to learn, I can learn on my own, from books and from life."

She had to admit he was probably right about that, and it made her feel a little better to know he seemed sincerely satisfied with the idea of staying in Alberta. He didn't harbor any hidden longings to continue his academic studies. He seemed so intelligent, so philosophical at times that she had suspected he might want to study philosophy or literature. His paper and conversation convinced her otherwise. He had a practical plan that suited his interests.

"Okay," she said. "I wish you the best! But I sure hope I'll be able to get one of my students to university one of these days!" Again, he surprised her with his seeming insight, almost prophetic. "Don't worry, you will soon," he assured her. "I already know Inez will be a teacher and Allie will be a nurse, like Mama. Don't plan for Joe to attend; he may not even finish school with you, but that will be fine. What he really wants to do is carpentry. He's good at it and he loves it. But if you can keep Gene's attention, he might go on." Later, when all he had said proved true, she reflected that it should not be a surprise that he knew his siblings so well. He had, after all, raised them. For now, she just knew that she would miss his helpful, friendly presence and his sunny intelligence in her classroom next year.

She prepared a special graduation present, a warm sweater that she knitted herself, and gave it to Eddie after a small ceremony she arranged in his honor. "You'll need it on cold nights, guiding those wealthy hunters in the mountains," she said, kissing him on both cheeks.

Summer passed quickly. Papa and Joe were away working much of the time. Except when Mama was delivering babies, Eddie had lots of time to himself. The rodeo would be in town during July, so he decided to prepare Redwing for some barrel jumping and trick riding. He knew the pony would enjoy the challenge, and he was convinced he might even be awarded one of the rarely given cash prizes if he was able to win competing against professional cowboys. That, and spending as much time as possible with Chief, became his passions. Actually, spending time with Chief also helped him train his horse. The old man's way with animals was truly amazing.

"How do you do it?" asked Eddie one summer afternoon after watching Chief negotiate Redwing through one of the most difficult obstacle courses he could imagine with the smooth, poetic motion of man-joined-to-horse.

"Easy," replied Chief. "Redwing and I move together. Horse trusts. I trust. We see the same. You try. I already let horse know you okay. Horse knew, anyway."

Eddie shrugged. He mounted Redwing and relaxed, trying to see what the horse saw. Much to his amazement, they soon traversed the same difficult obstacle course Chief had negotiated, in record time. It seemed he had barely touched the reins. It was a strange, natural, timeless motion.

"Wow!" he said when they had completed the course. "That was unbelievable!"

"Keep your heart pure," advised Chief in his odd way. "Horse always move with you now. Knows you okay. Knows you never hurt unnecessarily. True, right?"

"Of course!" replied Eddie. He loved Redwing. He could never imagine harming her.

"Okay," replied Chief. "Animals like that. We're same family. Give us what we need as long as we respect their gifts. All life's like that. Important you remember, okay? Always remember."

Eddie couldn't imagine not remembering. The sensation of being one with his horse had been incredible. He had no doubt that they would win the rodeo competition now, as long as he maintained this strange rapport. "You do this with all the animals, don't you? That's how you know where they are. How you always track them and find them. How'd you learn?"

"Grandfather taught me," replied Chief. "Grandfather Sky. We all same family. Animals help if we live right. You forget what I told you already?"

Eddie wasn't sure he understood what "living right" meant, but he knew that, thanks to Chief's uncanny guidance, he and Redwing would have no trouble at the rodeo. He also knew he and Chief could make a fortune helping wealthy hunters, if Chief would agree.

"Dad's working on a hunting lodge," he said. "Lot's of really wealthy people from the East Coast will come here to hunt elk, bear, and moose. If we help them find the animals, it'll be really good for this area. We'll have more money to get what we need."

"Hunters need these animals?" asked Chief.

"They think so," answered Eddie.

"Animals always help. If they need animals, we help find. You know how, now. Horse trusts you. Moose trust you. I taught you well."

Eddie was elated Chief seemingly agreed to help in his new enterprise. He spent most of his free time that summer with Chief, learning many trails into the mountains and seeing the areas where moose, deer, geese, bear, elk and other animals congregated. He noted Chief rarely hunted. Only when he needed food did he take bow or rifle. Otherwise, he pointed out interesting aspects of places they saw and ways animals lived to Eddie, behaving much as if he was visiting friends.

"Will you come with me to help hunters from the East when they arrive?" asked Eddie.

"Okay," said Chief. "I am curious. I want to see strange hunters."

The next time his father returned home, Eddie shared the good news. "Tell your developer you have the best guides in the area for hunting," he beamed. "Chief will help! There's no one here or anywhere that can compete with that!"

"That's for certain," agreed Liam. "He agreed, did he? Well, I'll let Sir Rigall know. In the meantime, I'm back for a brief spell because I've heard from your mother that you plan to ride that obnoxiously difficult pony in the rodeo next week. Is that true?"

Eddie's smile grew even brighter. "That I do!" he said. "I'm going to start earning my fortune and Redwing is going to help me do it!"

Knowing his father would be there to watch his attempts to beat the cowboys at their own craft made Eddie nervous and happy at the same time. Because of his new connection with Redwing Chief had helped him establish, he was very confident they could easily tackle any barrel course set before them. He and Redwing were able, now, to move as one body. Their trust and their sight were connected, beyond any doubt. Still, making his father proud of his accomplishments was very important. Liam's presence meant he MUST succeed. Eddie knew that this should not matter. As Chief had taught him, he just needed to see the outcome, without any emotional attachment, and live through the movements of the horse. He spent many evenings meditatively reminding himself of this as the rodeo approached. His efforts were not wasted. The evening of the rodeo, all of his family came to watch, excited with the prospect of seeing Eddie ride alongside the magnificent trick performers they enjoyed.

Before the competition, Eddie felt the tension in his body and the queasiness and excitement in his stomach. Redwing picked up his anxiety and began tossing her head erratically, bringing Eddie's focus back on what Chief had told him. "You and the horse see the same," he reminded himself. "See successfully completing that darned difficult barrel course!" He brought his anxiety in check and the horse calmed down with him.

"You will notice, ladies and gentleman," came the loud voice of the rodeo's officiator, "that our barrel course looks even more treacherous than usual. Two defending champions, Slim Johnson and Merle Rogers, are competing for the title. To make this unusual and spectacular event even more interesting than usual, we have a young local boy who has challenged the champions! Yes, yes—" he continued to the oohs, aahs, and expressions of disbelief from the audience. "It's true. Young Eddie McCauslin thinks he has what it takes to be a cowboy! Let me remind you, ladies and gentleman, that in the spirit of fairness of competition, this fine rodeo always allows any man or woman who wishes to challenge our professionals. It's just rare when that happens. Most of you value your bones and know better!" The audience laughed in response. "So," continued the deep voice of the announcer, "let's get on with the show!"

On cue, Slim Johnson and his well-known black stallion Coal Miner came galloping out of the gate, parading in front of the admiring crowd. "Okay, Slim," came the announcer's voice. "This is timed and this is tough. Go back behind the gate, get ready, and begin on my cue." Slim and his horse made a few more passes before the crowd to wild applause, then complied. On cue, they set off on the difficult course, jumping barrels and hurdles while negotiating hairpin curves at speeds that, miraculously, toppled neither horse nor man. "A new record!" boomed the announcer over the crowd's wild applause. "This most difficult of obstacle courses was completed in only two minutes and seventeen seconds!" The exuberant Slim and his exhausted horse spent several minutes prancing in front of the cheering crowd.

Eddie was impressed but still confident. "We can do it, Redwing. You're a lot younger and quicker and more supple than that big old stallion. Besides, we've tried courses like this with Chief in less than two minutes!" His words reassured the horse. Redwing happily tossed her mane in response.

"Now," came the thundering voice of the announcer, "we will see former—and I stress former, since his record has just been overturned—former Canadian barrel racing champion cowboy Merle Rogers try to regain his standing!"

Merle Rogers, a household name among most rodeo fans, emerged from the gate in all his sequined leather splendor. His spirited Appaloosa, Ghost Dancer, pranced before the crowd.

"He looks a little haggard," noted Eddie. "He's nervous about winning. That isn't a good way to start." He surprised himself with his analytical detachment from the competition at hand, still calm and centered with the assurance he and Redwing would leave the arena as champions. Because of his earlier observations, he was neither surprised nor upset, as the rest of the crowd was, when Rogers fell from his racing mount on the third hairpin curve and was trampled beneath her tangled feet.

The drama of a painful accident kept the crowd in the stands riveted to their seats. Although the chance of such an event attracted some to the rodeo year after year, it was rare such accidents actually happened. Eddie, still in that clear, detached state projecting forthcoming victory, watched his mother descend from the stands to offer medical attention to the injured cowboy as the crowed sighed and moaned.

"It's too bad she won't be able to watch us, Redwing," he sighed. "She would enjoy seeing how well you glide over those obstacles and dance around those turns." As if in a trance, he moved with his horse toward the starting gate.

"Given the turn of events on this treacherous course," came the voice of the announcer, "it would be perfectly understood if our amateur contender for the title and the purse of barrel-racing champion withdrew. In fact, given that a record has been set today, and a national champion injured, it is advised. There is no dishonor in such a decision." The eyes of the crowd turned to Eddie. He smiled.

"No," he said. "We're ready to go." A hush followed his announcement.

From the time of the starting gun to the finish of the course barely two minutes later, all Eddie remembered was a poem of motion. He and the horse became a sort-of liquid substance that flowed over barrels and around curves. He was intensely alert and yet not alert at all. He and Redwing moved together. When it ended, and the horse slowly drew to a stop just inside the gate, the roars of applause were deafening.

"This is a day that has never happened before and will likely never happen again in the history of rodeo!" exclaimed the announcer. "The amateur challenger has defeated the champion. In addition, the amateur challenger has set a new national record in claiming the purse. Two minutes, twelve seconds for the most difficult barrel course yet to be negotiated in a Canadian rodeo! I daresay a new rodeo cowboy has emerged today on the soil of Alberta, able to challenge the best cowboys currently riding now in all of America. Come, young man. Claim your prize!"

Eddie imagined he heard the voice of Chief saying "Live right, and all of life will support you," as he and Redwing trotted across the arena to claim the prize. *That was for you, Flo,* he thought.

"Thank you," Eddie said humbly as he took the purse. "I'm glad you all enjoyed the show." The applause of the crowd was deafening.

After his spectacular performance, he became quite a celebrity in the region. The rodeo boss invited him to join up and ride on with the performers. "If you're that good at your age, I can only imagine how great you'll become," he enthused. "I'll pay you a salary on par with my best pro cowboys if you'll join up now. I know you're worth it!"

Eddie was tempted. The travel appealed to him, as did the challenge of riding. "I have something else I want to do first," Eddie said, thinking of his plans to lead hunting parties. "Besides, I can't leave my family just yet. But if I change my mind, can I join you later?"

"Offer's good for the next two years," the boss said magnanimously. "You change your mind anytime during that time, you only need to find us and you have a place. Just look for me, Mr. Tom Ruby. Don't you forget, Eddie. You're a natural!"

"I won't," promised Eddie. "I appreciate the offer." He stayed and watched the rest of the rodeo, remembering last year when he had tried bull riding and suffered several bruises for his efforts. He wondered if he could use Chief's advice to be "one with the bull" and avoid similar pains in the future, but decided not to try today. After the rodeo ended, he rode to Chief's before returning home to share his good news and his winnings.

Chief was neither surprised nor impressed. "What I need money for?" he asked. "Get all I need from hunting and trading. Money just attracts robbers. Brings bad luck."

"Fine," said Eddie. "In that case, I'll open an account for our hunting business. We'll use the money for provisions and whatever else we might need to get started. It's yours, too, Chief. And Redwing's. You both deserve it more than I do. I'll get her a fancy new saddle and tack, and some special oats. The rest will begin the business that will make us rich!"

Chief laughed. "Why be rich? Already have all you need. I go once to lead the strange hunters. Then we'll see."

Eddie's family was far more enthusiastic about his success and his prize than Chief. Papa and the children had lots of ideas about how to spend the prize money, too. Although it was difficult for Eddie, who was generous by nature and delighted in getting everyone whatever they desired, he insisted that the money was going to be used for only two things: a good saddle for Redwing, befitting her championship status, and provisions for the business he planned to start as soon as the lodge opened. Although Papa grumbled a little about needing new carpentry tools, Eddie could tell he was proud of his resolve. "Okay, son," he agreed. "I can tell you are serious about this hunting business. I'll talk to Sir Rigall and arrange for your try-out."

"Early autumn or early spring," said Eddie. "That's when we should make the trips."

"The lodge won't open until spring," Liam informed him. "But Sir Burt may want to try you out with a few of his friends this autumn. We'll see."

For the rest of the summer, Eddie eagerly plied his father about details. "Is he interested?" he asked each time Papa returned from the lodge. "When do we start?"

He spent every spare moment wandering the mountain trails—with Chief when possible and on his own when Chief was otherwise occupied. He noted streams and rivers, clearings and camp spots. He became familiar with the vast, beautiful territories surrounding Waterton, Banff, and Jasper, sometimes vanishing for days of camping and exploring.

One afternoon, returning from a three-day trek into the forests, he saw Miss Welch as he rode home. She was walking back toward her cabin at the schoolhouse from town. "Hi, Eddie!" she called. "How are you? I heard about your stunning victory at the rodeo last month. Congratulations! Has that changed your plans? Do you plan to ride with the rodeo now?"

"Maybe someday," he said, loping up beside her and reining Redwing to a halt. "But I still plan on trying out my hunting guide idea first. Papa is trying to convince Sir Rigall!" He beamed. "How have you been? What do you do in the summertime, anyway, when there is no school? Don't you usually go back home to see your family?"

"Yes, I'm leaving next week for a month in Toronto," she said. Then she visibly paled and Eddie wondered what was wrong.

"I'm sorry to pry," he said. "Is everything okay with your family? I mean—are you alright?"

She still looked a little dazed. "Who is Sir Rigall?" she asked.

"Why, that's the wealthy investor from the east who is financing the lodge down at Waterton Papa is building," he explained, a little puzzled by her reaction. "I've never met him. I don't think Papa has either; or maybe just once going over plans. But he is supposedly a famous hunter with lots of friends and acquaintances who enjoy big game hunting, too. They'll be coming here, and will need guides. Chief and I are going to do it!" His youthful enthusiasm for his plan couldn't be contained. "I wrote about my plan on my final essay. Do you remember?"

"Of course I remember," his teacher said. "It was a wonderful essay and it's a wonderful plan. Eddie, would you do something for me? When you finally meet this Sir Rigall to take him hunting, will you tell him that your teacher wants to meet him afterward to find out how well you did? I'd like that."

Eddie shrugged. The request only seemed a little unusual. He had a feeling somewhere deep inside his psyche that his teacher would always be checking up on him and on his accomplishments. This was actually a useful illusion. It is important to always have someone to make proud of your accomplishments, even if that someone is an illusion based on a past teacher. "Sure, Miss Welch," he assured her. "I'll do that. You have a safe journey home to Toronto!" He rode toward home, noticing that his teacher stared after him for a very long time, poised almost like a statue on the path.

The summer passed quickly. Eddie felt satisfied Chief had shown him most of the trails in the region. He was now able to locate animals with almost the same uncanny accuracy as Chief. Joe was hoping to continue working with his father at the lodge, and it appeared that would be acceptable. Once school began, only Maybelline, not quite three years old, would be at home. Mama could generally take her along when she was called away. One child was manageable. Eddie would be free to seek his fortune in the mountains—after taking care of the animals and garden and whatever needed repaired around the house, that is. Even this load was lightening. Gene was good with the animals and as Allie and Inez grew, they were proving to be responsible and competent. Gardening, gathering eggs, milking and bringing water were all chores they had now taken over.

Eddie had time, now, for socializing. His famous rodeo performance made him a popular companion among all the young men and women in the area. No dance, party, or celebration passed that he was not invited to. Now he often attended. Most of the girls in the region hoped to be his companion. He was a good dancer with a natural sense of rhythm and he enjoyed the idle conversation that accompanied dances. As autumn approached, Eddie was having more fun than he ever remembered, enjoying less responsibility and thinking only a little about the future. He still had hopes for the success of his hunting expeditions with

Chief and if for some unfathomable reason that didn't work out, there was always the rodeo offer. Life looked bright. When his father returned for Eddie's birthday in early September, the present he brought made life look even brighter. His father produced a beautiful hunting rifle.

"You'll need this soon." He grinned. "Mr. Rigall is planning to engage your services as a guide! If he likes the experience, he'll use your services exclusively for the hunters who visit his lodge once it opens in the spring. You'll have your hands full, and make a pretty penny, besides. I hope you and Chief are ready to help him find more big game than he's ever imagined. He's bringing along some friends from New York, too. He said to arrange for a week's odyssey for a group of four experienced hunters. They'll arrive late next week."

Eddie was elated. His excitement barely showed, though, as he began approaching the task ahead practically. "Will they have their own gear?" he asked. "What will they expect us to provide? And how much will they pay?"

"My son the businessman!" Liam grinned. "They'll have horses, rifles, knives, tents and bedrolls I suspect, but I'll make sure of that. You and Chief provide cooking utensils and food—preferably from game you find along the way —and the entertainment. And your own gear, of course. You can use some of that rodeo money to get whatever you are missing, like you planned. They'll pay you the same fee they're accustomed to paying the professional guides they've hired in Montana. That's fifty dollars per man per week, plus a bonus of ten dollars per animal. If it works out well, you can charge even more in the spring. After you split your earnings with Chief, you'll still make in a week what Joe and I make in two months. Not a bad start to your professional life, I'd say. Happy birthday!"

Eddie enjoyed the rest of his birthday celebration, too, but this was truly the highlight. Mama made him a delicious German chocolate cake, his favorite, and there was rich homemade ice cream to scoop on top. Each of his brothers and sisters brought small presents for him.

Joe had whittled a beautiful little wooden flute for him. "Now you can entertain those hunters around the fire at night with music!" he announced. Allie had knitted him thick, warm socks and Inez had made a wool cap with a scarf to match. Gene produced a hand-tooled leather belt with a flourish.

"Did you make that?" Eddie asked, surprised at the skill evident in the design.

"I helped," he said proudly. "Sergeant Brown is teaching me in exchange for my storytelling!" Sergeant Brown was the local mounted policeman in the area. He also served as game warden, inspector, dispenser of fishing permits and anything else vaguely related to law enforcement in southern Alberta. "You make sure to see him about your hunting trips!"

Maybelline and Lizzie proudly presented him with pictures they had drawn. Both looked vaguely like rodeo scenes, with someone riding a horse. Chief appeared later, with a brightly colored saddle blanket. Eddie shared the good news.

"We'll be leading our first hunting party next week!" he said happily. "This week, we'll need to take care of permits and make sure our gear's in order."

"You do that," said Chief, less than thrilled. "This your idea. Still not sure I like it. Just go because I'm curious."

Eddie sighed. "You'll enjoy it once we're there," he said. "You can tell these men your stories about all the endings of the different worlds. Besides, the country will be beautiful, with leaves changing color."

"We fish, too?" asked Chief.

"Sure, why not?" said Eddie. "Fresh trout will make a tasty dinner."

Eddie spent the week preparing for the venture. He checked with Sergeant Brown and made sure he had all the permits. He paid more than he'd expected for the fishing and hunting permits, realizing a permit was something neither he nor Chief ever had before. He knew Chief would complain about the idea of paying a fee to a government for the right to hunt or fish, so Eddie told Sergeant Brown that he would just hang on to Chief's.

The sergeant laughed. "Yeah, I wouldn't tell him, either!" he said. "This really is more his land than ours, in a way. You know I've never bothered him before. But if he's guiding, it's best he has this so there are no questions."

Eddie also obtained all the necessary paperwork for permits for the four hunters. "It'll be easier if I just take care of this, and get it to you before we leave or when we get back," he explained.

"Yes," assented the sergeant. "It would. I like your ethics, young man! Makes my life much easier! Keep in mind the limits, now—not that anybody ever reaches them, because you probably couldn't carry that much back. You got a wagon to take, too, just in case? If not, you can use my old one if you like. Government just provided me with a nice, new shiny rig so my personal wagon has just been sitting, taking up space. You keep up with this enterprise, and I'll sell it to you for part of your profit!" Eddie was delighted. He hadn't even thought about how they would get the animals back if they had more than each man could carry on his horse.

Next, Eddie rode all the way to Lethbridge to get gear and cooking utensils. He wanted to look professional. He even bought new boots and jeans for himself, and a dark green flannel shirt. He and his horse would both look just as well cared for as the wealthy hunters he planned to lead into the mountains. The rodeo money was put to good use. When it was nearly time to meet the hunters with Chief, he was certain they had everything for a successful journey.

Chief was skeptical about the wagon. "What for?" he asked. "Can't haul it down most trails. Loud wheel noises scare animals. Don't need."

"For now, we can store gear in it," Eddie explained. "Bedrolls, tents, fishing poles and rifles are things we need to take. So are beans and jerky and fruit and eggs and potatoes I brought for meals. These men will be used to being well fed. We'll leave it in a campsite—a clearing a little distance from where we hunt. I've already found several possibilities, depending on where we go. You or I can take turns staying at camp if necessary, if no one else wants to take a break from hunting. Don't worry. Besides, when we come back we can use the wagon to haul the game we shoot."

Now Chief looked really skeptical. "Why we need so much?" he asked. "No rifle for me," he added finally. "I use bow instead. Better chance for animals."

"Fine. Have it your way," said Eddie. "Just get everything you plan to take ready so we can leave for the lodge site in the morning. It'll take us two days or more to get there. You won't be complaining about the food I brought along the way!"

Soon, they were bound for Waterton. "When you go to school today, tell Miss Welch I'm off to make my fortune!" he instructed the girls. Then, remembering his promise to the teacher, he added "Tell her I'll ask the hunters to pay her a visit after the trip, too!"

Eddie and Chief took their time getting to the lodge. Chief was curious about what to expect, and Eddie really wasn't sure what to tell him. "They will be very wealthy, powerful men who like to go hunting to relax," he explained. "They think it is important to use their skill to hunt big animals. Somehow, this makes them happy. Other powerful men respect this."

"Strange," said Chief. "They need animals for food?"

"Not really," explained Eddie. "They do eat them, I suppose, but that isn't the real reason they hunt. They hunt so they can stuff the animals, keep the heads, and show other powerful men what they have accomplished."

"Very strange," said Chief. "It is important to hunt a big animal when everyone is hungry, and everyone needs to eat. Whoever

ROSES IN THE DUST

gets a big animal then is much respected. Hungry people are grateful. Animals know, too."

Eddie shook his head. "I can't explain it, Chief. Maybe there's some part in their heads that remembers that. They want to get the biggest animal so they can be important, even though people aren't hungry. We must help them find big animals. The reasons don't matter. That's just what we need to do."

Chief looked at him penetratingly. "You think so?" he said finally. "You have a good heart. I know. But reasons matter. Why more important than what. Why almost important as how, but not quite. Why is very important."

"Okay," replied Eddie. "For now, why is just because you know I have a good heart and you trust me. We help them find the biggest animals in the forest. Big, old moose and elk that have spent their whole lives waiting to be stuffed and displayed in fancy parlors of rich men. Big, old moose and elk who have done everything they need to do, and feel arthritis in their bones. Old, tired animals that want to be immortal. Okay?"

Chief laughed. "Strange ways," he said. "Meat can be tough, huh? Some animals may like that."

When the two arrived at Waterton, Liam and Joe met them excitedly. "Sir Rigall's been delayed, but he'll be here in the morning. He is bringing a very famous photographer with him to chronicle your journey, and two very wealthy, very famous hunters. Are you two up to this?"

"Of course!" Eddie said, looking at Chief.

"Sure," said Chief. "I know lots of old animals with big horns. Meat tough. But they die happy for us. They like to be pictures for a long time."

Liam smiled and embraced Chief. "C'mon," he said. "You two camp with Joe and I tonight. Tell us some of your stories. This is a great day for me. I am very happy to see my oldest son about to make his fortune!"

They stayed at Waterton until Sir Rigall and his entourage arrived two days later.

"Sorry for the delay," he apologized, with an accent that seemed more English than Canadian. "Travel out west is far from reliable."

"No problem," said Liam, taking charge easily in his friendly, gregarious way. "My boy and the Chief are ready to escort you into the mountains for the best hunt of your lives but first I need to show you what we've done so far to the lodge, and ask you a few questions about future developments. It seems…"

Sir Rigall walked with Liam on a tour of the premises after introducing his companions. Eddie asked if they were hungry, and set about making a welcome dinner from the canned provisions he had stocked on his wagon. Before he cooked, he passed out the paperwork for fishing and hunting licenses he brought along. He also offered them fishing poles and bait. He suggested they complete the paperwork, then head down to the peaceful lake with Chief to catch some trout for dinner. It was a pleasantly received welcome. When Liam and Sir Rigall arrived back from their tour of the development, they took the last two fishing poles and joined the men.

"Good job, Eddie!" Papa said. "Very professional!"

Thanks to the fresh, tasty trout from the lake, they shared an excellent dinner that evening. Everyone seemed happy. Eddie managed, in the course of the conversation, to find out what each man hoped to accomplish during their hunt. Sir Rigall wanted to down a moose. "The biggest carcass ever seen!" he intoned. "More horns than pipes on the church pipe-organ in Westminster Cathedral! Huge animal!" One of his companions hoped for a bear. This surprised Chief, but Eddie was able to smooth over the exchange. The third hoped for an ancient elk with antlers large and entangled. The photographer, John, hoped for pictures of the Alberta wilderness more beautiful and rare than any that had ever been seen. That seemed, to Eddie, to be the easiest request to meet of all.

The group talked and laughed over dinner, graced by several fresh and delicious trout, then slept under the stars. It was a beautiful autumn night, with no need for a tent. The next morning, over breakfast, Eddie remembered his teacher's request.

"Sir Rigall," he said, "since this is my first expedition as a guide, and since my beloved teacher Miss Welch has always taken interest in my success as I use what she taught me, she did ask that I make a request of you. After our expedition, she would like you to stop by the schoolhouse to let her know how I have done as your guide."

"Wonderful!" said the photographer. "I can use that in the magazine piece I do. 'Young Frontiersman Makes Good; Teacher Approves.'"

Sir Rigall looked even more interested than the photographer did. "What did you say you teacher's name was?" he asked. "Where is she from?"

"Miss Welch," responded Eddie. "Elizabeth Welch. She is from Toronto, I believe. She visits her family there every summer."

"Hmm," said Rigall. "Would it be out of the way to visit her on our way into the woods? Perhaps I could invite her to come along and see how well her star student does firsthand!"

Eddie was surprised. "I know she won't leave her students to come," he replied, "but we could go by the schoolhouse before we head to Banff, if you like, sir."

Burt Rigall indicated he liked that idea. "My photographer might like that, too," he said. "We can photograph the loyal school marm before and after, so to speak. We can capture her pride in her student."

Eddie also liked that idea. He and Chief both slept well that night, with stars overhead and the lake lapping rhythmically in the background. Everything seemed to be indicating a positive first venture into the beautiful Canadian wilderness.

Liam slept well, too. He was very proud of the initiative his eldest son had shown. He knew Eddie's idea was exactly what was needed at the time for Rigall's lodge and for the community. He was glad that Eddie had come up with such an appropriate livelihood; one that would keep him near, benefit the community and make him happy as well. He was also pleased Chief, with whom he had always felt a special kinship, was involved and seemingly in favor of his son's enterprise. Besides, he had managed to get Rigall to agree with the beautiful, elaborate latticework he hoped to do on the windows and ornate carving for the stairwells and benches. He'd even agreed to let Liam plant a rose garden at the lodge.

The next morning, Eddie set off for the mountains guiding his first hunting expedition. The men found good mounts, courtesy of Liam's requests to the locals, and everyone seemed well prepared. They headed back the way that he and Chief had just come since Sir Rigall wanted to meet Miss Welch. This was an advantage, for it allowed selective hunting of small game along the way, necessitating stops at the most beautiful clearings as they made their progress. They enjoyed a delicious rabbit stew on their first evening together, and they also enjoyed hearing Chief tell about the ant-people who had emerged from the ground after the First World ended.

The group was beginning to bond. They respected the eccentric Indian and the knowledgeable young boy. All had the feeling they were embarking on a great adventure. When they arrived at Miss Welch's schoolhouse late the next afternoon, their sense of adventure was heightened. They arrived just as the students were leaving. Eddie entered first, the photographer close at his side. "Hi, Miss Welch. This is Bob Renwick. He is photographing my first hunting expedition. I remembered you wanted to hear how it went. He wants to talk to you and take some pictures. Do you have a few minutes?"

"Sure, Eddie," she agreed. "I'll always have time for you. Mr. Renwick? Welcome. Please come in and photograph whatever you like. This is where Eddie attended school. He is certainly one of my most promising students ever, so I am confident you will have an excellent hunting trip! Would the rest of your party like to come in, as well? I can make some tea, and we can chat for a while."

Eddie, on cue, lit a fire in the small stove in the back and put on a teakettle. Chief, in the meantime, had been helping other members of the hunting party tie up their horses outside. About the time the teapot began to whistle, the rest of the party entered the schoolhouse. As Sir Burt Rigall walked in, Eddie watched how his gaze was riveted on Miss Welch. He could feel his teacher tense and watched her face visibly pale. She said nothing, so he thought perhaps she was catching a chill and quickly made her a cup of tea as he began the introductions. John began chatting immediately. "I understand you are the teacher of this enterprising young man," he said. "Would it be possible to take a picture of the two of you together, perhaps congratulating him on his great business idea and wishing him well?"

Elizabeth nodded. "Can I be in that shot, too?" asked Sir Rigall. Almost under his breath, he added, "It has been a very long time since Elizabeth and I had a picture taken together."

The three arranged themselves for a photograph. First, Eddie stood between them and Renwick snapped a shot. Then, Sir Rigall moved to Miss Welch's side and put his arm around her waist. "Take one like this, too, Renwick," he instructed. "The beautiful schoolmarm between her star student and his benefactor. This should make a good story. Would it be possible, lovely Miss Welch, to make this an even better story by accompanying us on our hunt?"

"I'm not a hunter," she said softly. "I am a teacher. And I could not leave my students. How long will you be gone? "

"We'll be returning next Tuesday," offered Eddie. "Maybe you could join us for the weekend, at least? My father and Joe were planning to meet us then; we've arranged a meeting spot already. Just ask Gene or the girls to tell Papa you've been invited and to stop by for you on his way. Maybe Mama can ask Joe to watch the little ones, and come instead. I know she would enjoy it, and it might make you more comfortable. She's not a hunter either, but you will both enjoy the scenery."

"And the company," added Rigall with a penetrating glance at the teacher. "That's a wonderful idea, Eddie! What do you say, Elizabeth? Surely you don't want to miss this opportunity."

"I would like to be part of Eddie's first expedition," she said a little stiffly. "That is a good opportunity. Okay, Eddie. I'll let your father know I'd like to join the group along with your mother for the weekend."

"Great! He'll stop by for you on Saturday morning, then, and we'll see you in the mountains! Bring blankets and warm clothes. It will already be a little cool at night."

She laughed. "I believe I'm the one who taught you geography and weather patterns, young man! Anyone for more tea?"

"We should go," said Chief. "Go far into mountains and make camp before nightfall."

"True," said Eddie. The men began gathering their jackets and finishing their tea.

"Could you get my horse, too, TJ, so I have time for one last warm drop of tea?" Rigall asked one of his friends. "I'll be there in just a bit."

He stayed behind for a few minutes as the others went to untie the horses and prepare to leave. Eddie noticed that he and Miss Welch seemed to be talking intently and seriously. He had a vague feeling they may know each other, but decided to see if either of them mentioned this over the weekend. Soon, he was too busy pointing out the many plants, trees and flowers along the way to wonder. He had learned the names and uses for each from Chief, and was proud to display his knowledge. The hunters were impressed. They were even more impressed when they began seeing tracks of some of the animals they were hoping to find—moose, elk and bear. Rigall claimed he wanted a mountain lion for a trophy, too. This request seemed to dismay Chief.

"What for?" he asked. "Meat no good. Cat leave you alone if you leave him alone."

This comment passed as they rode on, appreciating the beauty of the high pines and the rising mountain landscape. They reached a beautiful clearing near a stream, well into the Banff wilderness, by early evening.

"We'll be based here for at least two or three days, depending on how good the hunting is," explained Eddie. "We can set up a comfortable camp. Someone can watch our gear while the rest of us ride further into the forest for hunting. Chief or I will stay when you all want to go. Since we'll be here awhile, let's settle in tonight and make ourselves comfortable."

Everyone seemed to like the idea. They spent the last two hours of daylight setting up tents and unpacking gear. By nightfall, Eddie had a roaring fire going and began preparing dinner. Chief and Rigall left the group an hour or so before. Chief planned to use his bow to find a deer for dinner, and Rigall had never seen bow hunting before. He wanted to learn.

"Gotta be quiet," Chief said. "No talking. No footsteps."

"Fine, I'll barely breath!" He laughed. "I just want to see how this bow works."

They returned to the fire, carrying fresh deer meat. Rigall was plainly impressed. He continued to talk about the stealth, skill and aim required by the hunting he had witnessed. His mind was no longer set on a mountain lion. Instead, he wanted to learn to use the bow with Chief as teacher. This seemed to please Chief.

The other men laughed. "Great! Less competition for us! You use your bow; we'll use our rifles."

After lots of laughter, jokes, and story telling, everyone slept well. Their stomachs were full, surroundings were beautiful, and the trip was off to a promising start. Eddie had learned in the course of the dinner conversation his hunch had been correct. Rigall and Miss Welch were acquainted.

"Well acquainted," Rigall said in response to TJ's question. "She was my first love. I left on an expedition, and when I returned, she'd vanished to take a teaching position out west somewhere. I never thought I would see her again."

The next few days passed as enjoyably and successfully as the first. Chief and Rigall would leave at dawn for bow-hunting expeditions. When they returned, Eddie and the others rode several miles from camp to use their rifles, returning before dusk. TJ shot a large moose on the first day out. Simmons got an elk on the second, and TJ got a bear. Renwick only seemed interested in shooting with his camera, sometimes following the bow-hunters, sometimes the others and sometimes just hiking off on his own in search of scenery. They decided to stay at their camp until Friday, when they would move to the area where Eddie had agreed to meet his father. Chief had convinced Rigall they were at the best place to use the bow, and Rigall had no intention of leaving until he had been successful in his quest. To everyone's relief, he did finally shoot a deer with the bow on Friday morning, and his mood visibly brightened, bringing a feeling of elation to the entire group.

"Took me two shots, and Chief had to finish it—this time," he said. "But I'll master that one shot to the heart he does so well before we leave these mountains. Just you watch!"

He thought bow-hunting would be appealing to many of the men who came to stay at his lodge and scheduled another trip with Chief and Eddie for November that would be bow-hunting only. He planned to buy a bow of his own from Chief and master the skill. Eddie knew there would be snow by then, but he was confidant it would be a successful trip as long as Chief was there.

He often hunted in the winter with his bow. Rigall offered to pay $200 for the trip, regardless of whether anyone else went along. Everyone was satisfied as they shared a good late breakfast and broke camp before riding to their new site.

The new site, near a sparkling blue lake with the peaks of Jasper visible on the horizon, was awe-inspiring, as Eddie knew it would be. Unpacking and pitching tents took longer than usual because everyone continually stopped to admire the view and hike around the water. By the time they were finished, it was early evening. Fishing seemed more appealing than hunting and the trout were biting ravenously. Fresh fried fish for dinner was followed by music. Simmons had brought along a guitar and was actually a decent musician. He knew several popular songs, and everyone joined in for the songs they knew. After that, Chief told his story of the sky people before the group went to sleep. They rose early to begin exploring before Chief took the group out for a hunt. Now that he had arrowed one deer and arranged for a bow-hunting trip in two months, Rigall seemed happy to return to his rifle. Eddie remained behind at camp, awaiting his parents and Miss Welch. They arrived in the early afternoon and settled in before the others returned with several animals as trophies.

CHAPTER SIX

LOST IN THE SNOW

"So my son is showing you a fine piece of our countryside, eh?" said Liam to Rigall as they leisurely fished at the lake. "Didn't I tell you he and the Chief were the best guides to be found?"

"You did, and in this case you were not practicing your Irish talent for exaggeration," agreed Rigall. "This has been a very enjoyable week. With the bowsmanship, nature lore and knowledge of the region they demonstrate, as well as tracking skills, I'm confidant I won't find better guides elsewhere. They are naturals. As long as they can handle the demand, they can offer their services to all of the guests at the lodge. I guarantee they will be busy in the spring. That is assuming, of course, that you and that crew of yours have finished by then."

"Just take my advice as you did this time and keep the supplies I need at hand, and I'll be finished well before that!" boasted Liam before turning his attention to his fishing line, now pulled taught by a trout.

"Perhaps I will," said Rigall. "You've given fine advice this time. Excuse me," he added, seeing Elizabeth set off for a walk around the lake. "I think I'll leave the fishing to you, and take off for an afternoon stroll in this beautiful forest."

"You do that," said Liam, "but call Eddie or Chief over to watch your pole and keep me company while you are gone."

Eddie joined his father by the lake after Rigall left. "Good work," Liam told him, showing pride in his son. "You've had an excellent idea and it is off to an excellent start. This is the way to tame the wilderness and survive. Good ideas that make you money to survive on. Easier than farming by far."

They continued fishing as Burt Rigall caught up with Elizabeth on her walk. "May I join you?" he asked.

"Why not?" she said, shrugging her shoulders. "You're here." They walked in silence, turning away from the lake and into the forest. There was an electrical tension in the atmosphere between them. Burt finally broke the silence.

"If that young man is any indication of your talent, you've obviously become a fine teacher, Elizabeth," he said. "As I remember, that is what you always hoped to do. You've done it."

After more silence elapsed, she replied, "Thank you, but I'm not sure Eddie is credit to my efforts. He is just one of those marvelous children who, like hardy weed with bright flowers, are able to flourish anywhere, regardless of conditions in the weather or the soil. He would have excelled with anyone. It's a shame he won't continue his studies."

"Perhaps not," said Burt. "Not everyone is meant to be a scholar or a philosopher. Eddie seems to be perfectly happy as a hunting guide, and for his age, he is remarkable. I suspect the Alberta frontier right now will benefit much more from enterprises like his than from higher education, and I suspect he knows this. To your credit, I suspect you taught him that without even intending to, and it was a good lesson."

"I hope that was not among my lessons," she bristled. "I want each of my students to reach their highest potential."

"But he has!" Burt laughed, watching her expression. "Ah, Elizabeth," he added. "As feisty as ever. Believe me, I don't mean to start an argument. You know, I never thought I'd see you again…"

"That was obvious when you left without saying good-bye!" she retorted, then bit her lip. She hadn't intended to let this meeting upset her. It had been so long ago. She was a grown woman now, independent and content with her life, not a silly schoolgirl. There was no reason to react like one. She walked on in silence.

"Is that what you thought?" he asked, obviously surprised and puzzled. "Of course I meant to say good-bye. Word came up suddenly that I had an opportunity to go on an expedition with my uncle the naturalist, sailing round South America and to Africa. He'd been on Darwin's crew, you remember. We even talked about that once; you were impressed. You were always impressed by knowledge, Elizabeth. Always more knowledgeable than I was, and you made me so aware of that. Well, I decided I had a good opportunity to obtain some knowledge. I came by to tell you, but your father said you were unavailable, visiting a cousin. I thought you were upset with me for some reason, having left with no word. I wrote you the letter your father gave you. Wasn't that saying good-bye? I explained where I was going and when I planned to return, telling you I hoped I would learn enough on the voyage to interest you and I wanted to marry you when I got back, if you'd have me. When I did return, and your father told me you had taken a job out west and didn't wish him to tell anyone where you had gone, I assumed that was a clear no to my romantic young plea. You were right of course, as always. Wise beyond your years. We were far too young and far too different, and you knew that. But of course I said good-bye!"

Burt realized he was more emotional as he spoke than he wished; more emotional than he had been for a very long time. He took a deep breath and waited for her reaction. Much to his surprise, he thought he saw tears begin to form in her lovely, clear blue eyes. She shook her head sadly. "My father never gave me the letter," she finally said. "He never told me of your visit. And I never went to visit my cousin. I…" Her voice trailed off. "I wasn't as wise as you gave me credit for," she finished softly. "If there was any wisdom in the results, it's a credit to my father, not me." Burt thought he detected a note of sarcasm, even bitterness, in her last comment but he couldn't be certain.

Elizabeth appeared to recover quickly from this news, but that was only because it was such a shock that she immediately pushed it from her mind. She would have to think it over carefully later, when she was alone. The tragic heartbreak of her youth was a result of her father's deception! Burt had not abandoned her. She had impulsively run off to Alberta, sure there was no hope of being with the man she loved, when if she had only waited.... No, it seemed impossible. It was impossible, at least, to think of right now.

"Well, you can impress me with your knowledge now. How long were you gone? What did you learn?" The mood between them lightened as they walked around the lake together for nearly two hours. Burt told her about many adventures on his three-year voyage with his uncle. He told her of the other hunting lodge he had built, in Quebec. She told him about her students in Alberta and her years of teaching.

"You enjoy it, don't you?" he observed. "Do you ever plan to retire? To marry and have a family?"

"Probably not," she said. "I enjoy my independence and I enjoy my career. It's getting too late in my life to think about that now, anyway."

"It's never too late," he said as they arrived back at the campsite. She enjoyed his company as much as ever. She still felt completely comfortable with him. Life was a strange dance, like an Irish reel, whirling you dizzy and setting you off on unpredictable paths, then finally returning you to the partner with whom you'd begun. She shook her head; she had lots to think about.

"Just in time to enjoy those trout you left me to catch!" Liam greeted them brightly as they returned.

The evening passed pleasantly. The next day, the men arose early to hunt and the women stayed behind to break camp and enjoy the scenery. Liam had announced that, since he and Elizabeth both needed to be back at work on Monday and the hunters had enjoyed such success, everyone could return home with the McCauslin's for evening storytelling. Chief especially liked the idea. "We have more animals than we need," he said. "Time to go."

The photographer took several more pictures of Eddie with his teacher, the scenery, and the group on the way. "This will be a fine magazine piece," he observed. "Great publicity for my lodge, too," added Rigall. "You will of course remember, my friend, to point out I helped discover this young man and he is under exclusive contract to my lodge, won't you? And give information about the lodge for those who may be interested in seeing this hunter's paradise for themselves?"

"Of course," his friend laughed.

"Just make sure that exclusivity contract goes both ways!" added Eddie.

The group returned just before nightfall. The wagon was filled with moose, elk, and deer. Rigall was discussing having some of the animals stuffed and mounted, a concept which made Chief uncomfortable. "You want animals to look at, why you kill them?" he asked. "I take you to look anytime."

Rigall shook his head. "For one of the best hunting guides I've ever had, Chief, you sure miss the point of hunting."

Everyone settled in happily that evening. When Miss Welch said she really needed to go back to her cabin near the schoolhouse so she would be there in the morning before the children arrived, Burt offered to accompany her. "The rest of you stay and enjoy Liam's hospitality," he told his friends. "You can ride up to the lodge with him early in the morning and meet me there. I'll find a place to camp on my way in tonight. Just don't forget to bring that wagonload of beasts with you!"

The two departed after dinner, Burt to the friendly jibes and knowing winks of his friends. They rode back under the magical glow of a full moon illuminating the landscape. "You know, Elizabeth," said Burt, "This looks very much like the last night we were together, as I recall. Even though you broke my heart once, I have to say that it is good to see you again."

She smiled and nodded. "You broke my heart, too, you know," she confessed. "I truly never knew until yesterday that you ever made any attempt to see me again. I thought you'd just been toying with me, having your fun, sowing wild outs. I thought you had abandoned me and didn't even think the action was worth an explanation. I felt so used, so betrayed…" She was crying now. "I'm sorry," she choked. "I don't mean to be so melodramatic and emotional. It's just that…it never occurred to me my father would go to such measures to keep us apart. Do you know, the only reason I came out west was because I felt so humiliated and so betrayed and because…"

"Hush, hush," he said, reining both of their horses to a stop and reaching over to embrace her. "That was nearly fifteen years ago. Besides, your choices came out well. You've told me how much you enjoy your work. I am here now, and you know the truth. I must admit when I decided to build this lodge, a part of me hoped I would find you. Every time I came west to hunt, I thought I might learn where you had gone, and see you again. It was a whim, a fantasy, I was sure, but there was always that small hope…"

He stayed with her that night before returning to the lodge worksite in the morning, and found excuses to stay on in Alberta for another two weeks as well, spending weekends with her. Finally, he said he could find no further excuses not to return to business and family matters but assured her he would return in less than a month. Parting, even though temporary, was very difficult. Both of them were flushed and happy, drunk on the elixir of young romantic love even though they were well past the age such madness usually fades. Perhaps they were fortunate to be able to experience such intensity twice in their lives. Perhaps that was the balancing reward for the pain both had felt due to the earlier events that kept them apart. So they told each other, at least.

After Burt's departure, Elizabeth dreamed continuously of his return. Her students noticed the change. Although she had never been a severe or strict teacher, she was now constantly radiant, always smiling and laughing. Nothing upset her. She felt like she had been given back her heart. Although she had at first been skeptical of Burt's explanation, finding it difficult to believe her father could be so deliberately cruel, as she looked back the story seemed not only plausible but also perfectly true. How could she have missed it before? Why had it never occurred to her that Burt had tried to tell her good-bye—had even, as he claimed, wanted to marry her—and her own family kept the knowledge from her? Now she clearly remembered her father's disapproval of Burt from the beginning.

"Young men like that are only interested in British noble-women," he had warned. "He's not serious about you. His intentions are not honorable and I won't see you throwing yourself at some wealthy cad."

She had, of course, refused to believe it, disregarding her father's warnings and even directly disobeying his curfews. Family opposition only brought her closer to Burt. Her father's actions only served to more firmly cement their love for each other, as such actions often do. And yet, when his predictions had seemingly come true with startling speed, she never even questioned it. She assumed her father had been right all along and Burt deserted her. She had slunk away in embarrassment and despair. To now learn of her father's deception was almost more than she could bear. He had not only lied to Burt when he came to see her, he had never delivered what would have been the most important letter of her young life. Burt had asked her to marry him, proving her father's suspicions wrong. Rather than admit that, he had destroyed the letter. That someone who professed to love her and always look out for her best interests could have behaved in that way both shocked and appalled her. Perhaps it was fortunate her father had died three years before. Had he still been living, she knew that she would never have wished to see him again. Her anger was directed partly at him for his actions, but even more at herself for not believing in Burt. She should have had faith in their love. She should have known something was wrong when he disappeared and investigated it further. She should have waited, steadfast as Penelope. That her father could deceive her so was unfortunate. That she could allow herself to be so deceived was unforgivable.

These thoughts haunted her, but not enough to keep her from feeling that she was walking on air while Burt was near. The colors of the world seemed even more vivid than usual as leaves changed to gold and fell and as fresh, clean blankets of snow turned the world white. As Burt pointed out, she was happy with what she had achieved. Besides, they would be together again now. He had, she remembered, that afternoon in the mountains as they walked around the lake, asked her if she ever planned to retire from teaching and marry. He told her it was never too late. And though she said at the time she did not plan to, her new understanding of what had happened in her past between them changed that. She was confident they would marry. She was sure the happily-ever-after life she had foreseen for them in her youth would finally come to be. She felt again like a princess in a fairy tale. She again believed in dreams and in the overall beneficence of life.

Although she missed Burt, she was sure his absence was only temporary, and the anticipation of his return added a special sweetness to her longing. He was never far from her thoughts as she continued her work, happily anticipating his return. The days passed quickly until then. Eddie, in the meantime, was spending his free time with Chief learning not only how to bow-hunt and camp in the snow, but also how to make the finely-strewn bows and sharp, well-balanced arrows Chief used. Chief remained skeptical about the wisdom of the hunters, though.

"You gotta follow what you know," he told Eddie. "I follow what I know. One more time I go with you. Then, maybe no more."

Eddie hoped Chief was just talking, and would change his mind after another successful trip. But, just in case, he planned to learn everything he could. Eddie wanted to become as proficient at finding animals as Chief. He, too, wanted to be able to see through their eyes, read their thoughts and will them to stay still. He wanted to be able to hold the gaze of a deer as he sent an arrow sailing quickly and painlessly to the mark in its heart or head, just as Chief could. He had lots to learn.

Eddie was still optimistic about his venture. He knew Simmons and TJ would tell others about the success they'd had in the Canadian Rockies, and was sure the article Renwick wrote would attract many more customers. He'd taken the permits and fees to the sergeant after the hunting party returned and purchased the wagon.

"This business of yours is going to make both of us rich!" joked the policeman. The remainder of the money he had earned was deposited in the bank account he had opened for his earnings. This seemed like a good start, but he had learned to plan ahead. He knew that the next opportunity for earning any money as a hunting guide would be when Rigall returned for bow-hunting, and he would need the time between now and then with Chief in order to become expert enough himself to be a suitable guide. After that, it would probably be spring before he had another opportunity to lead a hunting party. So what about the winter? He wanted to join the rodeo, but didn't know if that was possible. Certainly not in Alberta during the cold winter months, at any rate.

Liam and Joe continued making progress on the lodge, and Eddie's bow hunting and knowledge of the wilderness areas surrounding Waterton continued to improve. The little ones were doing well at school and Mama was around more than usual; it seemed to be a winter of few illnesses and few births, as if the two kept each other in balance and at bay. Miss Welch continued teaching, radiating a special glow. She wrote letters to Burt nearly every day even though she knew, mail service to the east being as it was, most would never reach him before he returned. Still, the feeling of contact, of sharing her daily life with him, appealed to her.

Soon, snow covered the ground in white blankets. Winter had arrived. Rigall arrived not long after, more than two weeks before his scheduled hunt. He claimed he wanted to look firsthand at the progress Liam's crew was making on the lodge, but everyone suspected he also wanted to spend more time with Elizabeth. When the scheduled time for the bow-hunting expedition arrived, he even asked to push it back by a few days, a request Eddie and Chief were happy to comply with because of weather conditions. At last, though, they sat off for snowy regions in search of big game.

As far as Eddie was concerned, this expedition went even better than the first. They went far into Jasper, spending over two weeks camping in the snow. Rigall was delighted with the elk and deer he shot, and Chief didn't complain, as he had before, about the excessive waste of animals. He seemed to appreciate the man's desire to master bow hunting and he didn't seem to think the number of deer and elk they returned with was extravagant. Because of that, Eddie was especially surprised and disappointed when Chief told him, after Rigall had returned to his lodge and they were headed home, that he was no longer interested in helping with the hunting expeditions.

"Why, Chief?" Eddie asked. "It's going so well!"

"Goes well for you," said Chief. "You feel in your heart it is right, that's okay. Not for me."

Although Eddie tried to persuade him to continue, his attempts were pointless. Chief had made up his mind. He said he had only agreed out of curiosity. He wanted to see what the white hunters were like. Now that his curiosity was satisfied, he had no desire to continue on the hunts. Eddie was disappointed, but he knew Chief well enough to know that he could not change his mind once it had been made up. There wouldn't be any more hunting until spring, anyway. Still, he wished his friend would continue in the adventure. Ah, well. He'd let Papa break the news to Mr. Rigall when the time was right, or maybe say nothing until next spring just in case, as unlikely as he knew it was, Chief changed his mind. At least they had begun together. Eddie knew he owed the knowledge that would allow him to make this venture a success to the old Indian.

Rigall enjoyed the bow-hunting expedition. Everything he had experienced since beginning his business venture in Alberta suited him well. He loved the country. Liam was a superb carpenter and contractor. Rigall knew his finished lodge would be a showpiece. The hunting here was even better than he had imagined and the publicity he was already receiving as a result of his first expedition with Eddie and the Chief would guarantee success in the spring. In fact, he hoped the lodge would be finished ahead of schedule, as Liam had promised, as he already had several requests from hunters who wanted to be among his first guests.

Even better was finding Elizabeth again. That had been a very unexpected surprise, and a welcome one. Although a part of him had always hoped he would see her again, he long ago resigned himself to her rejection. To learn it had all been a misunderstanding was exhilarating. He felt like a young man again, capable of anything. There were a few complications, of course, but he was confident now that these were surmountable. After checking on the progress at the lodge when he returned from the mountains and determining his presence was not required there—indeed, things seemed to go more quickly and smoothly in his absence—he happily returned to Elizabeth's cozy cabin where he had been staying secretly for several days.

Elizabeth was still re-experiencing the light-hearted, life-expanding ecstasy of a first love. She had been thinking about the strange twists of fate that first separated and then reunited her with her love constantly, and even allowing herself to dream about the future. It looked promising, indeed. Burt seemed happy here. They could remain in Alberta most of the year at the lodge he was building, returning east occasionally. They could still have a family. It wasn't too late for that. She was hesitant to share her thoughts and dreams with Burt, unsure of exactly what he wanted and willing to bide her time. But she had faith that, soon, everything would work out. Her long lost dreams would come true after all. In this happy state, she welcomed him back and spent the rest of November in their comfortable world of two.

In December, he decided it was time to visit the lodge again and check on progress before Liam closed down the operation for Christmas. A few of the cabins were already complete, so he and Elizabeth could stay there. The last part of December until early February would be too cold to accomplish much, even though most of the outer structures were finished. Inner details and finish carpentry would be all that remained when work began again in late February. "How would you like to be the first guest at my lodge?" he asked before she headed to her classroom on Monday morning. "I think that would be an excellent way to ensure my success."

She laughed. "I told you I am not a hunter!"

"No. But you are a bringer of good fortune to hunters. How soon can you send your students home for Christmas season? Could you arrange to do that a little early?"

She considered it. She had never missed a day of teaching since first taking her position, always conscientious about her duties. If she were to stop classes a week early, she knew no one would complain. She could say it was due to weather or illness or any number of excuses—or just say nothing at all and extend a week in the spring. Besides, she was considering the possibility of retiring soon if her relationship with Burt continued as she hoped it would. Any repercussions would not worry her too much. The students would be happy for the extra free time and their families would likely be happy for extra time with their children, too. "I suppose I could arrange that," she said. "I would enjoy seeing the project that brought you here. After next week, I should be free until after the New Year. How long shall I plan to stay?"

He considered it. "My mother was expecting me back in Toronto at Christmas," he said. "Blazes, she was expecting me back already! I might as well stay on; I'd much rather spend the holidays with you, I have to admit. We'll have a winter-wonderland paradise for two! I'll ride out tomorrow and make sure one of the nicer cabins is ready and well stocked. Once the construction crew closes down, we'll have the place to ourselves. I'll even tell them to take off a week early, so they can be home with all of those children you plan on setting free." He left the following morning to make arrangements, promising to return for her that weekend.

When he arrived at the lodge, he was pleasantly surprised to see how far ahead of schedule Liam and his workers were. He praised their progress, and they all commented on his unusually cheerful demeanor and joked with him about just where he had been since his hunting trip.

"Thought you'd be back in Toronto by now!" Liam said in greeting. "This winter camping and bow hunting must agree with you more than it does with the rest of us. Well, let me show you what we've done, now that you are here." He showed him the premises. Rigall looked at the nicest of the finished cabins. There was a stove and fireplace inside. Although it was not yet furnished, he thought that could be arranged. He asked Liam about it.

"I do like it here," he said. "In fact, I'm of a mind to stay in that cabin over the holidays to keep an eye on this place and send you and your crew home early. Would it be possible to minimally furnish that place by the end of the week? Linens and cooking utensils, a bed, a chair, a table, a sofa…what do you think?"

Liam considered. "It would make more sense to stay in the cabin my men have been using. We've already added bunks and chairs and tables there. But, if you like, before we leave we can move the chairs and table to this cabin, and the cooking utensils and linens. I should have time to make a bed this week, if that is your wish. Will you want just one of the bunks completed?"

Rigall shook his head. "I've been thinking that maybe we should have at least one cabin that's set aside for a couple. Sort of a honeymoon suite, you know? It might be an appealing idea for some wealthy young couple who wants to do something different to impress their friends. Why not add a nice four-poster, as ornate and elaborate as your wood-artist's hand wishes it to be, and some more elegant furnishings to one of the cabins for that purpose?"

Liam shrugged. "Why not? Sounds a bit unusual to me— hunting on a honeymoon—but you're the better judge of what you expect your customers to want. I can finish the bed. Might be a little difficult to find a mattress unless you want to check with Eddie about taking his wagon up to Calgary. If you do that, you can get the nicer linens and curtains and utensils you have in mind, too. The stores there are well stocked. It's at least a two-day journey each way, though."

"That's a good idea," Sir Rigall said. "I'll hire my favorite guide again, only for shopping instead of hunting this time. You just get that bed finished before I return and tell your men that they have an extra week off for Christmas this year—with pay—for all of their hard work!"

"You know the way to my place," said Liam. "Ride on out and make arrangements with Eddie, and tell my bride to expect me home for the holidays this weekend. We'll take care of the rest here."

When Rigall arrived at the McCauslin ranch the next day, after first stopping to tell Elizabeth his plans, Eddie prepared the wagon and horses for the trip. Hunting for a mattress and furnishings certainly seemed a far cry from hunting for deer and elk, but as it still paid well, he was eager to go. He'd been to Calgary with his father once last summer and remembered the way. The two set off in the early afternoon, determined to make it a fast trip and get as far as they could before sunset.

The trip went smoothly. Eddie enjoyed Rigall's company. The Englishman told a series of wonderful tales about his voyage around the world with naturalists, classifying plants and animals as far afield as the Galapagos Islands, Chile, South Africa and India. He was well read and intelligent; they discussed books and politics, and Eddie again realized how much he wanted to see the world someday. The two also spent some time talking about Elizabeth.

"She is a wonderful teacher," Eddie told him. "The best I could have had, without a doubt. Until you came, though, she seemed— I don't know how to explain it—serious, I guess. Lately, she has been the happy person I always sensed she was."

Rigall told Eddie the story of how he and Elizabeth had first met in Toronto, by chance, at a library and fallen in love despite the disapproval of both of their families. He shared how he had planned to marry her despite family protests and how their communication had been waylaid by her father so they lost contact. He told Eddie what a surprise it had been to meet her again here in Alberta.

The story was not lost on Eddie, who always appreciated a good tale about the lives of people he knew and cared about. "Will you marry her now that you have a second chance? What a story that will be to tell your children on a cold winter night! At least as good as some of Papa's!"

Rigall chuckled. "I don't know that I am quite the story-teller your father is, but I must admit the thought has occurred to me. I'm not sure she would be interested, though. It would mean giving up teaching, and she enjoys that so much."

"You should ask anyway," said Eddie. "I have a feeling she would be willing to consider a career change!"

"There's other complications, too," said Rigall, looking a little pensive and distracted. "Other things need to be taken care of first if that is my intent…" His voice trailed off and, as he didn't seem inclined to continue that conversation, they rode in silence for a while until Eddie changed the subject to the types of furniture and supplies he was hoping to find in Calgary. When Rigall explained his overall intent as creating "an elegant cabin among the hunter's cabins; something for a couple's romantic vacation or a honeymoon," Eddie nodded knowingly.

"You'll end up marrying her," he said, convinced. "I'm sure of it now." They talked about marriage for a while then, a topic that Eddie, as a young man, felt he had already given serious thought to. He described for Rigall the "pros and cons" list he had devised in his head on the topic and explained why he didn't plan to marry. "Too much responsibility for someone who wants to see the world. Besides, unless I make my fortune first, I wouldn't even consider it! Mama and Papa are happy, I know, but it would be so much better for her if he wasn't working all over the country. I'd be unwilling to commit to a wife and children unless I knew I could care for them."

"Your mother strikes me as a woman who prefers not to be taken care of," observed Rigall. "You might consider that. Elizabeth seems that way, too."

"Maybe," said Eddie doubtfully. "Besides, you've already seen the world, and you have plenty of money. In your case, it makes sense. As for me…"

"Your plans sound fine," said Rigall. "Given your life so far, they make perfect sense. Just remember, life doesn't always seem to work out the way you plan it."

They arrived in Calgary the following day and checked into the hotel there, both looking forward to warm baths. Their shopping expedition went surprisingly well, and by the end of the day, the wagon was loaded down with a mattress, bedding, furniture, drapes, china, and a variety of other things that would turn the large cabin into a small palace. Rigall treated them both to a good meal at the hotel that evening. They headed back to Waterton the following morning.

By the time they arrived back the following Wednesday afternoon, Liam had completed a beautiful mahogany bedframe. "You told me to spare no expense and utilize my artistic inspirations," he told Sir Rigall, "and, as you can see, I took you at your word!" It was a magnificent piece. Liam had also completed a stunning wood-inlaid end table to match, with patterns of interlocked oak, maple, and pine on a mahogany base.

Rigall and Eddie stayed at the lodge, preparing the cabin, until Friday morning. Then, Eddie loaded up his wagon with his father's tools and supplies and prepared to return home with Joe and Papa. The other men also happily prepared to leave for a long holiday. As they cleaned the work site and packed their supplies, Burt headed back to Elizabeth's cabin, looking forward to the best Christmas ever.

The weekend was festive for everyone. When Eddie, Joe, and Papa arrived home, Mama and the girls had already begun baking Christmas cookies and making decorations for the tall pine outside the front window. The extra week for holiday celebrations was welcomed by all. The girls were delighted to be out of school early. Everyone was eagerly anticipating a month of enjoying each other's company. Liam was eager to spend some of his generous Christmas bonus on presents, and asked Eddie if he was up to another trip to Calgary with the wagon next week to shop for Mama's "wish list" and a few surprises. Eddie's wagon was getting plenty of use lately.

Elizabeth was joyously awaiting the holidays, too. She looked forward to visiting Burt's lodge at Waterton Lakes, which she had not yet seen. When he arrived back late in the evening, seeming pleased with what he had accomplished, she fixed them both a late dinner of soup, tea and cakes as he recounted the journey to Calgary. She suggested they spend the rest of the weekend at her cabin so she could do some Christmas baking. He was agreeable to the idea, so they spent a comfortable weekend together, sharing more of their life experiences with each other and rejoicing in their reunion. Falling snow outside formed a lovely backdrop. The fireplace burned brightly as they talked quietly in the evenings. Both knew the rest of their lives would flow smoothly together at last. There was a sense of destiny about the love they shared and neither remembered ever feeling so peaceful or content.

Once they arrived at the cabin, the holiday season was even brighter for them. They spent Christmas and the New Year in a quiet, comfortable world of two. Snow fell softly around them. No one else approached the lodge. As the cabin was well supplied, they had no need to venture out. Three weeks sailed magically by, and Elizabeth was sure her dreams of long ago were finally coming true. Then, a few days after New Year's, they both heard the clatter of a wagon outside.

Elizabeth looked out the window to see two women disembark from the sergeant's wagon. The oldest, past sixty, looked vaguely familiar. The other was young, wearing her hair up in the latest New York style and dressed regally.

"My God," said Burt as the women approached the door. "It's my mother." Elizabeth looked at him questioningly and he motioned her toward the bedroom. Although she would have preferred a frank introduction, she complied, closing the door to the room behind her as he went to admit his guests. She could hear the conversation.

"Good day, Sir Rigall!" said the sergeant. "This fine lady tells me she is your mother and, when you decided not to come home for Christmas, she arranged to come all the way here to find you. Some of the men told me you were staying at your lodge, so when she contacted me for your whereabouts, I took the liberty of bringing her here. This is coming along nicely! I can see why you want to keep an eye on the place, but surely you could have asked me to do that for you and returned home to your family for Christmas."

"Indeed," echoed his mother.

"Didn't you receive my telegram, Mother?" asked Rigall. "I told you I had business that would keep me here over the holiday season."

"I received it, but that did not deter me from finding you. I made plans to travel here as soon as I received it. You see, I wanted to bring you my present in person. I knew you had not seen Anastasia for many months and so we had arranged a surprise visit as your Christmas present. Since you didn't come to us, we found you, instead! Here, come greet your fiancée properly. Speak to Anastasia. She's first come all the way from Europe, then traveled across all of Canada to see you."

Burt spoke, instead, to the mounted policeman. "Thank you, Sergeant," he said. "I appreciate your escorting these ladies here to find me. Have they made arrangements for lodging yet?"

"We thought we'd stay with you, Burt," the younger woman said. She had a high, musical voice. "I've desperately wanted to see this lodge since I read the magazine piece about Alberta. It is lovely."

"The only other cabin ready is where the workmen stay," said Burt. "It isn't nearly as nice as this. Perhaps you should go to a hotel in Calgary or Lethbridge…"

"That's a good ways on," said the sergeant skeptically. "They've had a long trip already."

"I thought I raised a gentleman," interjected Burt's mother. "Did it ever occur to you we could stay here, and you could stay at that other cabin?"

"I would like a proper hello," interrupted Anastasia. "It has been nearly six months since I've seen you, and your letters have hardly been constant since you began this project. I'm beginning to wonder if we're still getting married this spring, as our mothers have been so busily planning!"

When Elizabeth heard this, her throat tightened and her heart fell to her stomach. She wrung her hands anxiously. How could she have been such a fool? Burt was planning to marry a lovely English noblewoman, just as her father had always predicted. He hadn't even bothered to tell her during their intimate weeks together. His story about coming to see her before he left with his uncle all those years ago was probably just that—a story. Now, as before, he had played with her emotions. He again planned to desert her. She could hardly believe she had been so blinded by love and nearly marched into the room right then to introduce herself. It wouldn't change her heartbreak, but it would give Burt a bit of explaining to do! With the sergeant there, whose children she taught, she could hardly do that. It would make her impropriety far too obvious and impair her career—which, at this point, was all she had. She fought back the impulse and listened to the conversation continuing in the next room, hardly noticing the tears that were rolling down her cheeks.

She still may have confronted Burt and the women after the sergeant left, had they not left together. Burt said if they planned on staying here, he would need to take them into town for some provisions. The sergeant offered to escort them.

"Your horse will hardly carry the ladies." He laughed. "They may wish to help select their own food!"

Once they left, Elizabeth tried to decide what to do. She couldn't. She could barely think, barely feel. She simply left as if in a trance, not even gathering up her things as she headed to the corral, trudging through the snow. She hurriedly saddled her horse and rode from this nightmare towards the mountains. By the time Rigall, his mother, and his fiancée returned, she had been gone nearly three hours.

Burt assumed she had returned home. He was despondent at the turn of events, wondering how he could possibly explain to her. As it was, he already must explain the recent turn of events to his mother and his fiancée. He had no idea what he even wanted to explain. He didn't know if Elizabeth would be willing to give up her career and marry him; he had a feeling she would not, especially now. Burt didn't even know if he was ready for marriage himself. His mother had been pressuring him for the last two years to marry Anastasia, and he'd assumed before he was reunited with Elizabeth that he would. It was a good match; Anastasia was attractive, from a good family and pleasant enough to be with. He always found reasons to put off the wedding, though, and had planned to continue doing so for quite some time. Now, Anastasia was in Canada and his mother had obviously been making preparations for a spring wedding. She told him she had planned to surprise him with Anastasia's visit at Christmas, and that Anastasia would then be staying with her in Toronto until he finished his lodge in the spring. By then, preparations would be finalized for the wedding. He couldn't stall so easily this time. If Elizabeth would marry him, he would break his engagement. But if she would not agree, he didn't want to "burn his bridges."

That meant he needed to speak to Elizabeth, but now she was gone. This complicated the situation even more. He sighed as he settled his mother and Anastasia into the cabin, and moved his things to the worker's quarters. Tomorrow, he would find some excuse for going into town and ride to Elizabeth's cabin. After speaking to her, he would know what to do.

"You seem distracted," Anastasia observed during dinner. "What's wrong?"

"It's just the surprise of seeing you," he lied. "Besides, I'm busy with this lodge. I need to ride into town to look at some lumber tomorrow, and there is really no way I can cancel the appointment. I feel badly that you and mother came all this way to see me, and will see me for such a short time."

"Surely no one at a lumberyard is working over the holiday season!"

"This isn't a lumberyard, it's an individual. Someone I really need to see." I'm only stretching the truth a little bit, he told himself.

"Well, wouldn't this person understand, given the situation? You can explain that we arrived for a surprise visit when you next see him and—"

"If I postpone, I may not have what I need for the lodge," he said. "I really must go."

"Will you always be so busy?" She pouted. "I suppose I must just learn to accept it. Go ahead with your plans. I will explain to your mother. How long will you be gone?"

"At least three days. Perhaps even longer. It's nearly a day's journey each way."

She sighed. "That will not leave very much time for us to be together. We were only planning to stay for a week, and our return tickets are already purchased."

He shook his head. "I don't know what to say," he said. That was certainly the truth.

The next day as he rode to Elizabeth's, he continued to ponder the situation. What did he want to do? He loved Elizabeth very much and could barely believe his good fortune in finding her again. But the problems they had before with family and background had not changed. Nor had her dedication to teaching. Perhaps it would be best just to accept that they were fortunate to have each other again, and be together when he was at the lodge, just as they had been doing for the past few months. Asking her to be his mistress seemed logical, but he worried that she would feel it disrespectful even though that was the furthest thing from his mind. So how should he proceed? Ask her to marry him first, realizing she would probably decline, and then bring up the idea wistfully? What if she did not refuse? Should he then explain his mother's plans? No matter how he approached it, there would be problems.

He loved Elizabeth. Of that he was certain. He didn't love Anastasia, although he knew she would be a good wife. But was marriage really about love? Among his friends and family, he knew that love was certainly not viewed as the primary factor when choosing a mate. If it was there initially, that was fortunate. If not, it was expected to grow over time. When he was young and first knew Elizabeth, he would have readily gone against his family's wishes for love with all of the impulsivity of youth. Now, more mature, he could see the wisdom of their advice. Life was complex; society was complex. Marriages required far more than love to be successful, and could perhaps even be more success-ful when love was not there to muddy the waters. He faced a dilemma, and until he spoke with Elizabeth, he had no idea what the outcome would be.

When he arrived at her door, his dilemma was not solved, either. She was not at home. He wondered where she could be. Visiting friends, perhaps? He decided his best course of action would be to wait for her to return. But after waiting all night and most of the next day, still seeing no sign of her, he began to worry. He decided to ride to the McCauslin's ranch. Perhaps she was visiting there, or perhaps they would at least know where she was. Eddie was resourceful. He would surely have some idea. It didn't occur to him that since she had been careful to hide her whereabouts for the last several weeks that no one would have seen her for quite some time.

Burt arrived and told Eddie that Elizabeth was not home. He was concerned and wondered if the McCauslin family had seen her recently or knew of her whereabouts. They had not. Eddie left almost immediately to check with neighbors. When he first heard Burt's story, he felt an eerie sense of foreboding. After determining that no one had seen her for quite some time, he decided a search was necessary. The snow was deep and cold, and there had been a blizzard in the mountains the previous evening. Although it would be unlike her to ride on her own into the forest, perhaps for some reason she had. His intuition told him that was what had happened and he wanted to organize a search party and scour the surrounding forests. Rigall agreed immediately.

Liam left to notify Sergeant Brown and round up neighbors for a search party. "You come with me, Eddie," said Rigall. "We'll see if Chief will join us. He knows these mountains like no one else." Like Eddie, he sensed that something was wrong. As they rode toward Chief's, he relayed more of the story to Eddie.

"I last saw her three days ago," he said. "She was at the lodge. I won't go into detail, but she left that afternoon rather upset, I believe." Eddie nodded. Somehow, he'd suspected as much. They rode on in silence, each thinking his own thoughts about how to find Elizabeth. Both were speculating about the events that had led to this search. Chief's suggestion, once they arrived and explained the situation, was to begin from the lodge and follow her trail. Rigall balked at this, pointing out that it had snowed and tracks would likely be covered. The Chief dismissed this. "Other signs still there," he said. "Besides, Eddie knows her. He'll be able to see through her eyes when we are close. Just like with animals, Eddie. Get supplies. May take long time." Chief put a few provisions in a knapsack and saddled his horse. "Now we hurry."

Rigall's next dilemma was whether to stop at the lodge to explain to Anastasia and his mother that he was going on a search for a local schoolteacher who was missing. He knew they would protest and it was likely to take him some time to extricate himself. With Eddie and the Chief there, perhaps he would need to explain everything and break his engagement. His alternative was to simply proceed without stopping unless by some chance he happened to see them outside. This might also mean he would be gone several more days, though, and he had told them he was returning today. That also could be problematic.

He considered trying to ride ahead, telling them he had business to tend to at the lodge, but he knew he would never get there
before Eddie and Chief. Both were riding fast, pushing their
horses on toward the lodge. Their pace expressed a sense of great
urgency. This, more than any other consideration, resulted in his
decision to simply continue with the search. He imagined that,
when he did not return on schedule, his mother and Anastasia
would worry and find the sergeant to report him missing. At
this time, they would learn of the search party he was a part of.
He hoped they would view his actions as heroic and return to
Toronto on the day they had planned, regardless of whether or
not he had returned by then. Silence seemed to be his wisest
course of action until he reached a decision about just what he
wanted to do. Once he came to this conclusion, he focused his
attention on the search.

"I'm not completely sure of the time she left the lodge," he
told Eddie and the Chief, "but it was sometime in the afternoon,
three days ago."

"How she leave?" asked Chief.

"By horseback, I guess. I didn't see her leave, but her horse was
gone when I returned."

"You said she was upset," added Eddie. "Did she take any provisions, to your knowledge? Could she have been planning to go
into the wilderness and camp for a day or two, to think?" He
was already beginning to have an idea about how she might have
reacted, where she may have gone.

Rigall considered this. He hadn't checked to see if any food
or bedding was missing. "I'm really not sure," he said. "I don't
think so, but I could be wrong. I just assumed she went home,
and when I rode there the next day to find her, she wasn't there.
I thought that maybe she was visiting friends. I waited for her to
return, and when she did not come back that night, I was worried
and came to your ranch. That's all I know."

Chief looked at Eddie penetratingly. "You see with her eyes," he said finally.

"I see the lake where we all camped on our first hunting trip. Where my parents and Miss Welch met us," Eddie said without hesitation. "And I feel numb and very cold. C'mon. We have to hurry!"

Without waiting for a response, he turned his horse abruptly and headed in another direction, seeking the quickest route to the campsite where they had all been over three months before. He surprised even himself, but for the first time, he knew without a doubt that he had mastered the intuitive abilities Chief had been trying to teach him to use in tracking. Redwing also seemed to sense the urgency and know exactly where to go, almost of her own accord. Chief caught up with him long enough to hand him a small bag of fruits. "You go first," he said. "We follow."

Eddie knew that his destination was over a day's ride from where they were; he also knew that it was important for him to reach his teacher as soon as possible. He felt the urgency, could feel her life fading. He rode without stopping, except briefly to allow his horse to eat snow for hydration and give her apples and grain. Silently, he thanked Redwing for her cooperation. She was quick and sure footed. Even after the light had faded and he grew tired, nearly dozing in the saddle, she continued as if she remembered exactly where they were headed. Rigall and the Chief had fallen far behind. Dawn was breaking as the lake came into view.

Now, Eddie knew it was important to call on all of his powers of intuition. He followed his instincts and headed around the lake, in the direction he had seen Miss Welch walk with Rigall in the evening as he and his father were fishing. He sensed this would be the path she followed. He slowed his horse and surveyed the area. Soon, he thought he saw a flash of red in the woods just off the path. As he turned, trees and boulders blocked his view, but he continued anyway. As he rounded one of the boulders, he noted freshly fallen snow mounded in an unusual way. He stopped abruptly and began digging. Clearing away the top layer, he saw his teacher's hand. His pulse quickened. How long had she been there? Surely she had suffocated by now, if she wasn't frozen. He continued clearing the snow. As he did so, he saw that, because of the way that she was laying among the boulders, a sort-of natural cave had formed around her. There was an open space; she had been able to breathe. And she was still breathing—barely. Her breath was slow and weak but he could feel the air as it was released from her nostrils. He found her wrist to check her pulse and saw that the area near it was reddened with blood. It didn't take him long to surmise what had happened. She had come here, perhaps initially to think. There were visible remains of a fire before the last snowfall. Then, in desperation, she had slashed a vein in her arm with a hunting knife, seeking to take her own life. She would have succeeded except that the snow and cold had frozen the wound and stopped the bleeding. He had arrived in time—perhaps only by seconds. She had not yet frozen to death and she had not yet bled to death.

Without another thought, he tore his shirt and made a tight tourniquet for her arm, binding the wound so the blood would not begin again once she was warmed. Then, he built a blazing fire and began massaging her body to restore circulation. Once the blue tint began to fade from her lips and he could see she was out of danger from freezing, he lifted her to his horse and mounted behind her, bracing her so she wouldn't fall before regaining consciousness.

"C'mon, Redwing," he urged his tired horse. "This has got to be a smooth, fast ride. Take us home." He knew his mother would be able to nurse his teacher back to health. It was difficult for him to imagine the wise, calm, sure, steady woman he had trusted so much throughout his youth attempting to take her own life. He knew emotions could be painful. Remembering the bitter tears he had shed over losing his little sister only two years before reminded him of this. Still, he hoped he would never experience or cause the level of emotional reaction that could result in an event such as he witnessed. Beyond that, he was relieved to find her in time. He had learned to follow his intuition as Chief had showed him. He felt that he had learned at last to listen with his heart.

CHAPTER SEVEN

GROWING UP

Elizabeth turned her head and watched the snow falling softly outside the window. The world was white and serene, silent and frozen. It seemed to reflect how she felt. She was propped up against pillows on a comfortable cot in a bedroom at the McCauslin's. The two youngest girls were sharing Allie and Inez's room while she recovered. They enjoyed this; it seemed like an extended slumber party where they could bask in the attention their older sisters lavished upon them. Elizabeth was still weak and disoriented, and a little unsure how she had gotten here or how long she had been here. She vaguely remembered riding wildly through a blizzard after leaving Burt's, angry with herself for making a fool of herself in love not once, but twice. How could she have believed him? She remembered the emotional pain she felt, and how she seemed to ride with no clear sense of where she was going or what she would do. She shook her head. Had she really been so foolish as to try to take her own life? She thought she remembered huddling in the cold near the lake where they had found each other again, weak and crying, and deciding there was no way out of the situation; that she no longer wanted to live. Had she used her knife to cut her wrists? It seemed that she remembered doing so, and then remembered falling peacefully asleep in the snow. So how had she gotten here? That part of the story was blank.

She watched the snow continue to fall outside the window, blanketing the world in an icy glow. Eddie came into the room with a tray of tea and biscuits, set them on the small table next to her, and smiled. "I thought you might like these," he said. "I'm glad to see you are awake and feeling better."

"Thank you," she replied quietly, and motioned to a chair. "Join me?"

"Of course." He pulled the chair close to the cot and poured the tea. Then he sat quietly, waiting for her to speak. It had been such a relief for him to find her in time and bring her to his home and even more of a relief when his mother stitched up the cuts he had tourniqueted and told him all would be well. "You and the weather were her guardian angels," Mama had announced. "The weather froze the wounds in time to save her from bleeding to death and you found her in time to save her from freezing to death. Now, rest and nourishment and human kindness are the only medicines she needs. I think we can offer that without any difficulty."

They drank their tea in silence for a few minutes. Finally, Miss Welch spoke. "What happened? I mean, how did I get here? I..."

"I found you by the lake, where we all camped last fall," Eddie answered simply. "I brought you here."

"I—I don't know what to say. I'm sorry. I acted so foolishly. I..."

"You don't need to apologize," Eddie said gently. "I'm just happy you are okay now. Only you and Mama and I know what happened," he added tentatively. "I mean—the rest of the town just knows you were lost in a blizzard and I found you and brought you here. That's all. We can keep it that way if you like; it might be better if—"

She nodded. "Yes, it would. Oh, Eddie! I feel so foolish! I..." Tears began to fall.

Eddie spent many hours with her as she recovered. He listened quietly as she described her childhood and her great romance with Rigall when she was a girl. He nodded with wisdom far beyond his years as she described the events and feelings of the past few months, and the situation at the ranch that had caused her to lose hope in her future and act with such despondence. He reflected silently on life and love and death as she spoke. All of the joy and pain in her words seemed to attach themselves to his own understanding of what it means to be human. There was little he could do to help her except listen and empathize, and this he did patiently over the next several days. When she did, at last, ask about Burt he reported that, after she had been found and he was sure she was safe, he had returned to Toronto with his mother. Eddie told her that he would be happy to help at the schoolhouse until she recovered fully; that the villagers were simply planning to wait until she was ready to begin classes again. The winter break was not yet over, so there was plenty of time. She shouldn't worry.

"Just promise me you'll stay until Inez is old enough to take over!" He laughed. "Don't run off and get married. We need you here."

Those words, as much as the listening, helped her refocus on life and renewed her will to live, speeding her recovery. Being needed by the community was a powerful medicine. It put her own childish emotional reactions in perspective for her once and for all. Her role was helping to prepare the children of the frontier for the future. She was needed for that, appreciated for that. It framed her identity, her role in life. It connected her to a web of life in a pattern with a destiny she understood and could fulfill. This strength, this understanding, made her realize that whatever she had gone through emotionally with Burt, as devastating as it had been, had been a part of some greater purpose. She was perhaps not meant to marry. She was meant to be here in Pincer Creek, teaching the children of this area and helping them grow into fine young men like Eddie. That was her destiny. Whenever she sought to fight it, the result was pain. She needed to accept it.

As she came to this understanding, she tried to explain it to Eddie, too. He wasn't sure he believed in destiny. He knew his parents both did, in their own ways. His father believed the Tinker's knowledge of the future and his mother in God's will, which implied the same thing. He knew Chief's stories repeatedly expressed a belief in some predestined plan and that he strongly believed Eddie had a destiny to fulfill. And he realized that this belief in some greater plan, some universal story, was a very healthy and necessary belief for his beloved teacher to have right now. Still, as he came to his own understanding of life, he sensed that destiny was perhaps more malleable than the adults in his world seemed to think. He suspected it might be something that each individual created for himself as he lived life, without any pre-written script or master plan.

Once Miss Welch regained her strength, he spent several weeks with her at the schoolhouse and at her cabin, helping her with teaching and household chores, keeping her company and making sure she was well. When the telegram from Burt finally arrived, apologizing for the events and asking her to return to Toronto and marry him, Eddie helped her compose her answer and rode it to the Western Union station in Lethbridge. It was a simple answer, and she seemed perfectly content with it.

Dear Burt,

As you know, I would very much like to be with you. But I have promised Eddie I will not retire from teaching until his younger sister has been educated to take my place. That is my destiny. It is likely to take at least eight years, so I will understand if you choose not to wait.

Love always,
Elizabeth

There was no response to the telegram, as far as Eddie could tell, but Rigall sent word to Liam that he was planning to slow down construction and delay opening the lodge. His father was nonplussed. "I'll go back and work on the railroad," he said. "There will be work there for most of my crew who are interested, too." Rigall also rescheduled his spring hunting trip for some other year.

Eddie thought he understood; he wasn't sure if that year would ever come. Chief hadn't been overly enthusiastic about their business venture, anyway. Eddie considered his options. He had some money saved and a good horse; maybe it was time for him to see more of the world. When summer came, if it was all right with Papa and Mama, he would join that rodeo after all.

As he had suspected, Papa was more supportive of his idea than Mama was. Rodeo was a dangerous sport, she pointed out. Look what had happened at the last one they'd attended. He could be hurt just like that other cowboy had been. Besides, he was so young to leave home. He was such a great help around the ranch with the children. Since Liam would be gone, she could use assistance. Couldn't he wait just one more year? Papa seemed to understand that Eddie was ready to test his independence, though. He gently pointed out it was time for Gene and Joe to take more responsibility. He reminded her Eddie wouldn't be leaving until summer; he would still be around to help while Gene and Joe were in school. He praised how mature and responsible Eddie had always been and reassured her that their son would be in no danger.

Finally, with tears and promises to send letters and telegrams as often as possible, everyone agreed he could leave home and join the rodeo when it next passed through the region. As that was still months away, Eddie found himself becoming very restless. He continued to work as hard as ever around the ranch—perhaps even harder. He frequently checked on Miss Welch and helped with her chores. He read even more than usual, devouring adventure stories and philosophy books in equal measure. Any book he could find, he read.

Eddie enjoyed square dancing and reels. He always attended the frequent church and town socials, and learned to call the dances. He became very popular with the local girls—even those considered a bit fast and racy. This worried Mama, who heard rumors that he had been seen chewing tobacco and drinking whiskey on occasion. She worried and nagged; his father joked and smoothed the tension during his brief returns from working on the railroad. The other children continued learning, growing and changing, gradually shouldering the responsibilities that had been Eddie's. As often happens when children grow up, his mother became resolved to his impending departure, viewing it with a mixture of pain, longing, anxiety, and relief.

For Eddie, it seemed life was dragging by at the pace of a very slow snail. Would summer never arrive? He worked with Redwing constantly, often visiting Chief for the wisdom the old man always so readily provided. He began dreaming of distant towns and wondering what life held in store ahead for him. *Whatever I make it hold,* he chided himself, remembering his skepticism about his teachers' and parents' belief in destiny. He watched snow melt and flowers of spring break through the ground to bathe the meadow in vivid colors. He swam in the creek when the surface thawed, relishing the beautiful land of his childhood as only one who knows he will soon be leaving can. He camped in the forests and hunted with Chief. Just as he was beginning to question his decision and regret his impending departure, word came that the rodeo would be in early this year. Then, caught in a whirlwind of change, he began his own life.

CHAPTER EIGHT

RIDE 'EM, COWBOY!

Eddie's life-changing whirlwind began when he rode to where the rodeo was camped outside of Lethbridge on a warm evening in early June. He'd barely dismounted when Mr. Tom Ruby came barreling towards him laughing. "Well, well, well. If it isn't young Eddie McCauslin, our next big star! I was hoping when we rolled into town early that you would've come to your senses by now."

The warm greeting surprised Eddie. "You remember me, Mr. Ruby?"

"Of course I remember you; you and that fine horse of yours, both. Eddie, riders like you are born, not made. But I intend to make you even better than nature did on her own. Tell me you are going to join us now, won't you? That is why you are here?"

Eddie nodded, modestly overwhelmed by the older man's enthusiasm.

"Good. I'd hoped so. I must admit I was amazed when you didn't come with us last year. Most young men would have jumped at an opportunity like that immediately. At first I was worried you were planning to check with some of the other rodeo bosses back east, or in the southern U.S. to top my salary offer. If they saw you ride, they probably would've done it. When you didn't appear on the circuit, I knew to get back to this little town quick before anyone else heard what a fine cowboy lived here."

From the beginning, Tom Ruby and Eddie got on well. Ruby was at times a gruff father figure and at times more like a mischievous older brother. He took Eddie under his wing, treated him fairly, worked with him mercilessly to improve his riding, and generally made him feel at home among the rough-and-tumble cowboys in his travelling show. It wasn't long until Eddie was realizing his dream to travel and see more of the U.S. and Canada. Ruby's rodeo was based in Saskatchewan. It stopped in all towns of any size in that province, Alberta, and British Columbia, as well as Montana, Idaho and Washington from May until September. Occasionally, the troupe ventured as far south as Wyoming or Colorado for championship events. Ruby was sure he had a champion barrel-rider in his ranks now, especially after watching Eddie ride the two nights remaining in Lethbridge with his friend and family cheering him on. If anything, the boy had improved since his feat last summer. Ruby planned on a long season.

Eddie's good-byes before he left town with the rodeo were brief but heartfelt. "I won't be gone too long," he promised Mama. "Just for the summer. I'll be back in September, in time for my birthday." He told Miss Welch the same thing.

"Maybe, Eddie," she said thoughtfully. "But maybe not. It is hard to predict where your life will take you now. It may be better not to make any promises."

As it turned out, her advice was correct. His mother seemed to sense this, too. "You know we always have a place here for you, and we always want you back," she told him with tears in her eyes, hugging him. "But this is your life now. You are a fine, responsible young man, and wherever your choices take you, Papa and I will always be very proud of you."

Chief predicted an eventual return. "You be back in a couple years," he said when Eddie thanked him for helping with the hunting parties. "Not done here yet. Still gonna make me hunt more." Actually, Eddie hoped this was true. He loved his home and he still wanted to continue guiding hunting parties for Rigall's lodge, but given what had happened with Miss Welch, he expected it might be several years before the lodge was finished.

He needed something else to do while he waited, and he found it. He would see the world, make a good living and live some of the adventures he had until now simply read about.

Neither he nor Ruby regretted the decision. Eddie's skill, youth and enthusiasm pleased the crowds and the rodeo's reputation was greatly enhanced. As word began to spread about the phenomenal young barrel-rider, audiences grew. The rodeo had a record season. Ruby promised Eddie he would be the best-paid rider he had if he continued on an exclusive contract for two more years. The contract included working with the rodeo through the winters. Ruby wanted to teach Eddie everything he could about his business, from the animal care, which the boy already seemed to be quite competent at, to publicity, hiring, staging acts, competitions, costuming, and budgeting. He'd found an intelligent young man to mentor, and he thought of Eddie as the son he'd never had.

The travel alone would have been enough to convince Eddie to remain. Seeing places he'd never seen appealed to his sense of adventure. The rough and tumble rodeo life, including the many dances with pretty young local girls who admired cowboys, also set well. "Most of my friends dream of this," he told himself with wonder. "I'm actually living that dream!"

Ruby watched his protégé with pride. Occasionally he felt a fatherly duty to warn Eddie against the whiskey and high-stakes card games that he also seemed to be developing a penchant for, but since Eddie generally came out well ahead on the gambling and Ruby generally shared the whiskey with him, the warnings were seldom and not taken too seriously by either of them. When Eddie's birthday arrived, he was with the rodeo at a competition in Jackson Hole, Wyoming.

The town was his favorite among those he'd visited. The men were camped on a high bluff overlooking the rodeo grounds, just outside the city limits. In the distance, the Grand Tetons cast their majestic shadow, already snowcapped and shimmering in the autumn light. The air was fresh and the leaves were just beginning to turn colors, splattering flecks of gold and crimson through the green canopies of trees. The town looked just as Eddie had always imagined a western town should look; the main street was wide and dusty, with wooden railings and sidewalks. Saloons, hotels, general stores, saddle shops, and brothels were intermixed. A sheriff's office and small jail, a post office, a church and a school were also juxtaposed among the businesses. Most of the residents lived in the surrounding area on large plots of land rather than in the town itself, and they all seemed like colorful characters from books he'd read to Eddie who enjoyed spending his free time wandering and chatting with the people he met. He remembered he'd told Mama he'd be back by his birthday, and he felt a little guilty as he sat down at one of the local restaurants to write a letter home.

He thought of his brothers and sisters at the ranch. He wondered if his father was home or away working. Had Rigall resumed construction of the lodge yet? Had there been an early winter or was the air still mild? Eddie was a prolific writer when he felt like communicating. His letters were long and full of news. He recounted his travels, telling of the towns and cities he'd visited and describing what the competition in Jackson Hole would involve. He shared brief anecdotes about Ruby and the other men. The friendly waitress watched him curiously as he wrote.

"Homesick?" she asked, refilling his coffee cup again.

He shook his head. "Not really. Just a little keyed up for the riding tomorrow."

"I figured you were with the rodeo crowd. You're a young one, though. Been doing it long?"

"Just over a year. I'm with Ruby's Riders, from up north."

She smiled. "Yeah, I figured you were that young barrel-racing wizard people have been talking about. Good luck to you tomorrow! I'll be watching."

Eddie thought about telling her it was his birthday to get some more attention. The men were talking about organizing a square dance out at the rodeo grounds tonight, and he could invite her. She seemed nice, and she was pretty in a hardened sort of way, although she was several years older than he was—in her thirties, at least, probably. He thought better of it, thanked her, and returned to his writing. After another cup of coffee, he finished, sealed the letter, and headed to the post office.

Sixteen years old, he thought. This was the age his father was when he set off looking for his sister. It was a good age for exploring, a good age to start life and go with the winds of fate to wherever you landed. He explored the town a bit more, then went into one of the shops and treated himself to a new pair of jeans and a bright red plaid flannel shirt for his birthday. He wasn't short of cash now, that was for sure. There wasn't much to spend his wages—and they were good wages—on during the season since all of his living expenses were covered. He usually came out ahead on the poker games. Ruby had advised him to save, to maybe invest in a couple of good horses, or even go in on the rodeo with him. He had saved, mostly, thinking he would give some money to his parents if they needed it when he returned, and save for supplies when he started guiding again. Since that was still his goal, he didn't seriously think he would stay with the rodeo beyond his contract. This was a way to travel and live the life of a rover and a cowboy. It was fun and exciting for now, but he didn't plan on doing it too much longer. Besides, he'd seen the injuries the long-term cowboys had sustained. It could be hard on the body. Although he hadn't told Ruby, he really didn't think he was cut out for this. He'd honor his contract, visit all the places the rodeo went and earn his money. Then he'd find something else to do.

Because he did have extra cash though, and because it was his birthday, it wasn't too hard for the man at the shop to convince him to get a fine beige Stetson hat to match his new duds.

The hat fit well, emphasizing his square jaw line, straight nose and thin smile. The shadows it cast over his green eyes added a touch of maturity to his appearance. He'd never owned such a fine hat. When he left the store, wearing his Stetson, new jeans, and bright shirt, he did feel like it was a special day.

It turned out that way, certainly. Ruby had managed to remember it was Eddie's birthday, so the "dance" the men had planned actually turned out to be a lively celebration. Local musicians were there, including a great fiddler. It appeared half the people from town had somehow been invited, including the waitress from earlier in the day, and all the pretty young women. Drinks flowed freely, and Eddie was alternately roasted and praised by the men he'd spent the last three months with. He laughed and danced all evening.

The next morning, when the sunlight finally woke him, he knew he'd had a great birthday, but he couldn't quite remember it all. Perhaps that explained why he didn't ride as good as usual in the competition. He felt foggy, his head hurt, and his stomach was a bit queasy. Redwing, as if sensing he just wasn't up for much action, took the course at a smooth, slow steady stride. No glory that day. Ruby was disappointed but blamed himself. "My fault," he told Eddie afterward. "I knew better than to have that party for you. But birthdays only come once a year. Just bad timing. You'll win next year; you're still the best in the business."

The words cheered Eddie a little. He spent the evening alone, though, resting and was quieter than usual as they packed up the next day. Most of the men scattered in various directions for the winter, jovially saying good-byes and agreeing to meet up next spring. A few, like Eddie, would be returning with Ruby to Saskatchewan to take care of the animals and prepare for the next season. Slim, whom Eddie had met the first day he rode, was among this small group. The clowns, Tiny and Tulie, and a young cowboy from British Columbia a couple of years older than Eddie named Zane were also included.

Because it was on the way, more or less, Ruby agreed that the group could stop at the McCauslin's for a couple of nights on the way back to his home. "The missus can wait a couple of days more," he said. "Especially if your mama is as good a cook as you've been bragging she is."

Thus, Eddie actually arrived home before his letter did. There were a few reproaches for missing his birthday, but when he explained the schedule, he was quickly forgiven and fussed over. Papa was away, working on a government building in Edmonton. Mama made a large dinner for him and the others, as well as a late birthday cake. In a way, he felt as if he hadn't been gone at all. On the other hand, it was a little humbling to see just how well everyone seemed to be getting on without him. Gene and Joe had taken over his chores without difficulty. The girls were growing and more able to help, as well. Life seemed to be going on as normal at the ranch. He promised to return at Christmas, then headed to Saskatchewan.

Winter there was not too different from what he had experienced in Alberta. Ruby had a large wooden house, a pleasant wife, and a ten-year-old daughter. There were also a couple of men and their wives who shared a small cabin on his land and helped maintain it when he was gone. They had been two of his first star riders and, when they got tired of riding and married, he kept them on. Eddie could see by the limps and movements that riding had not been easy on them. He knew Ruby well enough by now to suspect he felt responsible for them and would always find a way to pay them. Jack Ruby was an interesting man and a bit of an enigma. Eddie studied him carefully during the winter. He was a careful entrepreneur and also garrulous and social. He seemed to know everyone in the rodeo business, from Ontario to California. Every part of his show, from the costumes and skits of the clowns to the flyers that advertised the coming of the rodeo in the towns they visited, were created by him. His horses and bulls were investments as well as show animals. He often turned profits by training them, then selling them to other rodeos. He wanted to buy Redwing, and offered Eddie a very high price for her, which Eddie of course refused. That horse was a part of his soul, he felt. He would never sell her. Ruby shook his head over that one. "I'll just have to win her in a poker game, then," he muttered. He tried to, often. As much as Eddie liked poker, and as often as he played, that was never a bet he would put himself in the position of making.

Ruby bragged about having known Buffalo Bill Cody and was proud of his work. Most of the "stars" in the rodeo circuit had been with him at one time or another. Eddie knew the man had a lot to teach him about the rodeo business and, if his heart had been in it, he could not have found a better mentor. His heart wasn't in it, though. As the winter passed, he and Ruby both realized it. Still the months went by pleasantly and Eddie continued to receive his generous salary, learning all he could from the older man. He learned that Ruby, in addition to the money he made from the rodeo, also invested in real estate. He had built and rented out several small homes in the area, and he advised Eddie that, whatever business he settled on, this would always be a wise investment. He also invested some of his money in the New York stock market.

"It's a little like poker," he explained to Eddie. "Let me teach you how it works. You'll enjoy it, and you will probably be good at it!" With Ruby's assistance, he invested the money he had saved over the season in short term bonds and stocks. He told Ruby about his plan of eventually running the hunting parties at Rigall's Lodge, once it was finished, and Ruby approved. "Good, you can take me hunting sometime!" he said, trying to hide his disappointment that Eddie would not be the one to take over his rodeo legacy. "I'll bet I can bring you some good business, too."

Eddie returned home for Christmas, again vaguely surprised to see how well his siblings and parents were faring without him. It was great to see Papa. He could tell that his father was proud of his fame as a rodeo star. It was also great to be able to bring presents to everyone and to leave extra "pocket money" with Mama. He felt like a returning hero. He even became the storyteller now as the family sat around the fire. Everyone wanted to hear him recount his exciting rides and describe the towns he had visited and the cowboys he had worked with. He found that, with just a little embellishment, he was able to weave fine adventure tales, just as his father could.

The holidays were refreshing for him. His father told him Rigall had gone back to England and wasn't planning to resume the lodge for at least another year. As far as he knew, he still planned to finish it eventually. Eddie called on Miss Welch one afternoon, taking along a book of poetry he'd purchased for her in British Columbia and some of his mother's Christmas cookies. She was delighted to see him. They talked about how his sisters were doing in school. He told her what he had learned from Ruby about stocks and investments. She seemed to approve.

"You are such a fine young man, Eddie. I can hardly believe how well you've grown up. I am so glad I was able to be a part of that. You'll always be my favorite student." She didn't mention Rigall, so he didn't either. They had a pleasant visit.

Eddie was also happy to see Chief when he returned. The old man seemed ageless, and still seemed to emanate the same wisdom and humor Eddie remembered. He had a new pony he was training, and a pet wolf. The leather boots Eddie brought him as a gift were appreciated, and Eddie chuckled when he placed them above his hearth for decoration. "Pretty to look at," the old Indian said. "When these wear out, I'll take them down and put them on." He pointed to the scuffed brown leather boots he's been wearing for as long as Eddie could remember.

When the holidays ended, Eddie returned to Ruby's ranch. He enjoyed his experiences there. It was very interesting to help prepare for the coming season. He watched the clowns develop their routines, learned more about how Ruby budgeted and planned and took over training a couple of colts Ruby had acquired during the holidays. When the snow thawed, he began working with Redwing again on the barrels. She was still agile, but not quite as fluid as she had been two years ago. He worried a little, wondering if maybe he had ridden her too hard or not tended to her quite as well as he should have over the winter. He hoped she didn't have a minor tear or injury that hadn't been noticed, or that she wasn't prone to arthritis, even as young as she was. He loved the horse, and couldn't imagine riding any of the others in competition. Another problem, though, was her size. She was small and frail. When he had first ridden her, he had been smaller, too. But he had put on lots of weight recently. He was several inches taller now and had become muscular and solid. He was nearly six feet tall and weighed at least 190 pounds. He shook his head ruefully.

"Guess it's a good thing I didn't plan on a long-term rodeo career, Redwing," he said. "I've outgrown it, I think. But we can make it through one more season, can't we?" She turned and looked at him with her deep, gentle eyes and he had an eerie sense that she was saying no. He ignored it though, and continued readying her for the coming shows.

Spring had come early that year. The snow melted and flowers were dotting the landscape by mid-March. Ruby and his troupe decided to try a new route and have an extended season, going south into the Dakotas and Montana first, then up into the Northwest Territories and the Yukon after an early circuit through Saskatchewan and Alberta. Then, they'd travel down the coast through the mining towns in British Columbia and end in Washington. The rodeo had never visited South Dakota before, and had also never been to the Yukon. It would be a tiring season, but everyone seemed delighted about covering new territory, and Ruby was eager to see if there would be enough interest among the sparse populations to the north and south to supplement profits from the sophisticated crowd in Seattle. By April, they were on the road preparing for their first show.

Eddie had made several close friends among the cowboys. He'd developed a talent and appreciation for poker that would stay with him throughout his life and he had a reputation in the towns they had visited last year as a good dancer and a gentleman. The young ladies liked him, so the other cowboys liked to be in his company. The season began on an upbeat note. Visiting new places appealed to Eddie. The crystal lakes and towering pines in the untouched north were spectacular. He watched families of bear catching fish and large herds of deer and elk, imagining how much Chief would love the land here. It was a long summer, but a rewarding one. Their reception in the Yukon was warm. The miners and rugged pioneers welcomed the diversion. Many joined in the competition, and a couple of them even won! Ruby turned a profit and had new young riders to groom as cowboys. Their trek down the Cassiar trail through northern British Columbia was awe-inspiring, a panorama of unspoiled natural beauty. After five months on the road and many performances, the men and animals were exhausted by the time they reached Washington in late August, though.

Eddie liked Washington. Perhaps it was because he was again in the U.S., where he had been born, and he felt at home. More likely, it was the group of young men about his age he met when the rodeo arrived. They were the sons of a man who owned several apple orchards in the area, and they all wanted to ride in the rodeo. When Ruby's group first came into Seattle, they were waiting, hoping to find someone to teach them—and Eddie was the person they found. All three of the Pearson boys were friendly and eager to learn. They were all close to Eddie in age, ranging from sixteen to twenty years. They quickly struck up friendly conversation with him, offering to pay him well if he would tutor them for a few days before the competition. He liked them and agreed.

During the lessons, they became good friends. Eddie learned about their father's orchards and they learned how to ride. He even allowed them to ride Redwing occasionally, since their own mounts did not seem to be nearly as capable on barrel tracks. Tom, the oldest, formed a special bond with Eddie, and seemed to be a good rider, as well. Ruby didn't seem to mind the time Eddie was spending teaching the Pearson boys to ride. He saw them as potential recruits more than competition for prize money, sure that Eddie could outride them.

As the rodeo approached, they had all become fast friends. The other Pearsons were ready to compete with their own horses against Eddie, but Tom asked if it would be possible for them both to ride Redwing. "It'd make it more fair," he pointed out. "This way, it'd really be man against man, not horse against horse!"

Eddie was hesitant. It would be unusual, that was certain. But, more problematic, was the extra pressure it would put on Redwing. He wasn't sure she would be able to run the course twice in close succession, with different riders, without repercussions. He asked Ruby for advice. Ruby responded by seeing this as a great marketing opportunity. "I can advertise my rider!" he exclaimed happily. "I can point out that the competition is completely level when both men ride the same horse. We'll flip a coin to see who goes first. It'll be great! Do it!"

Eddie still worried. He knew it would be hard on his dearly beloved horse. He could sense, based on his work with Chief, that she was hesitant and it may not be a good idea. Ruby was very enthusiastic, however. He'd advertised the competition and said many people would come just to see one of their own well-known locals compete in the rodeo "on equal footing," so to speak. Tom was also very eager. Finally, against his intuition, Eddie gave in to the pressure and the competition was arranged. It would be on the final night of the rodeo in Seattle. He and Tom would have the last rides of the evening.

His biggest concern was that Tom Pearson, once the competition was arranged, seemed to want to practice continuously, at all hours. Eddie knew his horse was growing tired. Tom was even larger than he was, over six feet tall and nearly two hundred pounds. Redwing was a small horse. The constant practice with two large riders combined with the required rodeo competitions after the long journey, was wearing her down. Still, on the final day of the rodeo as the last rides of the evening approached, she seemed energetic and ready. The announcer explained the competition and the crowd, swelled by the many friends of Tom and his family who had come to watch, cheered. Eddie went first. He didn't set a new record; he was intentionally trying not to push Redwing since he knew she had another ride afterward and that Tom would likely push her hard. The two just flowed through the obstacles in the comfortable, automatic rhythm they had established. Eddie silently thanked his horse and wished her well on her next venture.

Tom came out in the ring next, eager but showing his nervousness through his stiff posture. Redwing seemed tense, too. Eddie watched critically as Tom pushed her around the tight curves harder than he should, and with less balance than he needed. He closed his eyes for a moment, and just then the roaring and moaning of the crowd brought him back to the present. His fears had been realized. Redwing had fallen rounding one of the barrels. One of her legs was twisted painfully beneath her, and she had fallen partially on Tom, who was moaning. Eddie cursed himself for allowing this to happen. He should have known. He *did* know; he just hadn't listened to his intuition. He cried out and loped into the ring, running toward his horse and his friend.

The night was one of the worst Eddie ever remembered. The veterinarian had suggested putting Redwing down.

"Break like that, she'll never be any good in the rodeo," the grizzled doctor said. "Probably won't be able to be ridden at all—

and that's if it even mends. She's in a lot of pain, too. Isn't much I can do."

Ruby advised Eddie to listen to the doc. He knew how much his young protégée loved the horse, but he was a pragmatic man. "We'll find you another barrel horse just as slick," he promised. "Let her go, buddy."

Eddie refused. He had no intention of putting her down and he had no intention of leaving Seattle until she was well. "Just do your best," he pleaded with the veterinarian, his eyes stinging with pain and with anger at himself. "Set the leg, give her something for pain, and tell me what to do. I'll stay with her; find a place for her to recover. I don't care if I can never ride her again. I'm not leaving her."

Ruby nodded. He knew Eddie could be stubborn. He was being very impractical, but he did love that horse. Ruby remembered his first horse fondly; he probably would have behaved the same if something like this had happened to Starlight. "Do as he says," he affirmed. "We'll be camped here for another couple of days, and then I'll use one of the wagons to move her if necessary."

"Better not be far," grumbled Doc. It bothered him that his advice wasn't heeded. He didn't like to see any animal in pain, and he didn't like to see any animal useless. This horse was both, and likely always would be. Despite his complaints, though, he dosed her heavily with a painkiller and worked long and hard to set and splint her shattered left back leg. "Probably broke a rib or two as well," he muttered. "This horse is gonna cost you a fortune. This pain medicine I'll leave with you isn't cheap, and neither am I. And I'll need to visit her often to check that splint and make sure there isn't any internal damage."

At first, Eddie didn't even consider how he would manage to pay the doctor, or where he and his horse could stay in Seattle while she recovered. She wouldn't be able to stay at the rodeo grounds for long, although he certainly didn't plan to move her until he absolutely had to. He had wages coming, so he would be able to figure something out. He knew Ruby would let him remain with Redwing as long as necessary; in fact, they had both come to accept that Eddie probably would not be renewing his contract and continuing with the rodeo after this season ended. It had certainly ended now. His thoughts were just occupied with his horse at present. It seemed he could feel her pain, then her relief and her drowsiness. It had been a long evening, and he was ready to curl up beside her, exhausted, for the night. Ruby brought him some bedding, and had his men carefully clear the track away. They both slept in the arena.

"Your friend has similar injuries," he told him. "Broken ribs, arm, and leg. His neck and back are okay though. That's always the biggest worry in a fall like that. I told him and his brothers you were asking after him. Figured you would be, once you calmed down. He'll recover near good as new in a few months."

"So will Redwing!" Eddie replied fiercely. Then his voice softened. "Thank you."

"It's nothin'," said Ruby. He would miss Eddie. "By the way, the father offered to let you bring Redwing out to the orchards. The whole family feels pretty bad about this. You can stay on with them; says he'll find some work for you around the place until she's good enough for you to get her back home. The boys and I will break camp real slow—then I'll help you move her out to their place before I leave. Okay?"

Eddie nodded. "Okay." He slept restlessly, seeing Chief and shattered bones in his dreams, watching Redwing running from rolling barrels as he chased after them, trying to stop the collisions. When he awoke just after dawn, he was cold and stiff. He comforted his horse and brought her some water, urging her to drink. He injected the medicine as the doctor had shown him to ease her pain. Once she slept peacefully again, he set about saying his good-byes to the many friends he'd made among the cowboys. That was difficult. He felt dazed, as if his life was not quite real at present. He had a sense he was still dreaming. He wasn't sure what he would do next. Nothing until Redwing was well.

As promised, Ruby's Riders stayed at the rodeo grounds as long as they possibly could. They amused themselves with square dances and card games, packed and repacked their gear and explored the town. After a few days, there seemed to be no other reason to linger, though. Doc, still grumbling at Eddie's decision, came to assist with the move. Hoisting the horse in and out of the wagon could be as harmful as the break, he complained. This was pure foolishness to do this to a good animal. She was still sedated, though, and the move to the Pearson's place went smoothly. Mr. Pearson had a clean, warm barn with a special area prepared just for Eddie's horse—and Eddie, too, he suspected although he'd also prepared a room in their large, comfortable home for him. With Tom out of commission, he knew he could use Eddie's help with the last round of apple picking and with preparing the trees for winter. Eddie was quick and reliable; he would certainly earn his keep, once he recovered from the shock he was obviously suffering from.

CHAPTER NINE

PLAY BALL!

This was how Eddie found himself living in Seattle in 1909. The city was beginning to grow. It was very different from the little village of Pincer Creek in southern Alberta. There were lots of buildings and wide streets around a bustling harbor with an active port. Opportunity seemed to be everywhere. The Pearsons were good to him. He worked hard at the orchard. He spent most of the rest of his time with Redwing at first and then, as she seemed to become more settled, he spent time with the restlessly recovering Tom Pearson. They played checkers, chatted and dreamed, coming up with lots of grand plans. Tom was fascinated by the horseless carriages that were now beginning to appear on the streets. Eddie shared the fascination, in part because he was not sure that he would be riding his horse again and couldn't imagine another. They came up with several schemes to make money on these new forms of transportation.

Tom was athletic and he taught Eddie how to play baseball—at least to the extent he could while perched in bed in traction. They planned to actually play when Tom recovered. Eddie practiced the game with the two younger Pearson boys, and they noted he was an excellent pitcher, capable of throwing the ball equally well with both his left and right hands. "Now that is a gift!" beamed Mr. Pearson. "Keeps 'em guessing!" He was also a sports enthusiast, and introduced Eddie to a friend of his, Steve Ryan.

Ryan sponsored a city baseball league that was considering affiliating with the newly formed American Baseball Association and joining in national competitions with eight other teams scattered across the country. The sport was becoming increasingly popular since it's beginning in the 1870s on the east coast. The city of Seattle was planning to finance a stadium, pay players and charge admission fees to games; something unheard of before, but an idea that many of the banks and financial institutions in town were intrigued with and willing to sponsor. Once Ryan saw Eddie's ability as both a pitcher and a hitter, he decided he would have a place for him on his professional team.

That was still in the future, though. For now, Eddie was helping around the Pearson's in exchange for room and board. His rodeo money and what he had been paid for working in the orchards went to the veterinarian for medicines and care for Redwing. Doc complained less as he saw how much money he was able to make supervising the horse's recovery; he predicted she would be standing again by Christmas. That was one present Eddie really hoped to have.

Christmas away from Alberta would be difficult. He'd written Mama that he would be staying in Washington, although he hadn't gone into much explanation as to why. He felt guilty and responsible for his horse's injuries, and wasn't too eager to share the story. He did tell her about the Pearsons, the apple orchards and his forthcoming opportunity to play baseball. He even arranged for Gene to come to Washington and learn to pick apples when he was old enough and ready to earn some extra summer pocket money. The family seemed to accept that he had settled in Seattle, found a city to his liking, and begun his life. They wondered if a young lady was involved in the decision, but figured they would find out soon enough if that were the case.

Spending Christmas with the Pearsons was actually pleasant. Mrs. Pearson was a big, warm woman who made everyone feel at home. Tom had quickly become Eddie's best friend, despite his initial anger over Redwing's fall. It wasn't Tom's fault, he decided. It was his own fault for allowing the situation to occur when he knew better. The younger Pearson boys were also good companions. He enjoyed learning about the city—the docks, the orchards, the banks, the shops—and watching the baseball stadium being built. Redwing was standing again by Christmas, but she had a limp that the doctor proclaimed she would never lose. Eddie could see that the doctor's early diagnosis had been correct. He would never ride her again and she would spend the rest of her days here in Seattle, more as a pet than anything else. He hoped she would adjust to that fate and not become too sad or restless.

Time passed quickly. The stadium opened and Eddie began training. Ryan was a tough coach and a stern taskmaster, demanding hard work, loyalty—even perfection—from his players. But he also treated them well, paid them well, and shared the glory his team was beginning to enjoy. Other cities began sponsoring professional leagues of their own over the next couple of years. The competition increased, but so did the excitement; Eddie was able to travel again, visiting cities down the coast into Oregon and California for games, and even going to Chicago once. Tom was disappointed that the injuries he had sustained at the rodeo seemed to have hurt his athletic ability. Running was more difficult for him, and his arm had healed at a slight angle, destroying his pitching aim. He was still a part of the team, though he speculated it was only Ryan's friendship with his father that kept him playing ball. Eddie tried to ignore it when his friend began one of his "pity parties." He was happy they were able to play together and travel together.

Redwing was safe at the orchard; she and Mrs. Pearson had bonded. Eddie had resigned himself to losing the close relationship he had once had with the magnificent horse. He was glad she had adjusted to her life; that she was alive and happy. His rodeo days had closed on a tragic note, but they would have closed regardless. His new adventures more than filled the gap. He was looking forward to seeing Gene and Joe next summer; they would be coming to pick apples at the orchard. Mama and Papa were planning to bring the whole family out so they could watch him play baseball. He sensed he was still a hero back home—first a rodeo champion, now a star baseball player—but he had no desire to go back to bask in his glory yet. The Pacific coast had been Redwing's home for nearly three years now—and, thus, his as well. He occasionally missed his family and Chief, or wondered about Miss Welch. He would have liked to ride into the mountains of Banff and Jasper once in a while. Overall, though, he was happy. His life was going well.

It continued to go well when his family arrived. He could sense their pride and took pleasure in showing them the city. They stayed for two weeks, making a holiday of the visit, then leaving Gene and Joe behind to work in the orchards. Eddie returned to Alberta with his brothers at the end of summer for a visit. Once he was home, Chief and Papa gave him the news. Rigall had decided to begin work on the lodge again. It should be ready to open the following spring. Rigall wanted to return for his hunting trip at last. Soon it would be time to leave Seattle.

✳   ✳   ✳

"Are you sure about this, Eddie?" asked Ryan. "You have so many possibilities here. This team and this sport have possibilities. You're at the right place at the right time, and you're a darn good pitcher, besides."

Eddie was telling Ryan that he planned on returning to Alberta the following year. "I know, Steve. I know. But this sport is hard on a guy's body, and even harder on his nerves. I still can't eat before our games, you know. Can't keep the food down. Whenever we lose, I'm sure it's my fault and I feel awful for days. My health and my happiness are the two things I suspect I should always guard the most carefully. The most important tools in life. I'll stay with you through this season, and I'll make sure it's a good one. I will have given you three good years, probably the best years in me for this game. Then it'll be time for me to move on before I do any real damage to this body!"

"You're wise beyond your years, Eddie. I know you've made up your mind, so I won't waste my breath trying to talk you out of it. I just hope you're making the right decision."

"I know I am. Besides, that new pitcher you recruited last season from Chicago is at least as good as me. Probably better. The team will be fine, and I'll be fine."

"Okay. But it ain't over until it's over, buddy. If you change your mind and want to stay, or even come back the following season, I'll find a place here for you. I appreciate you telling me your intentions so well in advance. You haven't burnt any bridges, my young friend."

"That's good to know, Steve. Thank you for all you've done for me," Eddie said. He was relieved that the conversation had gone so well. Once he'd decided to return to Alberta and resume his hunting business, the most difficult part had been trying to figure out how to resign. Steve Ryan was an intimidating, awe-inspiring coach and Eddie had been unsure how he would react. The reaction had been supportive. He knew he would be comfortable spending the season here. He'd stay on in Seattle for another year, continuing to play ball and work in the orchards. Then, he would return home for good. Tom had expressed an interest in coming out to learn to hunt, and Eddie looked forward to teaching his friend. If the business did as well as he expected, he was sure that Tom could stay on working with him, provided he liked hunting. He certainly had more interest and aptitude for business matters than Chief did!

The year passed slowly. Eddie was still comfortable with the Pearsons, and he liked Seattle, but since he had decided not to stay on permanently, he began gradually taking less interest in the political climate in the U.S. and the growth of the city, even though it was an interesting time. The industrial revolution had created a booming economy. Several of the wealthier

people in town had automobiles now. He planned to take a sewing machine back to Mama when he returned, a gadget he knew
she would love. It would save her countless hours. The railroads
made transporting goods easier, and all cities and towns, even his
little hometown in Southern Alberta, were enjoying increasing
availability of goods. People were traveling more, interested in
seeing the country now that it was possible. The rapid changes
were startling but exciting. Eddie decided it was a good time to
be alive as he realized how much easier his own life was likely to
be than his parents' life had been.

Mostly, Eddie focused on playing baseball. He'd promised
Ryan a great season, and he was determined to give it to him.
Ever since the professional teams had consolidated and developed game schedules and play-offs, Ryan had wanted his new
team to make a good showing. Eddie hoped this would be the
season that happened. He practiced even longer than usual, and
gave his all for every game. He did get some recognition in the
sports columns as a remarkable pitcher, and two other teams tried
to recruit him. He'd already made up his mind to leave the sport
so the offers didn't attract him, much to Ryan's relief. Seattle's
team earned praise and good reviews, but no championship. By
the time the season ended, Eddie was exhausted.

At last, it was time to say good-bye. Leaving Redwing was
painful. She was happy now at the orchard, with her quiet life as
the pampered pet of Mrs. Pearson. He knew that he must leave
her behind. Still, it was difficult. That horse had been a part of
his heart and soul for many years. She had taken him into all of
the major, formative experiences of his life—winning the first
rodeo competition, the hunting parties, finding Miss Welch in
the snow, all of her faithful, hard work with Ruby's Riders. She'd
been his companion and his confidant as he struck out on his
own, taught him about love and loyalty, about pain and hard decisions. He hated to leave Redwing, but knew she would be much
better off here. As difficult as it would be, he would need to find

another good horse for hunting. He hoped Chief could help with that. Redwing would need to stay behind. He would still be able to visit her, of course, and he was sure he would find a way to do so. But the bond would no longer be the same. He knew it had already perceptibly lessened. The horse had accepted her role as a pet, if not eagerly, at least with grace and aplomb. Much of her connection was already to Mrs. Pearson. Redwing would adjust— probably better than Eddie. He hadn't gone through a more difficult good-bye since the death of Baby Flo all those years ago. Bringing that long-ago event to mind made this good-bye even more difficult for him. He was choking back tears. Tom chided him a little at first.

"Ah, c'mon, I'll be joining you in the summer!" he joked. "Soon as Gene and Joe get out here to relieve me from toiling in this orchard. It's not forever." His joking was short-lived, though. He was a good friend. He could tell that Eddie's real concern was for the horse and that his feelings ran deep. He couldn't quite understand it, but was kind enough to just leave his friend in peace as he prepared to leave.

Once Eddie was back at the McCauslin's ranch, he was amazed how quickly he fell back into the daily routines of chores and stories, of his comfortable family life. A few changes occurred during the five years he'd been away. Joe and Papa had made stunning new wooden furniture for the house as winter projects—finely carved cabinets and chests with a matching sturdy oak dining table and chairs graced the house. Mama had new curtains and china, thanks to some of the money he'd sent home. Gene had planted apple saplings, based on his summer experiences, and the garden looked better than ever, well manicured and well maintained. Inez was attending normal school in Calgary now, although she would be home for summer. Allie was planning on studying nursing at a medical college in Utah next year. The two younger girls had grown up so quickly; both were in school now. He had missed watching them develop their sunny personalities. He regretted that. The wonderful changes in the garden were due to Maybelline, who had a natural talent for growing plants. She spent long, happy hours there. Lizzie was more beautiful and charismatic than ever. Not yet twelve, she already turned heads with her charm and grace. She had been awarded the starring role in every school play for as long as she had been attending. This Christmas, she was playing the Virgin Mary in the nativity play. Eddie looked forward to going with his family. Joe was working full-time with Papa now. He enjoyed carpentry and construction. Gene had taken to spending most of his extra time with Sergeant Brown, hoping to become a mounted policeman.

Pincer Creek hadn't changed much. The school, churches, and general store were still there. The only development was Chief's idea. One of the new horseless carriages had been through town last year. Chief, always fascinated by mechanical objects, had spent the day examining the contraption and badgering the no-doubt surprised driver with all kinds of questions. He'd studied the engine and would have dismantled and reassembled it if Papa and the car's owner hadn't stopped him. As a result of this experience, Chief had predicted that automobiles were soon going to descend on Pincer Creek in droves. He wanted to open a gasoline station and become the local mechanic. He'd even ventured south to Montana, where the motorist had told him such a station existed, to see what it was like. Papa had a little money set aside, mostly from what Eddie sent home, that he was willing to invest and he was checking into possibilities. Eddie, familiar with car service stations in Seattle, saw this as the best way to keep Chief involved in his business.

"Tell you what, Chief," Eddie said. "We'll take your share of the money you make, along with what Papa has, and open up a gasoline station. Once the lodge gets going, there'll be lots of folks driving up here. Wealthy hunters will be the first to get those machines. They'll need somebody to take care of their cars and supply whatever it is they need to run them."

"Oil," said Chief knowingly. "Gasoline. Comes from the ground. From old animals."

The gasoline station idea kept Chief interested in leading hunting parties. Now they were ready to tackle Eddie's next problem. He needed a horse. Sparky, his father's mare, was too old for long rides. Besides, the family needed her at home. He visited Chief's cabin, viewing the horses penned there. "You looking to sell any of these?" As Eddie had feared, Chief was suspicious about what had happened to Redwing. "You had perfect horse," he said. "Where she now?" So Eddie had to find a way to explain what had happened. That was a very difficult thing to do, for it meant he also had to be able to explain it to himself. He made it through the story without breaking down and crying, but only barely.

"Hmm," Chief said, then sat in silence. "She was good horse for you," he finally said. "You learn anything?" The question surprised Eddie at first. Then, he realized it was a valid one, and that he HAD learned from the experience. He had learned a lot. He had learned to go against the voice of authority by insisting on keeping the horse alive. He had learned to consider his decisions more carefully because of her tragedy, and been reminded again to trust his intuition. His loyalty to her had kept him from returning to the rodeo where he may have been injured himself, and his vicarious experience with her pain had taught him to value his own health and well-being enough to leave baseball before he suffered any physical damage from the sport. Leaving her in Seattle in consideration for her own well being despite his strong attachment to her had taught him how to let go emotionally when required and move on. Yes, he had learned a lot. As he recounted this to Chief, he realized it himself for the first time. He felt more love for his little horse than ever.

When he finished recounting the insights he had gained, Chief nodded. "Okay," he said. "Don't have horse like that one, but you don't need horse like that again. Spider's foal Paint will

ROSES IN THE DUST

do. Sturdy. Strong. Good hunting horse. Not yet two summers old. Still train him. High-spirited and nervous, but you handle that. Last horse was good for you. This time, you be good for horse." When Eddie headed home that day on Sparky, they went slowly, leading a speckled grey gelding.

Eddie had plenty to do now, training his horse while exploring trails and campsites. He repaired and painted his wagon, stocked provisions, and checked for changes in hunting laws. He persuaded Chief to take him along whenever the old Indian went hunting, to refine his skills with the bow. He planned to contact Rigall and reschedule that hunting expedition at last. The way time was passing, that would likely be very close to the time the lodge was finished. Papa had already resumed work there.

Tom would arrive before summer, and would learn how to hunt quickly. The first summer season of the lodge was likely to be an important one for their future success and, Eddie hoped, a busy one.

Chief would commit only to the bow-hunting excursion with Rigall that he had already agreed to, and helping Eddie teach Tom. After that, he expected to start working at his gas station. Papa had already begun construction on a little store and garage on their land where it met the main road into town. Chief had contacted one of the new gasoline companies to find out how to set up pumps and get fuel in. His mind was now on machines instead of animals.

Even Rigall, when he finally arrived, noticed. He had obviously been practicing his own bow skills, and now performed nearly as well as Chief when it came to hunting. He seemed to enjoy hearing about Eddie's adventures with the rodeo and the baseball league nearly as much as he enjoyed hunting, though. He was distracted and not as eager to conquer the woods as he had been a few years before. He'd lost some of his enthusiasm for the lodge, too, although he seemed proud that several wealthy and well-known hunters had already agreed to visit in the future, including Teddy Roosevelt and the Brazilian diplomat Rio Branco.

"I told them I had the best guides in the country," he told Eddie and Chief.

"They drive automobiles?" asked Chief. Rigall nodded.

"Probably. I'm not really sure how they'll get here, but it wouldn't surprise me."

"Good," said Chief. He told Rigall about his plan to open a gas station and become a mechanic.

Rigall laughed. "You are an original!" he said. "But who will help Eddie?"

Eddie told him about Tom, and Chief assured Rigall he would be available, too, if necessary. As they spent the fortnight in the woods, companionably talking around the fire, Eddie learned that Rigall had married the woman who had come to visit him with his mother upon his return to Toronto. "It was a mistake," he said. "I knew it at the time, but Mother was so insistent." His marriage had been short and troubled. His wife left him and returned to Europe less than two years after their marriage. He confided to Eddie that he still loved Elizabeth. "After that sad turn of events last time we were together, I doubt she would even speak to me now," he said.

"I think you might be surprised. She'll retire from teaching soon, you know. Inez finishes Normal School next year. It's worth a try, at least. Shall I talk to her first?"

Rigall didn't seem hopeful but agreed. As Eddie had predicted, she assented to see Burt, although a little reluctantly. It surprised no one, however, when a few weeks later they announced their engagement.

Both finally seemed happy and at peace with life. Their marriage was a happy one. Elizabeth took an interest in the lodge's operations. Rigall began consolidating and transferring his business interests from Toronto, planning to live permanently in

Alberta. He contracted with Eddie's father to build a large house on the lake near the lodge to live in with Elizabeth.

Rigall surprised Eddie one day by announcing he wanted to be the senior partner in the hunting expeditions. "Don't worry, you'll still have lots of fun and lots of money," he said. "I'll cover the business aspects and save you the headaches. Your friend can still guide for us, too, and we'll get Chief set up in his gas station right now, if you like."

Eddie was both relieved and disappointed. Obviously, Rigall was planning to stay and wanted to devote his considerable energy to operating the best hunting lodge around, with Elizabeth's help. It made sense that he would operate the hunting tours, too. It would be much easier. Eddie would just be the guide, for very generous compensation. Still, it had been his idea first, his dream. He resented a little that he would not be in charge of it any longer.

Chief's gas station started slowly and, if not for Rigall's financial backing, probably would have failed miserably in the first two years. But by 1916, it was making a profit. Papa no longer found it necessary to travel; he earned enough from the station. The children were grown now. Inez had taken over as teacher at the one-room schoolhouse. Allie was a good nurse and continued Mama's work, although as the area grew, small hospitals began appearing in the towns scattered across Alberta, so she only practiced in Pincer Creek. Lizzie joined a traveling theatre troupe and left home against Mama and Papa's wishes. Gene was a mounted policeman planning to marry Clarissa, a sweet local girl Eddie remembered from his school days. Maybelline, though barely fifteen, was engaged to a young man from Toronto, a nephew of one of the families who visited the lodge during summer.

As Eddie had expected, Tom was a quick study learning about hunting in the Rockies. He had an excellent sense of direction and a good memory. He was skilled with a rifle and quickly became an excellent tracker. He also had a good sense of humor and the ability to inspire trust among the people that he led. Eddie was delighted to have his friend near. They easily settled into a smooth routine. When necessary because of demand, they led separately, but went together otherwise. Rigall provided a generous salary regardless of how busy or slow the demand for their services. Eddie was certainly making as much money as he would have on his own, without any worry. Rigall handled publicity, booked and often accompanied the groups, especially when notable men were involved. He seemed to know everyone they guided. Eddie was amazed at how many intelligent and successful friends the man had. Industrialists, bankers, senators, presidents, and professors were among the ranks of hunters who descended upon the lodge over the next few years.

Eddie acquired a wealth of knowledge about the world from the experiences recounted in the conversations of his clients as they enjoyed freshly caught game around the campfire each evening. He was given firsthand glimpses into the lives, thoughts and concerns of most of the important businessmen and politicians in the U.S. and Canada.

Several of the campfire conversations lately turned to the war that Britain, France and Russia had declared on Germany and Austria. Although the conflict was far away from the soil of western Canada, the men were concerned about the potential long-term effects on the world. Tom was especially involved in these discussions, siding with the hunters who felt that the neutrality of the U.S. in the conflict was a mistake. "I've half a mind to join the Royal Canadian Air Force and fight with the allies," he announced during one such conversation.

"That would be only half a mind," retorted Eddie. "All conflicts can be settled peacefully with enough patience and compromise. I agree with Rio Branco on that point. The countries of Europe are acting like spoiled children. Taking up arms against one's fellowman is a grave mistake. Neutrality's best. It will pass."

This conversation was only the beginning of a debate between them that continued throughout the summer and fall. Both

ROSES IN THE DUST

resented that, although best friends, they could not understand each other's point of view. Tired of the continuing arguments over international affairs, Eddie finally responded to his friend's comments by saying "Well, if that is really how you feel, why aren't you there fighting? I'm doing what I believe is best—staying out of it. But if I felt like you did, I'd be over there fighting right now."

Tom looked stricken for a moment. "That's a good point," added Steven Durham, a colleague of Eddie's uncle, the geology professor who had recently gained international fame by his discovery of several intact dinosaur skeletons in the mountains of Utah and Colorado. "A man should always live by his beliefs. Actions and attitudes need to be congruent. I respect you for pointing that out, Eddie."

When hunting season was over, Tom joined the Canadian RAF and was soon on his way to fight in Europe. Eddie worried about his friend often, feeling at least partially responsible for the decision to risk his life oversees. His worry was well-founded. By the time the U.S. finally entered the war in 1917, Tom had already been killed, his plane shot down over Germany.

The loss of his friend haunted Eddie. He speculated about how someone could justify killing and dying for an abstract principal that, as far he could tell, was often just created to cover up the real reasons for fighting—greed and power. He could never understand it.

Durham, who had become a regular among Eddie's hunters, noticed that the normally cheerful young guide had become morose. "You miss your friend, don't you Eddie?" he said one afternoon as they tracked elk. "It's a sad situation. My son is over there in that hell right now, you know. A lot of our best and brightest young men are, and lots of them won't be coming back. They're hunting each other like we're hunting these animals."

The comment bothered Eddie. He came to see hunting, which he had previously enjoyed so much, as just another war. Many of the Chief's past comments about only taking life to sustain life became entangled with philosophical and ideological arguments. Did that apply to war, too? Was this any different than a war? He came to see his work as distasteful. "I'm a killer, too," he told himself. "This is unnecessary."

His existential crisis extended to his body. His stomach became extremely sensitive, and he could soon no longer eat the meat he helped to hunt. His mother told him he'd developed ulcers and needed to be very careful of what he ate.

Gradually, he quit eating meat entirely, and that seemed to solve the problems with his stomach, even if it had not dissuaded his dilemma about war, survival of the fittest, and higher ideals. When Durham suggested, during his next visit, that Eddie leave the Rockies for a while and accompany him as his driver on a lecture tour of universities across the U.S., Eddie eagerly agreed. "I need a change of pace."

"You certainly do," said Durham. "So do I. This will be good for both of us. I can probably match what Rigall is paying you. We've always gotten on well, you and I. I can't think of anyone else I'd rather be cooped up with for long hours of conversation as I see the country, except perhaps my son. In ways, I wish he had been a little more like you in his outlook on life." He didn't tell Eddie his son had recently been reported missing in the war, but Eddie suspected this was the case. He didn't ask, though. Instead, he tried to become excited about driving a wonderful automobile across parts of the country he'd never seen before.

He actually was able to become enthusiastic about the idea rather easily; he'd been eager to travel more, and watching Chief extol the virtues of the "little smoking boxes" for the last few years as he puttered around his station had developed an appreciation for these new forms of transportation in Eddie. Being in charge of driving and maintaining an automobile sounded appealing. He agreed readily with Durham's offer. All that remained before leaving was to tell Rigall his decision. The two had enjoyed a long, pleasant, and beneficial working relationship. It was difficult to end it.

"I don't know what I'll do without you, Eddie," Burt complained. "With Tom gone, and as busy as we are, I don't think I can lead all the parties on my own."

"I'm sorry, Burt, but I really have lost my taste for this," Eddie explained. "Maybe Papa or Chief will help you, or Gene. Maybe even Elizabeth. You're resourceful. I know you'll find someone to replace me."

"I suppose that I'll have to," grumbled Rigall. "Well, best of luck to you, anyway. Come back when you've finished with the tour, okay? You always have a place to work. This is your idea, you know; your business as much as mine. There is always a place for you here."

Eddie knew that place was no longer suitable for him. Since Tom's departure, he'd imagined he saw the eyes of his friend reflected in the eyes of every animal he helped the hunters stalk and sight. His days tracking big game in the Canadian Rockies were over. It was time to find a new dream.

CHAPTER TEN

A BOX OF CHOCOLATES

Music wafted through the house, an emotional crescendo of notes from Rachmaninoff's Second Concerto. Clarence Robinson, hearing the sound from his grocery store situated next to his large Victorian-style home, smiled as he went about his work. Inside the house, his daughter Charlotte sat at the keyboard of her ebony grand piano as gracefully as a princess on a throne, her pale, long-fingered hands moving smoothly across the ivory keys.

Professor Rubenstein watched the movements of her fingers. Since coming to the Midwestern U.S. from Russia, where he had been a well-known professor of music at the conservatory in St. Petersburg, he had not found a better, more capable student than the frail, beautiful sixteen-year-old daughter of the town grocer. Perhaps he never had found such a student anywhere before and never would again. He remembered his first meeting with the girl's father, arranged by Doug Farnsworth, a mutual friend and one of the wealthiest men in Topeka, Kansas. Rubenstein had traveled over ninety miles for the meeting, from Kansas City, where he was then living. Clarence Robinson had greeted him reticently, almost shyly. "I have a young daughter who has taken a fancy to the piano," he said quietly. "She wants to give concerts, and when Charlotte decides she wants something..." He shrugged helplessly. "She is my only child. Her mother died when she was only three. Charlotte means the world to me. I want to give her whatever makes her happy."

Rubenstein had tried to explain that he took only the best students, students who had already learned to read music and been trained by others, but Robinson didn't seem to hear him. "She plays already," he said. "I bought her a Steinway for her fifth birthday, because she fell in love with it. She's been making up her own tunes ever since, and they are very beautiful. My neighbor Mrs. Belson, the church organist, taught her how to read music years ago. I don't think you will be disappointed. Besides," he added, "I've done very well for myself. I can pay you whatever you ask. I want you to stay to be my girl's private tutor."

Rubenstein was aghast. "It isn't the money," he tried to explain. "It is my love for my art, my duty to take the best musical talent and help it blossom…"

"I think you will find as many fine buds to prune here as you do in Kansas City," Doug Farnsworth said. "I've heard your crop there at that Symphony Hall I invested in. At least hear the child, Alexi. That will do no harm." Alexander Rubenstein, thinking of the support Farnsworth had given to his music, had agreed.

That meeting, he thought, changed his life forever. He regretted leaving his position in Russia, sure he would not find the talent he had among his students at the Conservatory anywhere else. But he also had known he must leave. He was from a wealthy Jewish family in St. Petersburg; his father was a good friend of Tsar Nicholas II and Rubenstein had given music lessons to the Tsar's daughters, counting them among his first pupils. He knew that his money and his heritage would both bring him into disfavor in the era he saw coming in his native land. He left with regret, first for Europe and then on to the U.S. in 1916, knowing that if he didn't get out of Russia then, he probably never would. War was on the horizon and political unrest was boiling, promising to topple the Tsarist regime soon. He suspected that what came after would not be pleasant for him. So, with the assistance of distant relatives who had already settled long ago in the U.S., he arrived eventually in Kansas City and began taking on private students. He occasionally gave concerts. It wasn't the Conservatory, by any means, but he had little to complain about. His life was good.

Charlotte was eleven years old when he first met her. She was a delicate, pale child with haunting eyes of a shade he had never seen before, deep blue with flecks of lavender and purple sparkling through her irises. She had high cheekbones, the only remnants of her grandmother's Native American heritage evident in her face and a thick mane of rich, dark hair with auburn highlights curling wildly about her shoulders. Her soft, melodic voice and polite reserve gave her the manner he had learned to associate with the daughters of Russian aristocrats. She seemed very mature.

"Shall I play for you now?" she asked quietly. "Or would you like to talk to me first?" He asked her a few questions about her musical background, hoping to set her at ease, but he soon noticed this was unnecessary. She had an underlying calm and self-assurance that made him feel almost uncomfortable in her presence, a self-confident bearing uncanny in anyone, but especially in a girl of eleven. She explained she wanted to be a concert pianist, and her father had told her that she would need someone like Rubenstein to help her reach this goal. She told him she'd always known she could play the piano; that she often composed her own songs and, although she could read music, she preferred to learn by listening. He asked her what she meant by that. "If I hear something I like," she explained, "I can usually repeat it."

"Show me," he said. He moved to the piano and played the first few measures of Beethoven's "Für Elise." The child listened, smiled, and then repeated the performance almost identically, including the same flourishes, increases and decreases in volume, and irregular timing he had just performed. It was uncanny. Thinking that perhaps she had already known that piece, he experimented again, this time playing a more obscure work by Chopin.

168

"I don't like that as well," Charlotte pronounced, but then repeated it nearly identically to the way she had heard it. "I'm tired of listening now," she announced afterward. "This is something I like."

She played a beautiful, haunting waltz. "I call it the Magic Waltz," she announced afterward. "I made it up. Or, rather, I heard it in my dreams one night and remembered it. Do you like it?"

"I do like it," he said, convinced he had discovered a prodigy. He accepted her father's offer, moved to Topeka the following week, and began giving Charlotte lessons almost daily. He took on a few other students in the community as well, mostly the children and wives of the wealthy merchants and bankers who could afford his fees, but his true work became nurturing Charlotte's incredible gifts. She was an able student. By thirteen, she began joining him on the concert tours he periodically performed at colleges and civic centers in the region. Now, she would soon be performing on her own in the Kansas City Symphony Hall. Rubenstein never regretted his decision. This lovely girl had vindicated his long journey and his decision to leave the Music Conservatory in St. Petersburg all those years ago by her talent and dedication to music. He closed his eyes and listened as the last few notes of the movement lingered in the air, nodding to himself. Then he began the careful, relentless critique of her work, seeking always to improve upon perfection. She listened to his comments as patiently as she could, replaying certain passages with minor changes. Finally, Clarence heard the resounding, thunderous clash of angry hands descending on the keyboard in a crash without melody that he knew signaled the end of today's lesson. He chuckled. It meant Rubenstein and Charlotte had reached an impasse on a point of artistic interpretation.

His daughter could be as fiery and stubborn as she could be charming and demure. The old Russian teacher was learning this and, although it had taken him some time to be able to accept her moods without lectures and tantrums of his own, Clarence no longer had to intervene very often. He didn't think he would today, either, but the store was quiet so he locked the entrance, hung up his sign that said "Back in 15 minutes," and went inside the house. Charlotte was probably nervous about her upcoming performance today as well as her Kansas City performance scheduled less than a week from now. She didn't ever show it, but he felt he could sense her feelings and moods as part of the uncanny emotional bond they had shared since her birth.

Clarence was prouder of his daughter than of anything else in his life. He had turned the small grocer's store his grandfather had begun into one of the most profitable businesses in the capital city of Kansas and was respected by all of the community leaders. He credited much of this success to the steady growth of Topeka rather than to his own effort. Since his grandfather had come here from England and turned the haphazard farmer's markets that served what was then a small settlement of Buffalo soldiers, German farmers, immigrants from throughout Europe and local Native Americans into a small grocery store with a selection of local produce and dry goods imported from larger cities to the east, Topeka had become a bustling city. The Atchison, Topeka, and Santa Fe railroad not only came through town, but also maintained a large office here. Several factories, producing everything from dog food to textiles, had opened in the past several years, encouraged by the easy freight access provided by the railroad. Canneries and bakeries, making use of the wheat, corn, and other grains that grew so abundantly in the rich Kansas topsoil, expanded. The downtown area near the capital had flourished into a boardwalk of stores, including Sears & Roebuck, Woolworth's and J.C. Penney. A small university had been built; a large public library and a center for the arts had opened just after the turn of the century. A zoo and several public parks were being developed. Local families were prospering and new families were flocking to the city. Keeping up with the increasing demand kept Clarence busy, but he had always been well organized and worked hard.

His lovely wife June had worked hard right beside him, helping design the new store and home he had moved into in 1903. She was the daughter of a local banker. Her father financed the move and the expansion. Clarence had been able to pay back the loan within three years because his store had done so well. Charlotte had been born during the summer of 1905 and he had known then his life was perfect, that he had everything any man could want or need. Then, in 1909, June died suddenly of rheumatic fever when it swept the countryside, leaving him alone with his young daughter Charlotte, barely three at the time. She became the center of his life. He had been both father and mother to her, lavishing her with all of his love and attention. He devoted his life to giving her everything she wanted, including the expensive piano he purchased for her, with her grandfather's help, when she was five years old. Charlotte grew up at his side, helping him in the store. He missed her when she went to the local public school during the day, where she excelled in all subjects. He looked forward to summers so she would be home with him all day. Charlotte was without a doubt the most intelligent, beautiful, and talented young woman in town. Yes, he was very proud of her.

Clarence felt this pride swelling within him now as he came in from the entryway of their home to the ornate, high-ceilinged music room and saw the rays of light, which filtered in through the large stained-glass window, rippling through her shining, dark hair. Her head was lowered over the piano as she listened to Rubenstein explain she should slow the tempo during a certain passage of the concerto. She was shaking her head. "No," she said resolutely. "The tempo should increase with the feeling. It should NOT slow down, even if that's how you and everyone else play it." Rubenstein looked distraught, as if he was about to begin pulling at his beard or hair, as he sometimes did when upset. "Then what am I here for, if you always know best?" he complained, building slowly in tempo himself. "Why do you even need me? Why should your father be paying someone with a fine musical education to be sharing his wisdom with you when you always know best? What…"

Clarence chuckled, readjusting his wire glasses. Running his fingers through his thinning hair and squaring the shoulders on his small frame, he asked: "Having a little trouble, Professor?"

"Oy vey," said Rubenstein. "What a student I have. She thinks her own interpretation is better than mine is. She thinks…"

"It is," she said, simply. "What do you think, father? Listen to both, and tell me honestly which seems more right."

"I will, my sweet one, but not now," said Clarence. "Tonight, after you have calmed down and thought over the professor's suggestions, you can play both for me and I will decide even though I am far from a musical expert. For now, I need to get back to the store. Why don't you run on to the fair with Mrs. Smith? It seems to me there is a beauty contest scheduled for this afternoon. I seem to recall you are entered."

"Oh, that's right!" she said, springing up from the piano bench with youthful exuberance that combined energy and grace. "I forgot all about that! What time is it? Mrs. Smith!" She hugged her father, kissed him lightly on the cheek, and went in search of the housekeeper who would help her dress and accompany her to the county fair. Once she left the room, Clarence turned to Rubenstein. "I thought it might be good to interrupt," he apologized. "I know how stubborn Charlotte can be sometimes."

The old musician nodded. "She may actually be correct," he mused. "I never thought about the intent of the piece there. Perhaps increasing the tempo and the volume does add to the feeling. Changing a standard interpretation, when justified, is not always a bad thing. It's just that…I wish she would listen to me more."

"She means no disrespect, Professor," said Clarence. "Perhaps it is partly my fault for being so lenient with her. I know she admires your skill and trusts your judgment. It's just that, sometimes, when she sets her mind on something..."

"I know," said Rubenstein. "We will continue this tomorrow. Perhaps I am pushing her too hard, after all. But if she is to realize her dream, she must be able to withstand far more pressure. A young woman on stage in the great concert halls of the world... it will not be easy for her." Clarence nodded. "She is still young; she will eventually change her mind and marry, I believe. Now, though, is her time to dream. Now that women have the right to vote, she thinks she can do anything." He laughed. "Besides, you don't push her as hard as she pushes herself," he added. "She always has, with music. With everything, really."

Rubenstein walked outside with him. As he unlocked the door of his grocery store to admit the two ladies waiting outside, Clarence watched Charlotte and Mrs. Smith come flying out the front door of the house. Charlotte had changed into a beautiful summer dress, coral silk with white lace edging the low, rounded neckline and puffed sleeves. She wore silk stockings and delicate white high-heeled shoes matching the parasol she carried. Her hair was tied back and pinned beneath a trim, white bonnet. Clarence caught his breath. She was beautiful, and she looked far older than sixteen years. He blew her a kiss. "I'll be there in time to see you claim your prize," he called after her. "I'll close early today, as soon as my delivery from the bakery arrives."

Clarence shelved the fresh packages of bread after they arrived. Then he took care of another customer, Mrs. Belson, before heading for the fair. "You'll be the last for the afternoon, Gracie," he told the large, dark woman in her fifties who stood before him at the register. "I'm headed for the fair to see my daughter." Mrs. Belson grinned, a flash of bright white teeth against her black skin. Her family had been in Topeka nearly as long as the Robinson's, actively campaigning against slavery when the state was founded.

Her father had been one of the first Buffalo soldiers, an escaped slave from South Carolina who had followed the Underground Railroad to the North, and then enlisted to fight with Custer in exchange for freedom and land in Kansas. His farm had prospered; he'd opened up a leather goods store and, later, a small hotel and restaurant. The Belsons had been Clarence's neighbors when he was a child; he still fondly remembered the delicious cookies and lemonade Mrs. Belson used to serve him on summer afternoons while he played with her sons, William and Booker. She was the organist at the Baptist church, and the woman who had taught Charlotte how to read music.

"That beauty contest is this afternoon, isn't it?" she said. "Charlotte will be the youngest contestant and the prettiest. Not to mention the most talented. You sure must be proud of her. You've done a fine job raising that child, Clarence, and I'm sure that's been no easy task without a mother. You better hurry!"

He smiled in acknowledgement as he bagged her groceries. "I won't be late," he said. "How's Booker's boy doing?" He knew his friend's youngest son had stayed on the East Coast after the war to work on airplanes. "He's doing fine, last I heard," answered Mrs. Belson. "Sure do miss him, though. Miss that grandson of mine. He was a great help around the hotel." Mrs. Belson owned and managed the finest inn downtown, near the river. As she gathered her bags and left, Clarence locked up the store and headed towards the river, where the fairgrounds were located.

He enjoyed the brisk walk through town. It was a beautiful late summer afternoon. Lilacs still hung on the trees that lined the road, fragrant and lavender. The lawns he passed were green and well manicured. Topeka was a clean city, well designed and well maintained. There were many advantages to living in the government center of a prosperous farming state. This was the breadbasket of the country. Many diverse groups, including African-Americans from the southern United States, immigrants from throughout Europe and the remaining descendants of the tribes native to the region had settled here. Symphony orchestras, museums, libraries, stunning architecture, and a focus on cultural events blended with the flat, rich farmland. Clear streams and rivers stretched endlessly across the horizon in all directions. People who lived here were proud of their land and conscientious about maintaining their property. The streets were wide and clean; businesses and civic services prospered. Clarence looked around him at the city as he walked on, happy to feel the warm sun on his arms. As he approached the riverbank, scattered sunflowers and Indian paintbrush showed their bright golden and orange colors. *This is a good place*, he reflected as he approached the fairgrounds. *A pleasant place to live. A wholesome place to raise my daughter. My neighbors are honest, hard-working people who respect each other. My life hasn't always been easy, especially since June died, but I wouldn't trade it. I wouldn't want to be anywhere else but here. I wouldn't want to be anyone else but me. I'll stay here for the rest of my days; Charlotte will stay beside me. No man could ask for more than this.*

He breathed in the fragrant air, made more so by the elaborate flower arrangements he was passing now that he had entered the fairgrounds. He walked on past the bright displays of blankets and crafts toward the crowd he saw gathered near the stage. He heard the last notes of a young woman's voice singing "K-K-K-Katie," a favorite song of his, and realized he was in time for the talent competition. Just as he slipped into the audience near the front and center, where he could easily be seen from the stage, he heard Charlotte's name called and watched her walk lightly across the stage on her fashionable, high white heels. Her coral dress floated around her delicate frame, contrasting beautifully with her rich, dark auburn-streaked hair. She saw him and smiled brightly as she sat down at the piano. A hush fell over the crowd in anticipation. Most of the people in the audience had heard her play at one of the town concerts with Rubenstein over the past few years, and those who had not at least had read of her performances in the newspaper or heard their neighbors talk about her magnificent talent. Clarence took a deep breath and looked on proudly. He was very glad to be alive on this summer afternoon.

"Hi, Pops," said a voice just behind him. "My dad sure knew what he was doing when he introduced you to Rubenstein, didn't he? Let's watch our girl win!" He felt an arm on his elbow and turned to see Howard Farnsworth. Farnsworth was the eldest son of his friend Doug. "Of course," Howard added, "I much prefer to see her in a beauty contest than a concert hall. Much more fitting for my future bride!"

"Shhh," said Clarence. "Listen."

"I've rented the ball room at the Bellflower Hotel to celebrate when she wins tonight," continued Howard. "I know she will. You, of course, are invited."

There was something about Howard that Clarence had never liked, never quite trusted. The young man was tall, attractive, and lanky, with short blonde hair and intelligent green eyes. He'd attended a prep school in the east, and then studied business law at Harvard before returning to help his father handle investments. Howard was in his early twenties and had one of the few expensive sports cars in town, a fancy roadster that he flaunted. Most of the young society girls pined for rides with Howard, which he offered to them freely. He was always well dressed and invariably polite. His father bragged of his skill in business and he was a good conversationalist. Since returning last year, he'd often found excuses to see Charlotte, at concerts or social gatherings, even though she seemed to show little interest. Clarence usually insisted she was still too young to accompany him to parties and movies, although he knew he should be delighted that the boy showed a serious interest in his daughter. Still, there was a self-assured insolence about Howard that made Clarence uncomfortable. Perhaps, he reflected, he was just being overprotective. That would be natural, and the young man had never disguised his interest in her. He didn't think this explained his reaction, though. He seemed to have an instinct that said there was something dangerous about Howard's overconfidence, something frightening and cold.

Howard smiled and shrugged, acknowledging Clarence's request for silence as the announcer indicated that the next contestant would play a piano composition of her own creation, "Rose Garden Medley," written in honor of the recently-opened new rose garden in Gage, the city's largest park. Charlotte's fingers embraced the keys of the piano. A delicate melody drifted through the crowd, telling the story through sound of flowers budding in springtime and blossoming in summer, of young lovers strolling through quiet paths under moonlight, of joy and sorrow, deeply profound. Clarence felt tears come to his eyes. He hadn't ever heard this particular song before.

Clarence wasn't the only member of the audience with moist eyes. Eddie, standing near the back of the crowd with Steven Durham, also experienced the misty emotion inherent in Charlotte's melody. "That was amazing," he said after the song ended and Charlotte left the platform. "That was really amazing."

Eddie and Steve had arrived in town the weekend before, planning to rest and enjoy themselves a bit before Steve's lecture at Washburn University the following Wednesday. They were staying at the Bellflower Hotel, owned and managed by Gracie Belson who had just finished buying food for the meals she would make for them this week from Clarence. Eddie had been driving for Durham nearly three years now. They had crisscrossed the continent eight times, allowing Professor Durham to speak of archeology, fossils and the ancient past at nearly every interested campus and museum in the U.S. and Canada. Eddie felt there were few towns and cities he had not now seen at least once and was sure he was familiar with every major road in North America. Other than his visits home to Canada at Christmas, he and Steve had been constant companions. Steve, since the death of his son in the war, had developed a special attachment to Eddie. Eddie had enjoyed traveling, met many interesting people, taken several beautiful women dancing and was sure he'd become more of an expert on the Mesozoic and Paleolithic periods than anyone else living.

Steve looked at his young friend's face. "I didn't know you appreciated music so much, Eddie."

"I can't carry a tune myself and I don't know much about it, except when I hear a good dance tune. But that was amazing. I never knew what people meant when they called music 'haunting,' before. Now I do. I feel like I've heard it before, like I have always known that melody, like it is a part of my very soul." Eddie shook his head, as if trying to return to the reality he was more accustomed to living in.

"Yes, it was beautiful," agreed Steve. "So was the performer. I'm sure you noticed that!"

Eddie shook his head, surprised. "Actually, I didn't. My eyes were closed from the time the music began. Point her out to me in the next round, okay?"

Pointing Charlotte out to Eddie was very easy. As Howard and most of the town, including the local newspaper, had predicted, Charlotte won the contest. "I present this crown and these roses, from the garden about which she wrote the beautiful song she played for you today, to the fairest flower in our fine town," said Mayor Landon, "as I am sure you all agree. Our winner today, our Queen of the City of Topeka in 1921, is the lovely and talented Miss Charlotte Robinson!"

The audience broke out in applause as Charlotte walked demurely across the stage to claim her prize. "Thank you, Mayor," she said softly. "This is truly an honor of which I will try to be worthy."

Chuckling at her formality, he said "I am sure there will be no problem with that! And now, I would like to announce to those of you in attendance that my esteemed friend Doug Farnsworth, President of the Topeka City Council, and his son Howard, have reserved the Bellflower Hotel Ballroom to celebrate this occa-

ROSES IN THE DUST

sion. He has authorized me to extend an invitation to all of you in attendance here and to any friends, enemies and family members you deem fit to bring along, to attend this event. It will begin this evening at 7pm, and our lovely Queen of the City will, of course, be Guest of Honor."

Again, the audience broke into loud applause. A free party was always welcome, and Farnsworth had a reputation as an excellent and generous host. As the crowd continued clapping, Clarence, followed by Howard, headed for the stage to embrace Charlotte.

"Since the celebration is going to be at our hotel," said Steve jokingly, watching Eddie's eyes riveted to Charlotte as she descended from the platform, "I suppose we might as well attend."

"Far be it from me to miss a free chance to dance," replied Eddie, not removing his gaze from Charlotte's face. "I think I'm going to like this town better than most of the places you've dragged me to over the past couple of years."

"I've dragged you?" Steve laughed. "You're the driver. Technically, it is more the reverse!"

Steve and Eddie, along with the rest of the crowd, left the arena. "Say, Steve," said Eddie. "Do you know where that rose garden she wrote the song about is? I'd like to see it. My father has always enjoyed raising roses."

"I think it is in the main city park next to the zoo, in the southwest part of town," replied Steve, handing him a map of Topeka. "Here. You pass the cemetery and turn left. Gage Park will be on your right, just a little way ahead. See?" He pointed to the area on the map. "I'd like to freshen up before the party tonight. Why don't you drop me back at the hotel and then head over there if you are interested in seeing it? The Bellflower is on the way."

Eddie left Steve at the hotel, and drove on to the park. As he walked beneath the large, leafy trees he was struck by an odd sense of destiny. Just as he felt, earlier, that the song Charlotte played was familiar to him, he had the sense he had been here

SHERRI MCCARTHY

before, in this park, walking toward the rose garden. He took a
deep breath and looked around at the lush summer landscape,
wondering what this familiarity meant, or what it was based
on. He could tell the rose garden had been planted recently, but
he could also see the future grandeur of what it could become.
There was a central gazebo, and a series of seven paths radiating
outward from the center circle intersected by two more circular
paths. Each of the sections divided by the patterns made by the
intersecting paths was planted with different types and colors of
roses, all clearly labeled. The effect was stunning; a colorful patch-
work of flowers that formed a kaleidoscopic pattern converging
at the center. The song, he thought, captured this picture very
well, but more as a prediction of the future beauty this garden
would hold. The bushes looked healthy, but young. They would
be fuller and produce more flowers in future years. On impulse,
knowing he shouldn't but smiling as he did, Eddie selected three
of the loveliest, fullest pink roses, pulled his pocketknife from his
jeans, and cut them, leaving the stems long. He used his knife to
skin the thorns from the roses, then tied them together with a
fresh white handkerchief he pulled from his pocket. He planned
to give these, tonight at the party, to the lovely girl who captured
this place so well in her music.

After strolling through the garden, Eddie returned to the
Bellflower Hotel in time to shower and dress for the celebration.
He had a nearly-knew pair of Tony Llama cowboy boots and
a Stetson hat, both purchased when he and Steve had recently
stopped in Texas for a lecture. With fresh blue jeans, a red plaid
wool western shirt and a tooled leather belt, he looked again like
the championship rodeo cowboy he had been many years before.
He wasn't sure what prompted him to dress this way, as he knew
it would be quite different from the suits that most of the other
men would be attired in. It was what he felt like wearing this
evening, though. Steve laughed when he saw him. "Ride 'em,
cowboy!" he said in greeting. "I suppose they'll let you in look-

ing like that. I guess we'll find out!" Then, noticing the roses, he winked. "We haven't been getting out enough. I forget you are an energetic young buck," he added. "Regardless of your success tonight, we'll find us a couple of local girls to take to the moving pictures next week, eh? I noticed there was a theatre downtown, the Grand. Sound good? I'll even find the ladies."

Eddie smiled and nodded as they walked into the silvery-blue ballroom an hour or so after the event had begun. A line formed along the long table covered with sandwiches and cookies. Above, a stunning chandelier reflected on the ornate glass punchbowl. A five-man band played popular dance tunes on a low platform in the center of the room. Several couples were dancing. Groups of friends gathered to chat around small tables scattered with roses.

Eddie's eyes quickly took in the surroundings, coming to rest on the girl he had come to look for. Charlotte still wore the coral dress. She stood with a group of men and women near the band. Eddie recognized a few of the members of the group, including the mayor, from the ceremony this afternoon. The two gentlemen who had met Charlotte at the stage after the contest were also there.

"Let's find a table, Steve. I'm hungry, and I want to put these flowers down for a while, until they are needed." They served themselves at the buffet and then made their way to the vacant table closest to the group where Charlotte stood. It was still a safe distance away, but near enough to allow Eddie to observe and to eavesdrop on the conversation, if he was so inclined. As they walked, the eyes of several of the young women in the room followed Eddie. Part of it was certainly his unusual dress—unusual, at least, for a celebration at the Bellflower Ballroom in Topeka. Part of it was also due to the fact that Eddie was a very handsome young man. His face had matured nicely, giving him a look that was rugged but pleasant. He had a chiseled, angular face, with a straight, strong nose and intelligent eyes, green flecked with gold. His smile was striking, framed by narrow and well-shaped lips.

His shoulders and upper body were broad and strong, tapering to a narrow waist and hips. He had grown to nearly six feet tall, and he carried himself well. He looked athletic, limber, and sure of himself. He was aware of the eyes that followed him and accepted the glances simply, without arrogance. He was also aware that the one glance he wanted to follow his movements had not done so. Charlotte had not noticed him; she was listening to the conversation around her and her eyes were on an older man with glasses and thinning hair. He was one of the men who had met her at the stage. Eddie guessed, correctly, that he was probably her father. He then looked at the women in the group, hoping to see a resemblance to the beautiful girl and thus identify her mother, as well. He was unable to, thinking maybe this was one of those rare instances where the child bore no resemblance to the parent. Satisfied he had learned all he could through a visual appraisal, he focused on catching snatches of the conversation, instead. A large, smiling black woman approached. Eddie had seen her at the hotel; she managed the Bellflower.

The young man who had been speaking quieted as she approached, looking almost embarrassed. The older man with glasses greeted her warmly; so did Charlotte. The woman embraced her. "Lord, child," he heard her say in a booming, sure voice, "I sure was proud of you today, up there on that stage. I sure think teaching you those notes must be among the best, most worthwhile tasks I've had the blessing to complete in this old life of mine. You were magnificent!"

"Thank you, Mrs. Belson," Charlotte answered politely. "I'll always be grateful to you for that."

"It was Gracie who first taught Charlotte to play," said the man with glasses, speaking to another older man, this one bearded. "Professor Rubenstein, I don't know if you've met Grace Belson, but she was the best piano teacher in Topeka before you arrived."

"Nonsense," said Mrs. Belson. "I play the organ, not the piano. And this one taught herself, anyway. I had very little to do with it."

"I know what you mean," said Rubenstein with a thick accent that Eddie guessed was either Russian or German. "Indeed, I know what you mean." He spoke to Mrs. Belson for a few minutes longer; then, she said good-bye to the group, saying she must check on some of her other guests. Once she was a safe distance away, the man who was probably Charlotte's father addressed the young man and the rest of the group.

"That's an example of why I am so opposed to your position, Howard," he said, his voice sincere and almost angry. "If you keep pursuing a segregation policy, fine women like that won't be able to teach my daughter; or work in schools where she attends. What's wrong with all of you? Kansas has always been a state that stands for civil rights. Last century, we had fine, far-thinking men who opposed slavery from the time the state was founded. We've always had a good mix of all kinds of folks here, and they've always gotten on fine with each other. Just because most other states educate black and white children in separate schools, that doesn't mean we must. I think that idea is a foolish notion. No value at all. It will just cost the taxpayers money building new schools they don't need, that's all it will do."

"There's another side to it," said a distinguished-looking white-haired gentleman who stood with the group. "It would require the building of new schools, and the hiring of more teachers, which might be a very good thing for education in this state in the long run. Besides, you know that, technically, we've been violating national policy for the last 50 years by not segregating schools."

"Exactly! Clarence, I am not so sure you've considered your position well," said Howard. "Besides, if we want to continue attracting more people to this fine city—which, from the standpoint of the real estate my father and I are developing is something I sincerely hope we will do, Governor! —we need to give them the civil comforts they are used to. They don't want niggers in their neighborhoods and they don't want niggers in their schools with their children. That's what they are used to, that's what they want, and that's all there is to it. Why, the KKK up in Indiana has taken a very strong stand on that issue, and if we don't follow their lead, they'll be putting pressure on us. There's wealthy, powerful folks in that group who could help or hurt us as we grow as a state. We have to consider that."

"What I must consider most," said the Governor, "is how the voters of this state feel about it. Right now, I'm not too sure, but I have ears all over, listening in. I should have a better idea by the next election."

"Will you take a public stand on it before the next election?" asked Howard. "Might make a big difference to some of the potential financial backing you get for your campaign, Governor." He winked.

"What about the Indians we still have in this state?" asked Clarence. "What about the people from Mexico who came to work the fields and stayed? Will they need their own schools, too?"

"Why, they'll go to school with the pickanninnies, of course." Howard laughed. "What a silly question! You are either white or you aren't white. That's all there is to it."

"Anyone who knows anything about the history of this county knows that it was founded through cooperation between the English settlers and the Shawnee tribe who lived here," retorted Clarence. "Some of that history is in my own family, and not too far back. One of my grandmothers was Shawnee. When my grandfather came here from England and first opened a grocery store, she married him at the request of her tribe. So I guess that means Charlotte would not be able to attend a white school, is that right? The escaped slaves and Buffalo soldiers who settled in this region did more for our state than your ancestors, Howard, I'll venture to guess. Your father moved here from Indiana to work in a bank less than twenty years ago. Those men helped tame this land and make this region what it is today, what it already was by the time you arrived. Be careful of your ideas about separation of groups. That's all I have to say on the matter."

"I agree with Clarence," said Professor Rubenstein in his melodic accent. "I know from my own experiences in Russia that it is never wise to divide men into categories and place one group above another. No good ever comes of this. It brings no good end." He shook his head sadly.

Eddie thought of Chief. He didn't have much experience with African Americans or Mexicans, but he didn't think that was necessary to make up his mind where he stood on the issue. He agreed completely with Clarence and Rubenstein. Segregation, or any other practice that implied different groups of people have more or less value than others, was an evil practice. He could never sanction it. He wondered how Charlotte felt. It was difficult to tell, as she made no comment. She had been listening to the conversation carefully, however, and he thought he saw a trace of tension along her mouth that hadn't been present before.

Almost as if responding to his curiosity, she patted her father's arm. "I'm proud of you, Papa," she said. "If you'll excuse me, I'll go talk to a few of my friends while you continue this conversation." She walked purposefully to join a group of girls, many of whom were African American, chatting near the opposite wall. She looked back once to see if Howard noticed this and, seeing that he did, smiled with satisfaction.

Eddie was glad to see that she apparently felt the same way he did about the issue of segregation. He was also glad she had left the group. Approaching her to offer his gift now would be much easier than when she stood in the company of an obviously wealthy group of businessmen, including her father, the mayor, and the governor. "Sorry to be such a rotten conversationalist, Steve," Eddie apologized, realizing suddenly he hadn't said a word to his friend since sitting down. "Guess I was just enjoying my food."

"That's okay," said his friend. "I was eavesdropping, too. You don't have those issues in Canada so much, but they sure are a sore point in this country. Kansas is one of the few places where there hasn't been segregation before, but it appears to be coming. Already here in most of the rest of the country, despite the war fought over slavery barely fifty years ago. Although I suppose many would say that war was an economic one, like most wars are, and slavery was just the excuse to sell glory to the masses who had to die in the mess. I never really thought much about it before, myself. I think I agree with that old Russian, though. It can be a very dangerous thing. Here we are complaining about the Germans and that young leader of theirs, Hitler, who seems to hate Jews, and here in this country we're doing the same things, just in slightly different ways and to a different group of people. But you and I aren't likely to solve the problems of the world, Eddie. So, why don't you take those roses to that young lady, as I know you are chomping at the bit to do? I think I'll look about the place for a pleasant, unaccompanied matron who looks as if she might enjoy dancing with me."

Eddie nodded, picking up the bouquet. He walked toward the group of girls where Charlotte stood. As he approached, several of them noticed, preening and smiling as he came nearer. He joined the group at Charlotte's elbow, turned toward her, and bowed gallantly, presenting her with the roses. "Excuse me, ma'am," he said, hoping his voice sounded suave and charming, "I'm Eddie McCauslin. I'm just passing through town with Professor Durham on his lecture tour, and I happened to hear you play today. I just wanted to let you know that your song was—well, it was the most beautiful song I've ever heard. I brought you these to thank you." He handed her the three long-stemmed pink roses from the garden, tied together with his handkerchief.

"Why, how sweet," she said. "They're lovely." He felt a nearly tangible electric shock as he saw the lavender flecks in Charlotte's eyes when she met his gaze. He knew he had never met anyone as beautiful as this. Normally charming and self-assured with every girl he'd met, he wasn't sure what to say next. One of her friends in the group saved him the trouble of struggling for conversation.

"Where are you from?" she said brightly. She was a pert young African-American girl, about the same age as Charlotte. She was wearing a stunning red silk gown, low on her shoulders, and a diamond necklace.

"Canada," he answered, "although I've spent lots of time in the USA. I've been touring with the professor for three years. Before that, I lived in Washington, playing baseball. And I traveled all through the western USA when I was riding in the rodeo."

"Rodeo!" she exclaimed. "I knew it! I'm Rosie Brown. C'mon. I've always wanted to dance with a cowboy!" Rosie grabbed his arm and pulled him enthusiastically toward the dance floor. He followed, but his eyes stayed on Charlotte, watching her walk away from the group with her flowers.

Eddie prided himself on his dancing ability, but Rosie was also a fabulous dancer. She followed his moves easily, adding a few spins and flourishes of her own. Although he wished it were Charlotte that he could hold so loosely and easily in his arms, he began to enjoy himself, getting lost in music and movement. When he did look back in search of Charlotte, she had disappeared. He found her eventually on the dance floor with the tall young man who had been talking earlier about segregation. Eddie thought about cutting in, but Rosie stayed with him on the floor and they continued to dance through three more songs. He finally excused himself, explaining he needed to find the friend he had come with.

"When you find him," Rosie said, "bring him over to meet my friends. If he's half as good a dancer as you are, we're all sure to have a great evening!"

Steve was still sitting at the table where he had left him. "Couldn't find myself any unattached women," he complained. Eddie told him of Rosie's offer, and he was happy to comply.

"They're all young enough to be my daughters, but a dance is a dance!" he shrugged. Eddie was hoping that Charlotte would rejoin the group so he could dance with her, but she never did. Howard seemed determined to stay close to her for the rest of the celebration. She danced with several of the older men from the group, too—her father, the Russian music professor, the mayor, and the governor. She was, after all, the city's new beauty queen, he told himself. That was probably exactly what she should be doing at this party in her honor. Still, he wanted to find a way to interrupt. He continued dancing with Rosie and with several of her friends. Finally, near the end of the evening, he approached Charlotte as she danced with her father.

"Excuse me, sir," Eddie said, moving Rosie close to the couple. "Would you mind if we changed partners for a little while? I really would like to have just one dance with your lovely daughter. After hearing her play, I truly am enchanted. I'm Eddie McCauslin, from Canada. I'm just in town briefly on a lecture tour with Professor Durham. I promise to take good care of her during the dance and return her to you safely as soon as the song is over. I—"

"Certainly, young man," Clarence said warmly, saving Eddie from rambling further. "Professor Durham. He's the fellow who discovered all the dinosaur fossils in Colorado, isn't he? We're planning to go to his lecture next week. Perhaps you can introduce me to him later. C'mon, Rosie," he added, lightly releasing his daughter and pulling Rosie toward him. "I don't think we've waltzed since Charlotte's last birthday party, and everyone knows you're the best dancer in town!"

She laughed, and the two moved away. Once Charlotte was in his arms, it took Eddie a moment to regain his sense of rhythm. Time seemed to crawl to a stop. He could barely move. It seemed he could barely breathe. He was aware of the dizzyingly fresh scent of her hair, of the way the folds of her dress crinkled against his skin, and of the gentle grace of her movements. For the first time in his life, he could think of nothing to say. It didn't seem to matter. Charlotte, also, was quiet. But the silence was comfortable, as if no words were necessary between them. They waltzed across the floor together as if in a dream.

Eddie hardly remembered the rest of the evening. He continued to dance with Charlotte until her father reclaimed her and the two of them left after the band stopped playing. He went to his room soon after, wondering why he felt as if the rest of his life up until this day hadn't mattered. The dreamlike afterglow still surrounded him at breakfast the next morning. Durham smiled in greeting. "What do you say we drive out to one of the lakes near here for some fishing?" he said. "I hear there's great bass in the area."

"Sure," said Eddie. "We haven't used those poles for a while; might as well justify the space they take up in the trunk." They finished their breakfast, got directions from Mrs. Belson to nearby Shawnee Lake and left. On the way, Steve pointed to a grocery store. "Stop there, Eddie," he said. "We'll pick up some bread and canned vegetables to go with the fish I plan to catch." Eddie parked the large Ford Roadster next to the store. As they got out of the car, he heard familiar piano music drifting from the house nearby and stopped to listen. By the time he regained his bearing and entered the market, Durham was already at the counter with canned peas, instant coffee and a loaf of bread, talking to the grocer as if they were old friends. The grocer was Charlotte's father. Clarence nodded at Eddie as he entered the store.

"There you are!" said Steve. "What were you doing? Checking our rods? I was just asking Clarence, here, whether he knew of any young ladies who might like to accompany us to the movies this evening."

"I have a daughter who might do for the young fellow," Clarence said slowly, smiling at Eddie. "She has already told me what a wonderful dancer and fine gentleman he is. I'll have to think who might do for you. Most of our older ladies are married, you know. Some of the local boys are planning a poker game tonight. Perhaps that might suit your fancy?"

"I sort of had my mind set on a movie," said Steve. "I guess I can go solo if there aren't any suitable dates." He laughed. "A man of my age should be used to it. No kindly widows, huh? Wish my dear wife were still alive to keep me company. Well, if you don't think of anyone, maybe the youngsters can go and I will join you for poker. We'll see. I'll be here this evening about 6:30, at any rate. Thanks, Clarence!"

"Good luck with the fishing," said Clarence as they gathered the groceries. Eddie was a little dazed, realizing he actually was about to take the beautiful young woman he'd met yesterday to the movies. He was quieter than usual as they fished. Steve didn't seem to notice; they both were busy pulling their lines in almost immediately after every cast. Within three hours, they had a pile of nearly a dozen wall-eyed bass.

"Time for lunch!" announced Steve. Eddie gathered wood and built a fire, pulled their skillet from the trunk of the car and began frying fish. They ate well, enjoying the green expanse of trees around the lake. Shawnee Lake was only a few miles from town; it was a nice place to come for an afternoon outing. A family was visible several hundred yards away on a small beach, getting ready for an afternoon swim. "I like this place," mused Eddie as he finished his meal. "It seems strange to look in all directions without seeing a mountain in sight. The sky never ends. But the soil is rich, the lakes are full of fish and the people are good. Most of them, at any rate," he added, thinking back to the conversation he had overheard last night and wondering why it still disturbed him. "Besides, you got me a date with the prettiest girl in town!"

"That I did!" said Steve. "This is our last stop of the tour, and I thought you might as well enjoy it. We have a long drive back to Alberta when we're finished. Then I want you and Rigall to take me hunting one more time before I assume my new post in the geology department at Utah State University this fall."

"What? This is our last stop?" Eddie had known the three-year tour would be ending soon, but he didn't realize it would be quite this soon. He hadn't even considered what he would do once he finished driving Durham through the country. Eddie was in his late twenties now. He'd saved some money, but not a lot, sending most home to his parents. He supposed he could return to leading hunting parties, although he really had lost his desire to do that. Maybe he'd work with Chief at the gas station. "I guess I haven't been paying attention."

"I may not have told you," apologized Durham. "I wasn't sure until recently. But I need to get back to teaching. I've had a chance to recover from the deaths of my wife and son. I owe you a lot for helping me through that, whether you know it or not. But I'm not really a drifter. Giving up my position for this tour was out of character for me. I miss the settled academic life. If you like, Eddie," he added, "You are welcome to stay on with me in Utah. You see what's waiting for you at home. Then, if you want to drive me down to Salt Lake and stay on, maybe even study at the university, you will certainly be welcome."

"I'll think about it," said Eddie. But he was thinking more about the evening ahead of him than the rest of his life as they wrapped up the remaining eight fish to give to Mrs. Belson and cleaned up their lunch site before returning to town. He found he was still thinking about it as he showered and dressed for his date. Almost inexplicably as far as his own memory was concerned, Eddie soon found himself back at the store.

"You look nice, young man," Clarence greeted him. "Here, you might be interested in these; just got a shipment in today." He pointed toward a display of chocolates. Eddie grinned self-consciously and chose a small, heart-shaped box, wrapped in gold foil and slipped it into his back pocket. As he paid, Clarence continued his friendly banter, "I couldn't find anyone suitable for you, my friend," he was telling Steve. "But that's just as well. I'll appreciate your company at the poker game tonight. Perhaps you can help me talk some sense into the heathen community leaders. They seem hell-bent on dangerous paths and need intelligence in there midst before they head humanity on the same course as your dinosaurs. Besides, I'm sure my daughter will appreciate an unchaperoned evening. I've always been overprotective. It's just that I don't usually trust the young men who want to take her out." He shrugged. "Since I arranged this date and your young driver seems so honorable, I feel generous! Here, come with me to the door; she should be ready by now."

Eddie barely remembered the walk to the door; he remembered very little about the evening at all. Charlotte was wearing a light gold silk dress that made the auburn highlights in her rich, dark hair even more visible and accented the violet flecks in her deep blue eyes. She was light on her feet and her hand, which she slipped into his as they departed and left there throughout the evening, was warm and pliant to his touch. He couldn't recall anything about the movie or about the conversation he was sure they must have had. All he later recalled was that the box of chocolates he had intended to give her had been crushed. He had forgotten that he had slipped it in his back pocket when he walked toward the door of her home to meet her, and only recalled it after the movie when, kissing her goodnight at her door, she said, "Mmm. You smell like caramel, my favorite kind!" Sheepishly, wondering why he did it, he withdrew the crushed, melted box from his back pocket and offered it to her. They both laughed raucously, uncontrollably, until tears were running down their faces.

"What's the racket?" called Mrs. Smith, the housekeeper. She invited Eddie in for hot chocolate while he waited for Steve and Charlotte's father to return from their poker game. He and Charlotte continued talking; he found her amazingly easy to talk to. Without realizing it, he told her most of the important parts of his life in the hour they sat together over hot chocolate. He told her about his family, and Chief. He talked of his success at rodeo and brief career in baseball. He told her how, after his friend was killed in the war, he no longer enjoyed hunting. He even told her how Flo's death so long ago had made him decide that his life should really matter, should really make a difference. He had never shared these things with anyone else, but she seemed to understand. She, in turn, told him about her mother's death.

"I was little, so I don't really remember her at all except for what Father has told me. I know he loved her very much. He has always been so good to me." She also told him about her determination to become the best concert pianist in the world. "Professor Rubenstein says it will be impossible, that even though I am very talented, women just don't do that. But I don't care. I can be the first! Women are getting more accepted in movies and dance now. Since suffrage, there really isn't any difference. Look at the success of Isadora Duncan! Painting and music won't be far behind. I've never felt so comfortable with anyone before, Eddie," Charlotte continued as they began their third cup of hot chocolate. "How long will you be here? Do you have to go back to Canada?"

He almost found himself considering how he could stay, but realized that was impossible. He needed to go back with Durham. He had no work here, no family, no way to live. "Yes," he said. "As tempting as it is to stay close to you, I must go back next week. But we will write. You can always share your dreams with me and tell me about your life. And I will be back someday. I promise."

"Do you?" she said. "Do you really promise?"

"Sure." He laughed. "If you are still here, I'll come for a visit. But after you've had a long, successful career as the world's greatest pianist, you will probably marry a Count and move to Austria, or buy a villa in Italy. Or maybe you will come to Canada."

She shook her head. "Too cold," she said. "Besides, this is my home. No matter what I do in life, this will always be my home."

They exchanged addresses and sat quietly for a while. When Steve and Clarence finally stumbled in, evidently drunk on bootlegged liquor as they happily recounted their winning hands,

Eddie regretted he had to leave, but his friend was definitely ready to call it a night. He agreed to meet Charlotte again the following afternoon for a good-bye walk in the park, and departed.

"Well," his friend slurred as they drove to the hotel, "I see how decisions are made in this town, I do. That poker game is more than a game, my friend. More than a game." Later, on the drive back to Canada, he would tell Eddie about the many business and political deals Howard Farnsworth and his father had negotiated with the mayor, governor, and wealthy businessmen of the town that evening. Everything from stock investments to real estate zoning to public segregation had been decided, literally, at the flip of a card.

CHAPTER ELEVEN

ENVELOPES

Eddie slipped the letter from his pocket now that he was alone and opened it, carefully removing the scented pink paper from the envelope. He'd been back in Alberta for nearly five years. Professor Durham had enjoyed a final hunting trip in the Rockies and then driven to Utah on his own. Gene, now a Mounty, was working in Jasper and rarely home. Joe had joined a construction crew headed for California last year. Lizzie was still with the theater troupe, happy and successful. His other sisters had all married and moved with their husbands to different parts of Canada. Pincer Creek had grown. Four teachers from Calgary worked in the new school that replaced the one room cabin where Miss Welch had taught him many years before. He was surprised how much had changed.

Mama still nursed local families, but not nearly as often as in the past. Papa spent most of his time with Chief at the gas station or taking care of the ranch. He was aging rapidly, and happy to have his oldest son to assist. It seemed fitting to Eddie; his parents had taken care of him when he was young so now he'd take care of his parents. There was symmetry to it all. Besides, his successful careers with rodeo and baseball, his profitable hunting business and all of the adventures he'd had driving Durham around the country were enough to satisfy him for a while. He could always work with Rigall if he needed to, or with Chief. There didn't seem to be any need to think about the future. He was happy to be home.

Eddie acquired a small blue Chrysler from Chief that one of
the many wealthy hunters from the east abandoned at the gas
station because of engine problems. "I can buy a newer model
for not much more than you'll charge me to fix this one." The
man had shrugged. "Give me a ride into Calgary, and I'll just
leave it with you." Chief and Eddie painstakingly rebuilt the
engine and transmission, ordering parts that often took weeks
to arrive. It had been a great project for both of them. Eddie
took as much pleasure in it as he had once taken learning to
track animals and ride rodeo. He was happy to be home. But he
did find himself, more than he liked, remembering the time he'd
spent in Kansas with the grocer's beautiful daughter. The scent
of her hair as they danced and the soft, warm feel of her hand in
his at the movie theater slipped into his mind often. Sometimes,
unaware, he would catch himself humming the melody to "Rose
Garden Medley."

Their few days together had been magical. He told Charlotte
more about his own life, his hopes, and his dreams during those
days than he ever shared with anyone else. She knew of his grief
over Redwing. She knew of many days spent caring for his siblings, anxiety before baseball games and his pride at establishing
Rigall's now-famous lodge hunting expeditions. He shared his
tremendous relief at finding Miss Welch in time, his sense of
loss when Tom was killed in the war, and his sadness at how his
friend's death soured the excitement of tracking and hunting in
the Rockies. In just a few days time, she had learned everything
about him. He'd learned about Charlotte, too. He knew how
much she loved her father. He was aware of her loyalty to her
friends, especially Rosie Brown and the Belson family. Her dream
of becoming a concert pianist once she finished high school was
important to her. If it wasn't for that dream—and for the fact that
she was barely sixteen and her father's only child—Eddie may have
impulsively asked her to marry him and come back to Canada.
Because of those reasons, they simply exchanged addresses and

promised to write to each other. Charlotte had written faithfully at first, and Eddie returned her letters regularly. He enjoyed hearing the news of her friends. He liked learning about the concerts she gave. He shared her disappointment over bad reviews and her elation over good ones. Their letters had become less frequent and less personal lately, but he still felt a special excitement when he received the dainty envelopes addressed in her unmistakable handwriting. Last summer, she had gone on an extended concert tour with Professor Rubenstein, all the way to New York. He assumed she had been too busy to write now that her dreams were coming true. Besides, he hadn't known where to reach her while she was on the road. This was the first letter he had received for several months, so he wanted to savor it. He had been carrying it in his pocket all day, waiting until he was alone and would be undisturbed to read it. Now, in his room for the evening at last, he opened it.

As he read, he was struck by the change in tone. The writer was more mature, which was certainly to be expected. Instead of a girl of sixteen, Charlotte was now a woman of twenty-one. This letter held an underlying note of discouragement barely evident between the lines that bothered him in ways he could not quite identify, though. Perhaps it was more apparent in what she did not write than in what she did. He expected a thorough description of her tour. Instead, she barely mentioned it, writing she would go on tour of the western USA in a few months, but Rubenstein felt she wasn't ready to join him in Europe. He expected the usual, chatty news about dances, parties, and friends. Instead, she mentioned only briefly that Rosie was getting married next month and that Rosie's older brother had married Linda Belson. Howard refused to attend the wedding with her and felt it was not appropriate for her to go, but she went regardless. "Maybe he was right," she wrote. "Things have changed, somehow, as we've grown up. I was the only white girl there, and I felt out of place. Since the schools have become segregated, it's harder to be friends. Rosie says we are just growing up and getting busy with our own lives, but I think it's more than that." She ended by saying she hoped he was well and would remain her friend "regardless of where our lives take us and whether or not we ever meet again. I hope more than anything that we will. You promised to come back once, remember? Will you?" He wasn't quite sure how to answer the letter, so he didn't for several months. Would he go back? He didn't know. And what could he tell her about his life here that he hadn't already told her? There didn't seem to be anything to say. The next letter he got, several months later, seemed even more out of character and troubled. He read her words, seeing her haunting violet blue eyes and soft smile superimposed over the letter as he read.

Dear Eddie,

It seems like it was so long ago when we met, but I still remember our few days together as the happiest of my life. It is rare when one finds another human being so familiar and comfortable, with whom it is so easy to share thoughts and feelings, life views and experiences. I have never met anyone else I enjoyed talking to as much. I have never met anyone else I enjoyed being with as much.

It has been several months since I heard from you last. I hope you are well. I am sure you are happy to be with your family in Canada, and keeping busy with things you enjoy. Please know I am always eager to hear about your life and look forward to your letters when they arrive. Please know I am still waiting, too, for you to keep your promise and return.

Much has changed for me. I have become discouraged from becoming a concert pianist. Professor Rubenstein tells me that a woman pianist would find difficult acceptance in Europe. I am finding it difficult here, as well. My tour of the East Coast last year left me questioning my talent, which I had always taken so much for granted before. Perhaps I have been a big fish in a little pond. The pianists in New York have more rigorous training. The reviewers, although they were kind, were more likely to comment on my youth and appearance than my talent, and I found that disheartening. California was worse. How I looked was compared to movie stars, but not a word was written about my playing. Howard says I should give piano lessons, and stay in the Midwest where my talent is appreciated. We do not agree on many things, but he has been very supportive of my desire to play; he has even agreed to rent a concert hall for me in Kansas City each year to perform whatever I like. He says it won't matter if my shows make a profit, as he has plenty of money. He has more than tripled his father's investments in stocks and real estate, and his father had plenty to begin with. My father also prefers this idea; he is so lonely when I am far away. I know I could never leave him; I am all he has. Perhaps age brings wisdom and pares down one's dreams. This is my home, so I need to find a way to be happy and contribute to my community. Would you ever consider coming back here to live? You seemed to like it very much once.

Rosie Brown has a child now, a beautiful little boy. Her brother Mose and Linda Belson Brown had a little boy this year, too, Moses, Jr. He is so energetic. All of my friends have married now, and have children. I suppose it is time for me to consider doing the same. Do you plan to marry, Eddie? Do you have a sweetheart? I know I shouldn't ask, but I am curious, and we are friends, are we not? I hope you will forgive my curiosity. Well, enough for now. Please write to me soon.

Always,
Charlotte

The letter left him feeling sad and vaguely troubled, although he was not sure why. After a few days, he made an effort and wrote back, not quite sure what to say but sure he was expected to say something.

Dear Charlotte,

I am always happy to receive your letters. You are the most beautiful, talented girl I ever met in all of my travels. You will always be my friend and have a special place in my heart. I know you could succeed as a concert pianist—or anything you want to be. I respect your decision to stay near your father. Although I haven't thought about it in the same way that you have, and although my parents have each other and several other children, I guess I basically made a similar decision. It is nice to be close to my family. I may live somewhere else someday; it is always hard to predict what lies ahead. But for now, I am content here.

You asked if I had a sweetheart. You can always ask me anything. It will never offend me and I will always be glad to hear about your life and share mine with you. I don't have a sweetheart, although there are a couple of pretty girls I take to dances once in a while. I don't plan to marry. I may change my mind someday, but for now I am happy on my own. Thank you for your letter. I always wish you the very best of life and I eagerly await your letters and am always proud to be your friend and confidante.

Yours,
Eddie

Several months elapsed without a reply. The following spring, Eddie finally received a letter. Eager to hear from Charlotte, he tore it open at the post office as soon as it arrived. To his astonishment, the envelope contained a wedding announcement. Charlotte had married Howard Farnsworth. Eddie had the eerie sensation when he opened and read the announcement that the world was closing in on him. He must have looked pale as he left the post office, for Elizabeth Rigall, as she was entering, steadied his arm.

"What's wrong, Eddie? Lord, I haven't seen you for months! You and I need to talk. Come home with me after I gather my mail and have some tea." Still feeling a little lightheaded, he agreed readily and accompanied her home. He hadn't been out to the lodge, where she and Burt had built a beautiful home, for many months. The top floor of their home included an open loft and balcony; the main floor had a large fireplace, sitting room, kitchen, and two bedrooms. Large windows and beautiful woodwork, his Father's best carpentry ever, characterized the home. Many people had been entertained here, including Teddy Roosevelt, Henry Ford and Eddie's personal favorite among the great men he had met, Rio Branco. The Rigalls' lodge had become a stunning success, and so had their marriage.

"Welcome, Eddie," Elizabeth said, settling them both down at the clawed oak table his father had carved for tea and scones. "I haven't seen you nearly often enough over the past few years. I am so glad you are back. You really do need to come around more. Burt always enjoys your company and complains that he wants his favorite guide to go with him on expeditions. I always enjoy your company, too. Besides, today you look as if you could use a friend. What's wrong? Bad news?" She motioned toward the letter.

"Not really," said Eddie. "Well, maybe…" He showed her the wedding announcement.

"Ah," said Elizabeth, remembering the long-ago days when she had told Eddie about her early romance and heartbreak with Burt and sensing this may be a similar situation. "The carousel turns. What goes around comes around again. Will you tell me about Charlotte?"

Eddie talked to his friend and former teacher for hours. He told her about the days he spent in Topeka, about the dance, movie, walks, and long conversations with Charlotte. He was surprised how easy it was to talk about it, and how much he had to say. He told Elizabeth about the years they had exchanged letters, sharing his disappointment that Charlotte had given up on her dream of becoming a famous concert pianist. "She is so talented," he explained. "You just can't imagine how beautifully she plays." He even pulled Charlotte's last two letters from his breast pocket, where he had carried them for months, and showed them to his friend. "I guess I'm just sad she gave up on her dream. This makes it so final, like an empty envelope. I didn't expect it."

"You know, Eddie," Elizabeth said, after reading the letters and watching his face, "I don't think I've ever properly thanked you for saving my life. I hope it is not too late for me to save yours now. I think you are sad about more than Charlotte giving up a dream. And I don't think it was the dream of becoming a concert pianist that was hardest for her to give up."

"What do you mean?" he asked.

"Men can be so blind," she said, not unkindly. "The two of you have been in love for years, and you don't even know it. She loves you. It's plain as day in these letters. Your young lady all but begged you to come back and marry her for the past year, and you didn't even notice! She was probably crushed. Of course, she felt she had no choice but to marry someone else. Eddie, Eddie—and I thought my youth was difficult. Ah, feelings..."

After talking to Elizabeth the rest of the afternoon, Eddie felt better. It helped to sort his feelings out, even if it was too late to do much about them. Knowing how he felt about Charlotte and her marriage hurt, but it was slightly preferable to the dark confusion he felt when he received the wedding announcement. Now, he could accept his mistake, if it was one. He could justify it.

"It's better this way," he found himself telling Elizabeth. "Don't you think so? She needs to be with her father, just as my parents need me here. She obviously wants a family, and I don't. She doesn't want to leave Kansas any more than I want to leave Canada. I can just be happy we met. We'll always be friends and we'll write to each other still."

"You're quite the detached philosopher, Eddie McCauslin," she said. "I do hope you are right."

Eddie thought he was. He wrote a long letter to Charlotte. At Elizabeth's suggestion, he included an invitation for Charlotte to bring her husband, father, and guests of their choosing to stay at the lodge and go hunting with Burt as a wedding present.

Dear Charlotte,

I received the announcement of your wedding. I wish you complete happiness. From the time I first met you, I think I always knew you would marry Howard. He is the wealthiest, most powerful man in the city you live and wish to remain in. You are the most beautiful woman there. It is fate. Books and movies we both enjoy speak to the wisdom of that arrangement.

I know from your letters that you made your decision carefully and responsibly. It is important to you to take care of your father. You love your friends and are loyal to them and to your hometown. You made a good decision. You are very wise, as well as very intelligent, talented, and beautiful.

For my part, I will always be grateful for the time I shared with you. I will always remember our brief moments together in Topeka so long ago with joy. I will also always be here for you when you need me, to share whatever parts of your life you want to share with me. I will always be your friend and love you from afar. I see the highlights of your hair in the red roses of summer each year and the color of your eyes in the sky.

Love,
Eddie

He felt better after sending the letter, as if he had said things that needed to be said and were important to both of them to acknowledge. His words apparently had the same effect on Charlotte, because he was soon frequently receiving long, friendly letters again, telling him news of the community and her daily life. He answered them as soon as they were received.

Their letters commented on world events and personal victories; they exchanged news of family and friends, of favorite foods, songs, and future plans. Everything seemed comfortable between them again. When Charlotte told him Howard and her father were planning to invite the park commissioner, the governor and Howard's father along to take advantage, at last, of the wedding present he'd offered, he was delighted, looking forward to showing Charlotte his hometown.

Eddie got a new haircut and began planning where to take Charlotte while the men were hunting. Elizabeth and Burt looked on with quiet curiosity, exchanging knowing glances as the visit approached. "Youth," Burt said mysteriously, "is completely wasted on the young. It's fortunate, Eddie, that you won't be young much longer."

Eddie's parents noticed his mounting excitement. He'd told them little of his adventures with Steve, barely mentioning the friends he'd invited to visit before. Now he talked about them almost daily. His descriptions of how well Charlotte played the piano and how beautiful she was caught his mother's attention. Johanna began to wonder if her son's stubborn insistence on remaining single was rooted in some sad experience from his travels. She had an intuitive sense that the young woman he appeared so eager to introduce was very special. That she was coming as part of a wedding present seemed odd, but Johanna had no reason to doubt Eddie's judgment. He was very good at realizing his goals. He always made good decisions. She helped him arrange a community concert, 'impromptu, you understand, and only if she agrees,' for Charlotte to play at when she arrived. She smiled at how his appearance, always attractive and well groomed, improved even more. She chuckled when he sent a telegram to his old friend Steve Durham, inviting him to join the hunting party, especially since Eddie had already said he wasn't planning to hunt.

Eddie, for his part, felt the mounting excitement as the visit approached but, even with the improved insight into his feelings Elizabeth provided, he credited it to happiness over a reunion with a friend. He still thought that was the reason for the lightness in his step and heightened sound and color in the world around him when he went to meet the train in Lethbridge. Because there were six visitors arriving, Eddie and Burt both drove their automobiles to the station so there would be sufficient space to transport everyone back to the lodge. Eddie's car could accommodate four comfortably, five in a pinch. Burt had room for six. Durham would be driving directly to the lodge, arriving later that evening for dinner. Eddie also invited his parents and Chief to meet his friends by joining everyone at the fine restaurant Burt and Elizabeth had opened in the lodge two years before.

Eddie watched impatiently as passengers disembarked. He saw Clarence first, and waved. Howard and three other men, who he assumed were the governor, parks commissioner, and Howard's father, disembarked next. Where was Charlotte? He felt his heart stop as he wondered if she had decided not to come. Then he saw her step down gingerly, carrying her bag and talking to a frail, elderly woman who held her arm. He smiled and ran to take the bag. She wore a loose, light blue dress. A tan sweater was thrown over her shoulders. Her auburn hair fell full and wild from beneath a light wool cap, brushing against the wool in bright contrast. She was even more beautiful than he remembered when he had last seen her almost six years ago. Her violet eyes looked a little haunted now, and her face had acquired a gaunt, chiseled elegance. Her smile seemed a little more reserved and the childish bounce he remembered in her step was gone. She still radiated the calm, quiet assurance he remembered so well. He wanted to grab her in his arms, spin her around, and share the joy he felt at seeing her again. He knew that would not be appropriate under the circumstances, though. He kept his excitement in check.

"Welcome to Canada, Charlotte. I'm so glad you were able to come. I mean—"

"It's wonderful to see you, too, Eddie," she said softly, as if she sensed the underlying, turbulent current of emotions he was feeling. "It's been a long journey and I'm a little tired, but Mrs. Farnsworth has been very good company." She introduced him to the elderly woman who accompanied her, Howard's mother. "I hope you don't mind that she came along. She's always dreamed of seeing mountains, so I thought this would be a chance for her to do that. Besides, I want someone to keep me company while you men go hunting. I have no desire to hunt, camp, or ride horses through the mountains."

"Of course I don't mind," he said. "I told you the invitation was good for as many guests as you wished to bring. But I'll keep you company during the hunt. I don't plan to go, either. I haven't enjoyed hunting for several years now."

"Oh, that's right," said Charlotte. "I remember you telling me. I just thought…"

"Here's my car. Let's get your bags in. Oh, excuse me," he added. "I'd better see to introductions first."

He joined the other men and Elizabeth at Burt's car, parked next to his. Burt had seen Eddie wave to Clarence. Once this helped him identify his guests, he had greeted the men. They were all talking jovially.

"I must tell you, Eddie," Howard said, "I would have come much sooner had I realized when Charlotte told me about your wedding present what hunting lodge you invited us to visit. I'd imagined some rustic little cabin hidden in the mountains. Sir Rigall's lodge has been written up in major magazines! Teddy Roosevelt called it the best little getaway in the world in several interviews. I'd no idea this was the lodge mentioned in your invitation until the commissioner pointed that out to me at our poker game one evening. He recognized the name. I felt very foolish, then, for not having taken advantage of your generous gift immediately. Once these gentlemen learned of the invitation, they gave me no choice. Is it true you have a waiting list of at least five years for expeditions? And demand the highest prices of any lodge in America?"

"Eddie had lots to do with that," nodded Rigall. "If it weren't for him, this place might not exist. The hunting parties were originally his idea. He started the whole enterprise. I just bought him out so he could go sow wild oats with the rodeo."

"Eddie's a modest young man," said Clarence. "It surprised me when the commissioner pointed out just where the invitation was to. I made sure Howard knew then I intended to take advantage of your kind gift with or without him. The governor and the commissioner felt they had to invite themselves along, of course."

"I haven't considered the passenger arrangements back," said Rigall as he opened his trunk. "Perhaps the newlyweds would like to ride in the more comfortable car?" He pointed at his large sedan.

"I already put my things in Eddie's car," said Charlotte, who had quietly joined the group. "That will be fine. Papa can—"

"I'll ride back with Eddie and the ladies," said Elizabeth, as if picking up some subtle cue in Charlotte's voice. "Burt can amuse the men with his hunting stories while we have a scenic, relaxed tour of the town without discussing dead deer."

Eddie met her eyes and nodded gratefully, not quite sure why. After a few more introductions and small talk about the length of the journey, they piled into the two vehicles for the journey, well over an hour by car, back to the lodge. Elizabeth and Mrs. Farnsworth climbed into the back of Eddie's car; Charlotte sat comfortably at his side, admiring the leather bucket seats he had cleaned and polished with such care the evening before. It seemed so natural to have her there. He tried to keep himself from reaching for her hand, a motion that happened of its own accord, as if his arm wasn't under his control.

There was so much he wanted to say and yet nothing to say. Elizabeth saved him the trouble of trying to speak by keeping up a running banter befitting the best of tour guides. She pointed out the various sights they passed and summarized the history of the region. She included personal stories of some of the early settlers, along with information about climate, wildlife, agriculture, and government.

"You certainly know this place well," Charlotte complimented her. "Have you lived here your whole life?"

"Oh, no," said Elizabeth. "I was born in Toronto. I moved here when I was about your age, Charlotte."

"Elizabeth was my teacher," said Eddie. "I know I've told you about her. She taught me everything worth knowing there is."

"Oh!" said Charlotte. "I didn't realize…you are Miss Welch?"

Elizabeth laughed. "Not for a very long time. I'm Mrs. Rigall now, thanks to Eddie. He saved my life once, you know. Did he ever tell you about that?"

"Yes, he did. You were lost in a snowstorm, and he found you. I remember him telling me… It must have been very frightening."

"Not really. I don't remember most of it. But I am very glad he found me. Eddie, why don't you drive by your ranch, and stop at the old schoolhouse? I'm sure Charlotte would like to see those places. I'm sure you've told her about them, too." *I'm sure you've told her everything of importance in your life,* Elizabeth seemed to be saying by her tone.

They took their time driving back, stopping by the stream at the ranch first, then a store in town where Elizabeth bought a few supplies, including some bubble bath and scented lotion she gave to Charlotte. "This will relax you after your long train ride. I'm sure you would give anything for a nice, hot bath right now. As soon as we get you settled into the honeymoon cabin, that is exactly what you shall have. Burt and I," she added, "were the first residents in that honeymoon cabin after Eddie's father and his crew built it." Elizabeth didn't go into that story, though; she didn't really want to think of it herself, and was surprised she even mentioned it. Talking of her rescue from the snowstorm must have brought back the memory.

They stopped at the old schoolhouse, now used as a kindergarten. Eventually, they arrived at Waterton Lakes. Charlotte caught her breath. "How beautiful!" she said. "What a beautiful place. Oh, Eddie, I can see why you wanted to come back here now. I…" She didn't finish the thought, feeling she had perhaps already touched on a subject she should not speak about.

"It looks like the men are at the main lodge," said Elizabeth. "Choosing their weapons, no doubt. Let me help Charlotte get settled in for that bath, Eddie. I'll be along in a bit. Take Mrs. Farnsworth up to room five in the main building. I'm sure Burt already has other room assignments sorted out."

Eddie carried Charlotte's bag in. As he left, he reached out and took her hand again. "I'm so glad you are here after all these years. This is so much nicer than letters, though those are very nice. I just wish…"

She squeezed his hand. "I do, too, Eddie" she said simply, as if completing the thought he couldn't quite permit himself to finish. "I do, too."

Steve Durham had arrived by the time Eddie entered the main lodge. They greeted each other warmly. The men were all laughing happily like old friends as they drank brandy and admired the antlers and stuffed hides on display from Burt's many successful expeditions. They seemed to have gotten a second wind after their journey and were already happily planning an early start in the morning. "Sure you won't change your mind and join us, Eddie?" asked Steve. "This young man is probably the best tracker there is, next to Chief," he told the others. "He has a sixth sense about animals. I don't know what got into him to make him give up the sport."

Eddie shrugged. "It's not a sport to me any longer," he said. "Like you said, Steve, I have a sixth sense about it, so there's no challenge. I don't like killing."

"Killing!" said the governor. "You sound so melodramatic! It's hunting young man, not murder. Quite a difference, I'd say! Here I thought this was a wedding gift you gave so you could enjoy it, too. Certainly what would have been in my mind to do."

"Ah, well," said Burt. "There will be more game for us, that's all. Eddie's acquired an overactive conscience, decided man and the animal kingdom are at war, and become a conscientious objector. Those of us who aren't crack shots have a chance now. Let's toast to world peace! Where are the ladies?"

"Elizabeth's helping Charlotte get settled in. Then she'll go down to the restaurant to make sure everything is set for dinner. She'll meet us here. I left Mrs. Farnsworth in suite five; she plans to nap until dinnertime. Your wife said you'd get these gentleman sorted into rooms."

"That I will," said Burt. "That I will. But first, another brandy. Will you join us, Eddie?"

This time, they toasted the newlyweds. "We aren't exactly newlyweds any longer," corrected Howard. "We've been married over a year."

"Howard, Howard, if I had a bride as pretty as Charlotte, we would stay newlyweds forever!" joked Doug Farnsworth. "You work too hard, my boy. I'm glad we all twisted your arm to take this hunting trip. You need to get your nose out of the stocks and bonds occasionally. That Harvard education has made you much too serious, I'm afraid."

After they finished their drinks, Burt showed them to their rooms, asking Eddie to take Howard back to the honeymoon cabin. They agreed to meet in the restaurant in three hours. Elizabeth arrived just as they were leaving. "Charlotte's taking a hot bath," she told them, "and then she plans to sleep until dinner."

"If that's the case," said Howard, "I won't disturb her. She needs her rest. Eddie, would you mind taking me into town for a newspaper?"

"I'll do that, Howard," said Elizabeth. "Eddie needs to bring his parents here for dinner." Eddie was relieved. He had been very uncomfortable, inexplicably, with the thought of being alone with Howard. He had never known him well, and wouldn't really know what to say.

Later that evening, they all gathered for dinner in the elegant restaurant next to the main lodge. Burt and Elizabeth had opened it two years before, bringing a fine chef from Paris and a maître d' trained in New York City. Eddie arrived with his parents and the Chief just as the group was being seated at the large mahogany table in the special dining room reserved for hunting parties on the night before expeditions. Tiffany lamps spread multi-colored light across the somber room, decorated much like a British gentleman's club. Eddie and his family took this room for granted; they had helped build it and ate here often. The guests, though, were obviously impressed with their surroundings. The governor let out a low whistle. "This," he said, "is the life!"

"Just remember the next time I ask a favor," Howard told him.

"I'm sure you won't let me forget. As I see it, you still owe me for that stand on segregation of housing and schools I took before the last election. I'm still not quite sure how you convinced me it was for the good of the state and what the people wanted."

"It was," retorted Howard. "Look at all the new people who've moved in since. Look at the money they brought with them. You may not agree it is connected with that decision, but I surely do. You haven't had much trouble convincing the voters, either."

"No politics tonight, please, Howard!" said the commissioner. "Let's just enjoy our meal and have a good night's rest free of the heartburn your discussions always bring. Sir Rigall, I seem to remember reading about a voyage you went on to South America to catalogue plants and animals. Tell me, how many new species did you find yourself?"

Rigall, a fine conversationalist, entertained the group with his stories of adventure for the rest of the evening. Eddie listened absently; he had heard these stories many times before. His eyes frequently drifted to Charlotte, seated at the far end of the table. She looked lovely, as always. She wore a loose-fitting cream-colored gown, decorated with a stunning emerald brooch near the high neckline. Her hair was pinned up, piled high on her head. She spoke little, barely touching her food. Her father sat at her elbow, protective as always. "You eat like a bird, daughter," Eddie heard him say. "You need to keep your strength up, pet. I knew it wasn't a good idea for you to come now, given your condition."

"Nonsense, father," she said. "I couldn't very well not enjoy my own wedding present, could I? I'm just a bit tired from the journey. I'll be fine."

Eddie wondered if she'd been ill. He would ask tomorrow. After the others had departed for a week in Jasper, he planned to spend every possible minute with Charlotte. If she wasn't well, he would change his plans for hiking to the waterfalls and boating on the lake. They could just as easily drink tea at the lodge and chat or drive through the countryside. He looked forward to the time they would have together, remembering how easy it had always been to talk to her and how comfortable he felt in her presence. He ignored the fact that he didn't feel very comfortable at present.

Dinner ended. "I knew you would all want to rest tonight, so I will save the band and the dancing for after our venture, when you celebrate your success," Rigall announced. "Nightcaps, for those interested, upstairs in the main lodge. We'll meet for breakfast at 7am sharp. Be ready to depart. I'll have gear ready; just bring warm clothing and good walking boots. We'll go by jeep to Jasper, and pick up horses at the stable there."

"Lord," said the governor, "times have changed. I used to ride nearly every day; now it's been nearly ten years since I've been on a horse!"

"Riding lessons are extra." Burt laughed. "But our horses are very gentle and well trained. Most of my customers have similar sentiments, Governor. You know, when Eddie and I first began this enterprise, there were no automobiles. We used a wagon. It took us three days to reach Jasper. Now there's a paved road nearly all the way. I've certainly seen lots of change in my lifetime, gentleman. We all have."

"You'll see more, boys," said the commissioner. "You'll see more. Why, the way the economy is going and industry is developing with help from science—Eddie, you'll be going to the moon when you are my age the way I'm going to Canada now. Hard to imagine how small this world is becoming. Hard to imagine it, for sure."

Charlotte walked back to the cabin with Eddie, his parents and the Chief while Howard stayed at the lodge for a nightcap. He enjoyed this chance to introduce her to his family. They accepted her warmly. "It's so nice to finally meet you, child," Papa told her. "I hope we'll see more of you over the next few days. There's a little carnival setting up down at the rodeo grounds later this week. Games and fortunetellers. A little band of gypsies. Maybe we can all go together."

"Liam has a weak spot for gypsies," explained Mama. "I'm the scientist of the family."

Charlotte smiled. "Yes, I have heard you are a wonderful nurse. Still, I've never met a gypsy before. That sounds very pleasant, Mr. McCauslin."

"Good, it's decided, then," he said. "On Thursday, Eddie can bring you over for one of Mother's wonderful dinners before we visit the gypsies together. I think it's time Eddie got his fortune told!"

"I make my own fortunes, Papa," Eddie said. "You know that."

"Make 'em, and lose 'em, too," chided Chief.

When they reached the cabin, Eddie opened the door for Charlotte. Before stepping through, they embraced each other, just as they had when saying goodnight for the evening in Topeka so long ago. Charlotte felt warm and natural in his arms. He found it difficult to release her as he kissed her on the forehead.

"Goodnight, Charlotte," he whispered. "I am so glad you are here."

"Me, too," she answered softly. "At least, I think I am." He noticed her eyes appeared moist, but decided it was moonlight reflecting on the blue and violet hues, so unusually bright. "Will you see me tomorrow?"

"Oh, yes," he assured her. "I'll be here before noon. I'm sure Elizabeth will bring you some breakfast in the morning. Sleep well and eat hearty. Tomorrow, if you feel like it, we'll walk around the lake and I'll show you the waterfalls."

"I'd like that," she said as she stepped inside, quietly closing the door behind her. He drove the family home, looking forward to morning.

CHAPTER TWELVE

HALF A PENNY

"I'm so unhappy, Eddie! I know I've brought it upon myself. But I just don't know what to do." She buried her head in her hands. Eddie held her, rocking her gently in his arms as he would an infant. He watched her tears fall, feeling helpless and trying to understand how their happy afternoon had ended like this.

Eddie had arrived at the lodge well before noon. He joined Elizabeth and Charlotte for tea and muffins. The two women were talking companionably, as if they had known each other their entire lives. "Elizabeth is like the older sister I always wanted!" Charlotte exclaimed when he arrived.

"Much, much older" added Elizabeth. "More like an aunt, I suspect. What are the two of you planning to do today?"

"I thought I'd take Charlotte up to the falls," said Eddie. "It's a beautiful trail, especially now the leaves are changing. Would you like to join us?"

"I wish I could! But I do have a lodge to run, you know. We have a few other guests coming in today, and a party at the restaurant this evening. Now that Burt's off chasing elk and wildcat, someone needs to keep an eye on things." She sighed. "But I'll make some sandwiches for you to take along for a picnic. The trail isn't too difficult. Just go slowly, Eddie, and help her over the rough spots. She needs to take it easy in her condition."

Eddie raised his eyebrows questioningly. "What condition? Have you been ill, Charlotte?"

"Oh, no, not at all. I guess I never mentioned it yesterday. I thought you would notice from these awful smocks I'm wearing. I'm going to have a baby."

Eddie was shocked. "You are?" he said bluntly. "You don't look pregnant. When?"

"You are too kind," she replied. "I know I must look awful. The baby is due in March. I'm about three months along."

"I was telling Charlotte your mother delivered most of the babies in this province for years, until the hospitals and clinics were built just in the last decade," Elizabeth said. "You should ask her to check Charlotte over when you take her out to your place, just to make sure everything is okay after the trip," she added. "It certainly was brave of her to come all this way."

"Papa was worried, but I told him it was silly. I'm young and healthy. I don't like being treated like an invalid."

"I'm surprised Howard allowed it," said Eddie. "If it was me, I would have postponed the trip until…"

"Until after the baby was born?" She laughed. "Good heavens, then I never would have been able to come. No, it was I who insisted on doing it now, while I could still join the group. I wanted to see your home, Eddie. Once the baby is born, I won't be traveling for quite awhile."

Maybe, Eddie thought, this baby was the explanation for Charlotte's tears now. Although he never noticed any difference in his mother when she had been pregnant, he'd heard women in this state sometimes became overemotional and moody. Maybe the walk had exerted her too much. Her tears puzzled him.

It seemed she'd been enjoying the afternoon. He told her the names of all the trees and plants as they wound up the hill toward the waterfalls that fed the lake. He still remembered this from his days in the woods with Chief. He'd even shared some of the stories Chief told him about how the various plants had been created. He'd told her about rebuilding the engine on his car. He'd recounted the typical chores of his days and summarized two books he read recently. The last hour had been filled with conversation. He enjoyed talking to Charlotte as much as he always had, and it was a treat to have her company all to himself for the afternoon. Then, as they'd approached the clearing where the first view of the falls was visible, he realized he had been monopolizing the conversation. "So how's Rosie?" he asked, knowing she usually loved to talk about her friends. "You haven't mentioned her in your letters for some time. Does she have any more children? What has she been doing?"

"I don't know," Charlotte had answered. "I don't see her much anymore. I don't see anyone much anymore." Then, she had begun to cry. Eddie stopped and spread a blanket he'd brought on the ground. "Hey, hey," he said. "Let's rest for a while."

She continued to cry and he held her, wondering what to say. "What's wrong, Charlotte?" he finally asked. "It can't be that bad. Do you want to talk about it?" Now, as the falls gurgled in the background, the birds sang and the sun shone brightly down on her auburn hair on this lovely autumn day, she was pouring her heart out to Eddie as she told him how unhappy she was.

He learned that, since marrying Howard, she had become isolated from her friends. "I don't want my wife around niggers," Howard told her. She ignored him at first. Then, he began getting angry with her. Upon finding out she visited Rosie or Linda or Mrs. Belson, he would lose his temper and strike her. This angered Eddie. He found it inexcusable for a man to strike any woman, no matter what the circumstances. She had brushed his protests aside, telling him that she could accept that.

"He works so hard. I know he's very unhappy, too. I should have more respect for his wishes. He doesn't mean it."

The worst of it, she said, was that he had begun to harm her friends. He financed a new hotel for "white folks" that took away much of the Bellflower's business. He'd publicly spoken out against the Browns as 'rabble rousers who upset our fine community' when Mose questioned new funding policies that gave less resources to the black school even though it had more students. Howard told her it was because she insisted on seeing her friends against his wishes that he punished them. It had become an all out war between the African-American community, who were filing cases with the help of the NAACP and other organizations to protest the segregation of housing and education, and Howard, with the influence he exerted over politicians and business. She was tired of it, and felt like one of the victims.

"I know I shouldn't have married Howard," she continued. "I guess I always knew it. I didn't love him. I—oh, I might as well say it. It doesn't matter any longer, anyway. I love you, Eddie. But you made it plain you wouldn't be coming back and didn't want to marry me. So I decided it was the best thing for me to do. I—I knew I wasn't going to be a famous pianist, after all. I'd outgrown that dream. I didn't want to be an old maid. I wanted a family. I wanted father to be proud of me. It just seemed like it was the best thing to do." She wrung her hands. "But after a few months, I realized that I would have been better off an old maid than married to Howard. He can be so cruel. Part of it really is my fault, I know. He senses I don't love him. That makes him jealous and unhappy. What I did was very unfair. I know that now." She stopped, pulling away from Eddie and straightening her back. She clutched at the blanket. "I didn't realize it at the time, but I know now it was wrong, and I'm to blame for it."

Eddie watched in silence, waiting for her to go on. He felt her pain. *Oh, Charlotte,* he wanted to say. *I loved you, too. Didn't you know that? Couldn't you tell? God, I still do!* He couldn't bring himself to say it. What good could it do now? "I'm sorry," was all he said.

"Oh, don't be," she continued. "It's my own fault. I brought this on myself. Once I realized how hopeless it was, how our marriage was just going to make us both unhappy, I decided I was going to divorce Howard. I knew it would be hard on father, that it would create a scandal. But I knew it was the only way. It was

better for him as well as for me. It would be better for both of us."
She shook her head and laughed bitterly. "Then, when I finally
decided that's what I'd do, I found out I was pregnant. That made
everything different."

"How did it make things different?" asked Eddie.

"Don't you see?" she exclaimed, as if talking to an idiot. "I had
to think of my child first! My child deserved to grow up with the
natural father. I could bring disgrace on myself, but not on my
child. Surely you see that, Eddie! So now I am trapped. I have
to be a good wife to Howard, even though I think he is a vicious
man and I don't believe in any of the things he does. Staying with
him is the only honorable thing I can do, for my child's sake. I
have no friends anymore, except you. Rosie and Linda practically
disowned me when I married Howard, and they certainly have
by now, with good reason. I can't let Papa know how I feel. It
would break his heart. The letters you send me are like a lifeline.
The letters I write to you are my one chance to be myself, to talk
to a friend. Until my child is born, I have no life. I wanted to
come here so much once I learned about the baby. I just had to
see you, to talk to you, to be comforted by the one friend I have
in the world. But I didn't know it would hurt so much to see you.
I didn't know that…" She was sobbing again, and trembling.

"Oh, Charlotte," he said. "What a mess we've made of our
lives. What a mess."

She looked at him, puzzled. "I have, Eddie," she said. "You
haven't. You have what you wanted. You are back here in a beautiful place with your family. You don't want to marry—you told me
that many years ago, and again recently in a letter. You've always
done what you wanted. You are honest and kind. I made a mess
of my life, but you had nothing to do with that."

He stroked her hair. "But I did," he lamented. "I did. I was
blind. I just didn't see what you were telling me in your letters.
I didn't listen to my heart." He pulled her close again. "I do love

you, Charlotte. I always have. I always will. I should've told you long ago."

Inexplicably, that revelation stopped her tears. First, she seemed shocked. Then, she laughed happily. "You do, Eddie? Do you really? That's wonderful! That's amazing! That's more than I could ever hope…" She stopped and looked at him. "It doesn't make much difference, does it? I still need to think of my child. I still need to be a good wife to Howard. Except now I know you love me. Since I know, I can face anything that comes."

He realized as he held her in his arms near the waterfall she was right. It made no difference now to either of them, except that they knew of their love for each other and they also knew they would put others before their love. He realized that was part of why he did love her. She accepted responsibility for her actions, sometimes even beyond what was created by her own actions. She considered the effects her actions would have on others. He had those qualities, too—at least, he hoped he did. "Just promise me one thing," he said. "When you go back to raise your family, promise me you still will play the piano. Promise me you will give concerts and write music. That's your special gift to the world. Don't give that up."

"Okay." Her voice whispered of sadness and longing. "I haven't given a concert for a long time. Howard says it's silly since I don't need to earn a living. But you are right. I should. It will help me get through. I promise you, Eddie. I will start to play again."

They sat together in the clearing in silence until Charlotte's mood lightened again, then climbed to where the falls began to cascade down the hill. They splashed each other and laughed as they tried to drink the fresh, rushing water. After their picnic, they gave remains to the squirrels scurrying up to take pieces of bread from their hands. They enjoyed a slow, leisurely stroll back to the lodge where Elizabeth greeted them with tea and cookies. Eddie left just after sunset, arranging to pick Charlotte up the following afternoon for dinner at his house and a trip to the carnival his father wanted to attend.

After he left, Elizabeth stayed talking with Charlotte. "You had a pleasant afternoon?" she asked.

"Very pleasant," said Charlotte dreamily. "The best afternoon I've had for many, many years." Elizabeth looked at her sharply.

"Excuse me for prying," she said, "but you love him, don't you?"

Charlotte's eyes barely registered surprise. "It is that obvious, isn't it? Do you suppose anyone else has noticed? Yes. I love him. And he loves me. And that is all that matters, even though we live a continent apart and may never be together again. That's all that matters."

"Two philosophers," said Elizabeth gently. "You are as bad as he is. And, yes," she added, "it is quite obvious. I think others have noticed. Be careful, child. Be careful. But don't give up. Life can be full of surprises. Let me tell you my story."

She spent the rest of the evening telling Charlotte about how she and Burt met, and the many long years of desperation before they, at last, were married. "The funny thing is," she finished, "as painful as all of the waiting was, I don't think I regret it. Because it took so long for us to finally get it right, because of all the challenges, I think I value our relationship more. I think it truly lets me believe that love does, eventually, conquer all obstacles. Eddie means a lot to me, Charlotte. I hope true love will conquer all of the obstacles the two of you face, too."

Charlotte smiled a radiant smile and squeezed her hand. "Thank you so much," she said. "I am very glad I came. After talking to Eddie today, and to you, I remember what it is like to be happy. I remember what it is like to dream. I think I'll call Professor Rubenstein when I get home and arrange another piano tour. If the critics liked making a fuss over the fact that I was a young, beautiful woman last time, they should really enjoy commenting on my pregnancy this time! Thanks so much, Elizabeth. I'm ready to take on the world again!"

Elizabeth laughed. "That wasn't quite the response I expected," she said, "but good luck! You may get to begin your tour early, too. I probably shouldn't spoil the surprise if he hasn't told you yet, but I know Eddie was hoping you would give a concert while you were here. He's arranged something at one of the churches next week, I think. You might want to ask him about it tomorrow. You might like to practice a little. There's a piano here in the lounge you are welcome to use anytime."

Charlotte's smile grew even brighter. "Oh, thank you!" she said. Then, she excused herself and played the piano for the rest of the evening. Elizabeth finally interrupted her with a glass of milk and a light snack, suggesting she might want to get some rest. "You have a busy day tomorrow," she reminded her, "and your body does require more food and sleep than usual right now."

"Oh, yes," said Charlotte absently. "You are right, of course." She ate and allowed Elizabeth to walk with her back to the cabin. "Thanks again," she said, squeezing her hand as she said goodnight. "Thanks for everything. I'll see you in the morning."

The young woman who greeted Elizabeth in the morning seemed completely changed. Her face had lost its pallor and her cheeks were rosy. Her smile was bright and her eyes sparkled. There was a bounce in her step. She ate her breakfast with gusto and then headed happily to the piano. Elizabeth listened to her melodies. Some she recognized as well-known classical pieces and contemporary works by Russian composers. Others she did not recognize, but these were strikingly beautiful. There was no doubt Charlotte had talent. Elizabeth remembered concerts she attended in Toronto many years ago. Charlotte was better than the masters she'd heard play; she was sure of that. When Eddie arrived a few hours later, Charlotte was still playing. He stood and watched her for several minutes, struck by the graceful way her hands sailed across the keys, a sort of poetry in motion. He closed his eyes to listen to her music, full of sadness and joy. She noticed him as she finished, smiled, and began playing "Rose

Garden Medley," the song he remembered so well from that long-ago afternoon when he first heard her play.

"See," she told him after finishing, "I always keep my promises!" She jumped up from the piano bench, embraced him and kissed his cheek.

He noticed the change in her demeanor. "You look rested."

"This place is good for me. I feel so much better now, finally at peace. I was beginning to wonder about those tales of how a baby makes a woman feel happy and beautiful, but I guess they're true."

"I certainly agree," said Eddie. "I thought it was impossible for you to be any more beautiful, but today you are glowing. Sparkling."

"I hear you have a concert planned for me?" she teased. "I really shouldn't be the last to know these things, you know. When am I playing?"

Eddie looked at Elizabeth. "It's impossible to keep any secrets around here, isn't it? Well, only if you agree, but I thought next Wednesday, when everyone has returned from hunting, you could perform for a small group at the Catholic Community Center. I'm sure your father would want to hear you. I have notices ready. I haven't posted them yet, of course, but if you agree..."

"Let's start posting them!" She laughed. "I think the town should have at least a week's notice. I am accustomed to having a large audience, you know! We can do that today, if we have time. You can show me your hometown while I help you."

Eddie was delighted. She seemed happy and energetic. "Sure, we have time. Mama won't be expecting us until late afternoon. I can show you the town while we post the notices. Would you like to join us, Elizabeth?"

"I wish I could," she answered. "But you know I need to be here. Will you be late?"

"Probably. We'll go to the carnival after dinner. Just leave the key with Charlotte and I'll see she gets safely back to the cabin. You don't need to wait up."

SHERRI MCCARTHY

They spent the afternoon posting notices at the various shops and bulletin boards in town after going by the church to confirm the date. They also informed the newspaper and the local radio station. Eddie knew everyone in town. They all greeted him warmly and seemed delighted to meet Charlotte. The reception she received assured her the concert would be well attended.

Later in the afternoon, they arrived at the ranch. Delicious scents were coming from the house. "Mmm," said Eddie. "Mama's making berry pie, and we'll surely have homemade ice cream with that! And I smell her special chicken and mushroom casserole. You are in for a treat. Let me show you the place, first."

She walked with him to the stables, which he had described to her in such detail years ago when he told her about Redwing. They visited the garden he had spent so much time tending as a child. She saw the chickens and turkeys. They walked to the stream where he'd fetched water before his father installed indoor plumbing. They strolled through the meadow scattered with the last of the late-summer flowers, and looked at the expanse of trees that had not yet been cleared. "There were more trees when I was a boy," Eddie explained. "The wood for most of Papa's projects came from this land."

Charlotte enjoyed seeing where he had grown up. "It's just as you described it to me," she said. "I feel like I've already been here."

You have already been here, he thought. *With me, in my heart. With every breath I took. You've always been here with me. I just didn't know it until now.* He led her around the scattered auto parts from Chief's latest projects, and into the house. "Hi, Mama," he called. "I'll show Charlotte the rest of the house and then we'll come to the kitchen and help you."

"No need," answered Joanna McCauslin. "I have everything well in hand. Your father and Chief should be here soon. We'll eat early and head down to the rodeo grounds for that carnival your father is so keen to attend."

Eddie led her through the house, first showing her his room and then the rooms his sisters had shared, which were now used for guests. The upstairs room his brothers had shared now belonged to Chief. He'd moved in with the McCauslins a few years ago to be closer to the gas station. A small library upstairs had floor-to-ceiling shelves filled with books, and there was a large bathroom complete with toilet, tub, and shower that had been added recently. His parents' room and another bathroom were downstairs, along with a beautifully decorated formal dining room, a living room with a large fireplace, a breakfast nook, and the kitchen. His father had made a few changes and modernized the house, but it was not too different from the home he had grown up in. Charlotte recognized it from his descriptions. "This was a nice place to grow up," he told her, as if reading her thoughts.

Chief and Papa arrived while they were helping Johanna set the table. She brought out the good china and her best lace tablecloth. "This is quite the occasion," she joked. "Eddie's never brought a girl home before!"

"Mama," he said, "I'm over thirty, and Charlotte is married! That's hardly appropriate."

She laughed. "Just makes it all the more special. You've never done the expected, anyway, Eddie. Not in your whole life. No reason to expect you to now. And, whatever the circumstances, I like this young lady very much." She smiled at Charlotte. "You're rested, my dear. Good. You look much better! I was beginning to worry about you looking so wan. I was ready to pull out my medical kit and examine you before dinner if you were still peaked. I'm glad that won't be necessary."

They had a pleasant dinner, followed by pie and ice cream. It reminded Eddie of the dinners Mama cooked when he was a boy and Papa returned after months away from home. He almost felt as if they should be about to settle down by the fire for a night of storytelling. He realized, suddenly, that his father hadn't been much older than he was now when he told those stories. By the time Liam was in his early thirties, Eddie and most of his brothers and sisters had already been born. This house had been built. He'd been building railroads and coming home to tell his family stories around the fire, after crossing an ocean and a continent to find his sister. Eddie shook his head. Here he was, without a family and without a career. He felt a chill. His life was passing him by without his notice, without him bothering to live it. Still, he had the sense that something was waiting for him ahead, around the corner just out of sight. He'd find it soon. He only hoped Charlotte would be a part of what he found.

With everyone's help, the dishes were cleared away and washed quickly. "Let's go to the carnival!" said Papa. "Will we all fit in your car, Eddie?"

"Sure," he said. They piled in and drove to the rodeo grounds.

"It doesn't seem like very long ago we came to these grounds and watched Eddie win a championship," said Liam. "Has he ever told you about his days with the rodeo, Charlotte?"

"He's mentioned them."

"I'll bet he never told you about that first time. He was barely thirteen, and had this beautiful, wild, cantankerous little horse Chief gave him. No one in the world could ride that horse but Eddie. And he rode her better than the national champion rode his horse at that barrel race!" Liam went on, in his best storytelling form, to describe the night Eddie won the competition. As they sat in the car listening to his narration. Eddie found he enjoyed listening to his father describe that night from long ago. He had the odd sensation he was watching himself, or someone he had once been, ride Redwing around the arena they looked at. Instead of the brightly colored tents and booths now scattered across the field, he saw the barrels, and the cheering crowd, and his lovely little horse prancing at the gate, ready to propel him into his life. Dear Redwing. He fought back tears as he remembered his beloved horse and all they had shared. He knew she had ended her life peacefully at the Pearson's orchards. He hadn't thought of her for years. But he missed her now. He shook his head slightly. He hadn't felt so many emotions in such a short period of time since—well, since the last time he had been with Charlotte seven years ago. It was making him feel restless, making him question his life.

"You really are a wonderful storyteller, Mr. McCauslin," Charlotte said as they climbed out of the car and walked toward the carnival. "Eddie wasn't exaggerating at all when he told me how wonderful your stories were to listen to."

Liam beamed. "Mine may be good, lass, but not as good as the gypsy tales! Did Eddie ever tell you what the gypsies told me?" With that, he was off on another tale, recalling the fortune that predicted he would find his sister, with the help of potatoes and bread. "Now," he said, finishing as they approached the dark tent of a fortune-teller, "let's see what the gypsies have to say today, shall we?"

"Chances are, if whatever someone says is general enough, it can come true," chided Johanna. "Or we make whatever is said come true. Our own belief creates the situation predicted. There's no great mystery in this. I think I'll save my money for one of the pretty glass animals that woman is selling." She pointed toward a table where a young girl sat with several hand-painted glass animals spread out before her.

"Hush, Mother," said Liam. "Life is a great mystery, whether you believe it or not. The gypsies know how to look just a little more ahead and around the corners than you do, that's all. But if you would rather have one of those little blue chickens, that's fine with us. Now, children, where shall we go? Here's a crystal ball reader in this tent, or the cards over here. Maybe a palm reader? C'mon, Chief; let's see what our hands say to this old woman."

"I think I'll try this one," said Charlotte, pointing to a small black tent with a placard outside that said "I talk to the dead. Sister Grace, medium." A large, dark woman with haunting eyes, wrapped in a purple shawl, sat outside the tent. It was hard to tell if she was African, Indian, Mexican, or some combination of all three. She had a broad face and iron-grey hair, woven into a thick braid. The area near her was empty.

"Haven't seen her here before," said Liam. "Well, go ahead. Tell us what the dead are chatting about this evening."

Charlotte and Eddie walked over to the dark tent. Sister Grace nodded as they approached and motioned Eddie inside. "You first," she said. "I have a message for you. Got it as soon as you arrived." He shrugged his shoulders, looked at Charlotte, and stepped inside. "Okay," he said, settled in the dark tent. "Who is the message from?"

"Don't know," said Sister Gracie. "No one I know. You'll have to figure that out. Pretty young woman who says to thank you for the promise. Says she wants her life to count. Says you better get busy!"

"Is that all?" asked Eddie.

The medium shrugged. "That and the usual things. She's happy. She loves you." The woman watched his face. "Know who it is?"

Eddie shook his head. "I have no idea. I can't think of any pretty young women I've made promises to lately. I try not to make that a habit!" He laughed.

"Maybe she wasn't a young woman when you made the promise," the medium said. "These folks can look however they want after they leave this earth. Maybe she was an old woman. A grandmother."

Or a baby, thought Eddie. *Maybe she was a baby.* He felt a chill run up his spine and the flesh on his arms prickled, hairs standing on end. He remembered Baby Flo. He hadn't thought of her for many years.

"Want me to tell her anything?" asked Sister Grace. "Want me to ask anything? Sometimes they answer."

"Ask her if she means the promise I made near the tree," he said. "Tell her I haven't forgotten. Tell her I keep my promises."

"She's nodding," said the woman. "She knows."

A little shaken, Eddie paid and left the tent. Charlotte was outside, waiting her turn. She stepped inside, leaving Eddie to wait and remember a day long ago near the Old General. A day when he was questioning his life as much as he had been lately, trying to make sense of it. Trying to make it count.

Charlotte came out a few minutes later, looking a little puzzled. "Who was your message from?" asked Eddie. "Your mother?"

"You knew that's what I was hoping for, didn't you?" she replied. "But these are just carnival games. It didn't make any sense, really. Should I tell you?"

"If you like," said Eddie. "I'm curious. I'd be interested in hearing it."

"It wasn't much of a message, really. There was a young man who looked very sad. He said 'Mother, I love you. I must go away. I am very sorry. But I will be back, and these are for you until I return.' Then he handed Sister Grace a bouquet of roses to give me, and disappeared before I could ask any questions. She said that, since I don't have any children, the message might have been for someone else. Maybe someone I know. Lots of young men who were killed in the war come through with messages like that, she said. Sometimes, they'll just give them to anyone and hope they get through." She shook her head. "I don't know. It probably doesn't mean anything. She probably just made it up."

"Maybe," said Eddie. "I guess we'll never know. Let's find Chief and my parents." They found them at the table, looking at small painted animals. "How's your fortune, Papa?" asked Eddie.

His father laughed. "Well, now, if I told you it might not come true! Can't just be randomly sharing fortunes now, can we? Might upset Mother."

"Liam will only tell us if it does come true," said Johanna. "That's his strategy. He forgets all the ones that don't. Here, Charlotte," she added. "This is for you. I thought you would like it." She handed her a small, white ceramic lamb with a rose in its mouth.

They stayed at the carnival for the remainder of the evening. Eddie dropped his parents and Chief at home first, then drove Charlotte back to the cabin. The lights were off in the main lodge, indicating Elizabeth was already asleep. He walked in with her and sat down on the sofa. "Ready for your concert?" he asked.

"No; I have lots of practicing ahead" she said. "Elizabeth has a piano here I can use, fortunately, although I'd like to try the one in the church soon, too. Can you take me there tomorrow or the next day?"

"Sure. What else would you like to see? I hoped to take you horseback riding, up toward Banff, but that probably isn't such a good idea, considering..." He patted her tummy. "We could drive part way up, into the park, though. Would you like that?"

"I would. Eddie, I'll enjoy anything, as long as you are with me."

They talked a few minutes longer until he told her goodnight. She walked to the door with him, and they embraced. It felt natural to hold her near. He found it difficult to let go. The remainder of their time together seemed to pass far too quickly. Suddenly, the night of the concert arrived. The hunters had returned the previous afternoon with elk, moose, and a small mountain cougar. They seemed tired, but pleased with their trophies. Charlotte was scheduled to play tonight at the community center. The following evening would be a celebration dinner at the lodge with live music, dancing, and several more guests. They would board the train for their return journey the afternoon afterward.

At the concert, Eddie sat in the front row next to his parents and Charlotte's father. The recreation center was full; there were over one hundred people in the audience. Charlotte, poised and beautiful in a pale silver gown, walked across the small stage and introduced herself to the audience. She informed the crowd she was trained by one of the best Russian pianists in the world. She told them she had toured the USA twice, playing in major cities from the east to the west coasts, but more recently had confined her performances to the Midwest. This would be her first perform-ance in Canada. The pieces she would play included Beethoven's Moonlight Sonata, Rachmaninoff's Second Concerto and two of her own compositions. She would pause for a short break after each.

Eddie felt such pride as he watched her. She was assured and professional throughout her performance. She played flawlessly, and with such emotion that many of the members of the audi-ence were moved to tears, her father included. "She belongs on the stage," he whispered at one point, during a pause between songs. "She is so natural at the piano, such a talented performer."

"She belongs at home," replied Howard, who sat next to him. "Especially now that we will have a child. I hope she's enjoy-ing herself, but not getting any more grandiose ideas. This is her last performance."

Eddie felt himself tense up at this comment. How could Howard so easily deny her the opportunity to pursue what was clearly her passion? He thought better of responding, although he felt like telling Howard he was a selfish pig to stop her. It would serve no purpose.

After the concert, Eddie took roses to the stage for her, fresh from his father's garden, and kissed her on both cheeks. "Let this be the first of many concerts in Canada," he said, "and around the world. That was magnificent." The applause was deafening as the audience clapped their agreement with his statement. Her per-formance had been a success. He hoped, as usual, she would ride back to the lodge with him. Howard, though, led her possessively to Burt's car after the concert. Eddie drove the commissioner and the mayor, then returned home with his parents.

He didn't see Charlotte again until the following evening at dinner. He noticed tension, so noticeably absent for the last few days, had returned to her face. Her lips were drawn, and she seemed pale again as she sat next to Howard at the table. She was unusually quiet as the group exchanged stories about their hunting adventures. Howard and the mayor discussed local political issues. "I don't know, Howard," the governor was saying as Eddie sat down at the table. "Many of the judges are liberal. They're strong advocates of racial equality and civil rights. Those cases that have been filed recently or that people are considering filing may be successful."

"Good attorneys are expensive," said Howard, "and I think we'll see that earning a living becomes hard for those rabble-rousers. Besides, judges can be bought."

"I prefer not to think so," said Charlotte.

"Think what you like," said Howard. "It doesn't matter. Besides, I didn't marry you for your ability to think."

She met Eddie's eyes. The look in her eyes was not hurt or helpless from her husband's comment. It was defiant. She smiled.

Eddie joined the conversation then. "You played so well at the community center, Charlotte," he said. "Everyone has been talking about how talented you are. Have you seen the review in the local newspaper?"

She shook her head. "No, I haven't, but I certainly enjoyed the concert. In fact, I've already told Father that I plan to contact Dr. Rubenstein when we get back to see if he will let me accompany him on another of his tours this spring."

"Not likely," said Howard under his breath.

"I have a copy of the review," said Eddie. "I believe I left it in the car. I'll bring it to you after dinner." The band started; a three-piece ensemble of horn, cello and piano with a vocalist, playing popular tunes. The musicians were acceptable, but not outstanding; Burt brought them in from Vancouver for special occasions. "Maybe, if you feel like it tonight, you can join the band for a few numbers later," he added. "It certainly might improve the show!"

She smiled in gratitude. "I might do that, but first I want to eat and to dance."

The conversation turned to hunting, interspersed with talk of stocks, bonds and world events. Stalin had just assumed power in Russia after Lenin's death. This, and Hitler's attitudes, as expressed in his recent book *Mein Kampf,* had several intellectuals predicting another war on the horizon. "It won't affect us here," predicted the governor. "Things are going great in this country. It won't be our problem."

"Maybe not at first," said Steve Durham, "but problems like that have a way of spreading. Look at what happened in the war a few years ago."

The debate continued as they finished dinner. By then, a few couples were on the dance floor. Charlotte and her father joined the dancers, and Eddie excused himself to retrieve the review. He came back with it and approached her. "I have the article. Can we dance before you settle down to read it?"

Her father smiled at him, a curious look in his eyes. "It's been awhile since you've asked my daughter to dance," he said, remembering the dance at the Bellflower several years before. "Lot's has changed since then. I'm getting older. Sure am glad I got to experience hunting in the Rockies while young enough to enjoy it. If this trip and that delightful concert last night are what come of you dancing with my daughter, Eddie, you may dance with her whenever you like."

Charlotte moved into his arms and he enjoyed the sensation of time stopping that always seemed to occur when they danced. She was graceful and fluid, following his lead flawlessly. He held her close and they moved across the floor in unison for the next several songs. Howard interrupted. "Okay, Charlotte," he said, "Time to dance with your husband." He grabbed her arm almost roughly, putting Eddie on edge. "In a moment," she said. "For now, I want to read this article Eddie gave me."

"Fine," he said. "I think I'll pass on that. Don't get any ideas about touring again." He walked away and asked one of the other young ladies in attendance to dance.

Eddie and Charlotte sat down while she read. *'Her talent far exceeds any performer our community has ever had the pleasure to welcome*, the reviewer had written. *In fact, it exceeds some of the performances by leading pianists I have heard in larger cities, as well. She has a flawless sense of rhythm and expresses the emotion of each song she plays in a manner far superior to that of...'* "Oh, Eddie, this is wonderful! He doesn't once say I'm young or pretty or female or pregnant, he just talks about my skill. This is what I expected to see when I toured, but I never did. Maybe I should go on tour again, despite what Howard says. Maybe the time is right now."

"You should," said Eddie. "You did promise me, remember? Now, how about helping out that band? They could sure use some of that rhythm and emotion! Shall I volunteer your services?"

She glanced a bit nervously toward Howard before she nodded. He'd finished dancing and was talking to a group of men near the bar. Then she approached the stage with Eddie. Her performance rejuvenated the group. The piano player had been happy to take an early break. Much to Eddie's amazement, Charlotte performed as flawlessly on the popular tunes the band played as she had at her concert, reading the music the band provided and adding a few flourishes of her own. Soon, the audience was applauding the band after their songs, something that had not been occurring before. When the band announced that they would be taking a break, she remained and played a couple of her own songs, inspiring even more applause.

"Your wife is certainly talented," Johanna McCauslin said to Howard after one of those songs. "You must be very proud of her." Eddie noticed his eyes darken a little. "Sure I am," he answered, "as long as it doesn't get in the way. We have a baby due this March, so I suspect she won't have much time for concerts then."

She met his eyes. "I don't know about that, Howard. I had eight children and still found time to take care of this entire province before we had clinics and hospitals." Howard turned away without comment and rejoined the men at the bar.

Eddie didn't have a chance to dance with Charlotte again. His parents were feeling tired, so he left early. He planned to spend some time with Steve Durham tomorrow before his friend headed back to Utah, but assured Charlotte he would help transport the group to the station the following afternoon. She shook her head. "No, Eddie, don't," she said. "Sir Rigall's arranged to get us all to the station tomorrow, and it will be too hard for me to say good-bye to you with everyone there. Say your good-byes to everyone tonight before you leave."

He obeyed, a little disappointed. Clarence and the rest of the group thanked him profusely for the hunting trip. Howard acknowledged that it had been a wonderful present, adding ominously, "Whatever your reasons for giving it may have been."

Eddie stiffened. "Howard thinks it may have been a little marketing ploy," the governor said. "He's always suspicious about things like that, because it is so like what he does! Whether that was you intent or not, it certainly worked out that way, young man. The commissioner and I have already booked future trips with Rigall—even though we need to wait until 1934 for the next available opening!" After bidding good-bye to everyone, Eddie found Charlotte before departing. She was talking quietly to Elizabeth.

"Good-bye, Charlotte," he said sadly. "I so wish you could stay...I can't imagine being without you. For half a penny, I think I'd be willing to go back with you to Kansas."

"Would you, despite everything? How sweet," she said simply. "I love you, Eddie. I always will. I'll write often. I'll think of you always. Thank you—for everything." She embraced him and kissed his cheek, tears in her eyes. Then, unable to watch him leave, she turned away as he walked out. Later, emotions under control again, she joined Howard and her father, and stayed until nearly all of the other guests departed.

CHAPTER THIRTEEN

FINDING HOME

Eddie felt the excitement he always felt when he received a letter from Charlotte as he opened the envelope, addressed in her flowing handwriting. Although he didn't like to admit it, much of his life over the past several months had been marked and defined by her letters. His sense of time was demarcated by when a particular event occurred in relationship to the last letter he had received from Charlotte. They had not all been happy letters, but that didn't matter. Any word from her, no matter what she said, brightened his day.

From her letters, he learned she had enjoyed a pleasant but uneventful trip back to Kansas. She contacted her old music professor about another concert tour, despite Howard's objections. This pleased Eddie, for she was keeping her promise. Charlotte's excitement at resuming her dream of being a world-renowned pianist was evident. Her two-month tour, which Rubenstein arranged almost immediately when she asked him to, went well; she had written him often and those letters had been happy ones. After her return home, the letters had gradually become sadder. She missed her friends. She was unhappy. Then, tragically, she lost her baby. The miscarriage devastated her. Eddie felt helpless to offer her comfort, except through his words—and he knew that would be little comfort, indeed. Reading between the lines of her letters, he suspected that domestic violence, perhaps an on-going argument with Howard over her tour or over his actions toward her friends, may have been responsible although she didn't actually say this so he couldn't be sure. She didn't actually say much in her subsequent letters, except that she was weak and depressed. She considered the loss of her child to be her own fault. Her despondency lasted for months. In search of a way to alleviate her pain and keep her from blaming herself, as was so characteristic of her even when there was no reason for it, he reminded her of the night in Alberta they had gone to the gypsy fair. He wrote:

Dear Charlotte,

I know you always take responsibility for your actions and, overall, this is an admirable and moral trait. But this tragic event can in no way be your fault. I can only guess at what events may have transpired to make you believe you could possibly be to blame. Whatever they may have been, I know that you were in no way responsible for losing your child. Maybe my father's belief in gypsy fortunetellers should be taken seriously, after all. Remember when we visited Sister Grace at the rodeo grounds last summer? You told me she said a young man was bringing you flowers and calling you mother. He said he must leave but would return. He told you not to be sad. Perhaps that was a prediction of this event, and something to give you comfort, to assure you it was part of some greater plan. Fate is not under your control. He told you he loved you and would return, remember? Take comfort in that. Take comfort, too, in knowing how much you mean to me and that you are always in my heart. I would give anything to stop your tears. If I thought it would do any good or make any difference, I would be there to comfort you in person right now.

Love always,
Eddie

He'd sent that letter over a month ago, anxiously awaiting her reply ever since. This small lavender envelope was his reply. He opened it carefully. Inside was a card, an announcement from the

Topeka newspaper that she had filed for divorce from Howard Farnsworth and one half of a penny. He held the penny, examining it. He couldn't tell how it had been so cleanly divided. Sawed? Melted and molded? Then he opened the card. She had written only:

> You told me last time I saw you this is all it would take for
> you to come back to Kansas. I hope that is still true.

Momentarily stunned by this response to his last letter, he brushed his lips against the half-penny and placed it in his pocket. Then he headed home to pack.

"Are you sure this is what you want?" his mother asked, already knowing the answer. "It's a long ways, and there's a lot to consider. Will you bring her back here? Would she want that? Can you find work there, if you stay? Maybe you should write to her first, and plan this more carefully."

Papa was more encouraging. "I admire your bravery, son. It's a long trip. We'll miss you." Not nearly as long as the trip you made when you were young, thought Eddie. Not nearly as risky as that. But he appreciated the words.

Chief was more pragmatic. "Car won't make it that far," he predicted. "Engine's too old."

"I've still got quite a bit of money saved," said Eddie, suddenly realizing he would not be able to leave quite as quickly as he had planned, after all. "I'll get it from the bank on Monday, in U.S. dollars. I'll have enough to get there and to get by while I figure out what to do. I hope I won't have to buy a new engine with it, but I won't be stranded for long."

It was evident to his family he'd made up his mind. Eddie's problem was just waiting for the bank to open on Monday; he wanted to be in the car and on his way immediately. That evening, he drove out to the lodge to tell Elizabeth his plans. She and Burt were encouraging and wished him well. On Monday morning, as he was driving out of town, he sent a brief note to Charlotte. Very brief. *On my way* was all it said; he didn't even sign it. He hoped to arrive in Topeka before the note.

The road stretched out before him like a ribbon that tied him to an unknown future. He felt no hesitation, no fear of the unknown and no doubt in the correctness of his actions. Occasionally, he pulled the half-penny from his pocket to look at as he drove. It was early fall. There was no snow on the roads yet. His route took him down through Montana and Wyoming, into Utah and across Colorado. Gas stations were few and far between, so he carried fuel with him. He planned to be in Kansas in less than a week.

Chief's prediction about the engine, unfortunately, turned out to be accurate. The mountains and long hours of driving were too much for the car. Outside of Grand Junction, Colorado, it finally refused to move any further under its own power. There was a mechanic in town, but he had to send for parts and wait for them to arrive from Denver. The parts that arrived were not the correct ones, so he had to wait longer. Then he had to wait for repairs. Since the mechanic was also a farmer and more interested in harvesting his fields than in fixing the car by then, that took several more days. Eddie, restless and bored, finally hurried things along by volunteering to help with the harvesting in exchange for meals, and the offer was readily accepted. Still, by the time he could finally drive again, a heavy, early snowfall had made the road into Denver impassable. He would either need to wait longer hoping the road would be passable and more snowstorms would not follow, or reroute his trip, driving south. The roads down to Route 66 were unpredictable, at best. Once he reached that highway, he could go across New Mexico and Texas, and then up through Oklahoma. There would still be mountains to cross until he got to Texas, and snow could be a problem there, too. It was definitely the long way around. But he decided it was better than waiting.

Normally, he would have enjoyed a leisurely trip through the beautiful country of the Southwest his father had described so many years ago. Now, though, he was in no mood for sightseeing and he regretted the additional expense. He wanted to arrive and convince Charlotte to return to Canada with him. This part of his journey, too, was plagued with mishaps and mechanical problems. The trip from Canada that he had expected to take a week took over two months. It was November 15, 1929 when he finally reached his destination. He drove into a town that, like the rest of the country, was reeling in the aftermath of the stock market crash and entering the Great Depression. He had arrived in the dustbowl of America just after "Black Monday".

His first dilemma was whether to go to the address on Charlotte's letters, not knowing whether she and Howard were still living together, or to her father's store. He wasn't sure what to do, and he was tired from a long drive. He decided to stay at the Bellflower Hotel, which he remembered so well from his last trip. It occurred to him that Gracie Belson, the wonderful matron there, might even be able to give him advice. Glad to have finally reached Topeka despite all obstacles, he arrived late in the afternoon and went inside to book a room. The first thing he noticed was that the hotel, previously bustling, was empty. The next thing he noticed was the run-down condition. The hotel was still clean, but nothing had been replaced or redecorated since his last stay. He also noticed that everyone else he saw there was African-American. He approached the desk. Gracie saw him and greeted him warmly.

"Sure you want to stay here?" she said. "Things have changed in the last several years in this town. We aren't allowed in white folks' places and they generally don't come near our places, either. There's another hotel, the Grand, two streets over, where most of the town events are now. You might be more comfortable there."

"I wouldn't dream of it," said Eddie, "unless you would be more comfortable if I wasn't here. I was perfectly happy at the Bellflower last time I visited Topeka, and it's where I want to stay now. Besides, I'm Canadian. These local spats shouldn't apply to me anyway."

She laughed and replied to him in French. Embarrassed, he admitted that French was not a language he had studied; only Eastern Canada was bilingual. Then he asked if she had seen or heard from Charlotte or her father lately.

"Well," she said, "I know it's been hard for those two. All the problems we've had politically made them awfully uncomfortable, for sure. I don't shop at Clarence's store anymore, just because in these times I have to support my own community economically. I don't hold it against him, you understand. I hope he understands that, too. It's just these new policies make it so I need to take care of my own people. And Charlotte—my dear baby Charlotte—I know she's always loved me. But that man she married was just poison. He was. Took a lot of guts for her to divorce him; women in her position don't usually take those measures. I admire her for it to no end. She just finally decided it didn't matter what everyone thought, she had to stand by her own principles. She left him. It was hard on her father, though. Maybe if she had waited just a little longer… But we can't see the future, can we? There was no way to know what was coming. Still, I shouldn't admit it, but I'm glad he was one of those crazy bankers who walked out of high windows last week. Better for all of us, I say. But I'm talking more than I should, no doubt. What you are really asking is how to find her. I think she's back at her father's home. I'm not sure, mind you—I haven't seen either of them for quite some time. But I think that's where you'll find her. Now, let me see if I can find you a room." Gracie chuckled at her own joke, looking around the empty premises. "How long are you staying?"

Eddie relaxed, comfortable with her forthright manner. "I'm not sure," he said. "Can we just leave it open, and I'll let you know a day or so before I leave?"

"Sure, it's not exactly like we've been overbooked lately. Good to see you back, young man. Here's your key. Restaurant's around the corner, if you're hungry. Breakfast is included, and served at nine a.m. tomorrow. You let me know if you need anything else. Don't you worry about people staring at you, either. They will. That's just how it is now; never used to be. It's unusual for everyone here, the help and the guests both, to see a white man at this hotel, that's all. This place has changed since you were here last. It's changed a lot. It's like there's two towns now; theirs and ours. All the white folks moved to the new houses in the south part of town, by the new school our kids don't attend. It's a different world."

Eddie settled into his room and showered, then realized he was hungry. He went to the restaurant for dinner, eating a hearty helping of spareribs and beans with cornbread. The changes bothered him. He remembered the last party he had enjoyed here; the ease with which Gracie Belson and Charlotte's father had once interacted, and Charlotte's group of friends. He could understand more clearly now how difficult the last few years had been for Charlotte; even more difficult, no doubt, because her husband was one of the people most responsible for creating this unhealthy rift in the community. Ex-husband, he reminded himself. Then, something else Gracie had said registered. Howard was 'one of those crazy bankers walking out of high windows.' He killed himself, Eddie realized. Like many other men who could not accept the loss of their wealth when the stock market crashed and the banks failed, he had committed suicide.

Up until now, the reality of the depression had not registered. Eddie knew, from what he had seen and heard in the last month, that many people were out of work, that banks were failing— that the U.S. economy had suddenly and unexpectedly ceased to function overnight. It hadn't affected him. He'd retrieved all of his money from his bank account and cashed in all of his investments before leaving in early September. He had no job to lose, no family to support, no sense of loss to match what so many in this country were feeling. Canada hadn't suffered nearly as much from what he had heard. The lodge and the gas station might be losing customers from the U.S., but there would still be enough to sustain both. His parents had the ranch; they would not be suffering or starving. The mounting wave of suicides puzzled him. He never understood people who tied their personal worth to their monetary worth. For him, there had never been a connection between a man's worth and a man's wealth. If the explanation was a sense of failed responsibility, then totally giving up was the ultimate failure. It seemed illogical to him. But if Howard was one of these economic fatalities, he sensed that Charlotte might be imagining she was somehow responsible, too, because of the divorce. He was worried. Her emotional state now would be even more fragile than before. He hoped he had done the right thing by coming. Then he remembered she would have received the note saying he was on his way long ago, before the crash or Howard's suicide. His delay in arriving had been one more burden placed on her fair, frail shoulders. He should've sent word of his delay. Ah, well; nothing could be done to change that now.

Realizing his parents may also be worried about him given the news they were probably receiving of conditions in the USA, he stopped at the front desk for paper and an envelope after finishing his meal. Back in his room, he wrote a letter describing his mechanical mishaps, assuring them he had arrived safely and indicating he would have more news for them after he saw Charlotte. Then, he went to sleep. Throughout his life, Eddie never had difficulty sleeping. No matter what was happening in the world around him, he always slept well. His mother told him it came from living a good life. Maybe that was true. Even now, eager to finally see Charlotte, he dozed off immediately and slept soundly throughout the night.

The next morning, he dressed in the freshest shirt and jeans he had, leaving the rest with Mrs. Belson to launder and press. He enjoyed a leisurely breakfast of ham and eggs, lingering over his coffee longer than usual. He was surprised how much the town had changed since his last visit as he drove from the hotel to Clarence's store, first stopping by the post office to mail the letter to his parents. Then, trying to relax and decide just what to say when he saw Charlotte, he drove to the rose garden before stopping at the store. As he had done before, he wanted to bring a few of the beautiful flowers that bloomed there to her.

The garden, which he had expected to look much lovelier and more beautiful after seven years of growth, was in disrepair. Several of the branches needed pruned. The ground was dry and dusty; many bushes were badly in need of water. Weeds were choking some of the newer plants, apparently added to replace others that had not survived due to lack of care. Without thinking about what he was doing, Eddie, who had originally pulled his knife from his pocket to cut a few roses for Charlotte from the public garden, instead began to carefully prune the bush in front of him. He thought of his father's beautiful, well-tended garden. How sad he would be to see this one, which could be so lovely, suffering from such terrible neglect. Eddie spent over an hour tending the roses. He even brought extra water he had in his car for some of the most parched-looking areas. They needed much more. He wondered why the city had not been taking better care of this park.

As he continued to work, he became aware of a large, well-dressed man approaching him. The man watched him for a few minutes. "It's about time," he said at last, "that the commissioner finally found someone who knows roses. When I first contributed funds to the city for this garden, I expected it to bloom. I expected it to be a showcase. Instead, it hasn't been cared for properly until today. I'd heard the parks department was laying off workers. It's a pleasant surprise to find they added a good one instead. What's your name, young man? I'm Henry Schneider."

"Schneider is my mother's family name," said Eddie, standing up and dusting himself off. "I wonder if we're related."

"A few generations back, we're all related. There was just one original garden, after all—cared for much better than this, I trust! Half the people in this part of the country came from the same distant corner of Germany my grandfather did. I'm glad the commissioner found one of my distant relatives to get this garden back in shape!"

"I don't work here. I was just passing through, and it's such a shame to see roses like this ..."

"Volunteer work?" Schneider laughed. "I like that, but I don't think the superintendent will be able to count on it on a regular basis, will he? Come have lunch with me and tell me how you learned about roses. I plan to convince you to stay on tending this garden"

Eddie spent the afternoon telling Schneider about his father's rose garden in Alberta and his life up to this point. He learned the man was a wealthy philanthropist who made a fortune in the steel industry in Michigan, then retired in Topeka to be close to his youngest son, a city attorney here. Schneider donated the money to establish the rose garden to the city, and he was disappointed it had not been better cared for. He told Eddie he frequently walked in the area just to keep people from cutting the flowers, and check on the condition of the garden. He had been out of town for the past few months, visiting his daughter in Michigan. "I'm particular, and I plan to make the commissioner's life hell until he corrects the condition of this," he said. "Believe me, I can do it. Do you need a job, friend? Lots of people have been drifting into town lately looking for work. Between the drought and the stock market failure everyone needs a job, but it is clear you know roses. If the department says they can't hire someone, I'll pay you myself. I won't give them a choice."

Eddie grinned sheepishly. "I actually came here with every intention of cutting a rose or two," he confessed." When I saw the condition of the bushes, I changed my mind." He liked this man immediately. There was something about his gruff, forthright manner that reminded him of Chief. As they continued talking, he told Henry of his visit to Topeka seven years before when he had first seen the garden, expecting it to be a showcase by now. Without mentioning names or going into detail, he told Henry he'd returned because of a beautiful young woman. He didn't know if he would be staying in town long or not, but the job might be useful. "Besides," he added, "someone needs to tend these roses. This garden could be a masterpiece in five years if it was taken care of properly." They spent the afternoon together, working side by side after lunch weeding roses.

"You're taking care of my garden," Schneider announced when they finished. "I'll see to that!" He handed him a card. "Where are you staying?"

"At the Bellflower, for now," Eddie told him.

A shadow crossed Henry's face. "You don't know this town, do you? Why don't you get checked into the Grand? Much better accommodations. Follow me. I'll show you where it is."

Eddie shook his head. "No, no," he said. "I don't want to change hotels. I remember Mrs. Belson from when I was here on tour with Professor Durham. She's a gracious hostess. I'm very comfortable there."

Henry looked at him sharply. "You were here with Durham? I've heard of you, young man. This may be trickier than I thought. Never mind. You call me. You'll need that card, and you'll need me as a friend." With that, he stood abruptly and left.

Once Schneider was out of view, Eddie cut one red American Beauty rose, fully opened. He knew it would wilt soon, anyway, and he felt he had worked for it. Then, looking down at his dirt-covered clothing, he realized he would need to go back to the hotel and change before visiting Charlotte. As he feared, his laundry was not ready, and he had nothing to change into. He considered buying new clothing, but that seemed wasteful. Still, when he learned it would be two days before his clothes were ready, he decided it was necessary. He cleaned up as much as he could, and asked for directions to a shop.

The late afternoon air was crisp, but his leather jacket kept away the cold. A light wind brushed across the November land-scape as Eddie walked through the downtown area. Mrs. Belson had suggested a men's clothing store close to the capital, fairly close to the hotel, as the place he would find the best quality clothing. Following her directions, he turned a corner to see a familiar face across the street. Rosie Brown, two young boys in tow, stood waiting to cross at the light. She'd gained weight and had a more serious demeanor than when he had danced with her at the Bellflower many years ago, but he still recognized her.

"Rosie!" he called. "It's Eddie McCauslin. Remember me?"

She waved and crossed to join him on the corner. "Of course I do!" she said. "Charlotte's cowboy. I'm so glad you came back. She told me you were coming, last time I saw her. I was so glad to hear that. She's had a rough time. Have you seen her yet?"

"No, I just got into town. I'm going in search of acceptable clothing for a visit," he said, motioning to his muddy jeans.

She laughed. "You been gardening or something?"

He told her that, actually, he had. She chuckled about his story of the rose garden. "That Schneider has a reputation in town for being quite a character," she said, not kindly. Then she introduced her sons to Eddie and offered to help him shop "I was just taking these two over to play with their cousins," she explained. "If you don't mind waiting a little bit while I drop them off, I'll help you find some clothes. We should talk, anyway."

As they walked, he learned Rosie and Charlotte had grown apart over the years. Since the divorce and Howard's death, Rosie had made a point of visiting her friend again. "She needs me," she said simply. "She's been so lonely. Now that she's back at her father's, I don't worry about going by to check on her once in a while. I was over a couple of weeks ago. She told me then you were coming. I hadn't seen her so happy about anything for a very long time."

Rosie told him about her husband, John, who worked at the pet food packing plant in town. When they entered the clothing store together, he noticed the clerk gave him an odd look before turning back to his other customer. He assumed it was probably his attire that drew the unfavorable response. This seemed to be a rather exclusive shop. He recognized the other customer, too, he thought. It appeared to be the parks commissioner. He tried catching his eye and smiled, sure he would recognize him since it had barely been a year since he had been hunting in Alberta. The man simply turned an icy gaze toward Rosie and resumed talking to the clerk. Eddie shrugged, thinking maybe he was mistaken. He began to look at shirts.

"You know," said Rosie, after the clerk had pointedly ignored them for several minutes, "maybe it wasn't such a good idea for me to come with you after all. I was so glad to see you, I didn't even think of it. And I didn't know you were planning to come to this store. But…"

He realized, suddenly, that the cold reception he had received from the other customer and the sales clerk may have been directed toward Rosie or towards him because he was with her. Stunned, he immediately turned and left the shop. "Take me to a place we'll both be welcome," he said loudly. "Not too many people have cash to spend these days. I do, and I'll spend it where people are civil."

"Bravo," she said, as they exited. "That certainly put them in their place! C'mon. If you can live with jeans and a checkered shirt, Wilbur's shop will do just fine. Save you some money besides. Follow me."

They walked almost a mile; as they walked, Eddie noticed the town began to change. "Yeah," said Rosie lightly, "this is where the black folks live now, Eddie. Streets don't get cleaned as often and trash isn't collected by the city. Streetlights are always burnt out. The school is old and run down; bad teachers and big classes. The police here don't protect us; they threaten us. You know, I don't remember it being like this when I was growing. It's all changed for the worse in the past few years. A shame my boys have to grow up like this." She shook her head. "My brother and Linda—they're trying to fight it, trying to mobilize people to take action. It's tough, though. Just gets them hassled by the police, mostly. Makes it hard for him to keep a job. People see that, all the trouble it brings on him and his family, and they just stay away and put up with things. I can understand that, I guess. It just isn't right. Well, don't mind my complaining; I don't, usually. Here's Wilbur's place."

Eddie found a comfortable pair of jeans and a brightly printed red and blue collared shirt made of a shiny material. "Not bad," said Mr. Wilbur. "If you'd just trade those boots for some nice leather shoes, now, you might look okay." He and Rosie both laughed. They walked back to the Bellflower together, talking more about the changes.

"I almost wish I could go with you when you visit Charlotte," she told him as she collected her sons. "I'd love to see her face! But I need to get these two home. You tell her I said she's always welcome at my house. Bring her over. It's not too far from Wilbur's shop." She wrote the address on a piece of paper and handed it to Eddie. "John and I expect to see lots of you two, hear me? Don't be strangers." She patted his shoulder as she left. Eddie took his other clothes back to his room before heading to his car. Now he would see Charlotte. At last, his journey would reach an end.

As he pulled his car up to her father's store, he noticed it hadn't changed much; still in the same place, clean and well maintained except the trees in the yard were larger now. Glancing at his watch, he realized it was after 6pm and the sign on the door indicated that was closing time. There were still lights on inside and looking through a window, he saw Clarence stocking shelves. Eddie knocked on the glass. Without looking up,

Clarence shouted "Closed. Come back tomorrow," continuing to remove cans from an open box at his feet.

Eddie knocked again, calling out his name. "Just need a box of chocolates. I hoped you might have one." Clarence looked up, annoyed. Then, recognizing Eddie, he smiled and stood.

"About time you arrived," he said as he opened the door. "I was beginning to think my daughter had become hysterical and just imagined you were coming. I suppose it is quite a drive. Well, come in; I just might have a box of chocolates. The cash register is closed for the evening, so you can't pay for them, which is just as I prefer. After that hunting trip, you have quite a credit here. Come in." Seeing his shirt, he chuckled. "You've changed your style. That's flashier than I remember."

Eddie entered, suddenly self-conscious of his appearance. He told him of the garden and shopping with Rosie. Clarence Robinson nodded sadly. "Well, then you've seen how our town has changed, and made a friend you'll probably need. After Howard's suicide, I'm not sure how welcome you'll be here. You see, Farnsworth and the boys may think the divorce was because—I mean—with you coming down so close after the trip, and Charlotte's obvious enchantment with you—I don't know quite how to put this, but..."

"Put it honestly," said Eddie. "That's all I ask. Do you think it's a bad idea for me to be here? Will it be harmful to you and Charlotte? If so, I'll leave right now..."

"Gracious, no. I'll take any consequences that group tries to direct at my store. They've been pretty unfriendly ever since Charlotte filed for divorce, anyway, trying to create new zoning and taxes to make my life difficult. I lost a lot in the bank failure and stock crash, too, so it's been difficult. I haven't been invited to a poker game for quite awhile." He shrugged his shoulders. "But it would be much worse for her now if you weren't here. She's been worried about where you are and pacing like a cat on a hot tin roof wondering when you'd arrive for the last month. Besides, what's done is done. That can't be changed and there's no reason to dwell on it. Just don't be surprised if everyone isn't as happy to see you as she is. And don't be surprised if she's a little worse for the wear. The past couple of years have been hard on her. She hasn't smiled much since she lost the baby, and Howard's suicide was really hard on her. I've tried and tried to convince her it was related to the stock market crash, not to anything she did, but I haven't had much success. Maybe you will have better luck. I hope so."

"Is she home now?" asked Eddie. "Can I see her? If it would be better to give her some warning, to come back tomorrow…"

"She's home. She's always home, lately. Hasn't been out at all. I worry about her. No, you go on up to the house now. I'll take my time. Our housekeeper usually serves dinner around seven thirty. I'll be in for that, and you plan on staying, too." He handed Eddie a large box of assorted chocolates in a gold-embossed, white box. "Here. Russell-Stover's. She likes these best. Time to get rid of them anyway. Not much call for chocolates lately around here."

Eddie walked up the path to the front door, a box of chocolates in one hand and a red rose in the other. He reflected that the colors around him, even though it was nightfall, seemed more vivid than usual. He had the sense that, whatever happened in his life ahead, whatever the outcome of this visit, the moments he would have with Charlotte would make it worthwhile. Their time together would justify anything that came. He took a deep breath, lifting the brass knocker on the heavy wood door. Waiting after the knock seemed to last an eternity. He heard footsteps inside. At last, the housekeeper opened the door. "Could you please tell Miss Charlotte that Eddie McCauslin is here?" he asked. This was not the same housekeeper he'd met before. This woman was a large, broad-faced African-American wearing a brightly colored apron.

"Who is it, Ginny?" he heard Charlotte call. Her voice had the soft, musical quality he remembered. He took another deep breath.

"Young man to see you, Miss," Ginny answered. "Says his name's Eddie McCauslin."

Within seconds, before Ginny even had time to invite him in, Charlotte ran to his arms. "I was so afraid you'd changed your mind," she said. "I didn't know how long it would take you to get here, but I got the letter saying you were on your way over a month ago and…"

"Shhh," he said, holding her and stroking her shining auburn hair. "I'm here now. It just took a little longer than I'd planned. I'll tell you all about my journey. But first, these are for you." He handed her the chocolates and the flower. "You'd better take the candy before I sit on it again! This rose needs some water. I brought it from that garden you wrote such a lovely song about." He noticed her eyes were moist as she stepped away to take the presents he offered and looked up at him. The beautiful violet highlights in her eyes were still hypnotic, but there were dark circles beneath, suggesting she had not been sleeping well for some time. Her face was paler and more drawn than when he had last seen her. She had lost weight and looked very fragile. As he looked at her, the enormity of what he had done and of what he was planning to do finally struck him. He'd traveled thousands of miles, to another country, with no plan other than to be with her. He, who had planned never to marry, wanted more than anything else he had ever wanted in his life to be with this woman. He pulled the half-penny she had sent from his pocket.

"Here," he said, handing it to her. "This piece of copper is seeking its other half. Save it. We'll pass them on to our children someday. It will make a good story."

Her face relaxed a little and she laughed through her tears before embracing him again. "You really are here," she said. "I can hardly believe it. I can hardly believe after all these years that we will finally be together."

They walked inside holding hands and sat together on the flowered velvet sofa in the room where her piano was. At first, they just looked at each other, still holding hands. Then they talked. They had lots to talk about. Eddie told her he was staying at the Bellflower, and that he had seen Rosie. "We're both invited to her house," he said. "I promised we'd visit often."

Charlotte smiled. "Good," she said. "We will. I'm so glad you are here."

He recounted the shopping trip. They talked about the changes in the town, both as a result of the strict adherence to segregation policies and the stock market crash and bank failures. He wasn't sure if he should tell her he knew about Howard's suicide, and decided it would be best not to mention it. They would have plenty of time together; she could talk about it when she was ready. He was sure that, as with the miscarriage, she had found some way to blame herself for that event. He also considered discussing how soon they could head for Canada, but decided that, too, could wait. They could make plans slowly, after they became accustomed to being together. For the next few days, they would just enjoy each other's company. He told her about his trip. Before he had completely recounted his mechanical misadventures, Clarence joined them while Ginny got dinner on the table.

"How long are you staying for?" he asked.

"I don't know," said Eddie. "I haven't really decided yet. I mean..."

"I only ask because you don't need to waste money at a hotel," said Clarence. "We have an extra room here. You are welcome to stay as long as you like."

Eddie noticed that Charlotte looked at her father with gratitude. "Yes, Eddie," she said. "Stay here with us."

"Thank you for the generous offer," he said. "Let me think it over. I'll need to go back to the hotel for my things, and I told

Mrs. Belson I would give her at least a day's notice before I left. I'll stay there through the weekend, and then we'll see."

Dinner was enjoyable, although Eddie remembered little of the food. They talked about world events and his meeting with Henry Schneider. Charlotte laughed at that story.

"You really just started pruning the roses in all that dust?" she said, incredulous. "And that feisty old character helped you, instead of threatening to have you arrested? He's very possessive about that garden, you know."

"I know," said Eddie. "He told me it was named for his deceased wife. It really has been neglected. I think he appreciated seeing someone trying to take care of it. Besides, you wrote such a beautiful song for the garden. It should live up to that someday."

After dinner, she played the piano. Eddie and her father listened to masterful, emotional renditions of well-known music by Debussy and Prokofiev. At last, Eddie said goodnight, promising to come back the following afternoon. "We have lots to talk about," he told her. "I guess we can start then."

"I love you, Eddie," she whispered. "I always have. I always will. I am so happy you are finally here." He was, too. It felt strangely right.

CHAPTER FOURTEEN

BATTER UP!

Eddie was glad he'd played baseball in Seattle, as it turned out. In a strangely serendipitous way, his previous recognition as a pitcher made it possible to obtain a secure, well-paying job in the dust bowl of Kansas during the Great Depression. He was probably the only man hired by the city in the early 1930s, and he was hired for a permanent position with the public parks department even though he was an "outsider" and made no attempt to hide views considered controversial. If he hadn't met Schneider in the rose garden the afternoon after he arrived, and if he hadn't played baseball professionally, it would have been impossible for him to remain. As it was, his certainty that his impulsive journey to a new life would work out was well founded, but only because of these two serendipitous events. It gave him a sense there was an organized pattern to the universe. He called it God, like his mother. He was not particularly religious, at least in a traditional sense, but he did have a deep faith in some underlying framework of destiny now, much as his father always had.

He returned to the Bellflower long enough to reclaim his laundry, pack, and visit the local jewelers. He spent some of his remaining money on a diamond and gold wedding ring set, then appeared at Charlotte's door the following afternoon to propose marriage. In retrospect during later years, he felt if he had stopped to think about what he was doing, he never would have done it. But he never regretted acting without thinking on that particular occasion.

Even planning the wedding was a matter of impulse and circumstance. A large church wedding would have been his preference. This was a special occasion that would only happen once in his life and it was a cause for celebration. Then, he quickly realized everything that made wedding traditions important didn't apply. He was far away from his family and childhood friends. Charlotte was near hers, but given her recent divorce and the suicide of her ex-husband, a festive ceremony would be viewed as inappropriate by her community. She didn't want it.

"I love you, Eddie," she said. "As far as I'm concerned, we don't need a wedding at all. We've always been married in my heart."

That was a little too unconventional for him. He wanted a church wedding. But, what church? Eddie had always preferred the Catholic faith. The ritual and ceremony appealed to him. He connected it to his Irish heritage and remembered his father's story of nearly becoming a priest. But Charlotte had been divorced; their marriage could never be sanctioned by the Catholic Church, and she wasn't Catholic anyway. Another option might be his parents' adopted-by-circumstance religion. But there probably wasn't a Mormon church in Topeka. Even if there was, the Mormons didn't allow blacks to actively participate in their religion, so that would not be an acceptable choice. The exclusion soured him on that particular religion. Once he considered it, tradition seemed irrelevant, so they were married at a quiet ceremony conducted by the local justice of the peace. Charlotte's father arranged it and attended the ceremony, along with the Browns and the Belsons. Then, Eddie moved in with Charlotte and Clarence.

Eddie wasn't comfortable with that idea at first. He wanted to get Charlotte her own home. When she had been married before, she had lived in one of the finest houses in town, and he didn't want to give her anything less. He told her he wanted them to have a place of their own, noting that living in her father's home would make him feel as if he were not providing for her as he should. He suggested they return to Canada, where he could provide well for her, but Charlotte wanted to stay in Topeka. Her father and friends were here, she told him; her life was here and she was sure his was, as well. Although he hoped eventually she would return to Canada with him, he didn't pressure her. As long as he'd known Charlotte, she had spoken of her ties to her hometown.

The top floor of Clarence's house was actually designed as a separate apartment for the housekeeper, with a small kitchen, living area and bedroom. Charlotte insisted on letting the housekeeper go to save money and help contribute to expenses which, due to the worsening depression and Clarence's habit of extending credit at his store to anyone who needed it, were rapidly mounting. She took over those duties and they moved into the upstairs apartment, tiny but cozy. They were incredibly happy in the small, comfortable quarters. Charlotte began to give piano lessons to the children of families who could still afford that luxury to supplement their income. Because her skill was well-known in the area, and because her own music teacher had since moved back to Kansas City, leaving several of his former students, she was able to make a good income. Eddie encouraged her to continue touring for concerts, but she refused, pointing out that, given economic conditions, travel expenses—since she would refuse to go without him—would be more than the profit. That wasn't practical.

Once Eddie resigned himself to staying in Kansas and their home was established, his remaining funds were rapidly depleted. He didn't want to rely on Charlotte's income and her father's generosity. He needed to find work. At last, he contacted Henry Schneider. Henry was delighted to hear from him. He asked if they could meet at the rose garden and do a little weeding and pruning together, as they had at their last meeting. "You haven't been volunteering your skill as a gardener lately, Edward, and my roses are dying," he lamented.

Once they began working, a tall young black man in a security uniform approached. "What are you doing, may I ask?" He looked familiar to Edward, although he wasn't sure why. "Oh, it's you, Mr. Schneider," the security guard added as he approached.

"That parks superintendent hasn't got a green thumb himself and can't seem to find anyone among his men who does. The commissioner will certainly get an earful from me when I see him next, I assure you, Mr. Brown. I just can't walk by this garden when it is in such disarray."

"I don't blame you," the young watchman said. "Don't worry. I won't report you to my supervisor for this."

"Good man, Moses. Heaven forbid that superintendent should begin to think he'll get free labor from me just because his men are incompetent." The watchman nodded, chuckling; Henry and Edward resumed their weeding.

"Give me some time," Henry said as the watchman walked away. "It won't be easy, but I'll get you on with the city. In the meantime, I'll pay you a decent wage out of my own pocket to come by here once a week and keep these roses from dying. I don't want to spend another fortune for replanting like last year. I haven't got so much of a fortune to spend anymore, anyway. But this garden is important to me. I dedicated it to my dear, dead wife Rosie, and I want it to become a showpiece. You're the only person I've met so far that shares that vision and has the skill to make it happen. So, give me some time with the boys who think they run this place, and you'll have a job. It won't be easy. Since you've married Clarence's daughter, Farnsworth is blaming the breakup of his son's marriage and his subsequent suicide on you. Because of that, you don't have friends in high places right now, believe me. Except for me. But if we time it right, I have an idea. You used to pitch for Seattle, didn't you, Edward?"

Edward nodded, noticing he liked Schneider's use of his given name. It sounded more mature and respectable. Clarence and Charlotte had also been calling him Edward ever since the wedding for some reason. It felt comfortable now. He decided to ask the few other people he knew in town to start using it, too.

"Think you can still pitch left-handed? Think you can still play? Not like you used to, mind you, but reasonably well?" asked Schneider.

Edward considered. "It's been a long time. But I'm in good shape. I can still run fast and, with a little practice, I'm sure my pitching and hitting will pick up again—with both hands!"

"Well, my friend, I suggest you begin practicing. That skill is going to be very important in helping me convince the City Board of Supervisors to hire you as the keeper of my rose garden. I'm a conniving old scoundrel and I know those boys. This is my plan."

Schneider told Edward that the first thing he would do, formally through the commissioner at a board meeting, and informally at the poker games most of the leaders in the community still regularly attended, would be to voice his dissatisfaction with how his philanthropic gift to the city was being maintained. He would make sure everyone knew he had no intention of paying for another major replanting, as he had already done once, and that all other monetary gifts from him to the community could be expected to cease if this one wasn't appreciated and cared for. "I created that garden in honor of my deceased wife, who loved roses," he would say. "Right now, it's a disgrace it bears her name, and I'll make sure everyone knows how I feel." When the politicians and supervisors tried to pacify him, as he knew they would, he would negotiate a compromise. If the parks department would create a new position, the chief duty of which would be twenty-four-hour care of the rose garden, he would make one more donation—a small caretaker's house built near the garden. This could be used as part of the salary for the new employee, figured into the city wage formula. He would also arrange that a small percentage of whatever profits he made from a couple of his existing investments that were still solvent would be donated toward the salary to fund this position. He would insist he needed to approve the person hired, and his donations would not begin until he had approved someone for the position.

"Because of all the policies and red tape and seniority rules for employment this city has, it'll be a nightmare. But my son's a good attorney; he'll find a loophole, and they'll work with him to pacify me," he predicted. "It might take a little time, though. Once that's arranged, I'll have to start by vetoing all of the many relatives and current workers and who knows who else that the commissioner and the board recommend for the job, which is what all the red tape is supposed to prevent but never does. Then I'll get the park superintendent to recommend you, and that will be the toughest part because of old Farnsworth and his pull. So, this is what I propose…"

He went on to explain that each of the departments within the city budget—police, fire, and parks—had amateur baseball teams for their employees. They played in a city league. It was popular entertainment, highly competitive and the source of quite a bit of betting among the poker club members, besides. The parks team frequently won, but for the last couple of years, as their players aged, the fire department had been more of a threat. In fact, they won the tournament last year, much to the chagrin of the parks superintendent. Schneider's plan was for Edward to apply for the position as gardener, but not until just before baseball season started. Schneider would pass the word, as an "inside information advantage" to everyone on the hiring board about Edward's previous career in professional baseball and hint his pitching and playing was still top quality. That information to the right people, along with his assurance he would finally approve someone for the position, thus allowing more funds to flow into the city coffers, should be enough to overcome the hurdles to getting Edward the job.

"You won't make a fortune, and you'll work hard. I'm a tough taskmaster and I'll want that garden perfect. I'll make your life hell if it isn't. But if it is perfect, I'll be a very valuable ally for you and your wife here, and you'll need that. What do you think?"

Edward agreed without hesitation. "I'm good with roses and I need a job," he said. "If you can arrange one, in this depression, I'll be very grateful. Your garden will be well-cared for."

"Keep this our secret for now," said Schneider. "Like I said, it may take a while; maybe several months. Can you get by until then on the little bit I secretly slip you to keep the garden going? Oh, and make sure no one ever finds out about that, either. You may have to do it at midnight and come up with lots of stories to keep the night watchman in the dark or this won't work." They shook hands on their agreement.

Edward liked the man. He had a gruff demeanor, but he was kind. Over lunch, he told Edward a little about his wife, who had been dead for several years. "Only person on this planet I trusted completely," he said. He wished Edward well with Charlotte, and gave him some money to buy whatever garden tools he needed to begin taking care of the roses. "Practice that ball game, now," he told him when they parted, "and keep this agreement of ours a secret. I don't want any word of it getting back to the boys. Walls have big ears in this town."

Edward tried to take the warning seriously, but he felt telling Charlotte was excusable. She was, after all, his wife and he planned on keeping no secrets from her, ever. She was delighted by the story. After her marriage to Howard, she knew the kind of control his father wielded over local businessmen and politicians. Schneider's plot appealed to her. She shared it with Rosie, John, Mose, and Linda one evening when they were visiting. These two couples had become their closest friends, despite the racial divide that now seemed to permeate the town. Charlotte had long ago begun to call all of her other friends "my high society fair weathers." They had abandoned her whenever she no longer seemed to be able to offer them social status through affiliation, but she observed it had been that way as long as she could remember so it was no surprise now. Rosie and Linda had always been loyal. Now, they frequently visited each other's homes for dinner or cards.

"A Canook and a divorcee," Mose had observed the first evening Linda invited them over. "You're outcasts in this community, too, aren't you? Sure, you're welcome here. We know the feeling." When Linda had given him a sharp look and kicked him under the table, he'd grinned. "Hey, sugar, I'm just calling a spade a spade. That's the thing to do now, isn't it?" he'd said, cynically making use of a current racial pejorative. "It may be different among womenfolk, but as I see it, this country just isn't structured in such a way right now that black men and white men can truly be friends. There's a difference in the power balance. Just can't get around that and no matter what the people are like, it makes friendship implausible. But these two—the white folks that run this town, for the most part, don't seem to like them any better than they like me. So maybe it doesn't apply quite the same way. In fact," he mused, "could be it applies in reverse. At least I ain't cast out from my own people, like they are. I feel for them."

Edward met his eyes sharply. "Nor am I," he said. "My people are still in Canada, except for Charlotte and her father and the four of you, because of your friendship with her." He was open about his anger with segregation laws. "I could live with the separation if it was fair, though I wouldn't much like it," he asserted. "If the schools really were of equal quality and the city resources that went for upkeep in your community was comparable to what the folks across the river get, I'd be okay with it. But that isn't how it is."

The two men respected each other's underlying honesty despite the risks it implied. Because the parks department employed Moses Brown as a watchman, and because he had already been a witness to Schneider and Edward weeding the roses, telling them about his agreement with Schneider made sense. He didn't mind that Charlotte did so. Not only did they enjoy hearing about anyone trying to outwit Farnsworth with the "city bigwigs," as they called them, Mose also became a close ally in the plot. He'd recently been moved to the night shift.

"They're trying to get rid of me," he said, "to punish me for trying to organize the folks around here to take action and fight the unfairness in this community economically and through legal means. The city employment policies say they can't let me go without cause, and they know if they tried it, I'd have so many NAACP attorneys breathing down their necks it would make their lives miserable and give me even more support in my efforts. So they'll keep looking for a cause, but they'll never find it. I am the best watchman they have, squeaky clean. In the meantime, they'll just do what they can to make me quit of my own accord, like put me on graveyard shift for some flimsy excuse of a reason. If times weren't so rough and I could find another job easily, I'd probably do it. As it is, I'll just work nights and thank the good Lord I have a way to feed my family—and that things aren't as bad here as I hear they are elsewhere where the nightriders resort to violence to keep black folks in their place. It'll probably come to that here, too, eventually but it hasn't yet."

Edward and Charlotte were thankful that Mose was the watchman on duty the evenings Edward fulfilled his temporary agreement with Schneider to keep the roses from dying. The cooperation was subtle; Mose kept a rotating schedule of approximately where on his rounds he would be throughout the nights he worked, including his break times. He posted this at home for Linda, in case she should ever need to find him in an emergency. Edward checked the schedule whenever he and Charlotte visited, then arranged his visits to the garden at times he knew their paths would not cross. The arrangement worked.

Another aspect of the arrangement worked, too. Mose, like most of the young men who worked for the parks department, played on the baseball team Schneider had spoken of. He arranged for Edward to start visiting their practice sessions as a "stand-in." Edward's skill, even after years without playing, was evident. He was an excellent pitcher, and equally good in nearly every other position. Also, based on his years in Seattle, he had several playing strategies he freely shared. All the men on the team soon welcomed his participation. "Sure wish we could get you a job at the department," many of them began saying. "Any position comes open, I'll sure tell my boss how much we need you for this team!"

They were true to their words. A few months later, when Schneider reported it seemed his efforts were finally paying off, several of the men on the team had already told Edward to go down and apply for the new position that was miraculously open even before Schneider did.

"This is going better than I thought," Schneider told him after he had filed his application. "Seems a lot of the folks were planning to recommend you even before I talked to 'em. They laughed at me and said they already knew from what the crew chiefs had told them there was a good ball player applying for the job, and they were eager to hire you, no matter whether Farnsworth liked you or not. They were just glad to know I wouldn't stand in their way." Thus, Edward had a job with the city parks department before baseball season began the following spring. He'd been in Topeka, married to Charlotte, for almost a year.

This was cause for celebration. They happily moved into the small cottage near the rose garden Schneider had built when he was officially hired. Between all the work required to make the garden a showpiece and the busy practice and game schedule, though, Edward was tired most of the time. Charlotte responded by taking on much of the responsibility for caring for the garden. She worked at his side for hours, tearing her fingers on the thorns as they weeded, despite his protests. She slipped out of bed at midnight to water the bushes. Whenever she wasn't giving piano lessons, she was busy in the garden.

Within a year, their combined efforts paid off. The garden was even more beautiful than it had been when Edward first saw it, after listening to "The Rose Garden Waltz." The garden was blooming beautifully, and the parks department had been reestablished as the local baseball champions. Despite Farnsworth's ill will toward Edward and Charlotte, he had been unable to make their lives uncomfortable, though not for lack of effort on his part. Henry, the garden, and the baseball team were protection enough. Henry was delighted with the garden, and had dreams of expanding it and making it the best rose garden in the country, entering it in national competitions.

In addition, Edward and Charlotte could socialize with Linda, Rosie, and their families without repercussion. In fact, because of his cooperation initially in allowing Edward to maintain the garden secretly, Mose also enjoyed Schneider's benevolent protection. He was moved back to the day shift, despite his continued activism in civil rights. This had been a shock to Rosie and Mose, who considered Schneider as one of the most outspoken racists in the community. Schneider now even asked his son, a well-known attorney in the area, to talk to Mose about the possibility of legal recourse to improve the schools and services in the northern part of the city.

"Now that Farnsworth's my enemy, I'll give him a run for his money," explained Schneider, chuckling. "An enemy of my enemy is automatically my friend. If he wants to champion white supremacy here, I'll fight him on it just for the sake of the battle!"

Schneider's son had been surprised by his father's request, but not uncooperative. He had begun to research the issue of school segregation, and was considering preparation of a civil case against the city school board. He also was searching through his contacts to find the best attorneys to handle such a case. Life was good. When, the following summer, Charlotte became pregnant, they were even happier.

"I told you the gypsy was right!" Edward told her, smiling. "See? Your son will come back now, at a better time of your life, in a better situation."

"What if this is a daughter?" she asked.

"I trust the gypsy," he replied. "But I will be happy, either way."

Many couples in the area, given the economic hardships of the depression and the draught, would have been troubled by a pregnancy. They were not. They were among very few people in the dustbowl of the American Midwest during the early 1930s who had no reason to fear providing for a new child in the family. Charlotte was worried, regardless. Her previous miscarriage haunted her. Because of this, Edward wanted to make sure she had the best care possible. As far as he was concerned, the only person who could provide that was his mother, a veteran of delivering hundreds of babies in a rough frontier environment. Besides, he missed his parents. He had remained in touch with them through monthly letters. He knew that they were both well. They were supplementing the income from the gas station with odd jobs and his mother's nursing skills. Canada had been less affected by the depression; the banks had not failed and, as his father had not relied on stocks or investments for income, he was surviving. Fewer tourists from the USA meant less business for the station, but his parents had always been self-sufficient anyway. They grew and raised the food they needed, supplemented by Chief's hunting. They were fine.

What Edward hoped was that he would be able to bring his parents to Kansas during Charlotte's pregnancy. He talked to Clarence; the apartment in his home was vacant now, and he was willing to offer it to Edward's parents during their stay. This meant the only hurdle was finding enough to cover the cost of their train tickets. Edward wrote, explaining Charlotte's condition and their fear because of her past miscarriage. He hoped his parents would be able to visit for a few months, at least until the birth of the baby. He wasn't sure if he could help with travel expenses, but their living expenses while they were in Topeka would be covered. Was it possible?

It was. Chief was able to maintain the house and gas station in their absence, as business was slow. They would be able to afford train tickets, and looked forward to seeing Edward's new home and seeing Charlotte again. They made plans to arrive at summer's end and stay until the birth of the baby in February of the following year. Edward was relieved. He knew, with his mother's care, Charlotte would have a successful pregnancy. He also hoped his mother would have more success than he had at keeping Charlotte from rising at midnight to water the roses and working at his side in the afternoons. So far she had been adamantly insisting that being pregnant did not make her an invalid. She felt better and had more energy than ever, she said. He didn't want to remind her of her last pregnancy, and he was sure the circumstances were different now. At least she didn't have the emotional stress and physical abuse she had dealt with before. But he was still uneasy that Charlotte didn't rest more, and he looked forward to his mother's firm, medical guidance to resolve the issue.

Edward's parents' arrival was a happy occasion. Charlotte, although she was tired and the pregnancy was obviously taxing her strength, welcomed them. She had always been very comfortable with them, as they had with her. Edward's mother, as he had expected, immediately took over most of the household tasks and ordered Charlotte to rest. His father, as he had hoped, immediately took an interest in the rose garden and began sharing his considerable knowledge and efforts to help make it even more beautiful. Having his family close made Edward keenly aware of how much he hoped to return home to Canada and be close to them always. Now was not the time to suggest a move to Charlotte, though. He would wait. For now, he was grateful his parents were close. When Edward stopped to reflect about it, which wasn't often, he was amazed that he was married. He was astounded he would soon have a child. He was also perfectly happy with this turn of events in his life, and he knew having a child was very important to Charlotte. Charlotte did eventually listen to his mother's advice to refrain from working in the garden. They had become close friends immediately and Johanna's gentle insistence that she wanted to "earn her keep" by taking care of everything around the house and garden was accepted. Charlotte insisted on continuing to teach her piano students as her pregnancy progressed despite his mother's stern warnings, though. "You are very frail," she told her. "Your hips are narrow and your body is delicate. I think, other than a brief walk each day, you should spend the last two months of your pregnancy resting in bed and worrying about nothing."

"I am worrying about nothing," Charlotte insisted. "I'm walking and resting. Sitting at the piano with my students is pleasant, not stressful. Let me continue." Johanna relented. She could see that Charlotte did enjoy her work, and it did not seem unduly taxing. Her long practice in medicine and her instincts, though, both told her that this pregnancy needed careful monitoring. She was grateful Edward had brought her here for the birth of her first grandchild, for she sensed that grandchild would need her very much when he entered the world.

CHAPTER FIFTEEN

BIRTH, DEATH, AND REBIRTH

Johanna's instincts were correct. The baby was late in coming, which was not a good sign. When she examined Charlotte carefully, she saw the baby had not turned properly and expected a breech birth that would likely require a forced delivery. When Eddie arrived after midnight one evening in late February, telling her Charlotte was in great pain and her labor had begun, she was prepared for the worst. She had to break Charlotte's water and forcibly begin the birth process, causing even more pain. The birth took many hours and when Johanna did finally succeed in the delivery, the child emerged blue and barely alive with an umbilical cord wrapped around his throat.

In all of her experience, she never assisted with a more difficult delivery, perhaps made even more so because this was her grandson. She loved Charlotte. She knew losing this baby would destroy her emotionally and that, in turn, would destroy her son. She HAD to succeed. Her considerable skill, faith, and strong resolve maintained her through the ordeal. After several long hours, she delivered and resuscitated the baby and laid him next to his exhausted mother. Then she called for her son, who she'd barred from the room hours ago, seeing how distraught he was becoming.

"You have a beautiful little boy, Eddie," she said. "I'll stay for the next few months to help. Charlotte will be weak and tired. It was a difficult birth. But everything is okay now. Mother and baby will be fine."

His mother stayed not just for the next few months but for over two years. When Charlotte became pregnant again not too long after the birth, Johanna insisted on remaining to deliver her second grandchild. She also insisted it would be advisable for them to have no more children after this one that was on the way, and made arrangements with a local doctor to perform an operation to insure this. Charlotte, who loved her son and loved being a mother, was reluctant. However, seeing the worry her husband and mother-in-law both shared, she relented. She did, after all, recognize her limitations. She knew how difficult the first birth had been. The second was arranged as a cesarean delivery in advance to avoid additional problems. Johanna returned to Canada only when she was certain both of her grandchildren and their mother were healthy. Edward enjoyed having the two women he loved most in the world, his wife and his mother, close to him and looking after his children.

When his mother returned to Canada, he finally knew he would be happy staying behind. Kansas had become his home. He enjoyed his work here and was very successful, rapidly moving up through the management ranks in the parks department, making good investments and active in the city. He had many good friends now. He was committed to the issue of desegregation and continued to find ways of supporting his friends in what he viewed as a very necessary and just battle. Everything in his life seemed richly fulfilling.

Edward's focus for the next several years was on family and work. He loved his children and their young lives were happy. The rose garden, true to Henry's wishes, had now won international acclaim and recognition. He had been promoted consistently at work and at last became the superintendent. His income allowed him to invest in several houses and other properties which, once the depression ended, were valuable assets. He and Charlotte became accepted as important leaders in the community and, with Henry's support, continued to champion the fight against school segregation. Many of his friends were even urging him to become active in politics and run for public office, perhaps as Commissioner. He decided to try. Charlotte worked beside him tirelessly as he campaigned, but in the end, he lost the election because of his active stand against desegregation.

The community still, sadly, did not seem ready to accept all groups of people as deserving of equal rights, education, and privileges. With the assistance of the local legal community through Henry's son, there had already been a case brought to court against the public schools. It had failed to achieve what was hoped, but the NAACP and a well-known New York attorney named Marshall were now assisting in challenging the case. Many years later, it would eventually reach the Supreme Court and become the seminal case mandating desegregation of schools, *Brown vs. Topeka Board of Education*.

Edward's children were growing up in a changing world. The depression had ended. Their childhood days were framed by World War II, and the returning veterans to the community were seen as heroes. Many of them were black, and this was rapidly changing attitudes. His children grew up playing with Rosie and Linda's children. Although prejudice was still rampant and they often lived with cruel comments from other children and experienced difficulty in their own schools as a result, it was clear times were changing.

He and Charlotte lived busy lives as their children entered adolescence. Community service and poker clubs for him and community charity events for her filled most of their free time while work filled their days. Edward's children experienced a very different life from the one he had known. There were no long rides on horseback through the snow to school; no days filled with chores; no responsibilities caring for younger children. In part, Edward saw this as a gift. His son would never know the responsibilities he had known as a child. His family would never live with long days when he was away. But he also sensed some aspects of a healthy childhood missing for them. His children had not known the wonder of stories at night connecting them to the past. They had not experienced the sense of family and community that came from the hard work and responsibility he had accepted from early childhood. These differences made them seem, at times, like strangers to him. They did not have the respect for their elders he had always known. They did not share his love of history, philosophy, and books. He suspected subtle changes in the way they were brought up accounted for this. Materially and emotionally, their childhoods were easier than his had been, just as he had intended. But perhaps there was an unintended consequence of this, a spiritual trade-off of sorts.

When James and Judy entered their teens during the 1950s, he felt almost as if they were from another species. Friends were important to them. Cars. Parties. Travel and clothes. Material things. They insisted their parents were "old fashioned." James dropped out before finishing high school and both Edward and Charlotte blamed themselves and their denouncement of public schools based on the segregation issues for this. He came to work for his father in the park briefly, then rejected this, wanting to prove he was independent and could make a life for himself on his own, without the help of his family. Remembering his own early search for success and independence, Edward thought he understood, and wished him well in whatever path he chose. James had his mother's musical talent, so he soon headed for California with a band. The easy success in records he hoped for didn't come. Too many parties and fighting, often due to drunkenness, took a toll. Most of the members of the band returned home, but James remained on the west coast, trying to achieve success. The path proved too difficult. He did not have the necessary self-discipline—perhaps, Edward feared, because his childhood experiences, smoothed by Charlotte, never required him to develop it. James drifted for a while, holding many jobs, from dance instructor to sales, to supplement his meager income from singing. When he finally returned home for a visit, somewhat disappointed and defeated since his desire for independence and success had not worked out quite the way he planned, his own sadness infected his parents, especially his mother. Sensing this, James left again shortly after.

Edward's daughter finished high school, married and moved to another state. Her marriage, as she often communicated to her mother, was not a happy one and she considered the five children she quickly bore to be more than she could handle. She felt she had been cheated of her life, somehow. This further darkened Charlotte's frame of mind. So much of her life energy had been invested in her children that their failures and misery became her own. She became depressed and despondent.

She had been so protective and maternal toward them when they were young. She had been hurt deeply by what she saw as rejection once they entered adolescence and then more deeply by what seemed to her to be their own unhappiness with life. Her father's death a few years before had also been an unbearable loss, from which she never fully recovered. These daily sorrows took a toll on her always-frail constitution. She developed cancer, seemingly from a broken heart. What had happened to her children? What had happened to her dreams and hopes for them? What had happened to her own dreams? What had happened to her life?

Edward also often found himself wondering what had happened. How had the world changed so quickly, almost overnight? And what had been lost in the changing? Why were the values and priorities of his children so different from his? What had he missed?

His own childhood had seemed so difficult in so many ways. He remembered still the emotional pain he felt when Baby Flo died. He remembered how hard he had worked and how much responsibility he had shouldered as a child. He remembered his father's long absences and his mother's sadness when he was away. The bitter cold that nearly took Miss Welch and his many struggles to establish himself in his own life seemed close still. The loss of Redwing still haunted him. He had always sworn to himself that his own children would not experience the early difficulties and pain he had endured, and they had not. He had kept this promise to himself. Their childhood had been easy and comfortable by comparison to his. The world they lived in, full of material optimism and scientific advancement after the war, was a very different world from the one he had known. Yet, he had a sense that somehow, for all of his conscientious efforts, he had failed to give them something. Some elemental wisdom, some sense of self-reliance and connectedness that his early struggles had given him, seemed lacking in his children. This missing element, whatever it was and wherever it had come from, seemed somehow responsible for his son's drifting and depression. This somehow-overlooked secret ingredient that had made his own difficult times good lessons for him had served to make their easy times bad lessons for them. What was it that was missing? What had happened? And how had the time passed so quickly? Where had the world he had once known gone? Where had the world gone?

He felt an overwhelming sadness as he looked at the lives of his children, and as he watched his beloved Charlotte become weaker and frailer each day. He lost interest in the work that had meant so much to him for the past twenty-five years and retired to devote his full attention to his slowly dying wife. There were still bright points in their lives. When Brown vs. Board of Education finally was resolved successfully by the Supreme Court in 1957, Charlotte's spirits lifted and her health improved. They happily celebrated the changes they had been such a part of.

The following year, when her health again took a turn for the worse, James returned. They had not heard from their son for nearly two years. It was almost as if he had sensed his mother needed him. He came home and returned to work for the parks department with his father's assistance, soon marrying a lovely young woman who worked at the local television station. She was stable and sturdy, from a respected farming family in the western part of the state. This reassured his parents who had been worried by his Bohemian lifestyle and the company he kept. When his wife gave birth, within the next year, to a daughter, Charlotte's zest for life and happiness seemed to be restored. It had been difficult for her to have both of her children and all of her grandchildren far away. She loved her hometown and hoped her family would remain close to her, as she always had to her father until his death. Now that James and his family were close, some of the shining shards of her shattered dreams seemed to be reforming into a new mosaic. Her earlier hopes for a comfortable life with her family seemed to be returning.

They did not return quite as she hoped, however. James was restless. His marriage was troubled, and he often disappeared for weeks at a time, perhaps still chasing his own dreams. These disappearances were devastating to Charlotte as well as to his young wife, who responded by burying herself in work and religion. Charlotte responded by burying herself in her young grandchild. She kept her granddaughter, Kris, constantly by her side. She returned to giving piano lessons, and the small girl, from the time she could barely sit, would stay beside her on the bench, watching and listening. The child, perhaps because of the constant attention she received, had a sunny personality and was energetic and very bright. She talked early and articulately. She developed some of the musical skill of her grandmother as if by osmosis. She became very attached to her grandmother. Young Kris and Charlotte depended on each other for happiness and emotional support. The child's presence seemed to slow the spread of the cancer the doctors had predicted would already have run its course years before. Charlotte, miraculously, lived on. Although Edward knew of the tremendous physical pain she experienced and how she struggled to hang on to the life so quickly ebbing away from her, he selfishly was glad the child helped her hold on to this world.

Still, he knew her departure from life was close on the event horizon. As if he sensed that it would be nearly as hard for his young granddaughter to lose Charlotte as it was for him, he began to spend more time with Kris as his wife became weaker. He took her for long walks in the parks he knew so well and told her the stories of his life. The young girl, barely five, listened eagerly and asked him many questions, fascinated by the snowy, mountainous world he described and by his many adventures. She became enamored with horses when he had told her about his horse and his days in the rodeo. He bought her a pony and taught her how to ride. She was interested in his baseball career, and learned how to play the game. They spent hours together watching the sport, now so popular, on television and she learned of all his favorite teams and players, and why he thought they were best. She listened as he told her of his regret for the animals he had assisted in killing. "My main regret in life," he would say. She noticed that now her grandfather would not even kill flies. Instead, his reflexes still quick and sure, he caught them in his hands and released them outside. They shared many adventures walking through the zoo he had tended for many years. She learned the names of all the animals, what their native habitats were like, and what they ate. She assisted in their feeding at times, with caretakers who still knew and respected her grandfather. He proudly showed her the rose garden, still one of the loveliest in the country and a tribute to the many years of hard work he and Charlotte had lavished on the plants. He taught her the names of all the varieties of roses in bloom there. On their long walks in the woods together, she learned the names of all the plants. Flora and fauna, ever since his days in the mountains with Chief, had remained Edward's special area of expertise

Kris was very close to Charlotte. Her grandmother patiently read her books and played games with her long into the night each evening. The child learned how to read on her own long before beginning school. She excelled there, immediately being moved ahead a grade and then selected for a special program for bright children funded by the National Defense Act, since it appeared Russia was getting into space before the USA. As Edward watched her grow, it occurred to him that he was giving her the attention he had not given his own children. He was giving her the attention his parents and his siblings and Miss Welch had given him. Perhaps that was the missing ingredient for James and Judy. He'd made sure they had an easy life. He'd loved them and played with them and been, by all outside standards, a good father. But he had never really told them the stories of his own life. They did not know of any world beside their own. He promised himself Kris would have what they lacked. He would give her the perspective, the history, and the understanding to contrast her own world to the world of the past. And by doing this, a deep part of his mind knew, she would also be his salvation when he lost the wife he loved so much.

Charlotte had been given new energy when James returned and had a family, but it was ebbing quickly. The dynamics within his family, his frequent disappearances and the responsibility—although in ways she thrived on it—of caring for Kris were taking a toll on her already-precarious constitution. The chemotherapy and radiation treatments she was taking to combat her cancer made her weak and depressed. Her doctors, already surprised she had lived as long as she had, could see the end of her life was near. As much as he tried to deny it, Edward knew it, too.

Kris also seemed to sense it, spending more and more time at her grandmother's side and endlessly questioning her about her condition. She was precocious and knowledgeable well beyond her years; the astuteness of her comments and observations and her awareness of the impending death of Charlotte surprised everyone. But emotionally, she was distraught. Her normally sunny personality became subdued. She began having problems with bedwetting, complaining of illnesses that kept her from school and otherwise exhibiting regressive behaviors, such as wanting to return to the bottle, something that in her young psyche represented closeness to her grandmother who so often held her and fed her when she was an infant.

Kris was experiencing severe difficulties coping with the impending death of her primary caregiver, her grandmother. Charlotte had indeed taken over the role of mother for the child almost from the beginning and the loss would be devastating as a result. Edward, sensing this, found himself torn between the desire to spend every available waking moment with his dying wife, despite the pain that caused, and the need to devote more attention to his highly vulnerable grandchild. Kris, for her part, had already announced she planned to become a doctor when she grew up and find a cure for cancer. He didn't doubt she would, or at least that she would try, but for now he knew she needed his attention and his love. The situation was painful for everyone.

The night Charlotte died, Kris was away staying with her aunt. Edward and Charlotte both had a sense that it would be her final night and arranged it that way, although in retrospect he wasn't sure it was the right choice. Perhaps it would have been better for the child, who certainly shared the same sense of finality as they did, to be allowed to remain and be part of the last goodbye. He wasn't sure. By the time Kris returned, two days later, Charlotte was gone. The atmosphere at the house was heavy with sorrow. The child entered, sensing what had happened, and ran immediately to her grandmother's room. Finding it empty, she began to wail—a reaction that continued for days.

Edward felt numb. It was as if all of his tears had been spent before Charlotte's death. Time seemed to move slowly. He was living in a dream world, swimming slowly through a thick, hazy dimension he hardly recognized. His normally sharp mind was dull. His memory, ordinarily unquestionably reliable, seemed to disappear. A thick, foggy sorrow permeated his very soul. So much of his life had been connected to Charlotte. He remembered when they had met as if it were yesterday. He still had, and daily re-read, all the letters they exchanged so long ago. He remembered her visit to Canada and the magical times they had shared there as their love grew. He recalled what she had endured for him, her divorce, her ostracism from the community, and the pain of her ex-husband's suicide. He recollected her father's hospitality toward him when he had finally returned to Kansas. All of those events seemed more vivid to him, more real than the current empty world he inhabited. The isolation enfolded him like a too-warm blanket.

Then, as the weeks passed, he suddenly began to notice that his young grandchild was as distraught and sad as he was. He remembered his promise to himself to give to her whatever it was that he had inadvertently failed to give his own children, to help her understand herself and her connection to the past. He decided that would be his final, enduring parting gift to Charlotte. Their legacy would rest in this child that was part of them both, linking them to the world of tomorrow. Fondly, he watched the little girl reading a thick book well beyond her years. He noted the shielded, distant look on her face, her closed posture, her legs and arms pulled into herself. He stood up from the chair in which he had been sitting for what seemed like a very long time and walked from out of a grief-stricken stupor and into her world. Walking to her, he tousled her hair and put his arms around her.

"Did you know, lassie," he said, trying to imitate his own father's rich Irish brogue, "that your great-grandfather was almost a priest?"

Her eyes met his with the light of interest. Soon she was sitting on his lap as he began to recount the story his own father had told to him so many long years ago. It was the first of many stories he told her as the years of her childhood continued. She learned to know and understand his life. This bond did, indeed, become a salvation for both of them and part of the on-going link to Charlotte in both of their hearts.

CHAPTER SIXTEEN

ROSES IN THE DUST

Kris laughed as she looked out the window. "You be careful, Grand-dad!" she called as she watched her eighty-eight-year-old grandfather lithely turn a cartwheel in the front yard.

"Bet you can't do that!" Edward teased.

"Can, too!" giggled four-year-old Elena, gracefully imitating her great-grand-dad.

"Try this!" challenged six-year-old Nathan, doing a handspring.

"Don't you dare!" shouted Kris. "I have no intention of setting broken bones!"

She watched the three as they continued to romp in the yard, reflecting on how fortunate she was to have her grandfather with her. If not for his welcome presence in her home, she wouldn't be completing medical school.

Edward had been an important part of her childhood, replacing both father and mother for her. He had been her teacher and companion for the first twelve years of her life. When she reached adolescence, she moved from Kansas to live with her parents and he returned to Canada to care for one of his younger sisters who had cancer. Cancer. That ghost brought a wave of sadness over Kris. On some deep, buried level, she was still grieving for her grandmother, who had died so long ago. She knew he was, too.

After he departed, without his assistance to keep her always-troubled soul in check, she experienced a tumultuous adolescence. It left Kris with two young children and more responsibility than she had ever planned to have before the age of twenty-one.

Always bright and capable academically, she completed public school early, at sixteen. Then, awash in the idealism and political activism of the early seventies and on her own, she had not continued to college. She traveled throughout the USA and Europe, then drifted until she became pregnant at seventeen. She married a man she did not really love, thinking that would be best for her future child. Her husband was kind but uneducated and unmotivated, unable to make a living. She returned to school, able to study on scholarships because of the innate intelligence she possessed. The financial struggles of supporting her young family required her to work while she studied. When, less than a year later, she again became pregnant, she was despondent and unsure what to do.

Never close to her parents, she lost touch with them completely once she finished school and left home. She had not seen Edward since he left for Canada over six years before. She felt that, somehow, she must have disappointed him. But now she was desperate, and he was the one person she needed. She had called an operator in the town where her great aunt lived to retrieve the number, hoping he was still there. When she heard his voice on the line, she burst into tears. Even across the phone lines and the distance, his voice comforted her. Sobbing, she told him about her life, about what had happened and what she was trying to do.

"Soon, you will have two great-grandchildren," she told him. "I can't believe you haven't known. I can't believe we haven't spoken for so long. I miss you so much."

They talked for several minutes, sharing their lives. The former closeness they shared had not disappeared. She learned her great aunt was recovering under the care of her doctors and Edward. She told him she was attending the university, hoping to become a doctor. But with her child and the necessity of working whatever jobs she could combine with her schedule—cocktail waitress, phone sales, factory night work, clerical jobs on campus— she did not know how she would ever be able to realize her goal.

Now, again pregnant and tired, she was considering giving up on her education.

"You always wanted to be a doctor when you were a child," he reminded her. "Remember? I am glad that is still your dream. My mother would be proud of that."

Kris recalled the stories of her great-grandmother, nursing the sick and delivering babies across western Canada. She hadn't thought of that for a very long time. She also remembered her steely resolve as a child of six, when her grandmother had died, to find a cure for the disease that had taken her away, leaving such an empty place in her young heart. She knew she couldn't give up that dream, no matter what the price. Thinking back now, she couldn't quite remember all of their conversation. But not too long after it had ended, Edward returned from Canada and moved in with Kris. From the time he arrived, her life became easier. He took over the care of young Nathan and her infant daughter, born just a month after his return. He cleaned and cooked, taking over all of her household duties. He helped financially with the pension he still received from his years working for the parks department in Kansas. More important, Edward's presence dissipated the loneliness Kris had been feeling and lightened her struggle. Her husband, too, responded well to his presence. Accepting Edward's unobtrusive advice, he began to work steadily at a job in construction he enjoyed and could do well.

Confident at last that her children were being well cared-for and the bills would be paid, Kris was able to concentrate on her studies. Since then, she had finished at the university and completed medical school. She had two more months of an internship to complete before she would become a licensed M.D. For now, her life was happy. She enjoyed her children. She enjoyed her work. Most of all, she enjoyed her grandfather's presence.

Her children had a luxury most of their peers did not. They had a strong link across time and generations to the past. She would watch joyfully, almost in tears of happiness, as Edward bounced his young granddaughter on his knee and sang her songs of the Canadian frontier and his rodeo days, songs long ago forgotten by the rest of the world. She listened almost in awe as he again retold the stories she remembered so well from her childhood. The stories his own father had told him when he was a child. The silver strands of love and life over time wrapped her and her children in a safe, warm cocoon through his voice and through his presence. Quickly, the children grew, beginning school themselves, making friends, and learning new skills. Quickly she sailed through the remainder of her own education and preparation for her career.

The most difficult task she'd faced recently, given the support Edward offered, was choosing her specialty area. Her earlier goals of medical research, seeking cures for cancer, had been supplanted by the desire to seek cures for AIDS, the new epidemic now sweeping the country. She had classmates and friends affected by this plague, and she did volunteer work at one of the local hospices with many of the victims. She explored the area of medical research to find cures for this blight. She discovered no cures, but she did discover that working in a lab was not something she especially enjoyed. She preferred working with people rather than bacteria, and seeing the positive results of her efforts in their lives.

Eventually, gynecology, pediatrics, and obstetrics were the areas she identified as most interesting for her. Women and their children needed women for their health care. Perhaps the many stories of her great-grandmother delivering babies on the Canadian frontier influenced her decision to become an obstetrician. She was completing her internship at a local hospital. Immersed in the long hours internship required, she had little time to notice anything else. The rest of her life seemed to be on hold, on automatic pilot as she finished it. She trusted her children and home were cared for by Edward. It caught her by surprise when, one day, her husband pointed out he had gradually been taking over Edward's tasks at home.

"You are a doctor, for heaven's sake," he said. "Open your eyes and look! He is nearly ninety years old. He is tired. And I don't think he is in very good health."

Forced to look, she had. Now, as she struggled to complete her internship, she had a new pain to face. Her grandfather, formerly such a pillar in her life, so invulnerable, so reliable was becoming frail. It was clear there were medical difficulties in addition to advanced age. He was short of breath and his formerly strong constitution was weakening. He spent long hours in bed and tired easily. Never one to willingly go to doctors for assistance, he protested now as well.

"My mother taught me all I need to know about health," he asserted. "She knew a darned bit more than most of these new-fangled doctors with their drugs and knives. I'm just old, that's all. My body is wearing out. Rest and blackberry brandy and the love of you and my great-grandbabies. That is all I need."

Kris was insistent, though, and eventually he relented. As she feared, there were problems. After several tests and long days of hospitalization, the diagnosis was given; he had lung cancer, and it had progressed so far that, given his age, there was nothing that could be done. Cancer again. Kris tried to fight back her tears but could not. The doctor recommended he remain in the hospital.

"It won't be long now, Kris. He will be better cared for here, and you know you don't have the time to do it yourself. You still have over a month of internship and your board exams to face. That is the most reasonable solution."

She knew it was, but she couldn't do it—especially when Edward was so insistent that he be allowed to leave. "This is a torture chamber," he declared. "All I want is to end my life at home with my babies. And I am not leaving this world yet, anyway. You still need me. You let me come home and take care of those kids while you finish your training. A man can live on will for a little while. If you leave me in this place, I'll be gone tomorrow. Let me come back where I am needed and I will keep this old body going for a season or two."

The request was irrational in light of her medical training, but she wanted to believe it. Besides, Edward wanted to be at home. Even if it meant delaying the remainder of her internship to care for him, that was something she would do. She informed his doctor of her decision.

"I was afraid of that," he said. "That old guy is stubborn, and you love him so much you'll give in to his wishes despite your better judgment. It really isn't wise, Kris. But I won't stop you."

So Edward returned home. To her amazement, he really did seem better and more energetic. He assured her not to worry, that he was fine during the day when the kids were at school. Her husband helped, too. Although it was necessary, eventually, to bring in a nurse to help when no one else was at home, Kris was able to resume her internship. Oddly, rather than distracting her, she found the situation caused her to focus more on her work in the hospital. With the death of the one she loved most in the world looming so close at her shoulder, it was truly a relief to immerse herself in bringing new life into the world. It was a way to fight death emotionally, to look it in the face and laugh and assert that there was no real power capable of stopping the continuation of life and hope.

Miraculously, it seemed, Edward survived. Although too weak to leave his bed most of the time now, he remained alert. He often refused his pain medication, saying it made him feel foggy.

"I'll leave this place when I am good and ready, not before," he said. "I have a granddaughter who is going to be a doctor. I plan to live to see it."

Sadly, Kris reflected that her own children were now experiencing what she had experienced so long ago when Charlotte died. They were losing the one person in the world they relied on most and, though young, they sensed this. She could see it in the changes in their behavior. Their usually sunny dispositions were clouded. Their usually compliant behavior was irritable. She knew she should now step in for them, as Edward had for her, to help replace the loss they sensed was just around the corner. But she also knew how much seeing her finish her internship and board exams and begin her medical career meant to Edward. And, she had to admit, it was important to her, as well. She hoped her husband would be able, at least to some extent, to take over the emotional needs of her family. She reestablished ties with her parents, too, in an effort to meet this need and was happy to see close relationships develop between them and her children. She sensed that she just didn't have the time or the energy to be there for them in the way they would need. Besides, the loss of Edward would be as hard, or even harder, on her than it would be on her children. True to his promise, Edward remained alive as she finished her internship, passed her exams, and began her career. He was now in great pain, though, and finally relented to the pain medication he was offered. The morphine dulled his senses. When Christmas came that year, sadness permeated the season. Everyone knew this would be the last time they would share the holidays together. The lights on the tree often reflected off tears in Kris's eyes—and in Edward's.

"I'll be going out with the year, Kris," he told her as she sat by his bedside on Christmas night. "I won't make it much past New Year's Eve. We both know that. Tell me, do you think my life has been a good one? Do you think I have made any difference in this crazy old world? I always wanted to. I remember when my baby sister died so long ago. I sat under my wishing tree, and I promised myself that I would live a life that made a difference. Have I, do you think?"

"Of course you have," she assured him. "How could you possibly doubt it?"

He shook his head. "It is hard to tell," he said. "Time stretches so far across the horizon and all of our actions count for so little. Who can tell?"

Overcome with emotion, crying, Kris could only nod and squeeze his hand. Then she had an idea. "If you put it all in perspective for others to decide, perhaps someone can tell, someday" she said. "Will you? I can arrange for a week or two off now. I want to spend it all with you. I know all the stories you told me of your family, but now I want stories of all the rest of your life, too. I will stay here with you, and bring a tape recorder. Tell me all you remember of your life. Tell me all you want to share. I know you made a difference. I will see that others know that, too."

"Ah, my child," he said, patting her hand. "You have always been so sweet to me. When your grandmother died, you were my salvation. Late in my life, when I thought I had nothing left to live for, you gave me these great-grandchildren. You gave me something left to live for. We are all only grains of sand upon the shore. In the end, the ocean washes all away. If you want to hear my stories, I will tell you. But I will tell you just because you want me to, just because you ask it. No one man can ever make a difference in the sea of time."

Of course you have, she thought. *How could you possibly doubt that? How could anyone possibly doubt that?* She stayed beside him all night, holding his hand. The tears ran down her cheeks unchecked. She arranged time off work and spent the next two weeks at his side. Sometimes, the children joined them. The morphine made him drowsy, but he still had the silver-tongued Irish gift of gab. His stories were vivid. She was amazed to hear the wonderful details of his life, his world, and all the things he had seen and done and felt. At last, as he recounted the final days of his life in Kansas, he lost consciousness. She stayed with him through the night. When, near dawn, she finally dozed, she thought she heard the sound of the piano in her dreams. Her grandmother playing the piano. Her grandmother playing the

"Rose Garden Waltz," as a welcome to the man she was now taking back into her arms in that black void of death buried within
the vacuums of space where they both would dwell with God in
an eternal dance beyond her comprehension. When Kris awoke
from her dream, Edward was no longer breathing. His eyes were
closed. His face seemed to have peacefully relaxed into some distant dimension far beyond time.

Time moved slowly through the next days as she, numb, made
arrangements for his burial. Here with her, far away from the
places he had spent his life, there were few people to invite to a
funeral. She saw that notices were posted in Topeka and throughout Alberta, but she knew most of his close friends and associates
were long gone. If they attended, it would be as ethereal beings
with the angels.

Edward wanted to be buried in an oak box. That was his last
request, a final connection to "The Old General." More, it was a
final statement about the beautiful strength, pattern, and simplic-
ity of his life. Kris, her family and the neighbors and friends in
attendance watched quietly as the oak box was lowered slowly
into the ground. At last, the others left. Kris and her children
stayed on, staring into the open grave. With her, she had a dozen
roses. Crying, she threw them, one by one, onto Edward's casket,
into Edward's grave. Roses. The Heirlooms and Cadenzas and
American Beauties he had nourished so well. Roses he had loved
so much. Roses in the dust.

ABOUT THE AUTHOR

Sherri McCarthy lives in Arizona with her two children, two grandchildren and her husband. Writing stories that are enjoyable and offer insight to readers has always been her passion. She has been a professor at Northern Arizona University for the last 20 years, following several years as a public school teacher in Arizona and Hawaii. She has also authored over a dozen books on topics related to education, child and adolescent development, cross-cultural psychology, counseling and other topics, as well as more than fifty chapters in academic texts and over seventy-five journal articles in psychology and education research publications. Sherri has given hundreds of national and international presentations around the world, and worked as a Fulbright scholar and visiting lecturer in countries including Brazil, Russia, Malaysia, UK and Italy. Her professional vita can be viewed at: http://jan.ucc.nau.edu/~snm3/. Prior to her teaching career, Sherri worked as a journalist and freelance writer. She has won several awards for her poems, short stories and articles over the past few decades. Through her novels, she seeks to entertain readers around the world as she paints word-pictures of growing up during different times and in different cultures for all to enjoy while viewing the feelings and values that tie us all together as human beings.